Aftershock

R.D. Shah spent his formative years in the north west of England before attending Rugby School in Warwickshire. At seventeen he attained his private pilot's licence in Florida and shortly after attended the University of Miami where he studied motion picture & psychology before returning to the UK to work in television & leisure. He has travelled extensively throughout Europe, Russia and the Americas. R.D. holds a scuba diving licence, which he gained along the shores of the Hawaiian island of Kauai. All this experience has prepared him for a career in writing. He lives in Wiltshire with his wife and young daughter.

Also by R.D. Shah

The Harker Chronicles

The Disavowed

R.D. SHAH

AFTER SHOCK

CANELO

First published in the United Kingdom in 2023 by

Canelo
Unit 9, 5th Floor
Cargo Works, 1–2 Hatfields
London SE1 9PG
United Kingdom

A CIP catalogue record for this book is available from the British Library.

Print ISBN 978 1 80436 095 8
Ebook ISBN 978 1 80436 094 1

Look for more great books at www.canelo.co

Printed and bound in Great Britain by Clays Ltd, Elcograf S.p.A.

I

MIX
Paper from
responsible sources
FSC® C018072

To Phillip and William. Two of my oldest friends. For adventures past and those yet to come. Cheers lads, I'll see you soon

Chapter 1

'Wait, there it is again.'

The man standing opposite pressed his headset even closer to his, his eyes squinting, as he strained to hear the sounds. He stood there motionless, his body rigid and primed for a response, but after a few seconds of hearing nothing he loosened his grip on the headset, placed it back on the small table and slowly shook his head.

'I can't hear anything, Lieutenant,' Captain Kelso noted with a grimace. 'Are you sure?'

Lieutenant Carol nodded firmly before the captain had even finished speaking. 'One hundred per cent, sir. It was faint and intermittent, but I heard it.'

Kelso eyed the young radar operator intently before expelling a slow, measured breath, now pondering the oddity.

'We're two hundred metres deep in the Atlantic Ocean, Lieutenant, and you're hearing... voices, somewhere out in the blue?'

'No, sir, not the sound of voices. The sound of music.'

As a ten-year veteran commander of HMS *Resolve*, one of the United Kingdom's nuclear submarine Vanguard class, Captain Kelso had come across many stories from deep below the cold foamy waves of the Atlantic Ocean. But never once had they involved music. He had encountered electrical issues, a couple of near misses with both Russian and American subs and, on one occasion, a collision with a humpback whale had damaged the ship's bow, sending them back to the port... but never music.

Kelso looked up at the small group of sailors who stood at their work stations in the command room in silence but were all staring at their captain for the next order.

'All right, gentlemen, unless Julie Andrews turns up outside singing a tune I don't want to hear about it. Eyes back on your stations.'

Kelso waited for his crew to continue with their duties before returning his attention to Lieutenant Carol whose focus was still on the headset as he listened for even the faintest trace of a melody, his teeth grinding back and forth rhythmically and his frustration obvious. No one on earth likes their judgement called into question, and that went a hundredfold for the sound operator of a Vanguard nuclear submarine.

'Pack it up, Lieutenant, back to the job at hand,' Kelso said stiffly. After receiving an accepting nod from Lieutenant Carol he stepped through the open grey hatchway leading back to the main command room.

'Sir!'

Kelso halted in his tracks and leant backwards so only his face appeared at the opening and he stared over at Lieutenant Carol who thrust his finger up in the air. 'I've got it, sir.'

Captain Kelso was through the hatchway and back to the sonar station within moments and snatching the spare headset off the table as Carol adjusted the volume. His first impression was of fluctuating static, similar to the sounds of waves crashing against rocks, but as the lieutenant set about adjusting his equipment further, the chaotic sounds took form until, after a few more seconds of mixing, Kelso heard it.

Music.

It was scratchy and fading in and out, but definitely music, and it sounded familiar. Kelso looked up in surprise to find the young lieutenant smiling at him, happy to have been proved correct. 'Is that Wagner?'

Lieutenant Carol's eyes widened further and he slowly nodded. 'Yes, sir. "Ride of the Valkyries".'

Both men stared at each other in a moment of shared bewilderment at the bizarre spectacle taking place two hundred metres down in the Atlantic Ocean, just less than twenty miles off the mainland coast of Spain.

Kelso opened his mouth, his lips beginning to form a word, but he never got the chance.

'Contact. One hundred metres off our port side.'

Kelso immediately shifted his attention to the radar technician on his left. 'Sub?'

'No, sir. It's going too fast... Contact, eighty metres.'

Kelso's stare hardened as he began to bark out orders. 'Hard rudder to starboard. Flank speed.'

Within seconds the command room was running like a well-oiled machine, each station performing their job as they'd been taught, but as the radar operator called out his revised distance Kelso already knew what was about to happen.

We've been caught dead in the water. But where the hell did it come from?

'Sixty metres until contact.'

'Release countermeasures.' Kelso ordered as he and everyone else in the command room steadied themselves as HMS *Resolve* pulled a full turn in an attempt to put some distance between them and the torpedo.

'Countermeasure away, sir.'

'Forty metres and closing.'

The entire hull creaked under the pressure of such a tight manoeuvre and the lights overhead began to flicker.

'Full speed ahead,' Kelso ordered. The throttles were punched to the maximum position as the radar operator called out the closing position of the torpedo.

'Thirty metres until impact.'

'Countermeasures have failed, sir. Object still approaching our stern.'

'Ten metres.'

'Sound the collision alarms,' Kelso ordered, and he then grabbed the metal steadying handle next to him, his knuckles white and his body rigid.

'Eight, seven, six...'

'Prepare for impact.'

'Three, two, one...'

The entire hull heaved violently, the force ripping two of the officers from their chairs, the deafening explosion so powerful that their seatbelts snapped from their fixtures, sending the sailors hurtling to the floor. Kelso clung tightly to his handrail as a second explosion sent the entire room into momentary darkness before the red hue of the emergency lighting bled through the gathering electrical smoke, which was rising in swirls from the damaged equipment below.

Kelso reached for the black handset dangling next to him and began to bark off orders. 'Damage report—' was all he managed. He felt the heavy popping of a pressure change in his ears and turned back to the open hatch entrance of the command room.

He could hear what was coming before he could see it, the thrashing sound of water filled the air like a death note and he watched in dread as a dark blue barrier of water flooded up the corridor towards him. Instinct pushed him towards the open hatchway. 'Get this hatch closed,' he yelled as the nearest sailor joined him and they pushed their combined weight against the door. Kelso grappled the circular twist lock and spun it into place, sealing it shut.

The pounding of the water hitting the other side sounded a car crash, metal on metal, and as Kelso stood back there came a sound from the other side that sent an unpleasant shiver through the seasoned veteran.

The frantic thudding of fists on the other side of the hatchway sent a similar shudder through everyone in the command room as the sailors outside desperately attempted to gain entry. The awful sound brought the room to complete silence.

Kelso said nothing. He didn't need to. Instead he turned and locked eyes with the small group of men and women left inside the room, and with great sadness slowly shook his head.

There was nothing they could do.

The thudding sounds fell silent. At their current depth hypothermia would have killed the sailors nearly as quickly as drowning would have. Kelso placed his palm against the hatchway door and dropped his head in respect. There were over one hundred and twenty lost souls in the now flooded part of the submarine. Good men... Kelso's men.

'Lieutenant Kale, how fast are we descending? What's the bottom depth at our location?'

The young woman wiped the debris from her station and scanned the numbers before throwing back the answer.

'Ground depth is five hundred feet, sir, but we're descending slowly, at twenty feet a minute.'

'Engines?' Kelso now asked, turning his attention to a thick-shouldered, blond-haired man at the far end of the command room.

'Engines are dead, sir.'

Although disheartening, this response had been expected. Kelso turned back to Lieutenant Kale. 'Release the distress beacon.'

Kale removed a key from around her neck and began to unlock the metal cover protecting the red eject button as Kelso sought to reassure what was left of his staff.

'We're deep, but not deep enough to stop a rescue mission. We're descending slowly, one of our ballast tanks must have held, so we'll make it to the bottom intact. What we have to focus on now is oxygen. It could be six or seven hours before they reach us… But we will make it.'

Of course, most of this was just for morale. He had no idea how badly HMS *Resolve* was damaged, and touching down on the bottom of the sea could cause the hull to crack. Six or seven hours to mount a rescue mission was also generous. It could take help days to get down here, and the oxygen they had was just a drop in the ocean, literally.

'Distress beacon away, sir,' Kale announced.

As Kelso considered what other, if any, options were open to him he caught sight of Lieutenant Carol appearing at the open hatchway leading to the sound room. In his hand he held his green headset, which he lifted into the air.

'It's started again, sir.'

Kelso raised his chin and the young lieutenant moved back to his station and pressed one of the buttons, flooding the command room with the sounds that had once again started playing through his headset.

The remaining sailors listened as Wagner's 'Ride of the Valkyries' flowed loudly from the speakers. It was eerie, and they remained silent until Kale spoke up once more, beads of sweat peppering her brow.

'Sir, I have contact.'

Staying calm and collected, Kelso licked his lips apprehensively.

'Is it a sub?'

Kale remained silent, uncharacteristically caught in the moment. When she replied, her voice wavered in disappointment. 'No, sir. It's going too fast to be a sub.'

–

Six hundred feet above, the yellow blinking light of the distress beacon broke the surface and began to roll among the towering waves as a heavy Atlantic storm descended from the night skies. Amongst the rolling waves and crashing rain it was barely possible to see the vast erupting bubble of air bursting from the depths like a foamy volcano. Within seconds the outline of the huge bubble disappeared and once more the shrieking wind filled the torrid night air. In the distance, the small yellow light of the emergency beacon blinked rhythmically as it was swept along by the heavy current, further out into the dark waters of the Atlantic Ocean.

Chapter 2

'This way, gentlemen,' the man in the grey suit announced, his French accent thick and guttural. 'You're the last to arrive.'

Hans Bauer gave a subtle nod and followed his guide along the craggy stone pathway leading upwards to their destination. He sensed the comment had been laced with sarcasm, but he ignored his suspicion and continued on in silence. The French had a strange take on humour, as far as he was concerned, but he was in no mind to mention it given the significance of what would take place within the next hour. It was going to be an important night, and one the Daedalus führer had been looking forward to.

Bauer glanced back at his chauffeured Range Rover still parked on the beach below and scanned the French city of Saint Malo, its streetlights twinkling just beyond the beachline. Located on the Channel coastline, some had considered it to be a logistically challenging location for the event, but Bauer knew better.

It was perfect.

He turned his attention back to his guide, who led him up the weathered rocky path, and gazed at the small stone fort ahead. He allowed himself a smug, nose-flaring smile.

Perfect indeed.

Constructed on a tidal island a few hundred metres off the walled city of Saint Malo, the fort was only accessible by foot during a low tide. It was built in 1689 to protect the city's port from the English, but these days it was nothing more than a tourist attraction. A place where sightseers could explore a time in history when travelling to an invasion point could be just as dangerous as committing to the battlefield itself. But tonight the fort had another purpose and Bauer was once again running the evening's plan through his mind with great relish. His guide stopped at the small wooden gate at the top and unlocked it.

'Just through here, Mr Bauer,' the guide directed, and then he paused for his guest to pass inside before locking the gate behind them. 'They are all waiting in the central room; we'll be ready shortly.'

Bauer was led inside the surprisingly cosy stone interior of Fort National and up a flight of wide stone shelf steps to a red door on the first floor. The stone walls held a number of woven tapestries, most likely replicas, celebrating the fort's history. The guide paused at the doorway and delivered two firm knocks.

'Come in,' a muffled voice called out from the other side. The guide pushed open the door and allowed Bauer to stroll though it before swiftly closing it and taking his position, standing guard, on the outer landing.

'Mr Bauer, good to see you,' a tall, balding man with unnatural looking cherry-red hair said in welcome, and he extended his hand.

'As with you, Ernst,' Bauer replied, shaking the man's hand firmly. 'The prime minister asked me to thank you again for all your help and input arranging this whole thing.'

Ernst Dupont was not a man who could be judged easily. The saying *never judge a book by its cover* was made for men such as he. At just over six feet tall and with a spindly frame, one could easily take the gaunt-faced Frenchman for a liberal arts professor, but to do so would be inviting peril. With his large hands and a seemingly clumsy demeanour, a stranger might be concerned the man would trip up over his own feet and tumble into them by mistake. Of course, anyone who knew him well would never entertain such idiocies. Because, simply put, Ernst Dupont was one of, if not the, most dangerous men among the attendees that night. Having served in the French Land Army since the age of seventeen, the talented soldier had gone on to be recruited by the special forces division of the 1st Marine Infantry Parachute Regiment. A nasty leg wound in Iraq and many clandestine operations later, Dupont had been promoted to Special Operations Command, a desk job... hence the seemingly clumsy walk. Still, as the unofficial representative of the French president tonight, he was a welcome addition so far as Bauer was concerned. Not because of his connections to the government, but rather those that only Bauer knew of. As far as everyone else in the room knew, Ernst Dupont was a patriotic nationalist with a rare dedication to everything within the sphere of the French government and its citizens. But in reality Mr Dupont had been a Daedalus operative since birth. The fascist organisation, the remnants of the Third Reich, had moulded the man since birth. He had a strong Germanic bloodline, the right bloodline, and it was Hans Bauer himself who had overseen and orchestrated Dupont's rise to this position of power. Dupont was a nationalist all right, but he was a disciple of the Fourth Reich.

Bauer stared into Dupont's blue eyes and raised his eyebrow slightly, acknowledging his young protégé's dedicated work in organising and pushing for tonight's affair.

'You're welcome, Mr Bauer, but you should know the American delegation has decided not to attend.'

The information brought with it a look of surprise from Bauer, but of course this little piece of body language was fabricated solely for the Frenchman.

'Well then, Ernst, it would seem that it's up to the French and British to move things along. Shall we get started?'

Dupont offered a firm nod and he stepped back and directed Bauer towards the only other people in attendance, a man and a woman both in black suits. The man was middle-aged with short curly brown hair, rosy cheeks. The woman was slightly older with a greying blonde ponytail and darkened teeth, a consequence no doubt of strong French cigarettes. The two guests said nothing and offered little more than a nod because everyone attending knew who and what would be going down that night.

Bauer turned his attention to the far end of the room, which formed a balcony, allowing attendees to look down to the lower level, a stone-floored room below and, as Bauer leant against the siderail and took note of a wooden contraption, bolted to the floor, he was joined by Dupont.

'We'll be using French servicemen to ensure it's legal, but unacknowledged. The men were handpicked by General Perdieu and are unknown even to me, which adds a layer of insulation for us.'

'Yes, I know. I left a message for the general on my way over, thanking him for the men, and his discretion. You've got a good one there.'

Dupont offered a smile before pulling a trim, black walkie-talkie from his inside jacket pocket and raising it to his lips.

'Bring him in.'

Down below, the thick oak door at the far end of the room slowly creaked open and a man wearing a plain army-green boiler suit was frogmarched inside by two red-beret-wearing soldiers. The man's hands were shackled by steel chains, which attached to a padlocked waist belt. Cuffs around each ankle made his short trip to room's centre awkward, his shoes scraping against the stone floor. The two guards brought him to a stop and then backed away before placing their hands behind their backs and looking down to the floor respectfully.

Despite unkempt black, shoulder-length hair and a few days' stubble on his face, the man looked unfazed by his predicament; even as he turned his attention to the slim set of wooden gallows before him, the beckoning rope noose hanging from it, he showed no fear. The prisoner simply took note of his method of execution and then gazed upwards to the group of four people staring at him from the gallery above, taking a moment to stretch his neck from side to side.

The gesture produced a smile from Bauer, whether out of respect for the man's courage or sheer enjoyment of the spectacle to come it was impossible to tell. But his expression fell blank once Dupont brought a piece of folded paper from his jacket pocket and began to read it aloud.

'Commander Marcel Lavigne, you have been found guilty by a military court of your peers of treason, and your involvement with the disavowed group DSV for the detonation of a one-kiloton nuclear device in New York

City, just over ten months ago. An act of terrorism that caused the death of over six hundred and fifty thousand people. Your crimes are grave, Commander, and I have been granted the power to see you are executed for your crimes under the Allied Security Act of 1945. Except for the leaders of the three allied powers, no one outside this room will ever have knowledge of what takes place here today. Your very existence will be wiped from the records and the name of Marcel Lavigne will disappear, as of tonight, from the face of this earth. For these crimes you will be hanged by the neck until you are dead. Your body will then be removed from this place and burned to ashes.'

Dupont lowered the piece of paper he was holding and stared down at Commander Lavigne who was still looking up at him silently, his demeanour remarkably calm given the circumstances.

'Do you have any last words?'

Lavigne remained still, and then sucked in a deep breath.

'Would they make any difference?'

Bauer leaned forward against the railing and grinned.

'No difference whatsoever, but hey,' he said, giving an uncaring wave, 'what have you got to lose?'

Lavigne lowered his gaze for a moment and then with a short snort he looked back up to his executioners before settling his gaze on Bauer.

'On the night that the weight of your own arrogance and deceit is brought crashing down upon you by my friends and their razor-sharp blades I want you to remember this moment. Remember me. Because, Mr Bauer... your time is nearly up.'

Bauer looked unimpressed and rolled his eyes.

'Yes, Yes, very poetic. But I'm betting that meeting will come sooner than you expect.'

It was an odd response, but neither of the other three attendees showed any sign of reaction.

But why would they? Bauer thought and continuing to smile smugly at Lavigne, because what they knew, and the commander did not, was that this whole execution was a set-up and, unless he had miscalculated, and he never did, DSV was already here.

After the brazen rescue of Colonel Jacques Remus mid-flight on his way to join Commander Lavigne for a secret military trial, Bauer had determined that there was no way Munroe and his merry band of DSV idiots would allow their teammate to be executed. Not if they could stop it. And so, a trap was laid, provided by Bauer and Ernst Dupont. If they could spin a tale of Lavigne's secret execution for treason and hold the proceedings somewhere away from any military bases at a location that appeared easy to compromise, then the temptation would be too great. DSV would be unable to resist a rescue attempt and, in doing so, the whole damn unit would be scooped up in one fell swoop. Or at the very least shot and killed during the attempt. Either way was good.

Bauer took a moment to rub his forehead, detecting the onset of a bad headache. He had been getting many of late and although he put it all down to his drinking these past few months, he knew in his heart that the frustration he felt from not pinning down DSV was likely the root cause. Hans Bauer did not suffer stress as most people did, his mind and decision-making was always clear and crystallised, but recently something had changed in him. Tonight he would excise those base human anxieties from his soul.

Fort National had proved perfect. The building, although a tourist attraction, was still considered military ground, which meant a military execution was legal by the terms of the Allied Security Act of 1945. This kept the politicians involved happy and covered them from any fallout if anything were to go wrong.

Which it won't.

The position was also well away from any other military installations or political institutions, allowing room for deniability, politically, should it ever be needed. The fort was also located away from most prying eyes and although it was close to the city of Saint Malo, the tidal island it was built on guaranteed privacy. At that time of night, the location would be irresistible to the morons of the disavowed, and Bauer had managed to convince the UK prime minister, Andrew Previn, to garner agreement from the French and Americans.

Unfortunately, the Americans had decided not to send any representatives: the superpower's need for deniability was greater than its want to play a part in it. It was understandable. With most of New York City deserted and the country in a financial meltdown, the president had other, far more pressing issues at hand, and scandals of any kind were not an option. For the Americans, revenge was most definitely a dish to be served cold. Bauer had no doubt they would get their pound of flesh at some point.

Bauer glanced over at Dupont and shrugged lightly.

'Now, can we please hang this bastard?'

Dupont looked down at Lavigne and then motioned to the soldiers.

'Prepare the guilty man. The execution will begin at twenty-one hundred hours, on the second.'

The solider to Lavigne's left pulled a folded grey canvas bag from under his belt as the one on the right slapped on a piece of black duct tape across the condemned man's mouth. The bag was roughly slipped over the commander's head. There was little resistance from their prisoner as he was pushed down onto a wooden bench that skirted the nearest wall. The two soldiers stood flanking him as the attendees pulled back from the edge of the gallery and now formed a group huddle.

'If you are right, Mr Bauer, that gives his friends just under twenty minutes to attempt a rescue,' Dupont said, glancing at his Tag Heuer wristwatch.

'Oh, I'm right, Ernst. They'll be here. The real question is, will we take them alive? And if we do, should we make them watch commander Lavigne executed as per the legal decree?'

At any other time, Bauer's comments would have been taken as revolting and unbefitting a man in his position, a position afforded by the prime minister of the United Kingdom, but these were not normal times. The devastation of the nuclear terrorist attack on New York had stripped many people of their empathy or moral code. The footage for weeks after the detonation was that of charred and burned children being brought out of what was now a quarantine zone; it had been chilling. There had been as many lives destroyed in the aftermath as in the initial blast, and along with all the radiation fallout that followed, the true toll on lives would not be known for years to come. In many cases, generations of families had been wiped out in a flash, and if the outpouring of anger after 9/11 had been considered potent it was a mere shadow of the rage now felt by most in the Western world and beyond. And as those expressions of sickening anger formed upon the faces of Dupont and his two special-forces counterparts, Bauer could not help but allow a feeling of pride to well up inside his chest. To think that he and the neo-Nazi organisation Daedalus, which he now had sole control of, were responsible for it all. It was, so far as he was concerned, a stroke of genius and a sleight of hand of logistical brilliance that only the master race could have accomplished. His race and the blood that ran through his veins would dominate the future of the world and restore a timeline that should never have been interrupted by the dismal outcome of the Second World War. The planet would now learn of his greatness through cast iron will and the slave races would serve his Aryan brothers and sisters for not only a thousand years but a Fourth Reich that would last ten thousand. Every conceivable whim would be catered for and every sordid act of filth would be enjoyed.

'Mr Bauer, are you all right?'

'What?' Bauer replied faintly as he awakened from his thoughts to see Dupont staring at him curiously. The special-forces officer stared at his midriff, causing Bauer to glance down and notice the bulge in his trousers that had appeared.

'I'm fine,' Bauer replied curtly, 'just anxious to get this over with.'

Dupont gave an understanding nod, clearly not having noticed the bulge. Bauer now pulled out a mobile phone from his pocket and gave it a shake.

'Just my phone,' he said, shooting the female officer a deflecting glance before sliding it back into his trouser pocket. 'Now let's go over the status of your men, Ernst.'

'Of course. We have three fire-teams. One on the edge of the city, just off the beach, in Jeeps. The second is on the water, two boats, six men patrolling from the English Channel side, and the third is located at the far end of the shoreline.' There was no arrogance in his voice, only confidence as he laid down the details of security in place. 'If they attempt to breach the fort—'

'*When* they attempt,' Bauer rectified, and it was met with a nod from Dupont.

'When they attempt a breach, from whichever side, we will be ready and waiting to take them into custody.' Dupont paused and gave Bauer an impressed look. 'I must commend you, Mr Bauer.'

'And that would be for?' Bauer replied, subtly making a final adjustment to his pants.

'For attending. Everyone here is special forces. It's their job, but for you to put yourself in the middle of this operation is—'

'Necessary,' Bauer finished, appreciating Dupont's words. 'Otherwise they could suspect a trap. But with me here they will know this execution is genuine.'

Dupont offered an appreciative nod and changed the walkie-talkie channel as Bauer took in a deep satisfying breath.

'We have just over ten minutes until the execution. Prepare yourselves.'

Bauer walked back to the edge of the gallery and pointed down to the soldiers still guarding Lavigne, whose semi-slumped posture made it look as though he had already given up, despite his earlier show of courage.

'Noose him up, gentlemen. Regardless of what happens, the court-sanctioned execution will be taking place tonight.'

Without hesitation both soldiers pulled Lavigne up by his arms and led their prisoner up the short flight of wooden steps to where the thick rope noose was placed around his neck and tightened. For the first time Lavigne struggled slightly against his restraints and his head began to jerk back and forward as he fought against the tight sensation around his neck.

'Not so tough now, are you, Commander Lavigne?' Bauer whispered under his breath before returning to face the others as the sounds of nasal groans could be heard coming from the grey bag. 'Here we go.'

Bauer's confidence in members of DSV making an appearance seemed unshakeable even though there were barely ten minutes until the execution. The time and date had been deliberately released by MI6 over channels that they knew the clandestine organisation could access. As was the information disclosing that just three officers and Hans Bauer would be attending and carrying out the secret execution.

The next few minutes passed as the four attendees waited in tense silence, each glancing over at Dupont's walkie-talkie periodically, but all remaining patient.

Two minutes.

Three minutes.

Four minutes...

The crackling from the walkie-talkie had Bauer jerking forwards in anticipation. Dupont raised the electronic device closer to his ear.

'We have a black transit van pulling up on the beach.'

Dupont placed the walkie-talkie on a wooden side table next to the door and pulled out his phone, which he began to scroll through.

At the same time, the other two special forces officers pulled Glock handguns from their concealed waist holders and readied themselves as Bauer strode over to Dupont and observed the small screen. The footage was sharp and taken from high up, probably from the top-floor window of the beach house where the first-floor team were encamped.

Out of the darkness, a black transit slowly rolled into view and proceeded to move along the beach but stayed as close to the coastal wall as possible. It then came to a stop at the darkest part of the shoreline, the gloomy shadow not allowing a clear picture of the driver's side.

'All teams maintain your positions,' Dupont ordered, and tilted the screen for a better angle so Bauer could get a view. As he did so the distant light of a vehicle heading into the city lit up the side of the transit van and everyone got a brief look at the driver.

Ethan Munroe sat hunched over the steering wheel with another two people on the passenger side next to him. The light afforded was only fleeting, but it was enough to have Bauer slamming his fist into his palm in excitement.

'That's them,' he growled as Dupont delivered his orders into the walkie-talkie.

'That's them. Approach and detain. We want them alive.'

Bauer drove his closed fist into his open palm for a second time with a satisfying thud.

'I knew they'd show. I knew it.'

'We're not finished yet, Mr Bauer. Let's see if we can take them alive, but I assure you we have them cornered. Either way, they are not getting off that beach.'

The smile on Hans Bauer's face was worthy of a Cheshire cat and he strode over to the balcony's edge and called down to Lavigne.

'Thank you, Commander, but your services are no longer required.' He then turned to the soldier whose hand was clamped around the release lever and clicked his fingers. 'Proceed with the execution. Hang that dead man.'

Without a pause, the soldier gave the lever a hard pull, causing the floor panel below to drop away, sending Lavigne freefalling for almost an entire body length before the rope jerked tightly, sending his body twitching wildly, his neck broken on impact.

Bauer barely watched, and even before the twitching had subsided he was on his way back to Dupont who was receiving a message through his walkie-talkie.

'Fire teams one and two into position... Sea team prepare to move.'

Dupont glanced up at Bauer and then over to the edge of the gallery.

'Maybe you should have waited, Mr Bauer.'

The comment was said with a distaste that made Bauer defensive. 'You focus on bringing them in and leave to me matters of State.'

Without offence, Dupont simply nodded and then pressed the button on his walkie-talkie. 'All teams are go. I repeat, all teams are go.'

Both men, with the other two special-forces officers behind them, watched the phone footage in silence as the transit van was lit up by powerful lights from three directions. Two from the beach and the third coming from one of the boats off shore, which illuminated the whole front windscreen and showing not only Ethan Munroe, but DSV members Sloan and Remus as well, each raising their palms and covering their eyes from the dazzling lights.

'Turn the engine off and exit the vehicle!' A deep voice from a megaphone blasted out from the darkness as half a dozen masked special-forces soldiers wearing blacked-out gear with no insignias, each holding a grey FN Minimi machine gun, cautiously moved towards the vehicle.

The transit van instantly sped off down the beach, leaving a spray of sand in its wake as short bursts of muffled gunfire could be heard, one of which hit the van's back left tyre but did little to slow it down on the wet and hard sandy shoreline.

On the coastal side, two boats filled with the second fire-team swept across the water, remaining parallel to the shore, with their lights following the van as it continued to race up the beach. Further up, the third fire-team were closing in on the van on foot. Their presence brought the van to a juddering halt as a burst of gunfire put a grouping of holes into the bonnet, sending a thick stream of steam puncturing the night air as the vehicle expelled its last gasp of life.

Ethan Munroe looked out the van's window at the special forces now approached the van cautiously, their machine guns raised. The two boats rode out of the water and slid to a stop on the beach, the armed occupants racing to join the soldiers already encircling the vehicle.

'Turn your engine off and exit the vehicle,' the same deep French voice demanded in English. 'You will not be fired upon.'

The whine of the transit van's engine suddenly cut out and the soldiers came to a dead halt, holding their positions having fully encircled the vehicle at a distance of twenty metres. They apprehensively waited for the doors to open... But they did not.

'This is your last chance,' the deep French voice bellowed over the megaphone. 'Slowly exit the vehicle with your hands up and get down on your knees. You will not be fired upon; I repeat, you will not be fired upon.'

Another ten seconds passed and still nothing. In fact, Munroe and the other passengers were still staring out of the car windows and not moving an inch.

'Captain, move in and secure the car,' Dupont ordered, and both he and Bauer watched as two of the soldiers slowly approached both sides of the van. With one hand holding their weapons towards the threat, they reached over, grabbed the handles and at the same time swung open the doors.

Bauer's bottom jaw literally dropped open as Dupont attempted to figure out what was going on. The inside of the van was empty except for a series of small rotating pistons that had been clamped on to the wheel, leading down to the accelerator and brake. Stranger still was the white screens that had been stuck with adhesive to the windscreen and side windows, a high-spec portable projector with three lenses was bolted to the middle seat and had been lined up to display the images of Munroe, Sloan and Remus. The clarity was remarkable until one got close and then the limitations of the technology could be seen, but from a distance and even with the powerful lights projected by the fire-teams it was near indistinguishable from the real thing.

'Shut down the area, now,' Dupont yelled as Bauer raced over to the gallery edge and looked down to see the soldiers gone but the body of Lavigne still dangling within the drop hole. The head was the only part of the body visible from his viewpoint. Bauer, followed by the two special-forces officers, flung open the gallery door and raced down the stairs to the ground floor where he kicked open the door and entered the execution room.

From this angle he could see almost the whole body and he raced towards it, coming to a sliding stop as something became apparent.

Lavigne's feet were still moving.

His breathing becoming ever heavier, Bauer reached up and on tip toe ripped the grey canvas bag from the prisoner and the face that stared back brought with it the realisation of what had happened.

'*Fuck!*' he screeched loudly, staring into the semi-conscious eyes of the guide who had greeted him initially. The rope had been wrapped around his waist underneath his green boiler suit and a short length of it ran directly up to his neck, giving the appearance of a single noose around his throat when in fact all the weight from the drop had been distributed around his midriff.

There were few times Hans Bauer found himself at a loss for words, but he stood motionless, his lower jaw hanging open in shock as his mobile phone began to vibrate. His eyes still wide, he slowly retrieved the iPhone from his trouser pocket, pressed the accept button and raised it to his ear.

'Hello.'

'Mr Bauer, I'm returning your message. I'm afraid I don't know what you're talking about.'

'What? Who is this?' Bauer huffed, succumbing to a feeling of light-headedness as his headache suddenly intensified.

'It's General Perdieu, Mr Bauer. I got your message of thanks, but you're mistaken. I haven't sent you any of my men for special duty.'

Bauer's hand dropped to his side and he let the mobile slip to the floor, its screen shattering against the stone.

'Munroe,' he hissed, as if just saying the name might cause some tangible damage in some way. 'You son of a bitch.'

Chapter 3

The sound of waves crashing against the side of the boat sent jolts through Commander Marcel Lavigne's body as the hum from the engine cut out and he could hear nothing but the gentle sound of water lapping against the craft's sides. He felt a hand carefully grasp the grey canvas bag on his head and slowly slip it off to reveal a face he welcomed, smiling in front of him.

'Welcome back from the dead, Marcel.' Ethan Munroe greeted him with a friendly tap on the shoulder. 'Sorry we were late.'

Lavigne expelled a relieved grunt and then took stock of his surroundings. He was sitting at the end of a black combat rubber raiding craft, which was in the process of being moored to the stern of an eighty-five-foot Princess motor yacht by Jacqueline Sloan, his British DSV counterpart. She secured the knots tightly, climbed up the matte aluminium boarding ladder and shot Lavigne a wave.

'Let's go, soldier. We've spent enough time saving your arse.'

Munroe took a small steel key from the top pocket of his French soldier's uniform and unlocked Lavigne's shackles before moving to one side and allowing the man to join Sloan.

He then watched as the two shared a brief embrace before disappearing deeper into the yacht's first floor and out of sight.

That had gone a hell of a lot easier than he'd expected.

Munroe glanced towards the distant glow of Saint Malo's coastline and imagined how Bauer was taking what must have been such a blow to his uber-ego. Right about now he was most likely formulating a plan to blame someone for not only blowing his little trap but allowing his prisoner to escape from right under their noses.

After rescuing Colonel Remus on his flight to Paris and replacing him with one of the world's most-wanted drug lords, DSV had gone dark; they had become nothing more than ghosts as they licked their wounds and figured out a way to get back in the fight. A fight which had become very clear real fast – comprising only two sides. Them against the entire Western nations' military and judicial apparatus, political leaders and everything in between. A fairly daunting prospect, by anyone's standard.

Hans Bauer, the newly proclaimed leader of Daedalus, had further strengthened his position with the British prime minister during that time, allowing his tentacles to reach contacts within the French and American spy services and beyond. Daedalus's private military contractors, Blackstar, had received the contract to track down DSV and bring them in, dead or alive – though preferably dead. And although, theoretically, they were assets of CIA and MI6, their free rein was long and all-encompassing.

There was a need for compartmentalisation and secrecy after the blame for the devastating detonation of a one-kiloton nuclear bomb in New York City months earlier had been placed squarely on Iranian terrorists. The global communities' outrage had proved so overwhelming that even Russia and China had backed away from providing Iran with political protection when war had been declared by the United States and its numerous allies, with the very vocal goal of regime change. As with most global events, and certainly political tracks, any and all opportunities were sought and gained, no matter what real truths had instigated the whole process. Invasion was expected within weeks and given that the Iranians had sped up their nuclear programmes, it was hardly surprising. The last thing anyone wanted was a nuclear Iran.

Munroe turned back from the glittering shoreline far away and climbed up the boarding ladder as both engines beneath the water began to propel the impressive yacht forwards, in the direction of the British coast. He steadied himself on the steel railing next to him, slipped off the soldier's beret he was wearing and let out a satisfied grunt with a shake of his head before tossing the piece of clothing into the water. For all Bauer's narcissistic belief in his own awareness of all things, the man was slipping. Perhaps his newly acquired power and responsibilities were weighing heavier on him than expected. The arrogant prick had not even realised that Munroe, along with Barbeau, his other DSV colleague, were the ones who had brought Lavigne into the hanging chamber in the first place. Their low berets had helped as had the little Nazi's choice to watch the execution from the gallery. As always, eighty per cent of an operation was in the preparation and when McCitrick had heard news of the execution on the intelligence grapevine, the planning had begun.

They knew it was a trap immediately. There was no way orders of a secret execution would be passed through that chosen line of communications because the powers that be knew damn well DSV could get access to it. But Bauer most likely had insisted it be used as a double bluff, which was his first mistake. His second was less his fault but caused by secrecy. To keep the execution as secret as possible, only a few people had been deemed trustworthy and only the most well-placed operatives used. Which, if anyone had stopped to think, were the exact type of contacts that DSV had been dealing with for years. So it was no surprise, yet still lucky for them, that McCitrick had a tight connection with one of the insiders arranging the event. The name of the contact was known only to McCitrick and even Remus was unaware of the whistle-blower's identity. The person in question had been adamant about secrecy and McCitrick had chosen to uphold the request. That aside, the old man always liked having an extra layer of insulation when it came to his top informants and that was fine by Munroe: there were few people he trusted as much as John McCitrick.

With security in their back pocket, it had taken just a fake phone call from General Perdieu using voice synthesisers to offer the guards for that evening's event and, once Bauer and the others had retreated out of sight of the balcony, the switch of Lavigne for Bauer's guide had been made. Munroe had stealthily subdued the guide within moments of Bauer entering the gallery and from there he simply had to go through the motions of the supposed hanging. With the audience's attention drawn to the raid on the transit van Munroe and Sloan had escaped with a shackled Lavigne to the waiting rubber raiding craft and back to the yacht anchored half a mile beyond French jurisdiction.

Munroe watched his beret disappear beneath the waterline before heading inside the first-floor cabin to join his teammates with a single satisfying thought in his mind.

Yep, Bauer would be going absolutely apeshit right about now... and that was nice.

'Good Job, Ethan.' John McCitrick congratulated, and he passed Munroe a silver can of Diet Coke and grinned. The DSV head was, as would be expected, in high spirits, although his outfit was what Munroe noticed before than anything else. The tan hunter's big-game outfit hung loosely from McCitrick's frame, with shorts down to his knees, making for an odd, almost uncomfortable costume.

'Thank you, sir. You do know you look like Orson Welles in that get-up?'

'Of course I do,' he replied, his grin unwavering. 'Anyone who has the finances to own this boat is going to be eccentric, believe me. If we get pulled then I'm playing the part. Besides, we were chasing some fairly big game tonight. Any problems?'

Munroe cracked the Coke's pull ring and took a well-deserved swig.

'It went well, and it might dent the trust between the prime minister and Bauer. Something we can work on expanding.'

'That's the plan,' McCitrick replied, nodding approvingly. 'Now join the others. I've got something to say.'

McCitrick made his way towards the eight-seat dining table at the far end of the cabin as Munroe greeted the others with a smile. Not all the DSV unit were onboard, purely due to security. If they were caught then having all the proverbial eggs in the basket was not an option. The American section, Dalton and Talon, were in a safe house Stateside while Remus was in a secure location just outside Saint Malo. He was there in case the mission went tits-up and additional logistics were required. Given that his skills had not been needed he would slip out of France and join them back in the UK. Some might have thought it ill-advised to hide out in the belly of the beast, right under MI6's nose, but in truth it was the safest place to be. What was the saying?

Keep your friends close but your enemies closer.

Well the same was true when it came to location and the monitoring of MI6 communication showed that most of the legwork to find DSV was taking place throughout South America.

Munroe stared over at Sloan as she watched Jean Barbeau deliver a back-slapping hug to his French team-mate making up the French section of DSV. As expected the two were close and the fact that Lavigne had spent months in captivity with his execution pending had been an understandable distraction for Barbeau. But as the two got reacquainted it was clear that with the entire team back they now had the best chance of shutting down Daedalus for good whilst restoring their own reputations. But how to do it with the whole world on your heels… well, that was the real question and as yet there was no plan.

'Nice work and welcome back, Marcel,' McCitrick announced before taking his position at the head of the dining table and, with a flick of his finger in a circular motion, the others, including Munroe, took their seats. He waited until they were all seated and only then did he continue. 'I had wanted for you all to take a few days R and R after a job well done but an opportunity has presented itself that we can't ignore.'

The entire team remained silent as McCitrick reached over to a varnished walnut side drawer, flipped open its door and pulled out an A3 roll of paper with a rubber band around its centre. He swiftly rolled the band off with his fingers, allowing it flick across the room, and then laid the sheet out across the table in front of him as Sloan and Barbeau unholstered their guns and placed them down on the two edges nearest them to stop the sheet curling up.

'Jean and I have already spoken about this,' McCitrick said, nodding towards Barbeau, 'so would you please go up top and let us know when we're approaching Southampton port.'

Barbeau nodded and gave Lavigne a final slap on his back before heading up the thin staircase to the upper deck.

Satisfied he had the attention of the what remained of the team and that the yacht was getting ever further away from the French coastline, McCitrick placed both fists on the table beneath him and began to explain.

'Eight hours ago HMS *Resolve*, a British Vanguard-class nuclear submarine, jettisoned an emergency beacon just off the coast of Spain. Since then there's been no communication with the vessel.'

Munroe's eyes widened slightly and he glanced over at Sloan whose look of growing curiosity mirrored his own. What it had to do with them though was another question entirely. Both they and Lavigne remained silent, yet their stares were questioning as McCitrick continued.

'On the surface it would appear to be one of the worst naval tragedies since the Falklands and little to do with us,' McCitrick acknowledged, tapping his finger on the map at a point just off the Spanish coast, 'but as I was able to syphon off more information it became all too apparent that there may be something in this for us.'

Munroe was already suspecting what was coming on down the line and he moved forward in his chair and leant over the map, focusing on the tip of McCitrick's finger and noting the printed depth.

'Hundred and fifty metres. It's deep but not too deep… we'd have heavy traffic though.'

Munroe sat back in his chair as Lavigne offered a small nod, with the only person looking concerned being Sloan.

'You want us to gain entry to a downed nuclear submarine which will have half the Royal Navy surrounding it and more divers crawling over the wreck than guards around the Queen's jewels!'

McCitrick smiled dryly as Sloan continued, calmly, yet with a seriousness that even the DSV section head would not have toyed with.

'You haven't forgotten that we're among the most wanted people on the planet at this moment, have you, sir?'

The smile evaporated from McCitrick's lips and he shook his head slowly in a manner that suggested he would never ask such a gamble.

'No, Captain, I am not asking you to enter the crashed nuclear submarine. I am, though, asking you to gain entry to the thing that brought her down.'

McCitrick slipped the ball of his finger a centimetre to one side and tapped upon the new location.

Sloan and Lavigne now also leant forward and took note.

'What brought her down, sir?' Munroe asked while noting the slightly shallower depth of around seventy metres.

'I'm not exactly sure but it took down a Vanguard nuclear submarine without a single warning and if the radar data is accurate, which it is, then whatever did manage such a feat is still there, lurking in the depths some one hundred metres away from the wreck.'

All three teammates sat back in their seats as McCitrick briefly eyed them individually. 'Intriguing, no?'

As Munroe and Sloan guessed at the possibilities, Lavigne undid the top button of his green boiler suit that he was supposed to have been hanged in that night and rubbed his unshaven chin.

'If we know there's something there then so does the Navy,' he stated in a thick French accent and McCitrick flicked his forefinger in the man's direction.

'They absolutely do, but at the moment the top priority and focus is on reaching HMS *Resolve* in the hope of rescuing any of the crew. But, after that, you can be sure that the Royal Navy will invest one hundred per cent of its resources into finding out what brought her down.'

Munroe glanced over at Sloan, then Lavigne, as they considered the problem. With a raised eyebrow he faced McCitrick again.

'How long do we have?'

'The Navy's been on site for the past four hours. They've had divers in the water for three of them. That they have not yet moved on to this other, nearby, mystery object would suggest that there are survivors, so it would appear time is on our side. Once the rescue is completed, the top brass will quickly turn their attention elsewhere. So, I'd say we have six to eight hours tops to get in and out.'

Given that the two-week preparation to breakout Lavigne had climaxed less than an hour ago, it wasn't surprising that the time estimate drew a few sighs, and McCitrick addressed them immediately.

'I've put together an insertion brief and the equipment's being readied for pick up once we reach Southampton port. Munroe and Barbeau will do the dive while Sloan, Lavigne and I will run support and interference. I know, the time frame is tight... but isn't it always?'

Munroe managed a smile. It was no surprise both he and Barbeau had been chosen. With his service in the British SBS and Barbeau's naval diving experience it made perfect sense. So the how, as always during his experiences dealing with McCitrick, was a sealed deal, which left the most important part. The part the DSV section head always left until last. The what and why?

'Well, sir. That's the small details taken care of,' Munroe said casually and on the cusp of sounding sarcastic.

His tone drew a smile from Sloan, who he could tell was just pleased she wasn't being asked to dive down into the cold, black depths of the Atlantic.

'So, what is this "thing" you want us to infiltrate? I'm guessing it's not a whale, sir, because Barbeau and I are not the Jonah types.'

His response drew a stern gaze from McCitrick and he lifted his finger off the map and stood up straight, resting his hands on his hips.

'Truth is, Ethan, we don't know. But what I can tell you is that whatever it is, the radar telemetry suggests it has not moved and oddly we can't discern its shape due to the coastal rockface behind it. All we know is that whatever it is, it somehow brought down a Vanguard-class nuclear submarine and we need to beat the Royal Navy to it.'

'And why is that so important?' Sloan questioned with her usual aggressive tone of voice as Munroe glanced over to see her deep frown. Tough as nails and with the bite to back up her bark the ex-military intelligence captain was a strong ally to have and there were few others Munroe would trust if his life was on the line. But a charmer she was not.

'Well, sir?' Sloan added, spurred on by McCitrick's momentary silence. 'So far you've been as helpful as a Bombay call centre.'

The DSV section head offered an unamused grunt. 'Because Jax, ever since HMS *Resolve* went down, a faint signal has been coming from that thing down there. A faint, yet unmistakable signal that the Navy picked up and passed onto MI6. It was from there I managed to pull it off the wire without anyone knowing. It's a signal that would have been made top secret and passed onto DSV if our organisation hadn't gone to shit.'

'And why would that be?' Lavigne asked, although given the clandestine spy organisations remit they all had a rough idea.

'When the SS began extracting top Nazis to safety, offering them new identities and livelihoods towards the close of the Second World War, their means of communication were highly secret and near impossible to decrypt. Of course, with modern-day super computers they would be just a keystroke away from being broken, but back then the channels and devices were of the highest technology. When DSV was established, one of its first challenges was to track and reveal this plan and what would soon become knowns as "Odessa". The name given to the largest relocation of war criminals the world has ever seen.' McCitrick pointed down at the map with his forefinger to the place of earlier interest and a coy snarl spread across his lips. 'And for the last eight hours, since

HMS *Resolve* went down, whatever is down there has been spewing one of those old Odessa codes. A response code. And as yet we are the only ones who know what it is. Whatever's down there it, no matter how old, must be linked in some way to Daedalus... or the organisation that would become Daedalus. And we need to know what.'

Both Munroe and Sloan looked pensive, but judging by Lavigne's thick black eyebrows, which were both raised, the man still had questions.

'Odessa's eighty years old, sir. How will that help with finding a way to take down Daedalus?'

'Well we won't know that until we've taken a look, now will we, son,' McCitrick answered gruffly, but his demeanour then tempered. It was easy to forget that Lavigne had been out of the loop for months and had no idea what DSV had been up to and involved in since his arrest. 'It's been a tough year, Marcel. You haven't had a chance to catch up yet but when you do you'll see for yourself. What's left of DSV is against the wall and our own people now see us as a threat. They've been chasing us down relentlessly ever since you were taken into custody.' McCitrick glanced over at both Munroe and Sloan reassuringly before turning back to Lavigne. 'Our only mission is to bring Daedalus's project of a Fourth Reich to light and show the world what they are. This is and always was our remit and if we can exonerate ourselves then that will be a bonus. But to do that we need to chase every lead available, no matter how lean it may appear.'

Lavigne needed no time to consider what he was being told and nodded agreeably, much to the satisfaction of McCitrick.

'The cold dark depths it is then,' Munroe announced loudly with unwavering confidence in his voice. 'OK then, sir. Let's go take a look.'

Chapter 4

Pitch darkness and a heavy fog embraced the flotilla of Navy ships that circled a point on the surface above the sunk submarine like a Native American war party preparing a raid. Their blurry outlines were just visible against the dark skyline as lightning crackled among rolling grey clouds, offering only flash frames of the busy work being undertaken below.

'There you go,' Sloan said as she slipped the harness over Munroe's shoulders, securing the single pressurised cylinder to his back. 'Your destination is sixty-two metres down. The tank should get you there and back.'

'Should?' Munroe replied, glaring over his shoulder at her, his eyes demanding clarification.

Before any operation, whether aquatic, land-based or airborne, any operator worth his salt maintained their own gear before heading into the theatre of operations. All parachutes were checked meticulously, firearms were taken apart and reassembled and any item that ensured survival, like a SCUBA oxygen tank, was filled and checked by the person using it. This time around, Sloan had carried out the equipment checks and even though the trust in his teammate was solid, her choice of words had caused a shiver of concern.

Sloan moved around him and began to lock the tank's harness across his chest, only replying to his questioning once all the clips had been secured.

'Don't give me that look, Ethan. The tanks are as full as the psi will allow, but we've no idea what you'll find down there or how long you'll need.' She continued her checks, reaching up to his rubber hood and adjusting it. 'You're carrying about an hour's worth of dive time due to the rebreather technology and the scooters have an additional mini tank for emergencies.' Sloan leant back and popped open the side panel of the compact black fan-propelled scooter sitting on the deck and retrieved the small grey canister of oxygen with a transparent mouthpiece protruding from its tip. 'This will give you an additional five minutes,' she instructed, waving it in front of him before slipping it back into the storage compartment within the scooter. 'You're covered.'

Munroe simply replied with a stern nod. He wasn't worried, but like any operator he demanded to know exactly what limits and options were at his fingertips for any unseen situation. He fell silent, but mollified, contemplating the task at hand as Sloan began re-checking his equipment and the outfit he was wearing. The black seven-millimetre-thick wetsuit would keep his body temperature stable in the cold waters of the Atlantic and the thin gloves ensured his fingers wouldn't numb up. For most underwater operations the initial dive was used for reconnaissance with the second executing the desired action plan, but for Munroe and Barbeau, who was sitting opposite and finalising his outfit with help from Lavigne, a single dive would encompass both tasks. As yet the Navy were still focused on the submarine and their rescue mission, but it was impossible to say when this urgency would temper and focus would be brought to bear on the thing that had brought the sub down in the first place. Hell, if McCitrick was correct and the information had been labelled top secret then it was possible the Royal Navy had not even been made aware of the anomaly. Not yet anyway.

'As I said, at the depth you're going the tanks will allow for about an hour,' Sloan repeated as he and Lavigne finished the final checks of both men's suits. 'So no sight-seeing along the way for either of you and you'll be fine.'

'Noted,' Munroe replied, and he and Barbeau stood up tentatively. They made their way to the diving platform at the rear of the boat and then sat down with their backs facing the dark choppy surface of the water.

On the white metal fishing trawler moored up next to them stood McCitrick. He had procured the vessel in Southampton port hours earlier and with a fake fishing permit and a roster they had been able to manoeuvre within a quarter of a mile of the rescue operation being carried out by the Royal Navy.

'All right, lads, it's now or never,' McCitrick said. He was wearing a pair of green rubber fishing slicks that looked like a pair of shiny dungarees, which allowed his paunch to protruded at the middle, so that he looked exactly like the salty seaman he was playing. 'Get to the destination point, find out what caused that sub to go down and get back safe and sound. We'll be waiting for you.'

McCitrick motioned to Sloan and Lavigne with a flick of his hand and they passed over the specialised headgear to the two divers, each man slipping them on to their head securely. The masks provided an air-tight space over their whole face, allowing both divers to communicate via mic, and a series of yellow LED lights lined the interior ensuring a dim view of them both.

Munroe offered a simple nod and a wink to Sloan before slipping the facemask fully into place. He then pulled up his wrist, as did Barbeau, and they pressed the buttons of their stop watches in unison.

'We'll see you soon, gentlemen,' McCitrick said, and then watched Munroe swivel around and drop backwards off the low diving platform into the water, followed closely by Barbeau. Sloan and Lavigne then lowered the two black, cylindrical military water scooters into the waiting hands of Munroe and Barbeau. With rotary fans at one end and protruding handles on either side, the equipment would allow the divers to cover the quarter of a mile underwater quickly. With a brief, single-fingered salute from Munroe both men disappeared beneath the foamy black waves.

The small fishing crew watched for a moment until McCitrick gave a satisfied nod of his head and rotated his finger, high in the air, towards the increasingly darkening storm clouds swirling above them.

'OK, get to your stations. This could be a long hour.'

'Aye, aye Captain,' his crew mates replied, both getting into the role as McCitrick reached into his rubber dungarees and pulled out a grey speckled woolly hat and tossed it over to Sloan.

'Put this on, please, Jacqueline. For the next few hours you're a sea dog.'

Without hesitation Sloan slipped the hat on and tucked her blonde hair in at the sides as heavy rain began to pour from the skies. She looked past the stern towards the dim lights of the naval rescue taskforce, which were now becoming more visible as the fog began to disperse.

She could make out the smaller boats near the centre of interest. Her main hope was that the fog would just hold for a few hours longer. Of course, they would be on the ships' radar at this range, but a visual sighting of their fishing boat may cause additional interest. Interest they did not need. Still, the fog was thick enough to provide a veil of protection for the time being. It was so thick, in fact, that she did not notice the blinking red light far off in the distance as she made her way back towards the cabin: a light that appeared to be getting closer with every passing moment.

Chapter 5

The quarter–mile trip took twenty minutes, give or take. The water was surprisingly clear, not murky as the briny topside had suggested, and as Munroe looked down at the satellite positioning display velcroed to his wrist, he could see they were close. Close to what was still unknown but as they got ever nearer they began to make out the faded circular glow of lights far below in the distance.

'Must be part of the rescue operation,' Barbeau said, his voice crackling over the mic, and Munroe glanced over to his colleague who was being propelled forward on his own scooter and gave an exaggerated nod. He could of course just have replied via the face mask mic but it was purely an instinctual gesture. His time with the Special Boat Service, or SBS, had seen him undertake many sub-aquatic missions, although most had relied on hand gestures and no transmission mics. The SBS did down below what the SAS did on land and given that he had served in both regiments, he knew the excellence they stood for. The British Special Forces had been the mother of them all and although the American Navy SEALs definitely had the better technology, as only a wealthy superpower can provide, the SBS's saying 'By Guile and Strength' was not only the motto but the reality for its soldiers who had historically ensured the regiment such exceptional success.

At one hundred and fifty metres away the dampened lighting of the ongoing rescue operation below them was hazy at best and Munroe signalled a complete stop. Their current equipment meant it was impossible for them to descend any deeper and Munroe now pressed down on the top tank of his scooter, releasing a small panel that popped open to reveal a compartment containing a square, rubber-coated box. He quickly retrieved the box and held it up to his mask. With a press of a button the green screen it up with a night display and he positioned it on the activity below and began manipulating the two small joysticks. The image was remarkably clear and as he zoomed in, the telescopic camera began to provide a close-up view of the operation being under taken. There were multiple lights surrounding something dark and massive and it was then that he saw a single beam of light from one of the rescue divers fall across a gigantic black propeller as the massive hull of what must have been HMS *Resolve* loomed into view. For most people, the overwhelming sight of such a structure could be daunting, even unnerving, but for Munroe it was a wonderous sight to behold.

Without getting closer it was impossible to get the full picture of the damage incurred by the Vanguard-class submarine but even from this distance the cause was clear. He could make out a partial opening of twisted metal about twenty feet along from the propellers, but only when the lights of the naval divers passed over it before disappearing into the dark gloom of the Atlantic.

'Could be a torpedo hit,' Munroe said, waiting for another beam of light to hit the submarine's stern, which came soon enough. 'Heavy damage though. Bloody lucky if anyone is still alive... but...'

Munroe paused as he caught sight of what looked like the side of a much smaller hull pass between the massive hulk of the Vanguard-class submarine and one of the diver's beams. The light moved quickly but was close enough for him to make an educated guess. 'There's a small rescue sub down there. Maybe someone made it.'

'Hope springs eternal,' Barbeau commented and he was met with a nod from Munroe.

'Maybe. C'mon, let's get on with it.'

Munroe shifted his scope in the direction of their destination and began scouring the rocky incline of a drop-off wall leading straight down into the canyon where HMS *Resolve* had come to rest. The surface was jagged and uneven, which was to be expected, but as he used the in-screen compass and directional finder he soon came across the only part of the rock face that stood out. No more than seventy metres away and nearly exactly where his finder was directing him, still picking up the radio signal it had been continuing to emit. The uneven toothy outcrop gave way to a far smoother surface set flat into the rock face itself and Munroe finally settled on a shape that looked out of place and unnatural in its surroundings. He couldn't be sure from that distance, but it appeared to be a rectangle in shape with rounded edges.

'We may have something,' Munroe said, noting the exact direction on the satellite display velcroed to his wrist before returning the scope to its compartment and clicking the scooters panel shut.

With a whirring of fan blades, both men made their way over as far below them the dogged activity around the Vanguard submarine continued. Up until that point they had both been using their glowing instruments to guide them but as Munroe came to a full stop he now reached to the side of his scooter and pressed a single plastic covered button, his fingers feeling it click into place.

A small lightbulb from the nose of his craft emitted a beam of light and illuminated the shape he had seen on his camera. It was covered in barnacles and wispy green algae but it was immediately obvious they had found what they were looking for. It was a hatch, rectangle in shape and part of a larger metal wall buried into the rock. A circular grab handle protruded from its centre with a footrest sticking off the side to allow traction when opening it.

Munroe moved his scooter off to one side and grasped it, pulling himself closer for a better view. At the top of the hatch was a small porthole window no more than six inches wide and after rubbing away the thick green algae, he peered through it, detecting the faint glow of light coming from within. The interior consisted of a small chamber about eight feet high by eight feet wide and on the ceiling a round hatchway with a circular grab handle stuck out from it, identical to the one he was currently holding.

'It's an entrance pool,' Munroe said with surprise in his voice and after noting that the inside hatch on the ceiling looked secure he grasped the outside handle and steadied himself. 'You better move back.' He glanced back at Barbeau who was already putting some distance between them.

Munroe placed his heel on the foot rest allowing his flipper to hang over the top of it and gradually applied pressure.

The handle began to swivel effortlessly and after one entire turn, and without feeling any pressure resistance from the other side, Munroe ground the handle into place and pulled with his free palm pressed against the wall for leverage.

In the short time it took for the hatch to be swung open Barbeau was at Munroe's side and they now entered, one at a time, bringing their scooters with them.

'Thoughts?' Barbeau asked as Munroe slowly locked the door behind them and turned his attention to the access point in the ceiling above.

'None yet, but if the size of the barnacles on the outer wall are anything to go by, it's been here a long time.' Munroe reached up and grasped hold of the circular handle above them. 'Give me a hand.'

The small chamber allowed more than enough room for both men to manoeuvre and Barbeau grasped the handle as well. He grunted as they began to apply pressure.

The handle swivelled around with ease, still well-oiled, before it clicked into place and rose upwards on air-hydraulics until it was upright, bathing both men in artificial white light from above. At the same time, four white metal steps slid into place from thin crevices in the wall, allowing for an easy exit.

'Interesting design. I've not seen that before,' Barbeau noted as Munroe kicked of his flippers, unstrapped the tank from his back and passed it along with his harness to his teammate whilst keeping his facemask on.

'Let me take a look.'

Munroe placed his foot onto the first step and began to pull himself up until he broke the surface, then he pulled himself over the metal lip of the opening and took a look around, only now able to tell how large this underwater building was. The entrance room was modest with two rows of metal benches bolted to opposite sides of the walls. On the far end was a row of metal lockers, all closed except one whose door hung half broken on its hinges. This wasn't the only thing that looked broken: the white tiled floor contained mostly cracked plates smeared with black dirt and the cast metal walls of the room looked worn with brown stains of decay. Whoever had been using this place had not done so in a very long time.

Munroe planted his hand over his mask and prepared to remove it. He planned to slip it upwards to reveal just his lips in case the air was unbreathable. This place had pressure but what gas made up that pressure was an unknown. With this in mind he cautiously pushed the mask upwards and gently drew in a breath.

Still alive.

Munroe now slipped the mask fully off his head and then paused as he sniffed at the air, taking only a small volume at a time. It smelt musty and stale but breathable and, satisfied he couldn't smell the odour of anything harmful, he dropped the mask over the metal entrance lip, onto the floor, before climbing all the way out. Once done, he remained kneeling and turned back and drove his hand back into the water to feel his tank harness being thrust up towards him, which he pulled up out of the water and placed it to one side. He then reached back in to find Barbeau's tank harness waiting for him and he slowly pulled it out, allowing time for his French colleague to follow him up the steps.

Barbeau slowly broke the surface. When he saw Munroe he took off his own mask off and sniffed the air, his nose wrinkling.

'Smells old,' he said as Munroe placed his teammate's tank next to his own and helped him out of the water.

'Smells abandoned,' Munroe replied, making his way to the only exit, another rectangular door with the same, now familiar grey circular handle as Barbeau slipped back the rubber headpiece of his own wetsuit.

'Keep a hold of those tanks, Jean,' Munroe said, motioning to the two harnesses that Barbeau now held tightly in his hands. Who knew if the other side of the hatch was flooded and Munroe was taking no chances. 'OK, let's see if our luck holds.'

Munroe grasped the handle and swivelled it open with ease; a light hiss escaped from the edges of the hatch as the pressure of the chamber they were in equalised and then he swung the metal door open with a creak. He paused before glancing back at Barbeau with raised eyebrows. 'Take a look at this.'

The dining room was impressive given that it was deep below the waves of the Atlantic Ocean. A large, lacquered wood table sat in its middle with benches running either sided of it. The walls were, of course, made of the same metal bulkheads as the entrance room but in addition what had once been fine French crepe wallpaper now hung from it in strips, revealing the amber sticking glue behind. The table was covered with a white linen cloth with silver cutlery placed for a total of eight people. A large wooden dining chair was at its head, the only place setting to have gold silverware. At its centre sat an ornate white china serving dish, empty, but with a large silver ladle propped up inside it and a stained drinks' table on the left-hand side held a crystal decanter the contained brown liquid, along with a dozen or so crystal tumblers that still sparkled in the light despite the layers of dust. From the ceiling hung a modest yet lavish chandelier wrapped around three flickering light bulbs which projected a myriad of colourful reflections across the tablecloth below, causing the silver handle of the ladle to glint regally in the light.

Munroe felt Barbeau's head crane over his shoulder and he now took a step further inside.

'Impressive,' Barbeau remarked as they took in the surreal sight of such extravagance, yet it was not the furniture and condiments that drew their attention but what hung on the wall at the far end.

The large red and black swastika flag hung there proudly, covering the top portion of the back wall as a statement of reality rather than a decoration, and its colours looked as vibrant as Munroe guessed they had done upon the day of its making.

'Jesus,' Barbeau said, and Munroe slowly walked past the dining table and stopped beneath the flag.

'I don't think Jesus has any place here, Jean.'

Munroe had heard many stories about the Odessa network, the Nazi organisation created in the last few years of the war to aid escaping Nazis to a new life, but he had never considered the full logistics or scope of exactly what it had entailed. A lifeline for the worst psychopaths and zealots the twentieth century had been able to offer up and yet the lengths they had gone to only now truly hit home. 'This must have been a staging post for escapees. A halfway house for Hitler's finest before the long trip to South America by U-boat. We may be the first people to step foot in this place in almost eighty years.'

Barbeau walked along the opposite side of the dining table and also came to a stop underneath the hanging flag as Munroe continued, his voice tinged with tempered respect.

'The first modern SCUBA diving gear was created in German-occupied France in '42.'

'By Jacques Yves Cousteau,' Barbeau added, sounding surprised by the notion being alluded to, 'but he didn't sell the patent until 1945, at the end of the war.'

'It would seem the SS got their hands on it before that. Who knows, perhaps with the idea of this very hideout in mind,' Munroe said, shaking his head with a smile. 'How else could they have carved out this place without such equipment? And who knows how many of these hideouts there are.' Munroe contemplated the ingenious nature of creating such a place, this deep in the Atlantic. The Nazis may have been the scum of the earth but damn they were organised and resourceful.

Barbeau looked just as surprised as Munroe, but he shook his head and asked the very question that was now at the forefront of Munroe's mind.

'So what does an eighty-year-old Nazi hideout have to do with the downing of a British Vanguard-class nuclear submarine?'

Munroe stepped back from the flag and looked around the room, noting the closed doorways with thin turn handles along with the one directly before them beneath the audacious flag.

'Let's find out. We'll work our way through, front to back.'

Without hesitation Barbeau took the door on the left as Munroe moved to the right side of the dining room, grasped the handle and slowly made his way inside to be greeted by a sight straight out of a forties home-refurbishment catalogue. Two long steel tables sat at the room's centre with porcelain sinks placed in between steel cutting tables and a cream-coloured double-doored Lieb-herr refrigerator positioned at the farthest corner. Various pieces of baking equipment sat upon the tables looking pristine and the whole layout was centred around a sturdy four-door cast-iron oven with thick doors. The walls were covered in white tiles, none cracked, and apart from scuff marks on the metal flooring it appeared remarkably untouched by the passing of nearly a century of disuse.

'A kitchen fit for a king...' Munroe muttered under his breath, 'or the antichrist.'

He made a final scan of the place before moving back into the dining room to see Barbeau appear at the opposite doorway.

'I've got a leisure room, sofas and board games,' the Frenchman said as he made his way back to the top of the dining room. 'The master race at play.'

'Kitchen,' Munroe replied, nodding towards his own discovery before joining him at the only other exit, underneath the hanging flag. 'There's an oven in there that must weigh a tonne. They must have used a U-boat with the ability to connect to the entrance hatch and brought it in, piece by piece.'

'Heavy work,' Barbeau said as Munroe reached over and gripped the door handle. 'Not if you don't do it yourself. It's amazing what cutting-edge technology of the day and an unlimited number of slave workers will get you.'

Barbeau offered a despondent grunt as Munroe turned the door handle and allowed the heavy slab of metal to swing backwards, revealing a corridor. With his eyebrows once again raised in curiosity he headed inside with Barbeau close behind him.

The passageway ran ten metres in either direction and had more doors on its opposite wall, and a number of paintings hung from the grey steel girders, giving it a somewhat cosier feel than the previous rooms. On the floor a thick red carpet ran its length, adding to the exclusive ambiance, and side tables on opposite sides of the corridor held white china vases containing desiccated flowers whose crisp black petals had fallen onto the carpet below.

'You take that end,' Munroe said, nodding to his right before heading off to the left and down to the first doorway. The cherry-wood frame had been overlaid on top of the metal giving it a more lavish feel. He reached down and gripped the still shiny brass doorknob, slowly turned it, and made his way inside.

The room was a modest-sized bedroom containing four bunk beds and a thick black woven rug on top of the grey carpet. On the walls hung framed propaganda paintings from the Nazis' time period, but their images were unlike any Munroe had seen before, their content unique.

One displayed a picture of a young, blond-haired, blue-eyed man staring out from the poster, a thin black line running down the centre of his face from the forehead to the chin. On the left half, the man wore an SS officer's hat and his expression was stern and unyielding. The right side had smiling lips and a rosy warmth exuding from the cheeks. Running across the top of the poster in black, bold font, the German lettered headline read, '*Never forget who you are.*' Beneath it ran another banner headline in a much softer font, '*Be patient. You will be needed in the war to come.*'

Above the other bunk bed another one of these instructional posters displayed a young family in a park with the father pushing his son on a swing as the mother and daughter sat on a light-blue picnic rug eating sandwiches, while in the background other park goers enjoyed themselves. Behind the father a flagpole rose into the sky flying the red, white and blue of the American flag – an image of forties' life in the USA, the American dream. And it would have been too if not for the shadows cast. The father cast a shadow of a German soldier in jackboots, holding a rifle instead of pushing his son. The mother's shadow cast the image of a proud German woman with braided hair, wearing a short-sleeved T-shirt with a swastika on the front, reminiscent of the outfits worn by the Nazi organisation, The League of German Girls. Even more unpleasant were the shadows of the children who both stood to attention, their tiny hands outstretched in Nazi salutes as from above the American flag projected a shadow of a swastika down onto the ground.

A hope of things to come, Munroe thought. He turned his attention away from the posters to an old-style cedar-wood butler's desk which sat between the beds with its front panel pulled down, creating a desk to write upon. An arch back desk chair sat in front of it and Munroe approached and pulled it back a few inches to reveal the moulded indents under each leg. Judging by the heavy impressions in the carpet it had not been moved in a very long time and even though he was sure this safe house had not welcomed any inhabitants recently he felt unsettled.

Why are the lights on and why does the air smell so fresh?

Sure, the whole place smelt pretty ripe, but not the stale stench one would expect from eighty years of disuse.

Munroe moved back into the corridor and with Barbeau still out of sight he headed down to the next doorway and found a conference room with a large oval board table and chairs. Apart from the oversized portrait of Adolf Hitler hanging above the head of the table in his usual arrogant pose, there was nothing of real interest, except a single closed doorway on the opposite side of the room.

Munroe made his way over and entered, the laid floorboards beneath him creaking with each step. He pushed open the door to find something of far more interest, even if only from a historical standpoint. The room was a smaller area with bare bulkhead walls and again a portrait, yet smaller this time, of Hitler overlooking a single lacquered wood table with a series of white painted metal stack trays upon it. Next to these sat a unique-looking piece of equipment with a metal rod bolted to the table, sticking vertically upwards from its surface. A hinge connected to another, thinner piece of metal with four magnifying glasses attached to them. Munroe pushed each of them with his finger to discover each could be positioned in front of the other and adjustable hinges were attached at the base of the main rod, allowing for the whole device to be move to any position above the table.

The metal trays were empty, but it was obvious to Munroe what this room's purpose had been.

Passport and documentation forgery.

Escaping Nazis would not have gone far in their new lives without documentation and it was here, in this place, that their new lives had been constructed... at least on paper.

Munroe began checking the desks, one at a time, and was still doing so as Barbeau appeared at the doorway.

'Ethan, you need to see this,' he said with insistence as the odd apparatus on the table caught his attention. 'What's that?'

'Forgers' tools. Everything needed to create new identities to the new world. Nineteen-forties style,' Munroe replied, still searching what quickly became evident were empty drawers. 'McCitrick was right. This place is Odessa. No doubt… What did you find?'

'I found what took down HMS *Resolve*.'

Munroe needed no more encouragement and he pulled back from the desk and began following Barbeau through the conference room into the corridor and along to the far end.

'Take a look at this.'

Barbeau stood at the doorway and allowed Munroe to enter first, who in turn came to an abrupt halt as he surveyed the interior. The room was the largest yet and divided into two sections. One was an observation room, which they now stood in, with a glass panel looking out onto the larger part of the room. The observation room itself contained a dashboard of controls, all unrecognisable to Munroe, but as he gazed through window he realised what they operated. A storage rack containing half a dozen torpedoes was bolted to the back bulkhead, explaining the use of the two large cylindrical tubes that had been drilled directly into the rock with a hardened-looking sealant paste around the join to keep the ocean water from seeping into the facility. Next to the rack stood a table with a crank attached to it for moving and loading the munition and it was then that Munroe noticed that the torpedo had two empty spaces.

'An underwater hideout with defensive capabilities,' Munroe said, admiring not the builders but the effort that must have gone into creating this whole place. 'So, who the hell fired them?'

'Not who,' Barbeau replied and, pointing down at the array of knobs and switches, added, 'but what.'

Munroe stepped back from the window and ran his fingers lightly across the dashboard. 'Automated firing? Was that even possible back then?'

Barbeau was himself also admiring the technological accomplishment before them. 'Seems so. I'm guessing the place has a basic radar net which when breached automatically fires the torpedoes. There's no way they have guidance systems but if something passes close enough, the torpedoes fire and hit whatever's straight in front of it.'

'In this case HMS *Resolve*. The first submarine to pass close enough in eighty years?' Munroe noted, but he was astounded by the innovation itself.

'Apparently. The ocean's a big place and with this type of technology you'd have to get very close to activate it.'

Munroe reached down and slowly swivelled the only knob with a label on it. *Volumen*.

From the desk's speakers the music of Wagners 'Ride of the Valkyries' could be heard and after a few seconds he turned it off.

'A welcome song?' Barbeau remarked with an eyebrow raised. 'Either death by torpedo or a song for arriving visitors. Looks like they thought of everything.'

As an operator, Jean Barbeau was second to none, as were all DSV agents, but his experience and knowledge in the mechanics of underwater munitions surpassed Munroe's. If the man said it was possible then it was possible. But there was still one thing that seemed sketchy in Munroe's mind.

'Jean, this is a hideout, right? An Odessa halfway house for escaping Nazis.'

Barbeau offered a simple nod of his head as Munroe continued.

'Then why go to all the trouble of creating a system like this? It was just a stopping-off point.'

Munroe could immediately tell that Barbeau knew more than he was letting on and he stared over at him, his expression demanding. 'Well?'

'Well it depends on who needs protecting. Who the guests were.'

Barbeau raised his finger and pointed to an open doorway at the back of the observation room that Munroe noticed only in his peripherals upon initially entering the room.

'Take a look at this.'

Munroe followed as he was led into the room next door, a reception room, for all intents and purposes. A small space with a desk and chair but the décor was far more exotic. Dark wood panelling and expensive white marble tiling covered the floor, and symbols engraved in gold print displayed the insignias of German military brigades on the walls leading up to a black doorway at the end of the corridor. To Munroe the sight appeared ceremonial, like something you would find in a museum or place of worship, and he followed as Barbeau pushed open the door and ushered Munroe inside.

'Plush,' Munroe declared as he gazed across the large room carved up into bedroom, work and leisure areas. The bed had four posts, each with gold tracing and twisting upwards from its frame to an overhanging roof, from which were suspended white, decay-stained drapes. The flower-patterned carpet covering the sleeping area ended where the leisure area began, becoming light red. Here a fine mahogany coffee table stood surrounded either side by light-green armchairs and on a three-legged sideboard sat an empty ornate china cake display surrounded by bone-china cups. The work area on the other side of the room was separated by navy blue carpet, offering a contrast to the two other areas, like a border, and a large Victorian-style Wootton desk sat within it. Made of dark aged wood, the desk had two large doors, which hung open to reveal the additional storage compartments allowing for the green leather desk top to be lowered into place.

The room was literally fit for a king and as Munroe scanned the exotic and expensive furnishings his eyes came to rest on an object that piqued his interest. An object placed down on the floor just a few feet from the doorway he had come through. He took as step over and hovered above the object, inspecting it before picking up the item and examining it more closely. It was an ice bucket, made of pure silver with a layer of dirt covering its interior, or perhaps due to an oxidisation of the steel layer inside. Two holes had been cut into the edges, offering handles, but it was the two initials finely carved into the silver exterior on the bucket's front which were the focus of his interest. Munroe rubbed his finger across them.

A. H.

'Adolf Hitler,' Munroe murmured to himself as Barbeau moved over to join him and tapped his own finger on the initials. 'Fuck me,' Munroe near blurted out the words, realising that this place had been created for one purpose. To hide the leader of the Third Reich until his new life had been created.

'Yep,' Barbeau said softly, 'and that's why this place has torpedoes.'

Chapter 6

Munroe was still rummaging around Hitler's master bedroom as Barbeau was taking a closer look back in the torpedo room. The whole place had been left in a clean and perfect state and although there were signs of rot on the bedsheets and one of the armchairs, it was remarkable how well preserved the things inside this eighty-year-old dugout were. In fact, it made sense and also lent evidence to the theory that it was only since the defence system had initiated its disastrous automated attack on HMS *Resolve* that all the systems had turned back on, which must have included the air recycling. The whole submersed hideout had been pressurised, eighty years ago, and without further investigation who knew if a vacuum had descended upon the place until just hours ago when the defence systems had activated. Perhaps the life-support systems had started back up again. It would certainly have explained the good condition of everything, but the most remarkable thing was that the systems had started up at all. Another demonstration of the famous German efficiency.

Munroe finished checking the beds side drawers and even though they were empty he couldn't shrug away the uncomfortable feeling he had. If they were right then this place had been Adolf Hitler's sanctuary, a place where the genocidal maniac had avoided prying eyes whilst those on the surface above believed him to have committed suicide, and perhaps were still expelling the last few breaths of a nation that had put all their faith in the man. It was a hell of a thought.

Munroe made his way now over to the oversized Victorian writing desk, the only thing in the room he'd not scoured over and began to nose through the multitude of small drawers and boxes. He rustled through the side panels first and upon finding nothing he turned his attention to the rectangular wooden panel at the desk's centre. He gripped the small round white porcelain knob and pulled, only to feel resistance. Of all the drawers in the room it was the first he had found to be locked and Munroe reached to his side and released the pressure lock on his plastic holder for his Tekna diver's knife with his thumb. He got down on one knee and held the small, five-inch, serrated blade before him and pushed the tip of it into the thin gap between the top of the small door and the desk top. He then gently slid it across until at its middle he felt the tip connect with something metal.

'There we go,' Munroe muttered to himself and began slowly leveraging the blade deeper into the gap.

'You find anything?' Barbeau asked, appearing suddenly at the doorway with a picture frame held tightly in his grip.

'Maybe,' Munroe grunted, his focus on jimmying the drawer away from its small metal locking mechanism as Barbeau waited patiently. The Victorian security prevention was no match for the strong modern alloy of the Tekna knife, and after wedging it inwards as far as the weapon would go Munroe applied increasing pressure to the handle until there was a loud crack and a small central portion of the wooden drawer burst into a shattering of shards, the force bending back the metal lock imbedded into it, allowing the drawer to pop open. Munroe then slipped his finger into the gap and pulled the drawer towards him, revealing a black metal strong box with the emblem of the Nazi eagle imprinted on its top.

'It's probably just his cocaine eye drops and amphetamine pills,' Munroe joked, knowing of the führer's drug addiction, which he'd seen on some History Channel documentary.

'Then we can party later,' Barbeau replied with a smirk before thrusting the framed picture he was holding into Munroe's line of view. 'Take a look at this.'

Munroe took the offering and turned it over to find a full layout of the very hideout they were standing in. The entrance was marked in red and the various rooms they had been in all as one would find on a hotel floor map. None of this was surprising, but what really stood out was the size, the plan showing multiple additional areas. Munroe pressed his forefinger against the map and tapped against the thin line leading deeper into the facility. 'You've got to be kidding me. Are those train tracks?'

'Not sure,' Barbeau replied, sounding just as surprised as Munroe, 'but there's an access door inside the torpedo room leading to the additional sections. We've only seen a fraction of this place.'

'We better take a look then,' Munroe said, and he handed the frame back to Barbeau, placed his knife back in its holster and picked up the black metal strong box. 'OK, let's go. This is the only thing I could find in here anyway,' Munroe said, getting to his feet. 'We'll take pictures of the place for the record as we go. Where's the camera?'

'The compartment in my scooter.'

'I'll get it,' Munroe said, heading back to the obser-vation room with Barbeau behind him. 'You locate the door.'

Barbeau replied with a nod and Munroe left him and headed back through the dining room into the entrance area and down into the entrance pool. The light was still on and he could see Barbeau's scooter at the bottom of the steps, so he reached into the only pocket built into his wetsuit and retrieved a pack of plastic bags with blue-coloured zip locks. Once the lock box was zipped up tight in the largest bag, he placed it on the side and climbed into the water before thrusting himself downwards until his feet hit the floor. The cold water on his face was refreshing. He reached over to where he knew the scooter was and grabbed hold of it before returning to the surface. Without getting out, Munroe turned the scooter around to face him and popped open the compartment before recovering the compact waterproof digital camera. He then reached up over the lip of the entrance tube, picked up the plastic-encased strong box and slipped it into the compartment. Once it was closed, he pushed the scooter back down before climbing up the steps and into the entrance area.

Munroe clicked on the camera and began snapping off shots of the entrance room. McCitrick had rightly instructed photo evidence be taken of whatever they found. As he tapped away at the cameras button liberally something caught his eye. A glint of something during one of the flashes coming from the partially open locker on the far said of the room.

Munroe lowered his camera and looked in the direc-tion of the anomaly, in the far corner of the dining room, and took another picture. The room lit up momentarily in another flash of light and again he saw the glint.

With the camera outstretched in one hand he moved towards the storage locker, snapping off a couple more pictures until he was just metres away, and then he gently reached over and pulled the metal door towards himself. What he saw caused him to freeze.

A shiny set of divers' oxygen tanks sat neatly inside, along with two standard black face masks, all still dripping wet.

Shit, we're not alone.

Munroe closed the door and made his way through the dining room, heading to where he had left Barbeau, all the while cursing himself for not being more precise upon entering the underwater hideout. No one had followed them in, they'd have heard.

Christ, they were already here when we arrived!

Munroe pulled his knife from its holster and raised it in front of himself defensively as he approached the observation room and, upon hearing nothing, he poked his head just slightly inside. On the far side he found Barbeau staring at something out of sight and the Frenchman looked over at him, his smile fading as he noted Munroe's knife.

'What?' Barbeau said with both palms held upwards.

Munroe slid his finger up to his lips and swiftly made his way over to Barbeau's position. 'There are two sets of diving equipment in one of the lockers back there, still wet.' Barbeau's whole body stiffened and he pulled out his own waist knife.

'We weren't the first guests to arrive.'

Barbeau nodded to what had drawn him here in the first place. 'Well that explains why this is missing.'

Munroe looked over to see a long railroad track running deeper into the bedrock, disappearing from sight at a right turn about fifty metres along. The steel tracks were small, suggesting an electric cart of some kind, and when he noticed the thick set of rubber cables running up the wall to an old-styled handle switch box he realised his guess was correct.

'It's your call, Ethan. What do you want to do?'

Munroe needed little time to decide and he pointed his knife down the dank-looking tunnel.

'We're outnumbered, three to one, and all we're packing are blades, but we need to find out who's here and why.'

Barbeau looked in complete agreement and he now jabbed his finger down at the tracks. 'The tracks will be electrified, but given that we're wearing rubber wetsuits, we'll be fine, just don't touch it with your bare hands.'

Munroe nodded his appreciation and without a wasting another second, they began heading down the rocky passageway in tandem, blades drawn, moving as quietly as possible.

Neither man said a word as they edged closer to the right turn. Upon reaching it Munroe peered down it to find it ran for maybe another hundred metres and at the far end, through the gloom, he could now see an empty metal-and-wood carriage parked up at the line's end. To its right beams of yellow fluorescent light shone through an open hatchway imbedded into the tunnel wall, illuminating half of the carriage, but so far as he could see, there was no one in sight.

'It's not far,' Munroe whispered. As the two men continued along the tracks Munroe found himself distracted by the scope of what had been achieved here.

The map had showed multiple floors, and the electric carriage served only to show what a massive undertaking this place was. During the war, the Nazis had moved production of the V2 rockets into enormous underground caves to escape Allied bombing, so this style of facility was not uncommon. But building underwater with the technology of the time was a feat in itself, although how many bones of dead slaves had been accumulated in reaching the achievement was anyone's guess.

Munroe extinguished these thoughts and came to a stop at the edge of the carriage with Barbeau close behind him. He then slowly leant in towards the open hatchway and sneaked a peek, the sight before him dwarfing anything he had seen so far.

The hulking shape of a Second World War, German-made U-boat submarine sat in its watery dock about forty metres below him. The room was the size of a large warehouse, all grey concrete, with a munitions loading bay on one side and a control centre on the other. The was an ageing metal walkway running the width of the room, directly over the sub and the proud but cracked painted numbers 'U-4173' ran along its stern in white paint.

On the far side of the warehouse a truly mammoth steel door, as big as the sub itself, was set into the rock, no doubt the mechanism by which the sub had entered and exited the base long ago.

'Shit,' Barbeau whispered in Munroe's ear as he stole a glance at the magnificent sight. They now retreated back into the darkness off the tunnel.

'They couldn't have Hitler getting his feet wet, could they!' Barbeau whispered sarcastically and Munroe offered a smile before looking back into the huge concrete cavern just in time to see a bearded man with dark skin and wearing a green wetsuit exit the top of the submarine. He made his way down the outer ladder of the fin and onto the dock, at which point another, older man exited from the top of the sub. He had silver-grey hair and a red wetsuit, which had been rolled up to the elbows, showing off his thick hairy forearms. The bearded man waited for his companion to join him, at which point the silver fox unleashed a torrent of verbal abuse upon him in broken English with a heavy Albanian accent. The spat ended with a hard slap to the beard's face and then the older man flicked his finger at the concrete control room and the bearded man followed until they were both out of sight.

'Whatever they're looking for, I don't think they've found it yet,' Munroe said quietly and Barbeau now stared at him quizzically.

'That makes two of us, Ethan.'

It was a fair point and Munroe knew exactly what he meant. The whole descent was based on a long shot. They had been hoping that they would find a clue, something to help bring down Daedalus, and although the discovery was fascinating, they were no closer to achieving that goal. Although their new friends here changed the dynamic.

Munroe was still deciding what to do next when he heard one of the men begin shouting again.

'Bauer has killed people for far less, you idiot. We don't find this and it's on your head. You're in charge. You made the promise.'

Munroe looked at Barbeau and they mouthed the word at each other at the same time.

Daedalus.

Suddenly both men were all business.

'We take them both and interrogate. Whatever Bauer wants we want.'

Barbeau nodded his approval as Munroe got down on his hands and knees before venturing out onto the top of the metal stairs leading down to the dock itself. He scanned the surroundings and glimpsed the two men arguing at the edge of the concrete control room before pulling back to the safety of the tunnel. He began to lay out his plan.

'We stealth it down there and wait outside the control room. They come out and we subdue them. If they head back up here we take them in the tunnel. If it all goes wrong then remember we need one alive or this whole thing's been for shit. You're on point; I'll be behind you.'

Barbeau raised his knife and nodded as Munroe once more crept onto the stairwell and watched as the two men stopped their bickering. After a few moments they, luckily, headed back into the control room.

Within seconds Barbeau was swiftly heading down the stairs his rubber wetsuit dampening his footsteps, but he'd barely made it a few steps when the two men appeared again from the control room.

Barbeau screeched to a halt as the two men stared up at him and before he could retreat, the nearest reached to the back of his waist belt and pulled out a black Glock handgun, which he pointed directly at the Frenchman's chest.

'Don't fucking move,' the man yelled and, with a look of fury, Barbeau raised his hands as Munroe held back in the tunnel, having not been seen.

The two men were on Barbeau in an instant, the Glock held to his head as they began to rage questions at him.

'Who are you? What are you doing here?'

At first Barbeau said nothing but after a hard smack to the side of his head with the butt of the man's gun he began to speak and reel off the legend he'd made for himself before the dive.

'I'm here on a rescue mission for the downed submarine HMS *Resolve*.'

His response had the two men glancing at each other in concern.

'Who else is here with you?' The gunman was around six feet tall and in his mid-forties, with a black beard and short, damp hair. He backed away, now keeping his distance from Barbeau, as the DSV agent leant back against the steel banister of the walkway breathing heavily.

'I'm alone,' Barbeau replied amongst heavy gasps, portraying a person scared out of his wits at having a gun aimed at his head.

'Bullshit, my man. What are you? Royal Navy? You would come aboard in groups... so once again, how many people are here with you?'

The bearded assailant once more moved closer and thrust his gun at Barbeau's forehead before then turning the barrel in the direction of his left kneecap. 'Unless you want to try crawling out of this tin can on your hands, I suggest you begin talking. My friend here is not as patient as I am.'

The man with silver grey hair and wearing the red wetsuit, moved closer and produced what looked like a small, flat-headed butcher's cleaver with a serrated edge from his backpack which he tapped against his own cheek. He remained silent and now took to tapping the cleaver against his open palm menacingly as his counterpart gave Barbeau a swift slap across the back of his head.

'All right, there are others on their way, but I'm the first in,' Barbeau stated, doing a masterful job of looking fearful while at the same time attempting to appear resistant.

'Royal Navy?' the assailant demanded for a second time.

'Yes. Part of a diving party to determine what this place is. That's it, that's all I know.'

Both his aggressors glanced at one another before the butcher gave a nod and his colleague now clicked back the hammer of his gun, still aimed at Barbeau's kneecap.

'I can stall the rest of the team,' Barbeau blurted out loudly. 'Give you extra time to evacuate this place.'

The silver fox paused, considering the offer, as from the inside of the tunnel Munroe stood up straight, his knife still ready to be thrown and still out of view of the others.

'How soon will they be here?'

'Five minutes... but I can give you ten. My radio's back in the entrance pool,' Barbeau said and gently flicked his finger towards the tunnel. 'You'd have time to get out of here. You can leave me behind.'

Of course, all three of them knew that was never going to happen but in such situations, time equals possibilities and for anyone facing death, hope springs eternal.

'Please,' Barbeau continued. 'I'm not a threat to you.'

'No shit,' the butcher remarked gruffly, still tapping the cleaver he held against his palm.

There was a moment of silence and then the assailant waved his gun towards the tunnel.

'We better get your radio then, but you so much as twitch in a way I don't like and I'll put two in your back.'

Barbeau offered a shaky nod and then began to make his way back up the stairs towards Munroe, but after a single step he tripped over and dropped to the floor. The fall was as realistic as anyone could have asked for and Munroe immediately took the cue and slipped back down the tunnel as the sound of slaps and insults rained down on Barbeau in the distance. The deliberate fall gave Munroe exactly the time he needed to navigate back down the long tunnel, just making his way around the bend and out of sight as the three men boarded the carriage and began heading to the torpedo room.

The rubber soles of Munroe's wetsuit scuffed against the metal tracks as his sprint turned into a full gallop and the vibrations of the carriage approaching the corner behind him chimed up his legs. By the time he made it back the torpedo room, the mini train rounded the corner, the grating sound of metal wheels echoing down the tunnel towards him and he dove to one side and skidded to an abrupt halt, just managing to stay out of sight.

Munroe hugged the wall just metres from the metal track, his blade still drawn, preparing for the moment he and Barbeau's unspoken plan would commence as the screeching sound of rolling metal wheels filled the tunnel. He could also hear the voices of Barbeau's captors getting louder and more aggressive as they approached and Munroe now caught sight of a shadow cast beyond the opening followed by a heavy unyielding clank as the carriage came to a hefty stop.

'Get moving, sailor boy, you do good by us and you may just get out of here alive.'

A diluted mass of shadows appeared from the opening as Munroe, his muscles already tensing in preparation, raised his knife ready for a throw. His left hand was the weakest when it came to throwing knives, but from his position he was sure he could land it directly in the gunman's chest.

Munroe stepped back slightly, transferred the knife into his right and then lay flat against the side of the tracks as the trio moved closer, the scuffling of steps offering a near precise trace of their location relevant to him. The primary danger was the gunman, disable him and the butcher could easily be pacified, but Munroe needed at least one of them alive. He needed to know what Daedalus was searching for. This would be Barbeau's thinking as well, and so Munroe expected him to dive off to the right upon crossing the threshold of the hatchway, allowing Munroe to throw his knife directly into the chest of the assailant with his right hand whilst securing the man's weapon with his left. With the gun in his possession he would barge the dead man back into the corridor, knocking the butcher backwards and then controlling the man with the acquired weapon. If the butcher attempted any clever shenanigans, then a cap of lead to his kneecap would pacify the man and questioning could take place.

With the plan determined, Munroe waited, the steps getting nearer, and within a few seconds Barbeau appeared and did exactly as expected. The Frenchman didn't dive so much as zipped to the right in a swift sidestep as Munroe plunged the serrated Tekna knife deep into the bearded gunman's chest with a dull thud. This though is when the plan went off on a tangent as the force of the knife impact caused the assailant's right hand to swing across his own chest sending the gun tumbling over his shoulder and back towards the butcher who was in the process of jumping backwards in surprise.

The bearded man's body fell backwards to the floor with a weighty thump. Munroe and the butcher paused as they looked at each other and then at the handgun lying on the floor between them. It was an awkward moment, as if both men were waiting for the sound of the starting bell to rush for the weapon.

Munroe leapt forwards first and dodged the cleaver being plunged down towards him. He grabbed the man's wrist and bicep and drove his knee hard into to the back of his elbow, feeling it snap upwards as the joint shattered against the force. It was left hanging in the opposite direction.

Barbeau meanwhile whisked past Munroe and slammed his shoulder into the silver-haired butcher's chest, sending the man crashing backwards onto the floor clutching his forearm as Munroe bent down, picked up the handgun and pointed it directly at the man's head.

Sweat peppered the butcher's forehead as he began to scream in pain, his yells filling the tunnel before turning into a series of puffing grunts. Spittle flew from between his gritted teeth as he struggled to handle the intense pain.

'You all right?' Munroe asked as Barbeau rubbed a reddening and large bruise forming on his cheek.

'Nothing a strong coffee won't fix.'

Munroe offered no reply and instead turned his attention back to the butcher whose teeth were clamped together in agony, bullets of sweat now began to pour down his face.

'That's a bad break,' Munroe said wincing, 'but you'll live... that is, if you can answer the questions I have.'

'My fucking arm,' the butcher hissed, his body shaking as the shock of it began to manifest, but he received no sympathy from either Munroe or Barbeau.

'Yep, no doubt it's painful and you won't be playing with yourself for a while but believe me—' Munroe clicked the gun's hammer into place and stared at him unforgivingly '—it can get a whole lot worse—' the gun barrel was now lowered until it was pointing directly at the man's groin '—real quick.'

Chapter 7

The butcher winced and his nose flared wildly in anger as Munroe leant forwards and stared at the mark on the underarm of the man's flopping limb. It was a mark he had become used to seeing over the past year.

'So, Daedalus have started tattooing themselves again,' he remarked casually, nodding towards the black symbol of a maze within a triangle punched into the man's skin.

The butcher managed a pained grin, his cheek muscles bulging. 'And now I know who you are, Ethan Munroe.'

Munroe looked unsurprised. 'A my-reputation-precedes-me kind of thing?'

'Something like that,' the butcher snarled, his teeth displaying trails of blood from the self-inflicted bite to his lips he had made during his writhing in pain.

Munroe leant closer and allowed the gun to loll in his hand, his action an obvious show of not seeing the butcher as a threat. 'I don't need to know your name; I already know what you are. I just want to know what you're doing here.'

The question caused the silver fox's nostrils to flare as he attempted to look smug and he glanced over at Barbeau with his lips curled condescendingly. 'DSV's not as smart as I've been led to believe. The real question is what the hell are *you* doing here?'

The man had barely finished his sentence when Barbeau dropped to his knees beside him and held his own knife to the man's throat.

'Enough of the charade. It's always the same bullshit with you dickheads. You play tough until your life's threatened and then you spill your guts.' Barbeau put just enough pressure on the blade to break the skin and held it there as a single drop of blood dribbled down the silver fox's throat. 'Why don't we skip the script and go punchline?'

Munroe did nothing but stare down at the man and after a few moments of silence had passed he crossed his arms and sniffed uncaringly. 'Whatever Hans Bauer's got you searching for we'll find it. Just a matter of time and given the dirt you Daedalus boys have rained down on DSV this past year, I honestly don't care whether you live or die.'

Munroe now also kneeled down next to the man as Barbeau continued to hold his blade stiffly at his throat. 'So, either we need you...' Munroe leant over and slapped the shattered arm being held so protectively, 'or we don't. It's your call.'

The silver fox appeared unfazed by the threat initially, but his confidence quickly turned to nervousness as he winced in pain.

'OK, OK,' the silver fox spat, his eyes bulging with burst blood vessels. 'We were told to look for some box, but I don't know what's in it, I swear.'

'What box?' Barbeau grilled, never loosening his grip on the blade.

'Something Bauer needs. Something lost. It's an operation he's fixated with... Iron Phoenix.'

Munroe glanced over at Barbeau sceptically. 'Sounds like a music act.'

'Or more bullshit,' Barbeau added.

'What is Iron Phoenix and what the hell's it got to do with an eighty-year-old Odessa facility?' Munroe demanded, moving in closer to the silver fox's sweaty face.

'I don't know, I really don't. That's the truth. But he only found out about this place recently and this Iron Phoenix is a big deal.'

'Bullshit, Bauer's got his fingers in every pie there is. Not a chance he doesn't know every secret in Daedalus's arsenal,' Munroe pressed, but his comment had the silver fox shaking his head.

'Then think again. Bauer's not the genius you think he is. He pissed off a lot of people in the organisation when he killed Reichsführer Bormann. If you want power, you need powerful people behind you, and they're in short supply after what he did.'

'More bullshit; Bauer's got the whole judicial world at his fingertips. We've been feeling its weight for a while now,' Barbeau said bluntly, now adding pressure to the knife, causing blood to spread out across the top of his blade.

'Fuck you, it's true,' the silver fox continued, his voice becoming squeaky as the knife pushed ever harder against his windpipe. 'He's barely holding it together and without this box, this Iron Phoenix, he'll have all the main Daedalus players turning on him. His arrogance makes him believe he's invincible, makes him believe he can outsmart everyone, but it also makes him blind to the reality of it all. His position, his power.'

Munroe sat back on his haunches and stared over at the man with a blank expression. If any of what he was hearing was true, then it opened up a lot of avenues to be explored, to be exploited and given how deep in the shit DSV were they needed every bit of leverage they could get.

'OK, so if that is true then what's in the box? It's got to be pretty important. If Bauer is in as much trouble as you say he is.'

The silver fox was already shaking his head. 'I told you; I don't know. It's one of Hitler's relics, something personal to him. And Bauer believes it can turn the tide.'

Barbeau shot Munroe a raised eyebrow and began to smile.

'I think we may have found this box of yours already. In Hitler's personal quarters,' Munroe said, leaning in closer as the man's whole demeanour began to change. He genuinely looked shocked before a serene look spread across his face and he said, 'If you have it then I'm happy to give you all the information on Daedalus you want. I'm not afraid to die.'

The out-of-place comment drew a look of mistrust from both DSV men and it was then that Munroe noticed something. Not a lot, really, just the way the silver fox's eyes flickered downwards, focusing now on a small waist bag and his free finger that had slipped inside the corner opening.

Munroe reached for the small protruding black Velcro zip bag even as the silver fox attempted to wriggle away from him and in doing so twisted his shattered elbow, producing an agonising yelp of pain.

'You're telling us all this because you're not expecting us to tell anyone else, are you?' Munroe growled and urgently grabbed the bag and pulled out a small handheld device, rectangular in shape, with a flick switch and a green LED display.

'Shit.'

4:00.

3:59.

3:58.

'The whole place is rigged to blow... run!' Munroe yelled as he and Barbeau took off sprinting through the torpedo room and back to the observation room and out into the corridor. The sound of uncontrolled laughter filled the air behind them as the man let loose his last offering to them. As Munroe sprinted after Barbeau, he scooped up the frame containing the facility's layout and smashed the glass against the hatchway as they entered the corridor. He pulled out the layout and dropped the rest whilst stuffing the piece of paper into one of the blue Ziploc bags from his wetsuit pocket and by the time they reached the dining room he had it closed tight.

Barbeau yelled as he flew past the dining table, followed closely by Munroe who caught a glimpse of the red display of a CF4 charge just behind the door and easily missed on their initial entry. He saw a snap shot of the timer and called it out to Barbeau who had already reached the entrance room.

'Three and a half minutes.'

Munroe burst into the entrance room and immediately began hurling their diving tanks back into the dive-pool opening.

'Good luck,' Barbeau yelled as he plunged in and slipped on his face mask underwater as Munroe followed and did the same. He then kicked back up to the surface, reached up and pulled the hatch shut and turned it one full revolution until the steps slid back into the wall slits with the scraping sound of metal, then the hydraulics tightened the seal.

Barbeau was already twisting the main entrance circular handle as Munroe gathered the two scooters. The door was slowly pushed open and they were greeted by a cold rush of water as it infused with the entrance pool. Munroe pushed one scooter out to Barbeau and then turned his own on with a flick of the switch and allowed the spinning fan to drag him through the hatchway and out into the dark waters of the Atlantic.

In their rush both pairs of flippers had been left behind and so both men now relied solely on their scooters, but they had barely made it a few metres when they were illuminated in bright lights, blinding them both for a moment. Through squinted eyes Munroe caught the glint of metal in front of him and as his eyes acclimatised to the light he realised there were two men in green wetsuits plunging towards them with divers' blades in their hands.

'They're not Navy,' he heard Barbeau's voice spike over the mask's earpiece and they let go of their scooters and each took on one of the aggressors as an underwater ballet of sorts began to take place.

The coincidental timing of the second Daedalus team could not have been better, and Munroe now wrestled with his own knifeman as the two of them rolled into a ball, each one trying to get some leverage over the other. A few metres off, Barbeau was also committed to the same underwater dance except he still had his knife, whereas Munroe's was where he had left it. Back near the silver fox!

Wrestling in the water is all about one thing, muscular strength. With no floor to push against it boils down to just two things: technique and brute strength. As Munroe tussled tightly he caught a glimpse the face of the knifeman as one of the scooters' lights flashed across them both momentarily. The man glared at him before squinting and falling back into darkness. Munroe felt both the man's thighs tense around his waist, tightening his grip and now driving the blade towards his chest with increasing force.

The two men stopped swirling as they held each other firmly, neither of them willing to give in but as Munroe's muscles began to weaken and allowing the blade's tip to inch closer he did the only thing he could. He took all the downward force on one palm and with his free hand felt his way up the knifeman's neck until he was able to pull his facemask off.

The pressure on the blade released immediately as the knifeman twisted around and swiping his hands like a net in hopes of catching the falling mask but in doing so he fumbled his knife, which sank quickly into the Atlantic depths. Munroe raised his legs and slammed his feet against the flailing knifeman's body, propelling himself backwards in the direction of Barbeau's glowing green wristband, but he hadn't needed to. His French teammate had his own attacker taken care of and he was already pushing away from the motionless body as Munroe reached him, a darkened cloud of blood emanating from the attacker's neck in the short distance behind him.

'Jean, you good?' he asked as Barbeau made his way over.

With barely a confirming nod from Barbeau, both men swam briskly to their scooters, only metres away and began rapidly putting as much distance between themselves and the Odessa hideout as they could.

Five metres.

Ten metres.

At fifteen metres, Munroe glanced back over his shoulder to see his attacker reach the light of his own scooter and attempt to clamber back onto it. He couldn't tell if the man had managed to retrieve his mask, but as he felt a rumbling through the water he realised it didn't matter one way or the other.

The blast of the plastic explosives ripped through the pressurised hideout with such force that it launched the large rectangle hatchway towards them in an explosion of bubbles that came within a few metres of Munroe's legs before it descended down below them into the depths. Munroe turned to see a violent black eruption of bubbles flooding the area just as he was hit by the shockwaves that ripped through the water, tearing at his bones and muscles as his body was pounded by the force of the blast. His head felt like he'd been hit by the blow from a sledgehammer, and as nausea filled his stomach and chest, everything went black. Thankfully, it was only momentarily, and he awoke to find his thigh muscles spasming, but one palm still clung to his scooter, which had come to a full stop.

Through bleary eyes Munroe looked over in the darkness to the only thing he could see, the flickering light of Barbeau's own scooter, whose small dashboard gave him his only point of reference.

'Jean,' Munroe called out, but he received only silence of the radio. 'Jean, I'm coming to you.'

It took only a few seconds for Munroe to gather his thoughts before he pulled back on the throttle, the rotation fans of his scooter made a humming sound as it powered up. He began to manoeuvre towards the light.

The distance was no more than fifteen metres, but it wasn't until he was nearly on top of the other scooter that he saw Barbeau. His body was motionless, floating in the water, but as Munroe reached him he could make out a smile illuminated by the yellow LED lights of the face mask. The Frenchman had one hand still clamped around his scooter handle and his mask was facing Munroe, the dim lights of the small dashboard illuminating his features. Both eyes were open and wincing behind a slightly fogged up visor.

'That was a blast.'

The cheesy pun had Munroe grunting his approval and he reached over and grabbed his colleague's shoulder firmly. He then opened his eyes wide, looking surprised, and began to move his free hand back and forth.

Barbeau offered a wince of confusion. 'What the hell is that?'

Munroe continued for a moment and then lowered his hand. 'A shocked wave.'

Barbeau didn't even smile. 'Jesus Christ. That's terrible. I think I'm going to be sick… seriously.'

'Wait until we're topside, will you.'

The Frenchman nodded. Munroe checked his wrist and the satellite navigation display velcroid to it.

'C'mon. Let's get back to the boat. If the Navy divers aren't on their way already to check out what happened, they soon will be.'

Barbeau replied with a nod and in unison they pulled back their throttles and began to head to the boat.

'That wasn't the waste of time I thought it was going to be,' Barbeau stated flatly. 'We still don't know what "Iron Phoenix" is though.'

Munroe now thought of the black strong box he had taken from Hitler's private work desk.

'Maybe,' he said, focusing on the darkness of the black waters ahead. 'Then again maybe we do.'

Chapter 8

The antique cigar box hit the office wall with such force that it splintered into shards that dropped to the navy blue carpet in a pile, the small brass lid hinges visible in the debris. 'You fucking idiots!'

Hans Bauer stood stiffly behind his desk and allowed his throwing arm to drop to his side as his guest stood nervously in the middle of his office, both hands behind his back submissively. He wasn't sure if he had been the intended target but the cigar box had missed his head by barely an inch.

'First, we let that asshole Lavigne escape his own execution, and now that shit stain of a man McCitrick beats us to the Odessa sanctuary! And how the hell did he know about it anyway, you useless bastard?'

The guest looked nervous and understandably so. Bauer was not one for forgiveness and given the severity of such failures, the reprisal would be painful and swift. And as he watched his leader turn his back and stare out of the large office window across the wide green lawn of the French estate, he sucked in a deep breath and expelled it cautiously, the knot in his throat tightening.

'We're not sure if anything was taken during their snooping, sir, but the fishing boat they were using was seen by our team leaving the area in a hurry.'

His reply had Bauer spinning around and grabbing the edge of his desk with such energy that the brass-stemmed reading light was knocked over, its green lamp shade denting as it struck the cherry-wood surface.

'*Snooping?* This isn't a Victorian detective novel, you ass wipe, its real life, and you've just opened a Pandora's box I had no wish to reveal.' Bauer clung to his desk as he took deep breaths and ground his teeth in fury. 'Fuck.'

'Sir, with due respect, we don't know if they found anything in that rotting time capsule. We don't even know there was anything in there to find. I should add that the explosion was large enough for there to be nothing but twisted metal and debris left for the Royal Navy to find. They've been scavenging it for hours and we've received no reports of them finding anything.'

Bauer finally released his grip on the desk top and his demeanour appeared to calm, the thick protruding vein on his forehead beginning to soften.

'Really,' he replied sarcastically.

The past twenty hours had been a total disaster as far as he was concerned. What should have been a moment to celebrate with the court-sanctioned execution of DSV agent Marcel Lavigne had turned into a personal and, for him, a political embarrassment. The clandestine execution was supposed to create a deeper bond with Prime Minister Previn, as secrets of such magnitude should. He had hoped to forge a stronger inner circle with the prime minister and top military brass, fully cementing his importance and value to the operation – taking down DSV piece by piece.

The nuclear detonation at the United Nations building had been a turning point for the infiltration of Daedalus into the British establishment. Bauer had offered to lead the operation to track down and make the rogue agency pay. It was all off the books, of course and his private military group, Blackstar, had been at the forefront. But now Lavigne's escape had brought Bauer's own personal credibility into question, which could not be allowed. If Daedalus were not at the tip of the spear of the hunt, then control of information would be impossible. And there was always the possibility that DSV, given the information, could return to the fold and bring the true nature of Daedalus to light. And if that happened then, what was the British expression, 'one's goose was cooked'. The full force of the wartime Allied nations would crush them and eighty years of planning would be destroyed. The possibility of a Fourth Reich would be extinguished in a puff of smoke, and he was not about to let that happen.

Bauer placed his hands behind his back regally and slowly ambled over to his guest, his expression grim, and came to a stop directly before him, his eyelids tightening with menace.

'There were only two of us who knew the full picture of what we are trying to accomplish here, and when I made you the third, I had hoped it was the right decision. If the others in Daedalus knew what we were up to they would hang all of us as soon as they could get their hands on us.'

The guest licked his lips anxiously and gave a stiff nod. There were no beads of sweat below his blond hairline, but the wrinkles of a frown on his pale white skin offered a clue to his tense demeanour. His blue eyes glazed over, not wanting to make direct contact.

'I understand and am grateful you took me into your confidence, sir. You should know that my men followed the DSV team back to the coast and have eyes on them as we speak. I've provided your secretary with all the details.'

The information brought a thin smile to Bauer's lips and he nodded.

'Well you didn't mention that.'

'I didn't have the opportunity, sir,' the guest replied, his confidence beginning to return. 'I have two teams in place.'

'Blackstar?'

'Yes, sir. No outsiders.'

Bauer snorted in relief and although his smile evaporated he was nodding favourably. 'Good. How many DSV?'

'Five of them, including Munroe and McCitrick. They abandoned the fishing boat at Portsmouth docks and as of a few minutes ago were heading north towards the Wiltshire border.'

Bauer mulled over the information. 'We should have a team at the airport just in case. That will be their exit strategy.'

'I'll arrange that immediately,' the man offered, but Bauer wasn't paying attention, instead he was going over the plan of action for himself.

'Five of them off the board at once will make for a good peace offering with the PM.'

'Yes, sir. It will.'

'Huh,' Bauer said as his attention was brought back to bear on his guest. 'Yes, yes, of course.'

Bauer reached over and placed his hand on the guest's shoulder and began nodding.

'Do you know what is better than three people keeping a secret?'

The guest looked puzzled and he slowly shook his head. 'No, sir. What would that be?'

Bauer pulled his free hand into view, which had been hidden behind his back, and revealed the stainless-steel dagger, which he plunged into the man's chest, just below his sternum, digging it in all the way up to the black leather handle. 'Two people keeping it.'

The act was performed so swiftly that his guest didn't react in time. He grasped at the knife's handle with one hand as red blood began to spread across the front of his grey shirt. He looked at Bauer in complete shock, his eyes bulging and with mouth wide open as the blade was twisted to one side, drawing a high-pitched whimper from the man.

'Good job, but I could never forgive the embarrassment you've caused me.'

The man's legs began to buckle and then he sank to his knees, both hands now attempting to grasp at Bauer's suit jacket. He swatted them away and allowed the man to drop to the floor.

'The last thing I need is blood on my attire. You've caused enough trouble to me already.'

Bauer walked past the still twitching body and back to his desk. He picked up the shiny stainless-steel telephone receiver and pressed one of the buttons.

'Send him in.'

The gurgling of the guest's last breath was ignored by Bauer as he sat down in his chair and swivelled it around to once more take in the view of the expansive lawn outside. He looked to the tree line bordering the property and was still watching the security men with guards patrolling it when he saw the door open in the window's reflection and watched as a man entered. The newcomer closed the door behind him and made his way over to the desk, pausing at the now still body splayed out on the carpet.

'You just can't get the help these days.' The newcomer spoke in English but there with a coarse drawl of a Russian accent and he came to a stop by the desk and stared at Bauer's reflection. 'Didn't go as you had hoped, then?'

'The end result is positive but the road he took has been, well—' Bauer flicked his finger over his shoulder, motioning to the dead body on the carpet '—unacceptable.'

There was a moment of silence and the newcomer waited patiently until Bauer tapped his finger on the armrest of his black mesh office chair.

'It is just the two of us now who bear the burden and I would like you to take care of it personally. Five of them, including McCitrick and Munroe, are heading north from Portsmouth. I want teams in place ASAP.'

'Should have come to me first time around, Hans. You're letting things slip. It's not like you.'

The faint accusation had Bauer spinning around with both eyes wide in anger and he glared at his newest guest with menace.

'Things are going exactly as I envisaged and I don't need anyone telling me otherwise. Especially you.'

The guest remained relaxed even under the evil stare of his führer though he stiffened in demeanour, now showing a modicum of respect.

'The crown of power weighs heavy for all men, Hans. I don't doubt you. I believe in you, but as someone who knew you before you rose to the lofty position you now hold I would be committing a great disservice if I didn't point out that there are many who are still at odds with your speedy succession to the position of führer.'

Hans Bauer was a man that had been in control of his life since his first memory. A man who had been taught the importance of his being since birth, with an unnatural ability to predict events, and he always came out on top. In the ancient days of druids and soothsayers he would have undoubtedly been the high priest. Who knew, perhaps even seen as a man who could predict the future, but of late those senses, on which he relied so heavily, appeared to have been tempered, at a time when the wolves of his own clan were circling, cautiously but circling nonetheless.

What had brought about this swift change in Bauer's nature, his guest could not be sure, but Bauer's inability to deliver the final blow to DSV had definitely something to do with it. The Hans Bauer he knew would have already sent out the order have Munroe's current location pounded to dust, but yet here he was, focusing on the failures and not on the solution.

'I only mean to say, Hans, that perhaps we should admit to ourselves that disposing of Reichsführer Bormann so soon was a tad hasty.'

The mere mention of such a mistake had Bauer springing out of his chair, the sharp look of confidence back in his eyes.

'The timing was necessary, my friend. Any later and we may not have been able to act as we did. Do not think you are able to see the world as I do.'

The response was not what his latest guest had hoped for, but at least the look of focused determination was back in Bauer's eyes.

'You're right, but not many of our colleagues have such an acute ability either and it might be more beneficial to keep that knowledge in mind when dealing with them. I've been receiving their concerns about what they still refer to as "the regicide of Reichsführer Bormann". Many are not happy, Hans.'

Bauer was displeased by the analysis and a look of suspicion descended across his face. 'My base are bringing you concerns about me! I wonder what you tell them, old friend?'

The question was asked accusingly, and Bauer's mistrust was self-evident.

'I'm sure you offered them the support and advice they clearly could not get from me.'

The guest hesitated, his lips flickering nervously as he attempted to clarify his comments and cool down the building wrath that burned in his führer's eyes.

'Many are nervous of approaching their new führer, but after speaking with them they will come to see your greatness in the fullness of time. DSV's demise and the Iron Phoenix will ensure that, but until that moment I would, humbly, recommend you give our brothers and sisters some… leeway, let's say, because once we achieve our goals, surely that will be the time to balance the books. But first things first: please allow me to take care of, once and for all, our DSV problem.'

Bauer knew he was having his ass cleaned and he did so love a brown tongue, but although he would never admit it some of what his friend was mentioning had resonated with him. For the past few months Hans Bauer's natural instinct and prowess had been waning, like a high tide receding, and it concerned him greatly. He did not know why, but he could feel it slowly ebbing away and his usual clarity of all things had become clouded. Of course, that was something never to be spoken of, it displayed weakness, but without the Iron Phoenix's location he felt something he detested more than anything else in the world: he felt vulnerable.

Bauer considered the request and then slowly walked back to the desk and sat down in his chair. He raised both his hands and formed a cradle with the tips of his fingers.

'I agree; I had thought it best to let you sit this one out, given your history with Munroe, but not anymore.'

A smile crossed the guest's face and he expelled a chuckle. 'You worry too much; personal history never did much to influence my actions.'

'It's not your dedication to duty that ever concerned me. It's your enthusiasm. I want them all dead, as quickly and efficiently as possible. And this time you sever that bastard Munroe's head off and don't leave until you see the life extinguished from his eyes. Understand?'

The guest nodded, and he then turned around and headed towards the exit, sidestepping the bloody body as he did so. As he reached the door, Bauer called out after him.

'And, Davit,' Bauer said, now swivelling his chair around to face him. 'No playing with the bodies. Just kill them and return to me.'

Davit Gasparyan paused and turned back to face his führer, his eyes sparkling with excitement at having the chance to rectify his mistake with Munroe the first time around. He raised his right hand in the air, offering the Nazi salute. 'It will be swift. It will be painless, my führer. I shan't make the same mistake twice.'

Bauer looked pleased with his reply and he returned the salute, although not with the same zeal.

'Good, my friend. And there's no need to emphasise the painless part.'

Gasparyan lowered his arm and grinned slyly before reaching for the door handle.

'And ask Dupont to come in for a moment,' Bauer called out. Gasparyan bowed his head respectfully and Bauer then waited as the door closed and then opened again. Ernst Dupont strode into the room and came to an abrupt stop before raising his arm in the air.

'*Heil*, my führer.'

Bauer sat silently and watched keenly before saluting back and allowing his protégé to relax somewhat. Ever since the escape of Lavigne, the blue-eyed operative had been acting sheepish and feeling responsible for the mess. Bauer, though, did not blame him, but there was something that had pricked at his soul. Something he couldn't put his finger on, but something going on nonetheless, and the conversation with Gasparyan had brought it into focus.

'I need your services, Ernst. I would like you take a hard look at someone for me.'

'Is there a problem, my führer?' Dupont replied and looking highly suspicious.

'Maybe. I'm not sure.' Bauer tapped his palm lightly on the table as he mulled over his concern. 'Lavigne's escape and now the Odessa mess isn't sitting well with me. We've not seen these types of failures since…'

Dupont waited patiently as Bauer's eyes tightened and became ever more menacing. 'Do you find Davit Gasparyan an ambitious man?'

The question was vague, but it was clear that Dupont knew what he was getting at. 'Ambition is a noble trait, sir. Prevalent in many of our ranks, one that Davit possesses in spades and he's certainly more independent than most, but he respects the hierarchy, the order of things.'

Bauer smiled lightly, but then his cold stare returned.

'It's the independent part that concerns me. I've tasked him with finding a solution to the DSV problem and I would like you to keep an eye on him. A close eye, as of this moment.'

Dupont looked surprised but he nodded his agreement.

'You don't think he would actively thwart his mission, do you, sir?'

Bauer considered the notion and then he replied with a clear voice. 'I don't know, but if DSV were to remain at large then I would be affected by it more than anyone else in Daedalus, would I not?'

Dupont's eyebrows raised and a look of anger began to develop at the insinuation.

'I will look into it immediately, sir, and report back directly to you.'

'Good, you do that, and let us see what your fishing trip brings to the surface.'

Dupont snapped his heels together with a loud click and after a stiff salute made his way back to the office doorway as Bauer called out after him.

'And, Ernst, have somebody clean that dead piece of shit of my carpet, will you?'

Chapter 9

Munroe pulled the curtain back and stared up the long muddy road leading to the high street. The entrance gate was padlocked and the open area surrounding the farm house gave a three-hundred-and-sixty-degree view of anything or anyone approaching. McCitrick had rented the property under a false name, of course, with the credentials to back it up. The fifteen-mile drive from Portsmouth had taken only twenty-five minutes in the white Vogue Range Rover that was now parked outside. Munroe took a final look before pulling away from the window and, after a quick re-check of the door, satisfied it was securely locked, he headed back to the bustle of the living room.

The swim back to the boat had taken a little over twenty minutes and by the time they reached it the Navy had already deployed boats to the area where the explosion had taken place and were preparing to deploy divers of their own. Munroe and Barbeau been met by Sloan and Lavigne who helped them out of their tanks as McCitrick pumped the throttle and made a beeline for the Portsmouth coast. Sloan said they had felt the rumblings of the blast from their position and had considered them both lost at sea. They had been about to head back to the coast when Munroe and Barbeau reappeared from the depths.

That's what she said, anyway.

Truth was that any longer and she would have thrown on a wetsuit and taken a look for them both herself.

Their time waiting for Munroe and Barbeau had passed without incident. They had seen another boat, keeping its distance, but although they had kept note of the position it was thought to be nosy Spanish fisherman come to get a look at all the naval activity. The sinking of HMS *Resolve* had not yet hit the news cycle, but it would. There was no way an event like that could be kept under wraps for too long and the MOD would have to make a statement. As it turned out, it came over the radio on their way to the farmhouse. The details were sketchy but the short report stated that one of the UK's Vanguard–class nuclear submarines had broken contact and the Royal Navy were conducting a search in its last known location.

Munroe had a feeling, no matter how unlikely it was to be true, that there would be survivors. Few submarine accidents ever resulted in survivors, it was the nature of operations, being so far underwater, but Munroe just felt that this time would be different.

Ethan Munroe was prone to feelings in his gut, what most people called a sixth sense, and he nearly always acted upon them and was nearly always right to do so. Who knew how it worked, perhaps a glitch in the matrix? Whatever and however these things functioned, it was a feeling he had come to trust and had served him well on many of his operations with the SAS and SBS.

Right now, that gut instinct began to prickle as he walked into the living room. The feeling of being watched spiked once again. It was that same feeling that had sent him peeking through the curtains of the farmhouse multiple times since they arrived a few hours ago.

Lavigne was upstairs taking a well-earned hot shower after his months in prison with only cold water, and McCitrick and Sloan were sitting at the dining table watching Barbeau pick the lock of the black strong box they'd retrieved from Hitler's personal quarters. Sloan also had the hideouts layout Munroe had stashed upon their escape and had spent the past five minutes scrutinising it. From what she could tell, the other half of the facility was made up a water- and oxygen-recycling facility, impressive tech for 1945, and another larger room labelled 'food production'. Whether it had been for cattle or vegetation, they would never know, but it suggested the facility had been designed for residents to live in for extended periods of time. Weeks? Months? Maybe even years?

Who knew but given that it had been created as a halfway house for Adolf Hitler, the butcher of Europe himself, the SS had thrown the most cutting-edge technology of the time at it to ensure the special VIPs made it to the New World.

Any historian worth his salt would have sold their own grandmother to have made such a discovery, but Munroe couldn't help wondering how many other facilities of this type had remained undiscovered. Was this the only one, built especially for the führer and his henchmen? Or was this just one of a lost network of hideouts used by Odessa to help the master race escape?

Master race!

So far as Munroe was concerned – putting the genocide and atrocities carried out by Hitler and his buddies aside – any man who slept in a four-poster bed with a crepe ceiling was someone to be wary of.

'Got it,' Barbeau muttered as he turned the lockpick ninety degrees causing the metal top to pop open a centimetre on springs. He looked over at Munroe and with both palms facing upwards offered up the strong box. 'You found it. Want to do the honours?'

The last twenty-four hours had been a bittersweet affair for Munroe. Yes, they had rescued Lavigne, one of their own, from death at the end of a six-foot rope, but their delving into the depths of the Atlantic had so far provided nothing that could help them in their mission to drag Daedalus from the shadows. Like a vampire in the daylight, worldwide attention would fry the organisation to ashes. His only encouragement had been that the new-age Nazis had turned up there themselves, and that they would rather blow the facility to hell than let it fall into the hands of their enemies added an additional layer of intrigue. Why was Bauer so obsessed with this 'Iron Phoenix'?

Whatever it was the black box before him might answer those questions and it gave Munroe a sliver of hope and more importantly it could offer a chink in the psychopaths armour?

But what exactly?

Barbeau stepped back as Munroe approached the black box with the steel eagle emblem and prepared to pull back the lid. 'Let's see if our scenic dive was worth anything.'

With a firm tug he opened the lid with an oily creak. The inside was layered in a bright red velvet, pristine as the day it was made, and lying in the middle was a thin stack of paper with a bleached white envelope on the top. Everyone at the table now leant forwards in a synchronised motion and peered inside the twelve-by-six-inch-wide black metal box as Munroe read out the name written in black ink on the envelope's surface.

'Hans Baur!'

'Hans Bauer?' Sloan repeated, looking up at Munroe, her eyes narrowing in suspicion. 'It can't be. That little shit wasn't even a glint in his grandfather's pale blue eye.'

McCitrick reached over and gently picked the envelope up with the tips of his fingers and held it before him.

'It's not him,' he said, turning the envelope over to find nothing on the back. 'Our own crazy little bastard is spelt B-A-U-E-R. This was addressed to someone else entirely.'

'Hans Baur.' Munroe mulled over the name for a moment before a spark of recognition ignited in his eyes. 'Hitler's personal pilot.'

McCitrick was already nodding in agreement and he picked up a dinner knife from the table and began to carefully prise open the envelope. 'Perhaps our own Bauer is his namesake. An eerie similarity, to be sure.'

'And the reason the letter was never collected,' Munroe added over the crisp peeling sound of glued paper as McCitrick's knife was slid further along the join. 'Hans Baur was captured by the Soviets whilst making his escape out of Germany after Hitler's supposed suicide. If I remember, he lost a leg and spent ten years in a gulag before being set free to spend time in a French prison. He died in the early nineties, in West Germany.'

'Impressive, Ethan. You're a bit of a nerd really,' Sloan noted as McCitrick now pulled back the envelope's seal and plucked a single sheet of white paper from within.

'He wrote a book about his time with his führer, which I read.'

Sloan stared up at him with a condescending raised eyebrow.

'Didn't know you read books.'

'I can even write my own name as well,' Munroe replied with a thin smile. 'When you join a clandestine agency tasked with chasing Nazis it pays to do a bit of research. You should try it sometime, Jax.'

Sloan smiled patronisingly as the room now fell silent and McCitrick unfolded the single leaf of writing paper before passing it over to Munroe.

'Your German is better than mine.'

Munroe held up the piece of paper and took a moment to scan it, line by line. He zipped through it to the end and only then did he begin to speak.

My most loyal friend and the only man I truly trust. I write this in the knowledge that through your actions and obedience to myself the greater Reich is not lost. Your dedication to my instructions will see this war as nothing but a stepping stone to the thousand years of promise that has been ordained to our cause. By the time you read this I shall be awaiting your arrival with the confidence of a new approaching era. It is one you must take great pride in and one that will see the fruition of our aims. Never forget, Hans, the darkest part of the night comes just before the dawn, and a glorious one it will be. The attackers that have ripped so many German souls from the Reich's womb will be avenged and we will see the culmination in all its glory.

There is one last order I wish you to satisfy before we see each other once more and contained

within this lock box is the means for you to accom-
plish it and fulfil the solemn oath you made to
your führer. The instrument of its success has been
relocated and I wish you to retrieve it and bring
it to me. Take all the usual precautions during its
transportation and know you have the future of the
Reich in your hands. I look forward to receiving
you on success of your duty. I know you will not
fail me.

Munroe noted the unique zigzagging signature below the last line and with a thoughtful nod he passed it back to McCitrick.

'It looks like Hitler's signature.'

Sloan got to her feet and took a look before nodding along with McCitrick.

'Looks real.'

'Yes, but what the fuck does that mean?' Barbeau growled with a frustrated chuckle. For him, the reason for living was to expose Daedalus and some buddy letter between the most infamous person of the twentieth century and his old mate was not going to help one iota so far as he was concerned.

Munroe offered no reply, but instead delved back into the strong box and began rummaging amongst the other items with his fingers. Apart from a single circular gold badge bearing a Nazi emblem, there were only two other items. One was an address written in red ink on a small piece of cream-coloured business card and the other a single piece of blue-lined writing paper with nothing more than a short sentence written directly in the centre of the page.

EISERNER PHONIX

The blank faces of the team said it all as Munroe now translated it. 'Iron Phoenix. It looks like the silver fox we met was telling the truth. Whatever it is, Bauer wants it badly.' He passed the note over to Barbeau and wagged the cream business card in the air between his fingers teasingly. 'The address is Venezuelan, but nothing stands out.'

McCitrick took the card and read the words for himself in a whisper before offering it over to Sloan, who was looking as perplexed as the others.

'The box doesn't really give us anything we didn't know about already. I'd say our mission was a blowout,' Barbeau declared with a deep sigh, his French accent strengthening on the word *blowout*.

'Maybe,' Munroe replied, sounding unconvinced.

'Maybe! It's been almost a century since these were written,' Barbeau continued, shaking his head and with both hands raised dramatically. 'We have an old address and the name of something Bauer wants. What's their relevance in 2023?'

Barbeau was allowing his frustration to override his usually solid common sense and Munroe sought to calm his teammate down a notch.

'What use are they to Daedalus, all these years later? I don't know, but Bauer certainly thinks their important. They risked an operation to blow that Odessa hideout in front of a British Navy task force. Big risk for something worthless.'

'Mmmm,' Barbeau grumbled disbelievingly. 'They appeared far more interested in blowing the place up than searching it. And all we did find was this—' he pushed his lips upwards and stared in disapproval at the strong box '—treasure trove of garbage.'

'If it was us who were worried about the place falling into the wrong hands then wouldn't we have set it up to blow as a precaution firstly, then strip search the place second?'

Munroe's tactical assessment was logical but even so Barbeau continued to raise his nose as if he'd just got his first whiff of a bad smell.

'Perhaps… But I still think this is a waste of our time.'

Of all the DSV team members it was Barbeau who was the most proud. As an operator he was second to none and followed his orders regardless of the personal cost, but ask his opinion and he could be stubborn, always relying on his gut instinct as his bible. Even when he was wrong.

'Well I have no idea what this means,' Sloan said, waving the piece of paper before her, but it was McCitrick who appeared more confident. He reached over and plucked the card back from Sloan's fingers and read the sentence to himself silently.

'Ethan's right. Daedalus took a big risk to destroy that hideout. I can't see they'd do that if there wasn't something in there that could tie the Nazis to them.' He sucked in a deep breath and flicked the underneath of his chin mindfully. 'And there's one person who might know. Been a while though.'

The room went silent as the others now stared intently at the DSV section head as he continued to flick at his chin. Whether McCitrick was mulling over the pros and cons of such a prospect was unknown, but after a painful fifteen seconds it was Munroe who chimed in.

'Well, sir, who would that be?'

McCitrick looked up at him and then slowly met eyes with each of the others around him before letting out a light snort. 'One of the only members of Daedalus who ever turned on them and came to work for us.'

It was Sloan who looked most surprised and her eyes widened with curiosity.

'I didn't think anyone ever had. All the ones I know of are either in the ground or doing their prison terms in monastic silence.'

McCitrick scratched at his unshaven cheek and seeming irritated. 'There was one. Before any of you joined DSV. But he only turned on them after we applied the ultimate pressure.'

'His family?' Munroe replied, his lips curling upwards slightly at the distasteful notion he was suggesting.

McCitrick nodded firmly. 'The only pressure most people will succumb to and he was one of the few whose family we knew of. His wife was shot in the head and his daughter threatened with the same.'

There was a universal look of revulsion amongst the team and McCitrick barked back immediately.

'Relax, it was subterfuge. We didn't kill his wife... but he believed we did and the thought of his daughter going the same way had him yapping like a puppy dog.'

The truth of it had everyone at the table loosening up as McCitrick explained further the games everyone at DSV knew so well.

'After we talked and he subsequently learned his family was safe and sound he had a change of heart. He worked with us for a couple of years, everything from bank accounts to the internal structure of Daedalus. Of course, that was a while ago and when it got wind of a mole the organisation did what it does best... Reorganised and re-strategised but not before we did some damage. Put them on the back foot for a change.'

'And the turncoat? What happened to him?' Barbeau asked, shifting his chair closer to the table.

'We gave him a choice. He'd be charged and hanged for treason in a secret military court, much like Lavigne had been about to experience, or he would be granted a new identity, papers, documentation and he could live out the rest of his life in peace... under our surveillance, of course, and with the caveat that he return when and if his knowledge and expertise were ever needed.'

'And you think he might know what any of this means?' Munroe said and pointing over to the card still hanging from McCitrick's fingers.

'As you already said, Ethan. Maybe. But if it means something to Daedalus then it means something to us and seeing how old this is then the fact he's been out of the loop for some time is irrelevant.'

The team once more went silent except for Sloan who was making clicking noises with her tongue and looking at McCitrick with more suspicion than concern. 'If it's that cut and dried and only a phone call away, then why do I sense such hesitation in you?'

McCitrick smiled immediately. He'd always loved her sharp perception and that she was always the one to call him out on such matters. Christ, it was one of the many reasons he'd brought her into DSV in the first place.

'Because, my dear Jacqueline, with our office totally compromised by every secret security service in the world, and probably Hans Bauer himself, it's very possible that his identity has been compromised. Shit, he may already be dead as far as I know and, if so, organising a meet with the man could bring a lot of exposure to the whole team. That said, and given how deep in the hole we are, I'm willing to take the chance. But just me, alone. If it goes

106

tits-up then the rest of you are protected and can continue the fight.'

Munroe disliked the idea of McCitrick going it alone. Of course he was capable, McCitrick had more contacts and experienced than all of them combined, but it was a big carrot to dangle if it all turned to shit; the section head was someone DSV couldn't do without. Certainly not now.

'How about one of us does the meet and you guide us from a distance?'

'Thank you for the offer, Ethan. But fuck off. I may be older than you but I'm not dead in the ground just yet.'

'I didn't mean that,' Munroe replied, and the section head's response garnered a smile from everyone there.

'I know you didn't and I appreciate it. But it has to be me, son. This contact, well, he was a twitchy bastard at the best of times and I doubt he's changed since I last saw him. Also, he's as anally retentive as they come. He won't meet anyone he doesn't know and even then, it's a fucking process. No, thank you, but I need to do it myself, besides, if any problems come up, I'll need you all to be nearby.'

Munroe and the others nodded in silence as McCitrick reached down and lugged his laptop case onto the table before pulling out a Hewlett Packard ZBook Fury from it and placing it on the desk. He flipped it open and with a press of a button it whirred into life.

'All sensitive contacts with DSV have back channels separate from the main office... As Jax is well aware.'

As one of the few ex-intelligence officers on the Disavowed team, Captain Jacqueline Sloan was really the only one on par with McCitrick when it came to information and data lines and that was fine by Munroe. Every one of the team had been trained in all aspects of data retrieval and the ability to use data subterfuge in the digital age, but Sloan, like McCitrick, had a particular talent for code and numbers. As was, and always had been, the deal with DSV agents, they all brought particular talents to the agency, but each had a high level of aptitude for all the skills needed and Sloan was no different.

Sloan joined McCitrick at the laptop as Munroe headed back to sneak a look through the windows, but then changed his mind.

'I think I'll do a perimeter check, take a walk around.'

McCitrick offered a nod and with that Munroe head back to the kitchen hallway at the rear of the house, opened the nearest closet and retrieved the metallic grey Smith and Wesson M&P 9mm handgun from the top shelf. He pulled back his navy blue winter coat and slid the firearm into the waiting holster. The handgun was the smallest calibre of the weapons in the closet, which included a rack of two Ruger AAR automatic carbines and a further five LaRue tactical LT-15, each serving 556 calibre bullets. To top it off a box of twelve hand grenades sat nestled in packing hay ensured. Over the past year, DSV had adopted a simple protocol: subterfuge is always better than a full-on frontal assault but, if backed into a corner, a good defence is a strong offence. These weapons ensured that policy.

He picked up the nearest LaRue and tapped in a full magazine.

'You walking the perimeter?'

Munroe looked up to see Marcel Lavigne waltzing down the thin staircase, his hair still steaming from the hot shower he'd just taken. He paused and rubbed his hands down the clean white cotton jumper and then patted the sides of the blue jeans he was wearing. 'Christ, that feels good,' the Frenchman said, smiling happily.

'Feeling human again, Marcel?' Munroe said, noting the satisfaction on the man's face.

'You try wearing an itchy jumpsuit for months on end, my friend. Feels like fucking bliss.'

Munroe replied with a deep chuckle and he reached into the cabinet and pulled out one of the Rugers which was already loaded, and with his free hand offered it up to the Frenchman.

'Want to walk the perimeter with me?'

Lavigne's smile grew even wider and he ambled down the last few steps and took the waiting firearm from Munroe. 'We remote enough to have these babies on display?' he asked glancing down at the Ruger now held in his hands.

'There's ten acres surrounding the farmhouse and if anyone's out there they shouldn't be. Besides, it's dark enough.'

Lavigne nodded and cocked his weapon. It was clear that the agent had missed what it felt like to be normal during the months he'd spent locked up in a French prison with security tighter than a gnat's ass, twenty-four seven.

Normal of course for some.

'Let's go.'

Munroe reached over to close the closet door when he heard the sound of glass smashing as something thudded to the ground below and rolled into the very closet he was about to close. He looked down to see the green frag grenade coming to a rest next to the box of grenades as Lavigne lunged off the stairs and into the kitchen beyond.

Munroe slammed the door shut and dove towards Lavigne's position managing to scream out a single word before he hit the floor.

'Contact!'

Chapter 10

The explosion ripped through the centre of the house like an exploding beer can, the shockwave blowing out the kitchen windows behind Munroe as both he and Lavigne lay in foetal positions, their heads dug into their chests as charred debris from what had been the closet clattered down around them.

The blast had left both men momentarily dazed, but above the high-pitched ringing in their ears the sound of shuffling boots on broken glass had Munroe picking himself up, the LaRue automatic rifle still gripped in one hand with the barrel scraping against the kitchen floor as he groggily attempted to regain his balance.

Munroe spun around as the back kitchen door buckled under the pressure of someone's boot and it flew open to reveal a man in full black tactical gear with a Smith and Wesson AR15 hanging from his side. He was ripping the pin of a grey flashbang canister but was met with a short burst of fire from Munroe's rifle sending the attacker staggering backwards onto the patio outside with the canister dropping to the floor.

Munroe heaved Lavigne to his feet and they stumbled towards what was left of the closet as he unleashed bursts of fire randomly towards the doorway with his eyes closed as the flashbang now erupted in an explosion of light and deafening sound.

Fortunately the flashbang did more to disorientate the advancing team on the patio outside and those few crucial seconds allowed Lavigne to take a covered position at the bottom of the stairs and Munroe to head further into the house.

His ears filled with the painful pitched ringing for the initial blast, Munroe staggered up to the farmhouse front entrance, each step becoming more solid than the last. He could hear Lavigne popping off covering fire in short, measured bursts and as he reached the hallway he slid behind the nearest covering wall and turned his attention to the corridor leading back to the living room.

The front door was now flung open and Munroe fluidly opened up his LaRue automatic, catching the first incoming invader in the chest and the one behind him directly in the forehead, sending both balaclava-wearing men to the floor before they even managed to place a foot across the threshold.

Munroe rammed his shoulder against the door, but the incoming resistance bounced him backwards to the opposite wall as another balaclava-clad man wearing black tactical armour appeared from behind it, gun aimed directly at his chest.

In that moment, adrenalin spiked through his veins and his senses slowed, offering some control over the passage of time as he began to raise his LaRue, but it was too late.

They had him cold.

A single shot cut through the right side of the invader's cranium and erupted from the other side, spraying crimson pieces of brain against the open wood door and dropping the man to the floor. Munroe glanced over to see Sloan, her arm outstretched towards the doorway gripping the still-smoking black Glock handgun tightly.

Above the ringing in his ears, Munroe heard more bursts of gunfire coming from the kitchen. He leapt towards the front door and kicked it shut as Sloan moved to the corridor behind him and began squeezing off shots, backing up Lavigne.

Munroe flipped the door key as another round of bullets hit the outside of the entrance door and he slid down to a crouched position. From his left Barbeau appeared and tossed him a fresh magazine.

The second most important DSV protocol. Never store your weapons in one place.

'Lavigne's at the back, multiple incoming. Cover the front door,' Munroe yelled and Barbeau, with a nod, took up position, his Ruger semi-automatic raised as the gunfire back in the kitchen now fell silent.

Munroe moved to the other side of the door and towards the living room. He glanced back down towards the kitchen to see Sloan tossing Lavigne a spare magazine and, except for the four bodies lying motionless on the back patio, there was no one else to be seen.

Daedalus, gotta to be, Munroe thought as he sped back to the living room. With their first wave pacified, a second would soon follow. Such an ambush was all about momentum and as Munroe reached the doorway and saw McCitrick packing up his gear, he heard possible movement from upstairs. Maybe a shuffling of feet, or a window being forced open. With the ringing in his ears, he couldn't be sure. Perhaps the oak beams of the farmhouse creaking?

McCitrick looked as if nothing had happened as he quickly flung his laptop and small satellite transmitter into its leather case. A black 9mm Berretta lay on the table next to him and he now calmly glanced back at Munroe.

'Don't waste your time on me,' he said and then glanced up to the ceiling. 'Go take a look, would you, and meet back here. This farmhouse has a few more surprises to offer up.'

Munroe gave a sharp nod and then moved back the way he'd come. His initial plan was to grab McCitrick and make a move outside to the waiting Land Rover they had stored in the next field before an incoming second wave but given the sounds coming from upstairs there would be no time for that. Besides, McCitrick had been true to his reputation and had a plan for all eventualities. As prepared as an anal-retentive accountant whose arsehole was tighter than a snare drum, it was often joked that if McCitrick had children he would have toilet trained them at gunpoint.

Munroe passed Barbeau and pointed to the door and then held his hand out to stop Lavigne from following and flicked his finger at Sloan, who shadowed him closely as he headed up the thin staircase, skirting the wall as he did so.

The top floor of the farmhouse contained two bath-rooms and five bedrooms, two of which had been added on, and as Munroe reached the landing he looked right and then left to see the sharp bend in the corridor where the additional renovation had occurred. It created a blind spot between them and the other two bedrooms and as he came to a stop, Sloan moved to his side, her own weapon trained down the landing.

There was silence, and Munroe pointed down to his right, sending Sloan creeping along the corridor as he made his way down the left. With every step he expected the sounds of gunfire to erupt from downstairs, the second assault, because sending one person into a house of five was suicide, unless an entire team had been sent to breach the top floor.

Munroe reached the open bathroom just before the corner and stole a glance inside, the muzzle of his gun preceding him.

Empty, except for Lavigne's army-green execution outfit and a wet towel lying on the floor.

Munroe continued on to the corner and once again stole a glance before heading onwards towards the three bedroom doors, two on the left and the third on the right. He cleared the left-hand side quickly and stealthily, the doors already ajar. Finding nothing but clean bed linen and locked windows, he returned to the corridor.

The final door was closed and Munroe got down on his haunches and reached for the door handle, turning it until he heard the latch unclick and giving it a push backwards. With his finger back on the trigger, he cautiously peered in to see nothing but an empty room, the king-size bed made up with purple floral linen similar to the others. Munroe stood up and entered.

This final room was larger than the others with what looked like an original Joseph Farquharson watercolour painting of sheep being herded across a Scottish highland above the headboard and a large floor-length mirror standing in the corner of the room. Wardrobes set into the wall were on opposite sides of the room and as he moved further inside he noted the window, open by just a few centimetres and he immediately turned his attention to the wardrobe next to it.

He'd made only a single step when something caught his eye and his head snapped towards the mirror to see a man in a balaclava, blue jeans and a white T-shirt creeping from the wardrobe behind him with a glinting tactical knife aimed at his back.

Munroe spun around just in time for the edge of his gun to deflect the blade off to one side as the knifeman slammed his free hand, palm down, against the LaRue's barrel, forcing the business end to the ground. The move forced Munroe to release his trigger hand and grab hold of his attacker's wrist as the blade was pressed down towards him.

The two grappled in silence as each man attempted to overpower the other, both expelling nothing but short grunts, his attacker not wanting to draw the attention of the other DSV agents and Munroe not wanting to give away his position in the house to whoever could be just outside.

The man was strong, far more so than his size would suggest and as Munroe's gun was held downwards to his hip, the force of the knife from above began overpower him. With quivering hands, more force was applied the blade, and it started to move downwards and closer to Munroe's neck. The grunts from both men got louder as now even more pressure was applied to the knife and Munroe was faced with only one option. He couldn't headbutt the knifeman because the blade would penetrate his neck as he thrust forwards and the downforce was too heavy for him to raise his leg and kick the man in the groin. So he took the only option available. He released his grip on the gun, sending the man off balance and at the same time grabbed his wrist with both hands, using the additional leverage to speedily rotate the man's hand backwards so he could drive the blade deep into his neck.

The impact drew a wide-eyed stare of disbelief from the man as blood from the deep wound now spurted out rhythmically, his carotid artery having been severed. As his life force oozed to the floor and his arms became limp, Munroe pulled back the knife and dropped the man to the carpet. Without pause he then unleashed a punch squarely to the dying man's nose, the cartilage giving way like cardboard.

Munroe swiftly picked up his rifle and watched as the mortally wounded man let out an unpleasant gurgling sound before dropping backwards to the ground, choked on his own blood.

With the body lying still and no longer a threat, Munroe crouched down by the window and peered outside. The courtyard lights illuminated the small parking area in front of the house but the darkness outside of the cone was difficult to penetrate. Munroe narrowed his eyes, allowing his vision to acclimatise, and as he did so, the outlines of two SUVs parked up at the end of the long drive came into view. They were too far away to make out if there were any occupants, but it wasn't important. With their attackers' first wave failing in its surprise, he would bet every single one of them was nearby on standby.

Munroe eased himself to the other side of the window and peered into the night. There was movement in the darkness, multiple bodies waiting down by the small barn less than seventy metres away. Impossible to tell how many, they were all bunched up, but as a single mass he guessed maybe seven or eight.

Munroe pulled back from the window, keeping low, and did not get back onto his feet until he was in the corridor. There were no windows in this section of the top floor and as he made his way stealthily to the staircase he heard a light scuffle from somewhere up ahead. The faint sound was all the motivation he needed, and he was now running, each of his steps muffled by the carpet and upon reaching the staircase he caught a sound of someone knocking against maybe a dresser or a table from the bedroom on the left.

Munroe slowed, and with his LaRue raised, he slid into the half-open doorway using his shoulder to throw the door wide.

What he saw appeared in his mind as a static image, a moment frozen in time, a skill engrained from years of situational awareness. A moment when a decision had to be made on pure reflex and without even a hint of consideration, like muscle memory for the mind when every fraction of a second would mean failure. These were the moments in battle that could snatch success from the jaws of disaster and it was in moments like these that Ethan Munroe thrived.

The masked attacker with the build of a man, dressed in near identical gear to Munroe's earlier visitor, had one hand clasped around Sloan's mouth and with the other held a knife to her throat, his muscles already tightening to slice the blade across her neck. In his peripheral vision Munroe could make out the rifle lying at her feet. The static image he saw was not unlike looking through a lens, its point of focus and clarity on the knife blade becoming blurry the further out it came. He pulled the trigger.

A single shot hit the attacker's temple, blowing out the top of the occipital bone at the rear of his cranium and sending a bloody mess against the window behind, which shattered from the incoming fragments and allowed a cold gust of wind to fill the room. Sloan was already wrestling herself from the dead man's grip as Munroe reached her. She picked up the rifle as the attacker slumped to the floor behind her.

'Makes us about equal,' Munroe whispered, but Sloan never even had time to grin as the sound of gunfire filled the night air outside, sending them both plunging to the floor as bullets ripped apart the crimson-stained window above them.

The lead barrage lasted more than ten seconds and then as the night fell silent once more, Munroe stared up at the now fully collapsed window frame. A familiar voice called out to him from somewhere down below.

'Hello, Ethan, it's been a while since I last had the pleasure.'

Sloan looked over at him, her head still pressed against the carpet, and gave a curious grimace as the voice continued to speak.

'And no doubt Mr McCitrick, Sloan and the Frenchmen are with you. The pride of DSV... well, when it existed. Never has your codename "The Disavowed" been more apt. Such a foreshadowing of what would become of you is ironic, is it not?'

Munroe pulled himself up from the floor and carefully manoeuvred to the windowsill, just getting a line of sight, and there down below behind the parked Land Rover he could just make out the shadowy face. A face he had hoped to see again one day, but not like this.

'Davit Gasparyan. What an unpleasant surprise. Shouldn't you be off somewhere getting a hard-on by, I don't know, maiming small, helpless animals?'

There was an awkward pause before Gasparyan spoke again, his voice sounding less smug and his tone becoming impatient.

'I have no problem in seeing you die for a second time, Ethan. In fact, I'd very much enjoy it, but seeing as our initial breach has not gone as we expected I am prepared to offer you a one-time deal.'

The idea that that Gasparyan, a psychopath with an intense love for anything even resembling pain and suffering, would give them an out was absurd and Munroe glanced over at Sloan and pointed to the door.

'I'll keep him occupied,' Munroe whispered quietly. 'If McCitrick has a plan, it's time to deliver.'

Sloan nodded and then began crawling back to the doorway, disappearing through it as Gasparyan continued to deliver whatever distraction tactic he was attempting to deploy.

'All I want is whatever you found during your trip to the bottom of the Atlantic and you may all scurry away... to fight another day.' Gasparyan expelled a loud chuckle. 'I'm a poet and didn't even know it. Anyway, you have my word, and I want an answer in ten seconds or this dilapidated farmhouse will be remodelled using your blood as wall paint.'

It was about the level of a threat that Munroe expected. The Daedalus killer was far better at exacting pain than threatening it. One might say it was a personal hobby of his but that aside there was only one thing Munroe needed to gain from this exchange: time.

'And if we didn't find anything or choose not to accept your terms?'

'If that's the case then you could say you're up shit creek, Ethan. Along with your band of merry men and Captain Sloan. I'd very much enjoy spending a few excruciating painful days alone with her. Forgoing that, you should know we have enough ordnance to level the building you are holed up in. If we can't have what you found then no one will.'

Munroe caught the silhouette of an RPG rocket launcher; its missile's tip being held up in the air and resting upon the shoulder of one of Gasparyan's men.

'You know that all this commotion has most likely been reported to the police. Gunfire and explosions tend to attract the law in droves.'

'Then it's lucky they're on our side, isn't it, Ethan? We're not the ones being hunted by every law agency in the West as terrorists. You people have a lot of blood on your hands.'

'On *your* hands, you murdering bastard. How does it feel to know over half a million people were murdered because of your games?'

'Details, details. All that matters is you're in deep shit and stop pushing for more time. Give me what you have or I'm levelling that building with you and everyone in it... Ten seconds.'

Munroe let a few seconds slip by, just to give the appearance of truly considering the offer.

'OK. You're right, we did find something. Something you're going to want to see. Right up your alley, Gasparyan. Old Nazi stuff from dear old Uncle Adolf himself.'

The admission brought with it complete silence and Gasparyan even appeared from the shadows briefly into the farmhouse's entrance lighting. His expression held no smugness or anger, nothing but wide-eyed astonishment, and he looked up at Munroe's window in fascination, clearly captivated by the very notion, before dissolving back into the darkness.

'Really, Ethan? If that's true then you have something very special indeed, something I would love to see with my own eyes, but still my offer stands. You either give it to me and allow our chase to begin again or, as I said, if we don't get it, no one does.'

Again, Munroe allowed a few seconds to pass before replying, his voice as firm and serious as a man facing possible death should sound.

'McCitrick is downstairs; he makes the final call.'

'Stop stalling, Ethan. Don't treat me like an idiot. If he's downstairs he's been listening to this whole fucking conversation.'

'I heard it, Davit. And I agree to your terms,' McCitrick yelled from somewhere down on the ground floor. 'But not until we sort out how we're getting out of here.'

Munroe pulled back from the window and crept back to the main landing and then down the thin set of stairs as Gasparyan and McCitrick began negotiating an exit plan. It was, of course, all bullshit. There was not a chance in hell the Daedalus killer would allow any of them to leave unless it was in body bags. His master, Hans Bauer, had already made that mistake once. After Lavigne's escape from military execution, Bauer would need to offer results if his credibility with the British prime minister and others was to be maintained.

By the time Munroe reached the ground floor, McCitrick was demanding that all the surrounding forces disappear and that the Land Rover was left to facilitate their withdrawal, but as Munroe passed by the kitchen he found no sign of his teammates. Barbeau, Lavigne and Sloan were all missing, and trip wires linked to grey bars of plastic explosives had been attached to the entrance and kitchen doors. Munroe continued past the traps and, upon reaching the living room, found only McCitrick. He was still shouting his list of demands and standing next to a trapdoor leading into the ground. The floor rug had been pushed to one side, revealing it.

'You let everyone leave in the Land Rover except for me. Once they're far enough away. I'll come out and give you the lock box we retrieved. There's some interesting stuff inside that should be a real turn-on to a Nazi bastard like you.'

McCitrick glanced over at Munroe and flicked his thumb towards the opening, but Munroe paused and was met with an annoyed glare and a firmer flick of the thumb as Gasparyan yelled his reply.

'You're giving yourself up to save your people. Very heart-warming.'

'The fuck I am, Gasparyan. Some of my people will take sniper positions and if I don't walk out of here, I promise you, your head will be the first to explode.'

McCitrick now jabbed at the trapdoor furiously. 'I'll be right behind you,' he whispered. Reluctantly Munroe did as he was ordered and went down the short wooden ladder until he reached a long dug-out shaft with hanging yellow building lights running its length and wooden struts installed every few metres to prevent a collapse. Fifty metres up ahead he could see Sloan making her way along it in a crouched position. She glanced back at him and smiled before heading deeper, Munroe now closing the gap.

The tunnel was only a metre underground and yet the air was as cold as a refrigerator. As Munroe passed each of the support struts he noted their darkened colour, suggesting this escape route had been dug out many years ago. Most of the safe houses employed by DSV had hidden back doors, which, given the nature of their jobs, was to be expected, but given that the agency had been dissolved for over a year he was surprised the hideaway was still secure. McCitrick always kept his cards close to his chest, and it seemed that even when the agency had been operational there were places that even he, one if its sections heads, had kept off the books. What was the old saying of his, 'Just because I'm paranoid doesn't mean they're not out to get me.'

And thank God for that, because had his compass run in a different direction they all would all be in danger of being killed in one fell swoop by Gasparyan and his henchmen.

Munroe moved quickly but as silently as possible, reaching the end of the one-hundred-metre tunnel just a few feet behind Sloan, and then he climbed up another short wooden ladder, which led out onto a patch of ground surrounded by bushes. Through a pair of night-vision binoculars, Barbeau was checking the lights of the farmhouse, and Lavigne was already sitting in the black Range Rover they had stashed on the side of the road upon their arrival, all its passenger doors wide open and ready for a speedy exit. Sloan joined him, taking the front passenger seat, as Munroe crept next to Barbeau and nudged him for the binoculars, which were passed over immediately.

The cutting-edge night vison or ENVG-B they were using was not even in service yet. It used augmented reality in the tech. Instead of the green lighting view of old, these allowed objects and people to be outlined in white, just like a video game, giving clarity to the view like never before. It took Munroe a moment to adjust, having never used them before, and he pulled away from the lenses to see Barbeau smiling at him.

'Nice, huh?'

Munroe nodded and took another look.

'There's nothing McCitrick can't get his hands on,' he whispered, now getting a complete view of the men surrounding the farmhouse. As he'd surmised, three tactical teams surrounded the building, two of which he could see. A group of four men was dug in behind the barn to his left and there had to be a second group at the back of the kitchen. He couldn't see them, but they were there. The third team, along with Gasparyan, were using the Land Rover for cover but had they realised what they were siding up to they would have been anywhere else. What they didn't know was that Barbeau had placed a bar of C4 inside the front right wheel arch earlier, just in case, and wired up to a remote charge that was linked to the detonator that he was now holding in his right hand. Any problems and Gasparyan and one of his teams would be taken out of the equation before a shot was even fired. It would also make for the perfect distraction for a getaway.

'Did you know about the tunnel?' Munroe asked, and the question had Barbeau shaking his head.

'Nope, but you know McCitrick. Always the magician.'

From their position they could hear Gasparyan's replies and, judging by his increasingly irate choice of words, the negotiations were close to concluding.

'My patience is about worn out. No more talk, McCitrick. Let's get this done now or I'm lighting that place up like a Christmas tree. Screw whatever you found.'

Munroe couldn't hear the reply but whatever was said appeared to calm Gasparyan and he stood back, took a position behind his team and took the AR-15 that was passed to him.

Sure, you're going to let us walk out.

Munroe passed back the binoculars and the stuck his head into the tunnel to see the upside-down view of McCitrick hurriedly making his way along the escape tunnel towards him. Within moments, Munroe was pulling him up the ladder and out into the covering of bushes surrounding them as Barbeau got to his feet and jumped into the back of the Range Rover, waiting for them.

'We'll be on our way before they realise they've been screwed,' McCitrick said, heading past Munroe towards the Range Rover. Then he paused as Munroe retrieved his LaRue from the ground and turned to face him.

'I told you the place had a few secrets, didn't I? Not a chance I'd let them get us that easily.'

'Yes, you did, sir. You've always got our backs.'

McCitrick smiled warmly and then he turned back towards the Range Rover and in doing so brought the single man wearing a balaclava and holding an AR-15 directly into Munroe's line of sight.

'Get down!' Munroe yelled, raising his own weapon, but not in time. A burst of gunfire struck McCitrick in the side and chest, propelling him forwards and slamming his body against the open car door with a heavy thud. Munroe retaliated with a single shot to the man's head, dropping him to the floor where he lay in a twitching heap.

'Blow the Land Rover,' Munroe ordered. As he, along with Sloan, pulled the bleeding McCitrick into the back seat of the vehicle a bright explosion erupted in the distance, sending a plume of fiery smoke bubbling into the night sky.

'Go, go,' Munroe shouted as he leapt in to the back seat, the tyres grinding against the earth, sending soil flying into the air as the Range Rover took off down the road, its lights turned off.

'Get me a kit,' Sloan shouted as she pulled open McCitrick's shirt to find three exit wounds oozing blood.

Munroe grabbed the green first aid kit from its plastic container under the seat and flung open the lid as Sloan grabbed the bandages and went to work stemming the flow of blood. McCitrick's eyes fluttered wildly as he struggled to stay conscious. Barbeau pushed the Range Rover's engine to its limit, the whine from the torque filling their ears.

'How bad is it?' Lavigne asked, his voice calm but with the obvious hint of distress. Munroe could only watch, his own clothes spattered with McCitrick's blood, as Sloan injected something into the section head's arm.

'Have to stabilise him,' she growled above the whine of the engine. 'And keep the fucking car steady.'

Barbeau was doing his best, keeping his driving line near perfect as the Range Rover navigated through the winding road ahead, and as Sloan did what she could Munroe reached over and placed his two fingers against McCitrick's neck.

There was barely anything to feel.

Chapter 11

McCitrick's eyes flickered wildly and his whole body began to shake violently as Sloan continued attempting to stabilise his heart rate. Three of the gunshots had pierced his liver and right lung; the last bullet had fractured his sternum. The plastic bag taped to his chest ballooned and deflated rapidly as the DSV section head struggled with each breath as he lay akimbo on the Range Rover's back seat. With Sloan taking the lead there was little Munroe could do except grip tightly his boss's hand for reassurance, the coagulated blood sealing their palms together in a sticky binding. In the front seat, Barbeau continued to push the vehicle to its limits as Lavigne looked on with apprehension.

McCitrick's heart had stopped for over a minute before a shot of adrenalin had kick-started it and although his heartbeat was erratic it was at least beating.

The old man was tough.

The nearest hospital was less than ten miles away but contending with the tight, narrow and winding country roads it might as well have been a hundred as Barbeau struggled to maintain top speed. The blood loss had been immense and even though Sloan had got the bleeding under control, McCitrick unquestionably needed a few extra litres, as his ever-whitening face bore testament to.

Munroe glanced behind him to see no vehicle lights following them in the distance but that piece of news did little to change the mood in the car as McCitrick began to moan as he regained flashes of consciousness. Sloan snatched a piece of transparent rubber tubing bearing needles at each end began to roll up the sleeve of her shirt.

'You're all right, John,' she said hurriedly, yet her tone remained calm, and she slid one of the needles into the thickest vein in her bicep. 'I'm going to top you up with a few litres. I'll have you back on your feet in no time; just try to relax.'

Munroe watched as she now gently massaged the rubber casing and encouraging her blood to snake its way down the tubing towards the other end and only once it was dripping did she pierce into the bulging vein in McCitrick's wrist.

Asking if Sloan had the correct blood type did not even entered Munroe's mind. She knew what she was doing; the only question was, would it sustain him until they could reach the hospital?

'Six miles out,' Barbeau stated loudly as Munroe felt McCitrick's hand begin to squeeze his and he looked down to see his boss now staring directly at him, his eyes wide, bloodshot and full of questions.

'You took a few hits, sir, but you're OK. We'll be at the hospital within minutes. Just hang in there.'

The information appeared to provide a momentary splinter of relief before his eyes began to roll back into his head once again, which had Munroe delivering a series of light slaps across his cheek.

'Stay with us, sir. Listen to my voice.'

Recognition suddenly returned to McCitrick's eyes and he even managed to smile through gritted teeth and Munroe smiled back at him.

'Concentrate on your breathing and try to relax. You're not going anywhere.'

His words definitely had an effect but despite the blood being pumped into him McCitrick's complexion was getting ever whiter.

'Check the police bands; make sure we're clear,' Barbeau instructed, but Lavigne already had his radio out and was scanning for any local communications. Daedalus were juiced into almost any judicial organisation on the planet and the local police would be no different, perhaps even easier to control than the larger, more influential groups.

Munroe glanced up ahead to see the hazy glow of the town centre on the horizon. The sight brought a mild sense of relief. The hospital wasn't a general; they were too far out in the sticks for that, but it would have the basics and that was a hell of a lot better than what the first aid box had to offer.

With Sloan fixed on their patient, Munroe now turned his attention to the front seat as Barbeau skimmed past an old red telephone, nearly clipping the box.

'Give them a call and tell them to have a gurney waiting. Report it as a heart attack.'

Lavigne was already bringing up the hospital's details up on his phone with one hand as his other pressed his radio to the other still listening intently for any police reports.

Once inside the hospital they would have to take charge of the situation at gunpoint because after the doctors realised they were dealing with a gunshot wound a call to the police would quickly follow. If they could get McCitrick into surgery with minimal scrutiny, then there was a chance the team could control the situation with threats of violence. He had no idea exactly how big the hospital was, so decisions would have to be made on the fly but at the very worst they would ensure McCitrick was in good hands. Worst case was that he'd end up in custody, but at least he'd be alive and then a rescue attempt could be made at some point down the road, Lavigne style.

These were the tactical thoughts running through Munroe's mind as the glowing haze of the town's lights grew ever closer and his only personal contemplation was his hope that the detonated C4 back at the farmhouse had taken out Gasparyan and a chunk of his men with it.

'Four miles,' Barbeau shouted, most likely wanting McCitrick to hear the update. Munroe felt a small sense of relief, and he could feel eyes boring in to the back of his neck so he turned back to the back seat.

Sloan was staring at him, eyes dull and her face expressionless, and it was then that Munroe realised the tight grip on his hand had become limp. He looked down at McCitrick. His body was still and the muscles in his jaw were relaxed as he stared upwards with a peaceful gaze in his eyes. Munroe pressed two fingers into the gap of skin between McCitrick's jaw and neckline. He felt nothing.

'Jax!' he yelled. His voice appeared to shock her back into play, and her eyes flickered with a realisation of something.

Munroe watched as Sloan slung herself over the top of the back seat and began scrambling for something in the darkness of the boot before slinging herself beside McCitrick but this time with a thin white pen-shaped package in her hand, which she ripped open with her teeth and pulled the plastic covering off with her lips. The sharp tip of the needle glinted as she hovered it above McCitrick's chest.

'Keep us steady,' she yelled over to Barbeau who glanced back. Seeing what she was about to do he let up on the accelerator to maintain a constant speed, the Range Rover becoming steady.

'Last shot of adrenalin we have, and his heart may not be able to take it,' she said without looking up at Munroe. He watched as she positioned herself and then slammed the three-and-a-half-inch needle deep into her boss's chest and unloaded its contents.

The effect was near immediate. McCitrick's whole body began to shake and his eyes bulged as Sloan retracted the needle and once again began to work on his wounds. His breathing was erratic but the plastic bag sealing his pierced lung was inflating once again and as Munroe felt the grip on his hand tighten it was Barbeau who called out their distance only to be stopped halfway by Lavigne.

'Three miles, get ready t—'

'The hospital's a no go. We need a new destination,' Lavigne said, dropping his phone into his lap and concentrating on the radio still pressed to his ear. 'Local law's setting up a blockade around the town centre.'

'Jesus, that was quick,' Munroe muttered, but in truth he was not that surprised at Daedalus's quick reactions. Sickos, yes. But damn good at what they did.

'There's a vacant hotel a few miles from here. I saw it when I did the reconnaissance earlier. Nothing special, but it's four walls and a roof,' Barbeau said, already slowing to take the next turn leading off the country lane they were on.

'Take it,' Munroe ordered and noting the look of concern from Sloan. An empty building was no hospital, but it was all they had, and needs must.

The Range Rover slowed and turned off the road. Sloan continued to work furiously on her patient as their vehicle drove off deeper into the dark countryside. Behind them, the flashing of blue and red lights now began to appear from the town's outskirts a few miles away, lighting up the night sky. As Munroe looked back, what had always been a welcoming sight now appeared as a warning. *Abandon hope all ye who enter.*

Christ, at this point, hope was all they had.

Chapter 12

When Barbeau had described the hotel as vacant, he hadn't done it justice. The old, stone-walled country pub with guest houses wasn't just empty, it was ready to be demolished. There was even a mini wrecking ball parked up in the cracked tarmac car park, meaning the whole place would be coming down within days. Construction companies rarely left equipment like that unattended for long. The property was surrounded by wire fencing that had been easy enough to get the Range Rover past. Once McCitrick had been moved inside, the vehicle had been driven roughly into a high bush covered by towering oak trees. A close inspection from the ground would reveal it, but would be virtually impossible to detect from above, and if the sound of helicopters passing overhead was anything to go by it was a good thing too. Daedalus were pulling out all the stops to search the surrounding areas and going by the chatter Lavigne was picking up on his radio, it wouldn't be long before someone came knocking. An hour, maybe two.

The guest house they'd chosen at least still had curtain and a bed and, even better, running water, but it was no substitute for a hospital. The odd glances Munroe had been getting from Sloan said it all. McCitrick was lying on the bed with a temporary IV that had been hastily put together using an old trouser press and a couple of coat hangers, and even though he was falling in and out of consciousness, he was going downhill fast.

Barbeau was by the window of the single-floor residence, grasping his semi-automatic and scanning the entrance for any newcomers whilst Lavigne stayed glued to the radio and mapping the areas of the ever-widening police search.

'Ethan.'

Munroe look at Sloan. Her eyelids were drooping and she was slowly shaking her head from side to side in the dim light of the torch placed on the edge of the bed. Her shoulders then sagged and she gently rubbed McCitrick's forehead and made her way over to Munroe by the sink of the open-plan kitchen where he was washing his hands of his boss's blood.

'He's fading quickly,' she said, her lips tightening with frustration. 'I've done all I can. He needs medical attention, and soon.'

Munroe nodded his understanding, turned off the tap and dried his hands with a piece of ripped curtain lying on the counter. Getting him to a hospital would be like sticking one's head in the jaws of the tiger. No coming back from that. And they couldn't just leave him somewhere for the police to find, there wasn't enough time for that. It would be a death sentence for the section head and Munroe knew it.

He mulled over their options and then shot Sloan a cold stare. 'I'll take him in while you and the others make a break for it. Find Remus and get him all the intel we've collected. With any luck you can connect McCitrick's contact and—'

'Not a chance, I'll take him,' Sloan interrupted, raising her hand between them as Munroe opened his mouth to protest. 'Your skills are going to be needed more than mine going forward, I suspect. It's the right choice, logistically.'

The two stared at each other in silence and even though Munroe knew she was right he couldn't accept it. Once taken into custody it would not be long before she was delivered into the hands of Gasparyan and that he could not allow. Especially given Sloan's history with Daedalus before joining DSV.

'No. We've no idea whose skills are going to be needed and, besides, with me in their grasp they may ease up slightly and get complacent, and that's the type of environment DSV thrives in.'

Munroe could tell this was going to be a battle between them, but as her lips began to curl in preparation for an aggressive retort, a weak voice called out to them.

'Enough.'

They turned to see McCitrick staring at them, his head lolling to one side and his left hand limply calling them over. They did so immediately as both Barbeau and Lavigne looked up from their positions.

'You need medical attention, John,' Sloan said bluntly with no hint of emotion, but her assessment was met with a light wave of his fingers, his eyes closing momentarily.

'She's right, sir. Your wounds are severe,' Munroe added, hitting him with the reality of the situation. 'Without help you're not going to make it.'

McCitrick blinked slowly and then spoke in a whisper, each syllable uttered causing him immense pain. 'I'm going. I can feel it. You'll do as I say.'

Those softly spoken words still had the air of supreme authority and Barbeau and Lavigne also moved over to his torchlit bedside, their shadows shifting gloomily on the brown, water-stained ceiling above them.

'Captain Munroe, as of now you'll take my place as section head of DSV, UK division.'

The order had Munroe looking stunned but as he glanced over at the others he found them all nodding in agreement, and he slipped back into military character and nodded with a salute that his boss returned with a painful wince. McCitrick scanned each one of them and seeing no disagreement in their faces he continued, now speaking to them all as a team.

'Leave me here, find the others, meet the contact and bring the Daedalus house of cards down,' McCitrick growled as best as his wounds would allow, and as he struggled for an additional breath no one said a word. Once John McCitrick made a decision is was cast in stone, and besides, they knew what he was asking, they knew he was demanding not just his own sacrifice but theirs as well if necessary, and as hard as it was to admit, they knew he was right.

'There's a small airstrip, with a single engine Cessna. She's small, but enough to get you all out. It's on my laptop. File name "Extract Beta".'

'Sir—' Sloan began but with a spluttering cough, McCitrick shot her an angry look.

'I'm in no state to argue with you, Captain Sloan. You have your orders.'

Captain Jaqueline Sloan never shed a tear for anything and this was no different but that moment was as close to emotional as Munroe had ever seen her. She shared with McCitrick a level of bond above the others and she now reached over and gently held his forearm and smiled caringly.

'Yes, sir. We won't let you down.'

'I know you won't,' he wheezed, now looking over to Barbeau. 'Commander Barbeau, Captain Lavigne, you've made your country proud, as you have me, and I expect you to carry on until the job's done. It has been one of the greatest honours of my life serving with you both and—' McCitrick paused as he subdued the cough rumbling up his throat and reeking pain across his chest '—you tell Colonel Remus... You tell Remus I'll see him in Morocco, and I'll be waiting. He'll know what it means.'

'Yes, sir. The honour has been ours,' the Frenchmen said in unison, and both raised a salute.

'You will not be forgotten, sir,' Barbeau added, and McCitrick managed to raise his hand to his forehead before dropping his hand back down to his side, the effort clearly immense for him.

'Don't you boys dare get soft on me now. You may be family, but you're my soldiers at heart. Go forth and set things right. Whatever it takes.'

Barbeau and Lavigne lowered their salute and with bulging jawlines, both men's teeth clenched tightly, they nodded proudly before heading back to their positions as McCitrick ushered Munroe and Sloan closer with his eyes, his voice growing weaker as his strength began to desert him fully.

'Jaqueline, you know how I feel so I only have one thing to say to you. You are the person I am most proud of in my life and it has been the greatest honour to have known you. Never question yourself... ever! And support Ethan always, but never forget to keep him on track if he strays off course. You understand what I mean.'

'Yes, John, I do, and I will,' Sloan replied, and now fighting back tears she leant over and tenderly kissed him on the forehead. 'I'll see you on the other side, old friend.'

'And I'll be waiting for you.'

Sloan stood back up and gazed at her mentor one last time as he looked directly into her eyes.

'Now let me have a quick word with your teammate, would you.'

Sloan managed a smile before nodding sternly, and then she headed back to the kitchen area as Munroe knelt down so the two men were level which each other.

'You may be the newest member of DSV, Ethan, but you're the leader your team needs, and I knew it the moment I met you, so never be in doubt... ever. Remus will accept my decision and welcome it, but my only wish is that I wasn't leaving you DSV in the state it is.'

McCitrick managed to raise his hand, motioning him closer, and Munroe leant in so no one else would be able to hear, his boss's voice now falling to a whisper, his body beginning to shut down. 'There'll be times in this job when you'll be on your own; it can be colder than you can imagine being in charge of DSV. But trust your instincts, son, and never be swayed from what your gut tells you. Rely on your team and always listen, but never forget you hold their lives in your hands, so do what you must to protect them.'

McCitrick's eyes began to fade, but then he woke from the enticing slumber, his voice now barely audible, his face white as bone china. 'You take care of Sloan, she's the best of us but doesn't always realise it. Good luck, my boy, never forget they are your family now, your blood.'

His breathing was so light it became barely detectable as the bag taped to his chest inflated one last time.

John McCitrick managed his last few words, 'Bring the Disavowed home... to where we belong.'

McCitrick's arms slumped to the bed, his body motionless, only the sound of his last breath slipping from his lips filling the air. He stared up at the ceiling, eyes now blank and lifeless, and Munroe leant over to brush McCitrick's eyes closed before resting his open palm on his forehead. He then turned to face everyone and for almost twenty seconds no one said a word, each of them lost in their own personal grief. There were no tears, only a shared loss for the man whom they not only respected greatly but had come to rely on for stability during the nightmare that had become their lives. They glanced at each other, eyes conveying more than words ever could, before finally they all became focused on Munroe.

It was Barbeau who spoke first. 'Well, boss?'

Munroe offered a sad smile and then expelled a loud sigh.

'We need to keep moving. He'd expect nothing less.'

Each of the team barely managed a nod as Munroe turned back around, picked up McCitrick's hand and lowered it gently onto the section head's chest respectfully.

'Jax, get us the airstrip's location. We can contact Colonel Remus mid-flight and recall Dalton and Talon. We need the whole agency together if we're going to figure out our next move.'

'What's left of it,' Barbeau said, looking uncharacteristically disheartened.

'That's why we need them more than ever,' Sloan chimed in, and Barbeau now gave her a firm nod.

DSV's American team of Dalton and Talon had been deliberately kept at a distance for the weeks it had taken to complete the operation of getting Lavigne out of prison.

Not because they weren't trusted, but because they were. If the mission had failed then at least they had a DSV cell still active on the outside. Having all your eggs in one basket, so close together, was a risk. When everyone was after you it was just the sensible move, as it had been with Remus back in France, but things had changed. McCitrick's death was tantamount to ripping the beating heart out of DSV; even though Remus was one hell of a leader, it was John who had been the glue holding the DSV renegades together. His loss was incalculable, but it meant they needed each other more than ever.

Munroe glanced around his teammates, their pain etched on all their faces, when a saying came to mind. A saying he held dear and which had seen him through some of the most difficult times in his life. 'A famous writer once said, "I never saw a wild thing look sorry for itself".'

The line drew a genuine smile from the other three and they all nodded. 'I think it's time we got in touch with McCitrick's old contact. The ex-Daedalus creep.'

'And then?' Sloan asked, her chin up, confidence returning.

Munroe's lips curled and his eyes now blazed with a focused rage. 'And then we poke the bear... And we poke it fucking hard.'

Chapter 13

'Well, what did you find out?'

Hans Bauer held the Samsung mobile to his ear and ground his teeth as the familiar voice of Ernst Dupont crackled through the earpiece.

'We may have a problem, sir. It would appear Davit Gasparyan allowed the entire DSV team to slip through his fingers.'

'What!' Bauer replied in nothing short of a yell, causing the few people sitting in the waiting area to glance over at him in surprise, but after a few courteous smiles each went back to what they were originally doing. 'How? What happened exactly?'

'He tracked them to a farmhouse north of Southampton. He had them surrounded, but they managed to escape.'

'All of them!'

'Yes, sir. I'm afraid so, and the team took many casualties.'

Bauer resisted the outrage he was feeling and shot a pleasant smile at an attractive young blonde woman in her thirties as she passed him and made her way over to the main reception desk.

'How is that possible? He had enough ordnance to level the place,' Bauer said in a low whisper, his palm covering his mouth and the lower part of his mobile.

'Yes, he did, sir, but he took to attempting a negotiation with them during which time they escaped. I still haven't determined how, but I do know that Davit was injured in the process.'

Bauer was now shaking his head at the idea of such a weak operation and then he stopped, his eyes squinting like a predator about to attack.

'So not only did he survive, but he allowed every one of those bastards to escape.'

'That's about the sum of it, sir. It would appear your concerns may have been justified. He had them cold. They should never have escaped.'

Bauer exhaled deeply through his nose and then began to tap his teeth together as he considered the prospect.

'I think someone is trying to make me look bad. Perhaps he's become a bit too ambitious.'

The line went silent for a few seconds and then Dupont spoke, sounding unsure this time.

'Surely he wouldn't dare, sir? He'd have to be insane to try to depose you.'

'True, my friend, but the prospect of power and money have a crazy effect on weaker minds and, for all his bravado, Davit Gasparyan has always been a coward at heart.'

There was more silence, until finally Dupont spoke again, his tone of voice tempered but sombre. 'What would you like me to do, sir?'

Bauer ran the possibilities through his mind, but one thing that kept returning to him was his rocky position within the organisation. One that would be solidified, but not until Iron Phoenix was located.

'Do you have eyes on him at the moment?'

'Yes, sir. He and his team are still combing the area, but I would guess McCitrick and his boys are long gone by now.'

Bauer considered his words, and his lips began to curl in to a snarl.

'Stay close to him, but not so close he knows. If he is planning to betray me then he'll need Phoenix. Let him chase it for us and when he does find it, we'll close his account for good.'

'Yes, sir. I'll be in touch.'

Bauer hung up, slipped the phone back into his pocket and picked up a paper off the side table beside him, but he had barely read a word when a voice called out to him.

'Mr Bauer, the chancellor will see you now.'

Hans Bauer lowered his newspaper and looked up at the smiling receptionist with an unimpressed gaze.

'I've been here for over an hour, my dear.'

The complaint received raised eyebrows from the female receptionist and she stood backwards a step, straightening her grey work suit pants respectfully. 'I'm sorry for the delay but the chancellor has a very busy schedule.'

Bauer folded his newspaper and dropped it down onto the black chair next to him before slowly rising to his feet.

'Don't we all, young lady. The difference is, I make an effort.'

To her credit, the woman's smile never wavered and she nodded pleasantly and gestured towards the set of glossy doors behind a large glass-top reception desk. 'Please follow me and I will make the introduction.'

She barely took a step before Bauer called out after her, his voice low and with authority. 'I need no introduction, dear. The chancellor knows me well.'

He passed her, leaving her standing by the row of waiting chairs, and as he reached the door and placed his palm on the handle, Bauer glanced back.

'I'll have a cup of Earl Grey with one spoon of brown sugar. Chop, chop. Make yourself useful.'

It was only now that the receptionist's smile dissolved and her change in demeanour brought a smile to Bauer's own face before he pushed open the door and made his way in.

'Ursula,' he said, deliberately leaving the door open a moment for all to hear, 'I hope I don't have to wait this long every time I pay you a visit.'

His point made, Bauer now closed the door behind him and strode over to the thin black metal desk as German Chancellor Ursula Schneider got to her feet.

'Hans,' she said with an obviously forced smile. 'I apologise for the wait, but there is barely a moment of my day when I'm not sought after.'

Bauer shook her waiting hand and then sat down in the brown leather chair being offered him by Schneider's palm. He shuffled in his seat, the sound of leather crumpling beneath him, and once comfortable, he stared at the chancellor and waited for her to sit back down.

'You've been difficult to get hold of in recent weeks, Ursula. I hope you've not been ignoring me?'

'Of course not,' Schneider replied, her frown wrinkling in either earnest or annoyance, it was difficult to tell. 'I thought it best, given the current climate, that I focus on my job and not to draw undue attention to our close association, given your sensitive work at the behest of the British prime minister.'

Her tone was confrontational and she leant forwards in her chair. 'And the way you just treated a member of my staff out there shows I was right to be cautious.'

Schneider pointed to the small security monitor above the unused cherry-wood bordered fireplace on the left-hand side of the room. 'There are certain protocols you must adhere to, for both our sakes, as well as Daedalus's. Reichsführer Bormann insisted upon it.'

The name of Bauer's previous master made his eyes tighten and he waved his finger in the air.

'I surmise that your carefree mentioning of Daedalus means this room is secure?'

Schneider offered a slow nod of her head.

'I have the room checked every morning by my personal security team, so relax, Hans. You are free to talk.'

The room fell into silence and only once Bauer had deemed it uncomfortable enough did he cradled his hands together, fingertips touching his chin, and let out a growl-laden sigh. 'Before we begin, I think it important that I iron out the wrinkles and blow off the dust that appears to have settled on your character. First, I want to remind you who is in charge, because judging by your demeanour, and possibly the chair you now sit it, that ego of yours has swelled your big fat head more than ever. Second, never forget who put you here and where you allegiance truly lies. And third, if you mention that traitor Bormann to me ever again or call me Hans instead of my title—' Bauer also now leant forward, his lips curling venomously '—I'll have your fucking head ripped off and dumped in the Rhine to be gorged on by the crabs and whatever other vile slimy animals live at the bottom of it.'

For the first time since Bauer entered the room, Chancellor Schneider looked genuinely unnerved and her bullish expression evaporated. She sat up straight in her chair as Bauer sat back in his seat and lifted his leg upwards slightly and farted. He then craned his nose forwards and took a deep sniff before blowing the foul smell in the direction of Chancellor Schneider, much to her disgust.

'You are nothing more than a cog in a machine, a machine that I, and I alone, operate. I decide when to turn it on, or when to turn it off and how much worth your cog has rests solely in my hands. And no one, I repeat, no one, is big enough to take on the machine.'

Schneider, her nose wrinkling, nodded respectfully.

'Yes, my führer.'

The menace on Bauer's face faded and was quickly replaced with a playful smile.

'Good, my child. Then let us discuss our plans.'

'May I open a window?' Schneider asked, pointing to the glass frame behind her.

Bauer stared at her as he contemplated the request. 'Err, no.'

The chancellor forced a smile. 'As you wish.'

'Good. Now that's over with, how go the preparations?'

Ursula Schneider ignored the unpleasant smell hanging in the air and set about bringing Bauer up to speed with zeal.

'The terrorist attack in New York was exactly the catalyst we had hoped it would be. The push towards a politically global world has truly begun and not only do the people in power see the merit in it, but polls show the vast majority of free nations see a combining of armies and military budgets as needed if we are to fight a new age of nuclear terrorism.'

Bauer remained silent as Schneider continued with her appraisal of the Free World post New York.

'Wall Street is on life support, and with the economic fallout of the terrorist attack, much of the money market has diverted to Europe and developing nations. There is much work to do, and the path has only had its first stone laid, but I believe this is the beginning we all hoped for. A true path to a one-world government and once that much power has been consolidated, the world will be ripe for interests to prevail. Our interests.'

Bauer raised his hands in a calming manner.

'One step at a time, Ursula. There are many, many variables and much work to be undertaken, but you are right that this is the beginning of a new world order and we will be in the middle of it. Ready to exploit the opportunities as they arise, but for now what are the whispers coming from the United Nations?'

A deep smile crept momentarily across the chancellor's face and she tapped her red acrylic nail upon the desk.

'The G7 countries are drafting a proposal for the reformation of the United Nations. There's no name for it yet, and China is resisting, but I believe she'll come around once her own allies sign up. It will be messy and we've decades of manoeuvring ahead of us but as of now it's on the table. The beginning of a new world.'

Schneider's lips curled upwards in a delicious act of her own narcissism. 'And when all is said and done, and the levers, laws and security apparatus of world governance have been laid in place, Daedalus will attempt its true goal of a thousand year Fourth Reich.'

'All good things to those that wait,' Bauer murmured loudly, and he appeared content with the chancellor's work. 'And when will we have conformation of your position in all this?'

Schneider now looked doubly proud, her eyes seeming to radiate excitement as she spoke. 'My appointment as president overseeing this reformation of the United Nations will be confirmed within the week, and I will be giving a speech on Liberty Island in New York on the night of the announcement, as you know. We have positioned ourselves perfectly.'

One could never guarantee how the political winds would blow, but this was only when common voters were involved in the process. The politicisation of the European Union had shown Bauer, and anyone taking note, that when only a few politicians decided the appointments then most, if not all, could all be swayed into voting the right way, and if not then simply shorten the list of voting politicians. Power always corrupts, and a globe-spanning agency like Daedalus that dealt solely in power and money made anything possible.

'Good. Now there are some other issues I wish to talk about but let me say just two things before we begin.' Bauer sat up and crossed his legs before laying out both his arms on the armrests, like a chairman preparing to receive his staff. 'One, you've a right to be pleased. You are making us all very proud, Ursula. I hope you appreciate how much effort I've put into getting you this opportunity.'

Chancellor Schneider smiled and then nodded confidently. 'And two?'

Bauer stared at her intensely before reaching down and unzipping his fly. 'It's time to show me how appreciative you really are.'

Chapter 14

'Yes, sir. You may take the elevator to the restaurant,' the concierge replied, holding out her open palm towards the multiple glass elevators leading to the top of the famous Burj Al Arab hotel. 'Please, enjoy your meal.'

Wearing an open charcoal grey suit and black leather Oxford brogues, Munroe offered the woman a thankful smile and headed deeper into the world's first seven-star hotel. Given the décor of a golden paradise, it was not difficult to see why it had earned those stars. Built in 1994 on the sparkling blue coast of Dubai, with the huge oil reserves and billions received in petrol dollars from around the world, it seemed there was no extravagance the small desert country could not afford.

Munroe made his way up an escalator with a large pyramid-shaped water fountain on one side and an over-sized fish tank filled with exotic fish on the other until he reached the first level that was overlooked by the towering interior of the ceiling, which rose up to the highest floor. Expensive shops lined either side, filled with attractive young women partnered with much older, overweight men who looked on anxiously as luxury items were handled excitedly.

After passing another fountain, this one shooting out streams of water in arcs, he reached a group of chattering tourists, many whom would not have been able to afford the eye-twitch-inducing twenty thousand pounds a night rate per room. Instead they came to visit for the day and just admire the place before retreating to their own far less costly hotels during their visit to the Arab Emirates.

Munroe arrived at the elevator and pressed the gold call button; the button actually being made of gold and not some cheaper fool's-gold metal substitute that one would expect in any other hotel. The elevator doors slid backwards and with a glance behind him to the lobby, which looked like a physical representation of Aladdin's cave to him, he entered the elevator, satisfied he hadn't picked up anyone tailing him. He pressed the button labelled 'Al Muntaha Restaurant'. The doors silently closed behind him and he made his way over to the glass windows as the elevator began to ascend upwards at a remarkably fast pace.

The view out onto the expanse of glistening blue water that was the Persian Gulf was hypnotic, and Munroe gently held the silver handrail as the elevator reached its maximum speed, passing by the dozens of floors effortlessly.

Three days had elapsed since the death of John McCitrick and despite the entire DSV team meeting up in a Cannes safe house on the south coast of France, the reunion had initially done little to lighten their spirits. Talon and Dalton had had arrived first, having travelled from Morocco, and Colonel Remus had turned up only hours later, having moved to a safe spot in Paris after the rescue of Lavigne. The meeting had proved a sombre affair, but after sharing a dinner together and, with the help of five bottles of Cabernet Sauvignon that Remus had supplied, the mood around the dinner table had taken a turn for the better. Uplifting and amusing stories of John

McCitrick's undeniably unique character had been at the forefront, and even though the individual sense of loss was palpable at first, by dessert the reminiscing had become a real source of satisfaction. They were professionals and the grieving process would have to wait until their mission was over, and considering the heavy task of exposing Daedalus, the wait could be long.

Barbeau had found a funeral home to where a close and trustworthy contact of his had taken McCitrick's body and stored it in one of the refrigerated lockers on site. It was important that no one knew the section head was dead, firstly because it would renew what was an already worldwide manhunt for the former agency, and secondly because it would expose their weakness. Even though Hans Bauer's private military, Blackstar, was at the tip of the manhunt's spear, it was undeniable that DSV were still seen as the best of the best, near magical ghosts with the ability to evade capture. And there was no good reason to change that perception of them now.

Sloan had taken over McCitrick's role of central intelligence gatherer for the team and even though Colonel Remus was the only original DSV section head, he had made it clear that everyone would have a say in the course of action they would take. Democracy within the military or spy agencies was not a normal thing in anyone's book, but then again DSV, the Disavowed, were no ordinary team.

Sloan had contacted the only Daedalus member to turn mole, one Karl Gruber, and as McCitrick had predicted he had been a tough one to nail down. Two days of wrangling and then a final threat to expose him to Hans Bauer himself and the man had finally accepted their terms.

A single meeting with Munroe and the disclosure of any and all information asked.

They had decided to not mention the handwritten note from Hitler or the words contained within. After some checking, it turned out that the Argentinian address had been one of the first places Adolf Hitler had taken up residence after escaping the war-torn soils of Europe. His personal pilot had no doubt been expected to meet him there after his final mission had been completed, but obviously his capture by the Soviets had screwed that up, thankfully. The fact that it would not be McCitrick meeting him had made Gruber nervous enough, forcing him to betray his 'beloved führer' would have to happen face to face. The Daedalus traitor may have switched sides, but who knew if his true obsession with his führer was a strong as it was for the others in his ex-organisation. No, far better to interrogate the man in person. As the best interrogator in the team, it had been Munroe who'd been elected to carry out the operation.

As for Gruber having made a new life for himself in Dubai, it made perfect sense: he had got as far away from Europe and the Americas as possible. Munroe had travelled on his own under a false passport, pair of dark sunglasses and a false and bushy moustache. The addition to his upper lip had needed re-gluing after arriving in the stifling heat of Dubai International Airport. Thankfully, the airport was only fourteen miles from Gruber's demanded meeting place, and Munroe had gone from one air conditioner to another. The heat in this part of the world was like nowhere else on earth. Totally void of humidity, a relentless heat that could sap one's strength quickly if one was not used to it, and even if Munroe was experienced in such climates his moustache was most certainly not. Munroe was on his own for this one, although that didn't mean the others weren't close by and watching.

The elevator door slid open and Munroe was met by two smiling waiters standing behind a thick, glimmering gold desk.

'May I help you, sir?' the attendant with the whitest teeth of the two asked.

'I'm meeting a friend for lunch,' Munroe stated as the set of gleaming teeth turned to a red leather book and prepared to skim down the list with his finger.

'Your name, sir?'

'Dunston, Henry Dunston. I'm here to meet Mr Gruber. The booking may be under his name.'

Munroe had elected to use a different alias throughout his negotiation with Karl Gruber. The man may have been a trusted source of McCitrick's but to him he was an unknown quantity and as such Munroe had not wanted to throw his real identity into the ether. Who knew what lines of communication the ex-Nazi still had in his back pocket.

It took only a few seconds for the toothy waiter to bring his finger to a rest on the name and he then came out from behind his gold desk and proceeded to guide Munroe towards the front of the restaurant.

'This way, Mr Dunston. Mr Gruber has already arrived.'

Like everything else in this hotel, the Al Muntaha restaurant was unique. The hotel itself was in the shape of a giant sail, one side thinner than the other to give the appearance of being blown in the wind, and right at the top sat the restaurant. Like a horizontal piece of rigging that attached to the hotel's mast at its centre and with glass panelling making up the entire right side, it allowed an impressive view of the beach and the city of Dubai. In the distance one could easily make out the two artificial offshore islands of Palm Jumeirah which, as you would expect, looked like huge sandy palm trees in the blue sea where the rich and wasteful had private homes up and down each of the sand bars.

The view truly was impressive, but as Munroe was led up to a table, the occupant having his back to him, he was far more focused on surveying the place from a tactical perspective, working out where to position himself if things went pear-shaped.

'Mr Gruber. Mr Dunston has arrived.'

The waiter moved over to the other side of the table and pulled out the vacant chair in preparation and Munroe took a step over to it, stopping for a moment to acknowledge his host.

'Mr Gruber. It's a pleasure to see you,' Munroe said, and he held out his hand, which was shaken before he sat down and allowed the waiter to push his seat inwards.

Karl Gruber was in his early sixties with short, slicked hair. He stared at Munroe with blue-grey eyes and forced a smile. Wearing a plain red shirt underneath a navy-blue jacket, buttoned up, and a tanned pair of chinos, Mr Gruber looked more like a retired wing commander than an ex-Nazi with enough secrets to bury thousands of men. His demeanour was solid and, along with his chin held high, oozed confidence, but his twitching right eyelid suggested that this was the last place he wanted to be.

Munroe looked over at the cup of coffee on Gruber's side of the table and he looked up at the set of bright white teeth smiling at him patiently.

'Mineral water with ice and a slice of lime, please.'

'Of course, sir. I will be back with the menus.'

Munroe waited until they were alone before tapping his open palm on the table and settling back in his chair.

'Thank you for meeting me, Mr Gruber. And I firstly want to recognise you for all you've done for the agency in the past. John McCitrick speaks highly of you and sends his regards, and apologies for not being here in person.'

Gruber continued to stare at him in silence and then he spoke, his German accent still thick as it wrapped around the English words.

'Is he dead?'

'No, not at all. He's in good health, although his right knee has been playing up recently; apart from that, he's doing just fine.'

'Then why is it that you're sitting in that seat and not him?'

For a man described as being extremely twitchy, Karl Gruber appeared extremely at calm, although his eyelid was continuing to spasm rhythmically. Munroe now leant forwards.

'He thought it better to send an unknown, like me, so as not to draw attention to you. Your cover has stayed intact for all these years and he didn't want to take any chances, given that Daedalus has stuck their heads above the parapet recently. That is something you are probably not aware of. So, he asked someone he trusted, and I said yes.'

Gruber considered the justification for a few moments and then he took a sip of his coffee before gently placing it back on its saucer with a clink.

'That I did not know. And if I had I certainly would not have met you here today.'

Gruber began to rise from his chair, his intention to leave immediately obvious, but Munroe reached over and grasped him firmly by the wrist.

'If you leave now, we can't help you… Don't you even want to know why I'm here?'

Munroe's wide eyes and tone suggested unseen peril and he released his grip and sat back in his seat as the waiter returned with a mineral water, which he placed down on the table.

'Gentlemen, would you like some time to look over the menu?' the still smiling waiter asked, placing a menu in each of their hands and noting that one of his guests was standing he pointed to a set of gold mosaic lined doors behind him. 'The restrooms are just there, sir… Unless you're leaving?'

Munroe held Gruber's stare for a moment and then he turned his attention to the waiter and smiled.

'Both my friend and I have been looking forward to this meal for a while. We wouldn't miss this experience if our lives depended on it. Thank you. If you could give us a few minutes and then we'll be ready to order.'

With an extra near lip-splitting smile, the waiter disappeared back to the front desk leaving Munroe and Gruber alone once again.

'I wouldn't be here if it weren't of upmost importance, for both of us.'

Gruber eyed him with mistrust, but it finally melted away and he sat back down, straightened his jacket and placed his clasped hands on the table in front of him. 'Very well. You may have five minutes of my time.'

Munroe got straight to the point. 'The nuclear attack in New York. It wasn't some Iranian extremist, it was Daedalus.'

Gruber's eyes widened at the information and he sat rigid as Munroe continued.

'It's over for them, and everyone connected to them. The old game of cat and mouse in the shadows is coming to an end, along with the secrecy of their existence. You can't kill that many people and not expect the rules to change. The heads of the United Kingdom, America and France have been briefed and they have declared war on Daedalus, have no doubt. And they've tasked DSV with all the resources we need, covert and overt, in bringing the house of cards down. It's the end for them, Karl, and we need your help.'

Gruber was already looking doubtful at the tale being spun.

'I don't believe you. Daedalus would be insane to draw such attention. It's not how they operate.'

'It's not how they used to operate, but there's been a change of management. Bormann is dead and a man by the name of Hans Bauer is running the show. And he's a bloody maniac.'

The names drew a look of surprise from Gruber and he took a deep breath and closed his eyes momentarily before returning Munroe's gaze.

'I know Bauer. Used to, I should say. Long time ago when he was an up and comer. And Bormann is dead!'

'Yep. Dead as this meal that we're about to order. And I don't need to remind you of your place in all this,' Munroe went on, causing Gruber to look confused. 'Now it's all out in the open those governments are going to stop at nothing to track down anyone who ever had an association with Daedalus.'

'But I've been helping DSV for years. I'm a hero... not the enemy.'

Munroe sat back in his chair and made a clicking sound with his tongue.

'Well that depends on if you help us bring this quickly to a close, doesn't it?'

Gruber pulled his hands off the table and his nose wrinkled in anger at the obvious tactic being used against him.

'John McCitrick never would have blackmailed me, never. He was always the carrot and the stick type of man.'

'Like I said, Karl. The rules of the game have changed.'

Gruber didn't like what he was being told, but it took him barely any time to decide. A decision to save his own skin.

'Very well, what do you need from me, Mr Dunston?'

'Call me Henry.'

'No, thank you, Mr Dunston will do just fine. I not a man to be on first name terms with those who blackmail me.'

Of course, the whole story Munroe was dropping in Gruber's lap was bullshit. But how the hell would he know the difference?

'Fair enough, Karl. Then let's get to it. Does the term Iron Phoenix mean anything to you?'

Gruber's shoulders sagged suddenly, and he winced, clearly knowing what it meant, and given his expression it was of immense importance.

'Now that's something I've not heard in a very long time.' He crossed his arms and smiled dryly. 'Providence, you might say, or a failsafe. Very few people know about it.'

'What is it?' Munroe asked, watching as his dinner partner appeared to be enjoying being in the driving seat.

'What's it's value to you, Mr Dunston? Such information is worth more than what I have been promised.'

'I already told you, Karl. You get to keep the life you've made for yourself.'

Gruber was now wagging his liver-spotted finger in the air at him.

'Oh no, Mr Dunston. As you have already said so eloquently, the rules have changed and that goes for me as well. I may well have helped you for free, but as I mentioned, blackmail does not sit well with me. So, what have you got?'

At this point Munroe didn't care. If Gruber knew the real truth of DSV's position then he'd know there was nothing he could offer that would amount to anything.

'What do you want?'

Gruber now relaxed into his seat and placed his wagging finger thoughtfully against his lips.

'I would like eight million pounds deposited in to an account of my choosing.'

Even as Munroe attempted a reply, Gruber was stating his next demand. 'And I would like a new identity, because you forcing this meeting upon me has most likely ruined my current one... And I want it today.'

Munroe sat silently. If he said yes right away then it could clue in Gruber that none of this was going to happen, or that he was that desperate and this negation was going to take even longer. So, he waited for ten seconds and then he replied, 'Three million.'

'Six million.'

'Four million.'

'Five million.'

'Deal,' Munroe replied, much to the pleasure of Gruber, 'and a new identity.'

'Yes.'

Gruber chuckled to himself and smugly waited for Munroe to speak first. He wasn't going to make it easy.

'Well? What does Iron Phoenix mean?'

Gruber allowed himself a few more moments of enjoyment and appeared to revel in the knowledge.

Or it's because he believes he's just made five million quid.

'There are many levels of secrecy within Daedalus and for many of us on the lower rungs there was always talk, whispers really, of what plans had been laid in place to lead us towards the final glory of a new world order. A Fourth Reich.'

The very word sent a charge of excitement through Gruber, his body stiffening and his eyes brimming with pride at the herculean task of remoulding the planet's population into the Nazis' idea of perfection. Munroe had seen in before in the eyes of Hans Bauer and any other cult member he'd come across. Even still, he found the gaze unsettling.

'The whisper in connection with what you ask though was, as I said, a failsafe for ultimate power. And it came from the lips of only one person. The same person you now tell me is dead… If you are indeed telling me the truth.'

'Bormann?' Munroe replied, just the name making the old Nazi quiver.

'Reichsführer Bormann,' he corrected. 'And if it is true what you say then the meaning of the word most likely does not matter anymore.'

Munroe's eyes dulled and he tapped his palm on the table top. 'It's about to drop to three million if you don't get to the point.'

The threat made no impact upon Gruber as a smile crept in from the left side of his mouth and he leant forward, dropped his elbows on the table and cradled his fingertips together in the shape of a steeple.

'Holding power over men is a strange thing, Mr Dunston. Some achieve it through charisma, others through authority or violence, or the threat of it. Now imagine how one would maintain that control at the top of an organisation, when nearly all of its members seek to pull the throne from directly under you at all times. It wasn't always like that, not when the true führer was still at the helm. The power he held over all of us... was beyond spiritual. It was near magical. Just a single word of congratulation could light up one's world with confidence and a single dismayed scowl could drive you deeply into the depths of despair. This was the führer's power. Glorious times.'

Gruber pulled back from the table and settled into his seat with a sigh.

'I met him on numerous occasions, you know? And I can testify to the magnetic aura of Adolf Hitler. His hold on and direction of Daedalus was crucial in the early years.'

'That's funny. I heard he was a drug addict and riddled with Parkinson's.'

The truth had Gruber sitting up in his seat and waving his liver-spotted finger once again. 'No, no. He didn't have Parkinson's, but you are right about his addiction. You try waging war against the world single-handedly. Even you and your Disavowed boys and girls would need a little pharmaceutical help. Thankfully, Adolf Hitler was not a natural addict and as such wasn't in his DNA so once the pressure of the war had been removed from his shoulders he never touched anything again and his mind was restored to its former glory. You know I saw him dictate two separate letters at one time without a pause. Such was his ability. But then, when he died, the leadership became a mad scramble for power, those seeking to make proud their adored führer.'

Munroe found it hard to tell if Karl Gruber still believed in all the Nazi garbage or if it had been only his mesmerisation of one man, and he decided to keep the story moving regardless.

'Bormann took the reins.'

'Yes, but not without a fight. And a bloody one too. On the führer's deathbed he laid the trust in Bormann to carry out his final wishes. Now, as Bormann tells, it was he who was nominated to lead Daedalus, but there were many who said otherwise. The führer's wife, Eva Braun, and their son were also privy to his deathbed wishes and after Bormann announced his ascendency they were outraged and charges of usurping the position followed.'

'Hitler had a son?'

'Yes,' Gruber said with a genuinely loving smile. 'Shortly after the war and by the time the führer passed away in 1981 his son was almost thirty-three and was deemed the natural successor.'

The news of Hitler's lineage should not have been surprising to Munroe and he remembered back to the house in Key West, shortly after the attack in New York, where he and Sloan had seen Hans Bauer murder Bormann in cold blood. And the two offspring of Adolf Hitler who were in attendance and watching the sickening display play out.

'I saw his son at the same time I watched Bauer kill off Bormann and take control of Daedalus. He was barley in his twenties.'

Gruber beamed back at him with welcomed surprise. 'You have been busy, Mr Dunston. But I know for a fact that wasn't his son. The people I believe you're referring to were relatives of the führer but not his direct line. The reason I know this is because his actual son accused Bormann immediately after the führer's death of usurping his rightful position. The accusation could have stuck too, but sadly he and his mother, Eva, were killed in a terrible car accident near Buenos Aires soon after.'

'So, Bormann had them killed?' Munroe asked, hardly surprised, but Gruber looked sly about the subject.

'There was talk but nothing was ever proven, how could it be? What I am sure about though is the Martin Bormann, Hitler's first aide, became head of the modern and blossoming Nazi Regime and the steward of an organisation worth upwards of four and a half trillion dollars!' Guber allowed the amount to roll off his lips venomously, the gigantic number drawing a stunned gasp from Munroe. 'And that was nine years ago, before I became an informant for DSV.'

Munroe slumped back in his seat and let slip a shocked whistle. He knew Daedalus had money, but he never realised they had *money*.

'Jesus, that's a lot of cash.'

'Hard to get your head around, I know. That's not just "fuck you, money". That's "fuck you, I'm going to rule the world" money. You see, the billions that were stolen from Europe during the war was just to get Daedalus going. The real money came with seventy years of business building and the determined will to reach a goal of a Fourth Reich.'

Gruber noted how shocked Munroe was at the startling number and he chuckled deeply to himself.

'Now you see the true mastery of Daedalus and the genius of their operations and to give credit where credit is due it was Bormann's business mind the made all the difference. After a few years, the successes of these enterprises silenced any dissenters. And with that he was in charge... until very recently, it would now appear.'

Munroe was still reeling at the sum of money and understanding their ability to infiltrate pretty much anyone, anywhere, at any time. Most people would never admit it to themselves, but the truth was almost everyone had their price.

'OK, so what about the words I asked you about?' Munroe said, bringing the older man back to the core reason he was there.

'Ah, yes. Well, Bormann may have taken the top position and quelled the complaints but it didn't mean he didn't have wolves circling at all times and as such he established something that Adolf Hitler had set in motion years earlier that could protect him from internal treachery. The kind of thing that demonstrates an ability to bring the whole fucking thing crashing down if he were ever betrayed.'

'And that was?'

'As I told you they were only whispers, but whispers deliberately put out by Bormann to facilitate his grip on power. There was talk that there exists a place where every secret, every bit of information on Daedalus and their operations is stored. Enough intelligence to bring down Daedalus and its trillion-dollar empire in one fell swoop. Like I said, a failsafe. But if the whispers I heard were correct, its vaults were only added to by Reichsführer Bormann – the secretive cache was originally created by Hitler himself, preceding the war. It was said that what the true führer kept there was the true salvation of the Nazis, the key to a global Fourth Reich and a new world order.'

'What was it?' Munroe demanded, his attention piqued, but Gruber only shrugged.

'Dammed if I know, Mr Dunston. As I said, they were just whispers, but one thing is for sure, whatever it was didn't work because Bormann is dead and that asshole Bauer is still breathing.'

Munroe mulled over the information and considering telling his informant that the words he'd found had been written by Hitler himself. That alone suggested this vault, stash, whatever you wanted to call it, was or had been real and he was still deciding what to reveal when Gruber began offering him more.

'There is someone you might ask, but it's a long shot. It makes no difference to me if you want to waste your time.'

'Tell me,' Munroe said, ignoring Gruber's indifference.

'Well, Bormann had an aide, someone very close to him, but I heard along the grapevine she took off recently, divorcing herself from Daedalus and given what you've told me about Bauer taking over, I'm not surprised. They loathed each other.'

'You, an ex-Daedalus turncoat have a grapevine?' Munroe said, looking highly suspicious as Gruber now leant forward in a secretive manner.

'Just because I'm out of the game it doesn't mean I don't have a few pieces still on the board. Why do you think McCitrick kept me active?'

Munroe's sixth sense was beginning to tingle but he didn't show it.

'OK, who is she?'

'Freda Wilter. Where she's run to is anyone's guess but I'm sure you can track her down. Smart woman with a degree in nuclear physics and a Harvard law degree.'

'Smart? She sounds dangerous,' Munroe replied, and Gruber laughed and shook his head slowly from side to side.

'You have no idea.'

Munroe had heard enough and even though he felt something was off he decided in that moment to give McCitrick's contact a bit more information. He wouldn't reveal how deep a hole DSV was in, but perhaps something less to ensure Gruber would meet again if needed.

'We have...' Munroe began, but his attention was drawn away momentarily by two people being greeted at the restaurant by their smiling waiter. Munroe stood up and placed his chair next to Gruber's, not wanting the newcomers to overhear the tale he was about to spin. He leant in close and kept his face down as behind them the approaching guests were shown to their seats, just a few tables away.

'We have a problem at the agency,' Munroe said in a whisper, and his change in demeanour caused Gruber to look nervously at the couple being passed their menus before returning to Munroe's newly formed huddle.

'A serious problem?' he asked, and Munroe slowly rocked his head back and forth dramatically.

'Not serious, but a cause for concern.'

Gruber winced and then pulled away slightly with a dry smile quickly forming across his face. He then expelled a short and forced grunt of satisfaction. 'I would say, Mr Ethan Munroe, that being accused of unleashing a nuclear attack on New York City was a bit more than just a cause for concern. Wouldn't you?'

Munroe's poker face held as his real name was mentioned. Gruber knew more than he'd been letting on. Officially, the attack had been blamed on Iranian extremists who, if the papers were to be believed, had been killed in a single-strike action by American Special Forces. Only those at the highest levels, along with Hans Bauer, knew the truth and of the efforts to bring DSV to justice.

'You can't blame me for using an alias, Karl, not in such dangerous times. And I don't know who you've been talking to but I can assure you no one is blaming us for anything. Setting off a nuclear bomb resulting in the deaths of hundreds of thousands! I think you'll agree that is something we would remember doing.'

Gruber continued to smile, and he then patted Munroe on the thigh, got up from his seat and rested his back against the table opposite.

'I'm sure you'd remember it,' a voice called out from two tables back, and Munroe turned around in his chair see a man in a black suit and tie, his face covered by the bill of a New York Yankees baseball cap. Next to him, a red-haired woman in a grey work suit raised her right hand to reveal the barrel of a gun aimed directly at Munroe over the lip of the table.

'Because if you don't remember that then I'm hoping you will remember this.'

Munroe watched as the man raised his head, revealing the multitude of thick red cut lines covering half of his face and the dark black threads holding the wounds together. His left eye was grey and clouded and the skin of his cheek was red and rough with recent burn marks.

Munroe remained still and returned the stare, his expression calm and at ease. 'Gasparyan. If I knew you'd be joining us I would have reserved a table for four.'

Chapter 15

Davit Gasparyan got up from his seat and walked stiffly over to Munroe's table, leaving the redhead where she was, her gun still aimed at Munroe's chest. 'Don't do anything foolish,' Gasparyan said, nodding back at the woman. 'She may look petite but she'll pop two in your chest without a second thought. I trained her myself.'

'Poor thing.'

Gasparyan mustered barely the wisp of a smile before sliding his hand inside Munroe's jacket and then down across his waist, then he pulled back the chair opposite and sat down with a pained wince.

'Funny, but I'm not in the mood to joke, Ethan. Which is a shame because I do find it amusing that you didn't come armed. Anyway, the pain medication is doing very little to dampen the throbbing in my face. The doctor assures me I'll get my sight back in the coming weeks, just temporary, so that's one thing to be sanguine about.'

'All part of the service,' Munroe replied cockily as Gasparyan gently massaged his stitched cheek. 'We aim to please and, honestly, you look better this way.'

A flicker of anger rippled across Gasparyan's face and he slammed his fist on the table. But then he quickly settled and looked over at Gruber who was perhaps the most nervous looking of them all. 'Thank you for keeping him here, Karl. It won't be forgotten.'

'I hope not, Davit. And that you stay true to your word.'

'Despite what many think, there is still honour amongst friends. Even ones that betray.'

Munroe had realised the dynamic the moment he'd seen Gasparyan's torn face. Either Gruber had always been a double agent or, with his protectors at DSV gone, he had chosen the winning side and taken a gamble. Only time would tell but given what he knew of Gasparyan it was a long shot at best.

'I don't fancy your chances, Karl. Your friend here has a nasty way of keeping his word.'

Gruber said nothing, but Gasparyan appeared upbeat. 'Oh, Ethan. There is no better zeal than that of a convert and given the circumstances, Daedalus will be happy to bring our old friend back into the fold. So, what is it you were looking for?'

Munroe said nothing and instead slowly reached across the table, retrieved his drink and took a sip.

'Karl, perhaps you can tell me what he wanted?'

Gruber licked his lips in anticipation before answering. 'He's looking for the Iron Phoenix.'

The answer came as no surprise to Gasparyan and he managed a smile from corner of his mouth, allowing for as little movement in his stiches as possible.

'So you did find something of value in that underwater grave. Good, then this wild goose chase hasn't been a waste of my time. So then, what was it exactly?'

Munroe remained silent as Gasparyan glanced over at Gruber again who was more than happy to reveal what he knew.

'He didn't tell me exactly, just brought up the name, but that in itself is all you need to know.'

Gasparyan's nostrils flared and he stared at his new friend coldly. 'I will let you know what is of importance, Karl, and right now I want to find out what he discovered.'

His reply caused some excitement from Gruber and he stopped resting against the table and stood up to attention as fast as his ageing knees would allow.

'That I can help with, and now Reichsführer Bormann is dead I think it may be the only other person who knows of its location.'

This information had Gasparyan raising his eyebrow and he nodded, pleased at the thought. 'And that would be?'

'Freda Wilter.'

'She's dead,' Gasparyan was quick to correct, but Gruber was already shaking his head enthusiastically.

'No, she's alive, and I know where she is. If anyone knows about Iron Phoenix, she does.'

This further piece of intel truly garnered Gasparyan's attention and he swivelled in his chair until he was directly facing Gruber.

'And that is?'

Gruber looked over at Munroe suspiciously, apprehensive of disclosing what he knew in front of their adversary, so Munroe instinctively jumped in to keep the information flowing.

'Your vault of little secrets sounds fascinating, as important as Adolf Hitler made it sound in the hand-written note we found.'

The mention of a handwritten note caused a stir amongst both men, but it was Gasparyan whose eyes enlarged the most. 'Ah yes, the handwritten note from the führer you mentioned back in England! What did it say?'

Munroe settled back in his seat and smiled. 'C'mon, Davit. You know how this works. You get a piece; I get a piece. Quid pro quo.'

A gravelly chuckle slipped form Gasparyan's lips, his recent stitch work tightening.

'Do you really think you have a chance of getting out of here alive, Ethan? The best I can offer you is a painless death, and you know how efficient I am in that area of things.'

Munroe crossed his arms and stared back uncaringly.

'You've botched my demise twice now. You're not that good. So, do you want to know or not?'

Gasparyan's stare became cold, his lips curling – the only show of anger his wounds would allow for – and then in an instant he calmed and expelled a playful snort through his nose. 'I admire your confidence, it's about the only thing I do admire. But why not, third time's a charm.' He flicked his finger in Gruber's direction. 'Go ahead, tell this dead man your secrets.'

Gruber rested back on the table and clasped his hands together. 'She's in North Korea. She made a deal to focus her talents on their nuclear programme... For amnesty and a free life. Well, as free as you can get over there.'

Gasparyan looked impressed. 'Clever girl. North Korea! The one place on earth we'd have difficulty in reaching her... But it's not impossible. That's quite a line of information you have at your disposal, Karl. How so?'

'Oh, I still have many vines to pluck from. It's why DSV valued me so highly,' Gruber declared proudly, 'and I am now back where I belong. In the service of Daedalus... My true home.'

Gasparyan turned back to Munroe who was listing intently and he wagged his finger. 'And that is why we welcome Karl back into our loving embrace, Ethan. He's far more valuable to us alive. So, you have your golden nugget, no matter how pointless it is, and now for the favour to be returned.'

Gasparyan raised both his eyelids and waited silently as Munroe considered it and as Gruber crossed his arms smugly, content he actually had a future. Munroe began to speak.

'The letter was addressed to Hans Baur, Hitler's pilot and confidante, ordering him to take up one last mission. He was to deliver something to your Iron Phoenix; he didn't say what but the old Nazi seemed to think it held the key to Daedalus's success.'

Gasparyan now looked fascinated and he rolled his finger, encouraging Munroe to tell more.

'Baur was captured by the Soviets at the end of the war and therefore never received the letter, it would appear the trail runs cold. Whatever the item was, it never reached its destination.'

'Was that all!' Gasparyan demanded so aggressively that a single stitch tore and he winced at the pain. He retrieved a white linen napkin off the table and dabbed the small drop of blood that had appeared. 'Well?'

'Well there was something else. Something that could be very beneficial to you, but first I want to know what's so important about this vault. I mean, obviously having such sensitive information out there is a serious concern, but I get the feeling there's more to it than that.'

Gasparyan's eyes glistened with amusement and he placed both his hands on the table and rolled his eyes, not wanting to tear another stich.

'You never give up hope, do you? You've spirit, Ethan. Undoubtedly the German engineering we geared into your DNA. Very well, I will allow you this last taste, but then you put your final card on the table. Karl, give us a moment, will you? Head down to the foyer; there's a vehicle waiting for us and we'll be leaving in a rush.'

Gasparyan pulled back the breast of his suit to reveal a black Glock handgun, which he carefully pulled from its holster and placed in his lap.

'What car should I look for?' Gruber asked.

'Don't worry, our people will meet you at the entrance. Oh, and, Karl, I would never mention the name Reichsführer Bormann in the new führer's presence. Not if you value your life.'

Gruber gave a simple nod and without even a glance towards Munroe he headed back towards the reception desk and disappeared out of the restaurant doors.

'Good,' Gasparyan whispered menacingly. He now motioned to the redhead, who had been silent throughout, her gun never wavering. 'Wait for me by the door and once I'm done with Ethan here, put down the two waiters immediately.'

The redhead reached into her pocket and pulled out a black metal silencer, which she screwed on to the muzzle of her gun. She then slipped it into the slim holster under her jacket and headed for the entrance.

'Well, you asked and so you shall receive. You're correct that we could never allow any stash of information that could expose Daedalus to the public to just sit out there waiting to be found. Too much of a risk. It was though an oversight for Hans to kill Bormann without a few hours of interrogation first. You see, not only does the vault contain enough information to have us all lynched, but he stored details of bank accounts throughout the world containing most of the money, the life blood that allows Daedalus to operate.'

The mistake had Munroe smiling in satisfaction and he afforded himself his own smug chuckle. 'You mean the four and a half trillion pounds has gone walkabout?'

Gasparyan looked surprised. 'Karl has been running his mouth, has he? I must have a quiet word with him on the importance of keeping shtum. But, yes. A large chunk of our money has, as you put it, gone walkabout, but now I have a line on Freda Wilter's whereabouts it will soon be back in our hands. No wonder she took off so quickly after Bormann's death. We all knew she was his closest confidante.'

Munroe looked out of the large, panelled windows and down at the Dubai coastline, the gentle waves lapping against the spotless white beach, and he smiled.

'It's a beautiful view, isn't it?'

Gasparyan nodded in agreement but never took his eye off the man in front of him.

'It is. You couldn't ask for a more beautiful final image to end your wretched life with. But now it's time you repay my graciousness and tell me what else was in that letter.'

Munroe turned back and stared at him with a smile. 'All the answers you need are right over my shoulder.'

Gasparyan's line of vision remained firmly planted on Munroe, his eyes fixed with mistrust, but after a few seconds he positioned his head and then stole a glance.

Jack Talon stared back at him through the small gap in the restroom door, which had been pushed open slightly, and he was pointing a smoke-black Heckler and Koch handgun right at Gasparyan's head.

'That's impossible,' Gasparyan gasped. 'We've had the hotel entrances under surveillance since four o'clock this morning.'

'Then it's lucky he stayed here last night, isn't it?' Munroe replied, checking the small mirror on the opposite wall he had noticed upon entering the restaurant. It offered a solid reflection of the front desk and now the armed redhead standing next to it with her back turned. 'Now, Davit, I know this is painful but I want you to stay calm. You lose your head and I guarantee… you'll lose your head. You're going to call your henchwoman over to the table and tell her you've changed your mind. You want to take me somewhere private for a more invasive interrogation, understand? When she approaches, my man is going to knock her out and then we'll be leaving. I've no need to kill you unless I have to. If you're dead then Bauer will just send someone else after me, and at least you're predictable.'

Gasparyan's neck muscles tensed up and his nostrils flared as he slowly turned away from Talon, settling his eyes on Munroe. The word furious didn't do his expression justice. Both his cheek muscles clenched, creating further rips in his stitch work and fresh lines of blood around the healing wounds. 'I have three teams downstairs just waiting for anything to go wrong. You'll never get past them. You and toilet-feeder over there.'

'Oh, we're getting out of here, Davit, either with you alive or leaving your corpse behind us. Now, don't move,' Munroe said. He slowly reached across the table and pulled the handgun from the man's fingers. There was some light resistance at first, but after another glance over at the barrel of Talon's gun, the Daedalus killer released it and sat back as Munroe slid the firearm beneath his belt. 'Now call her over.'

Gasparyan glared furiously before raising his hand and blowing a sharp whistle from his lips that not only caught the redhead's attention but the waiters' as well, one of whom, the set of teeth, followed behind her. Munroe saw the procession in the reflection and he once more uttered his demands.

'Tell the waiter you need a few more minutes to decide. Let him return to his desk and then tell her to scarper.'

'Yes, sir?' the redhead said upon reaching them, but Gasparyan held his finger up and turned his attention to the waiter.

'I'm not sure what to have, would you stay here for a few moments whilst I decide.'

'Of course, sir,' the waiter replied, and he winced. 'Do you know you're bleeding, sir?'

Gasparyan picked up the already used white napkin and again dabbed his face. 'My apologies, I was in a minor car accident a few days ago. I'll happily pay for any cleaning bill needed.'

As the waiter shook his head and began to explain it wasn't necessary Munroe could see Talon's line of fire was now being blocked by both arrivals and he was about to send the waiter away himself when Gasparyan looked over at him.

'So, Mr Dunston, what would you like for your starter?'

He'd barely finished his sentence when the bloody linen napkin was hurled at Munroe's face and that's when all hell broke loose.

Munroe flipped the table, sending Gasparyan flying backwards to the floor, his chair cracking in two under the weight, and with the swinging motion of his left fist he smacked the redhead squarely in the jaw, sending her crashing into the waiter beside her. Next Talon sprung out of the restrooms and slammed the butt of his handgun down hard onto her cranium, finishing the job and rending her unconscious as Munroe pulled Gasparyan's confiscated gun and headed for the entrance.

Talon was only a few metres ahead when the first shot sounded off, the high-pitched scream zipping past his right ear as he launched himself over the top of the reception desk to find the other waiter hugging the front of it in terror. Talon was already returning fire and crouched down low to the right as Munroe scrambled back to the desk for cover, risking a glance around the edge to see Gasparyan hiding behind their overturned table. Who knew where he'd got the gun from, maybe his unconscious apprentice or perhaps it was a spare he had on his ankle, but none of that mattered and Munroe began laying down cover fire as Talon passed by, tapping him on the shoulder as he did so.

The covering fire was enough to get Talon through the entrance and taking up a position on the short landing outside the elevator, and Munroe now retreated behind the desk as Gasparyan unleashed another round. He looked over at Talon, his line of sight allowing Talon to see him and when the barrage stopped Munroe ran for entrance, firing shots as he went, aided further by covering fire from his American DSV colleague.

As Munroe passed through the doorway, Gasparyan opened up again but the dull thuds on the thick door frame told Munroe that he didn't have the right angle, and with Talon in the lead they skipped past the elevator and burst through the emergency exit door to begin racing down the stairs, two steps at a time.

'How far?' Munroe yelled as down below them the metallic sound of the exit door being flung open echoed into the shaft, and the deafening sound of gunshots clipped the underneath of the metal stairs.

'Two floors,' Talon yelled as they raced up to the next floor and barged their way through the upper exit roof door. More shots rang out, sending sharp vibrations through the metal arm rails. They were shots of desperation and as Munroe stepped onto the roof of the Burj Al Arab hotel and the blinding sunlight from above he slammed the door shut and Talon pulled a padlock from his pocket and secured the waiting chain that had been soldered to the door during his overnight stay.

'It'll hold,' Talon said confidently, both of them now jumping down a small concrete incline and sprinting off towards the green helicopter pad on the far side of the roof. Two parachutes were neatly secured and laid out on its surface. They were already strapping themselves into their harnesses as the sound of the first bullet hit the interior of the emergency door through which they had exited, sending light shrapnel past them. Munroe secured his main strap and then along with Talon carefully picked up the thin suspension wires connecting the parachute itself as even more bullets struck the inside of the emergency door.

'I said it'll hold!' Talon repeated confidently as Munroe shot him a look of doubt and then with a nod they ran forwards, the winds causing their canopies to balloon, and with a final leap off the edge, they were airborne.

The success rate of a low-altitude jump got higher the more planning one put into it and as they began to descend around the side of the hotel and down towards the blue waters of the Persian Gulf Munroe was glad the day's weather report had stayed accurate. The wind speed was as low as he could have hoped for and the short forty-eight hours they had had to plan this whole operation meant everything had to go to plan and today. Luck had been on their side.

'What a sight,' Talon yelled as they floated lower, but Munroe didn't reply, instead focusing on his glide path towards the pale blue speedboat waiting for them just off from the hotel's edge and the woman in shorts and bikini top looking like a tourist out for a day of fun.

'Hell of a rush,' Munroe yelled back eventually as he came within a few metres of the boat. He twisted his strap, releasing the harness lock, and dropping into the warm blue water with a splash. He was followed by Talon, who dropped a few seconds later, and by the time they clambered aboard the twin-engine cigarette boat the bikini-wearing Sloan was revving up the engines and slamming down on the throttle, putting ever more distance between them and the hotel.

'Remus is waiting for us in the helicopter. His rotors spinning and primed to go the moment we get there. See that dot?' Sloan yelled above the roar of the engines, pointing to the black object sitting out on a landing jetty, its edges blurry due to the heat ripples distorting the view. 'That's him. We'll be there in four minutes.'

Munroe grasped the handrail as the thin speedboat cut through the waves like a hot knife through butter with hardly noticeable bumps resonating through the hull. He glanced over at Sloan who shot him a satisfied smile, enjoying the feeling of power at her fingertips as the rush of salty air blew through her golden locks. The escape plan was purely a plan B in case anything had gone wrong, and Talon had been part of that as well as insurance in case Karl Gruber had turned out to not to be the informant McCitrick had believed him to be. Well he hadn't, but having Gasparyan show up was something none of them had expected and that he was aware of DSV's goal put one hell of a time constraint on their next move. That said, the information gleaned had been worth the risk and without the Daedalus killer turning up they would not have had any idea how important this 'Iron Phoenix' really was. And that piece of data was priceless.

'Well, did you get any answers?' Sloan yelled as a fresh spray of seawater covered their faces, filling the air with a haze of colours as she waited for him to respond.

'Oh yeah. We got some answers,' Munroe shouted back at her, now grinning deeply. 'Four and a half trillion of them.'

Chapter 16

'She's covered, even a satellite would have a hard time scoping her out,' Jack Talon confirmed, having spent the past few minutes covering the Bell 222 business helicopter with a sand-coloured military canvas.

'Good, take a seat,' Colonel Jacques Remus said, and turned back to face the entire DSV team as Talon sat with the others at the wooden kitchen table of the solitary residence on the outskirts of Habshan, over a hundred miles from the Burj Al Arab hotel.

The switch from speedboat to helicopter had been swift and uneventful, as had the trip to the sand-strewn suburbs of the small Dubaian village. No police or security forces had been encountered and apart from the surprise appearance of Gasparyan, the mission had exceeded all their hopes. Not only did they know what Iron Phoenix was, they now knew how to reach it. They also knew why it held such importance to Hans Bauer, and that small piece of information was golden. With Remus and the rest of the team back together, there was a renewed sense of hope and spirit that had taken a hit since the death of McCitrick, and as Munroe glanced around the table he found their very presence uplifting after what had otherwise been a difficult few days.

'The mission was executed perfectly, but before we get to that I want to put to bed the elephant in the room,' Remus announced, his voice deep, scratchy and unyielding as it always was. 'We all respected John McCitrick and his loss is going to stain our memories for a long time to come. He was one of the best operators I've ever known, and I am proud to have called him a friend... but if he knew any one of you was wasting your time preoccupied with his loss then you now as well as I do he'd stick a firm boot in each of your assholes.'

The blunt assessment drew nods and acknowledging grunts from all of the team.

'With so much at stake he'd be fucking offended, and to that end I want everyone to draw a line under it right now. They'll be time to grieve and we'll give him the send-off he deserves, but as of this moment I need everyone's head crisp and clear. Once we've ripped apart the shit-stain on humanity that is Daedalus, then we can mourn. Until then, people, it's time to pull down that house of cards. And its time Hans Bauer and his henchmen learnt what it's like to live in fear.'

There were no complaints from the six teammates as Remus stood before them, his shoulders pulled back and his neck stiff and straight.

'Thanks to Munroe we've got a lead on their precious little vault and if it contains what they think it does it will be enough to expose them. Rats don't like the sunlight. We shine a spotlight on them and they'll scarper like the rodents they are, and *we* will be the ones hunting *them* down.'

Remus leant down and picked up a rolled-up piece of A3 paper, which he unfurled and pinned to wall behind him before pulling a black marker form his pocket, popping its cap. He began writing upon it: 'First, we extract the location of the Iron Phoenix from Freda

Wilter. North Korea is one of the most secure countries in the world; getting in and out is going to be a challenge, but by no means impossible. I want Munroe on this one, with Sloan and Dalton running intel and distraction. Ethan, your operations in Chechnya and Afghanistan make you the best fit for the job.'

Munroe said nothing. He knew that everyone in that room was capable of carrying it out, but in terms of experience and improvisation on the ground, he pipped everyone to the post, with perhaps only Talon rivalling his skills in that area of expertise.

'Sloan, you do what you do best and give him an opening, and then get him out. Dalton, you're on the extraction,' Remus continued, writing their names on the blank paper with his squeaking black marker. 'This operation is going to have to run perfectly or you'll end up facing a hundred years in a Korean concentration camp and, given the risk, I want you to have the final say on getting in.'

Munroe considered the prospect and after glancing over at Sloan, who he could tell was already having the same idea as him, he looked back at Remus and made a clicking sound with his tongue.

'If we had the time I'd say I go in as a Western journalist, but considering Daedalus will be making their own plans to reach Miss Wilter as we speak, we have go in silent.'

'High-altitude halo jump,' Sloan added, and Munroe nodded in agreement.

'Quick in, quick out. But that's a lot of equipment. It's a heavy package to pull together on a dime.'

Remus was already smiling, his expression oozing confidence. 'You leave that to me. You need it, I'll get it.'

'I've got some options for extraction but...' Dalton said, looking unsure, 'if we don't know exactly where she is and when, then it's impossible. Unless you want us going door to door across the entire country? Ethan wouldn't get a few miles.'

Remus still looked cool about the idea and he glanced over at Talon's US counterpart, Zeke Dalton, and raised his eyebrow.

'The moment your little gunfight with Gasparyan ignited, his security teams left their positions outside the Burj hotel and headed up to the top-floor restaurant,' Remus informed them as Dalton left his seat and disappeared into one of the back rooms. 'Well, with them gone, we were able to pick up a rather helpful fellow. One Dalton and Barbeau were able to bring back with us.'

Dalton appeared from the back room with a man who had zip ties cuffing his wrists behind his back and a dirty grey linen bag on his head. He led his prisoner over to Remus, the man bumping into the table as he did so, and the sound of a muffled groan had Munroe realising immediately who it was.

'Guess who came jogging right out of the Burj's front entrance and right into the back of my van?' Dalton said as he tugged off the face covering to reveal a dazed-looking man, his thinning grey hair standing to attention due to the static electricity.

With his pupils wide and his nostrils flared, Karl Gruber looked like a rabbit caught in the headlights. A piece of sliver masking tape had been placed firmly over his mouth and as he gazed at the small audience before him Remus slapped his large palm on the man's head and tapped it jovially.

'They just don't make Daedalus agents like they used to, ex or not. Our little Nazi munchkin here has realised the silliness of choosing the wrong side, haven't you?'

Gruber began nodding obediently, the remorse in those blue eyes of his almost believable.

'I hardly had to threaten the man at all,' Remus added, continuing to slap Gruber's head. 'Just a single suggestion of a bullet to the head and voila, he realised the error of his ways.'

Munroe got to his feet and approached Karl Gruber menacingly as Dalton and Remus stood back and allowed him some free rein.

'Karl,' Munroe said with a mischievous chuckle, 'so you knew where Freda Wilter was all along?'

Gruber didn't even attempt to put on any bravado and merely nodded frantically, the silver masking tape wrinkling as he attempted to smile.

'Well, you are the gift that keeps on giving, aren't you?'

'He is,' Remus said, once more patting the man on his head like a good boy, 'and there's no stopping him. As it happens, not only does Mr Gruber know where she is, but he also keeps in regular contact with her. To add a cherry on that gateau he also has some details on Gasparyan's travel plans that may come in useful.'

'Birds of a feather?' Munroe said, he moved to within inches of the man's sweating face. 'And I'm sure you can arrange an introduction or meeting place? Maybe you wish to join her in the eternal paradise that is the DPRK?'

Gruber's masking tape wrinkled once again before Remus motioned to Dalton who marched the man into the back room once again before returning to his seat at the table, along with Munroe.

'With an exact location I can begin planning,' Sloan said, smiling at what had seemed impossible now becoming probable.

'Yes, you can,' Remus said, turning his attention to Munroe and raising his hand. 'Ethan, I believe you have something to say?'

Munroe stood up as Remus took his seat and with folded arms waited for whatever was to come. His taking over as the UK's section head of DSV had been greeted warmly by Remus, just as McCitrick had said it would, and the American team had also welcomed him to the position. With Sloan's help he had spent as much time as possible scouring through McCitrick's laptop files, which held more secret contacts and intel than he had expected – though he wasn't surprised. There was much the old man had kept close to his chest, but one thing had stood out more than anything else and Munroe felt it time he shared it with everyone.

'If the contact is correct and Bormann was able to hold power for so long because of the information he held over everyone's heads then it's no wonder Bauer is so desperate to find this information vault. He's gotta be feeling very exposed at the moment and I want to use it to our advantage. With the way he stole the top Daedalus position you can guarantee the cockroaches will be appearing from the cracks to challenge him soon enough. Live by the sword, die by the sword, and he knows it. I suggest we help the process along a bit. With that in mind I—' Munroe looked over at Sloan '—*we* discovered something recently that could cause serious turmoil within their ranks. None of us ever knew the insider who helped us get Lavigne out in France. John kept that card close to his chest and even though we have access to all his files, we're still no closer to discovering the person's identity.'

Munroe allowed the blank faces all staring at him to hang for a moment before continuing. 'But we did receive a communication from him, and if what he says is true then we've got someone on the inside. His codename is Saviour, which seemed appropriate, and he's someone who already turned their back on Daedalus and is now looking to bring it down... from the inside.'

More than one of the team were looking unsure at the incredible piece of information being dropped on them because it looked just like it sounded... too good to be true.

'Could be disinformation being hung out for us to pick up,' Lavigne said, and Dalton nodded in agreement.

'Sounds like they're fishing, brother, and I reckon they got their hook into you.'

Munroe waved his hand in the air and brought the growing rumblings to a halt. 'No. This came through on McCitrick's direct and secure line.'

'It's true,' Sloan chimed in, and she nodded over to Remus who also gave his seal of approval.

'It does appear genuine, and Ethan is correct,' the colonel added gruffly, 'it came through the same comms line used to bust your boiler-suited ass out of prison, Marcel.'

Lavigne smiled wildly and held out his open palm and waited until Remus slapped it down hard.

'There's something else,' Munroe said, and he clapped his hands together bringing the focus back on him. 'The contact won't reveal their identity, but has something in mind that could gain our trust as well as screw with

Daedalus, give us an edge. As we believed there is genuine turmoil within Daedalus after Bauer murdered his way to the top. It's left a sour taste in their mouths and many are unhappy.'

'Then why doesn't your contact take Bauer out of the picture? Do us all a favour,' Dalton asked and looking annoyed at being left out of the loop when it came to such an important asset.

'If "our" contact did that then Bauer would be replaced by someone we don't even know. Someone we can't predict, but if he fakes an assassination from within, one that fails, he'll have Bauer so paranoid he'll be ripping his own people to shreds and any time wasted on internal strife and not focused on the Iron Phoenix can only be good for us.'

Everyone fell silent, the rumblings no more as the common sense of it became clear and Munroe gave a little nod in Sloan's direction before he finished making his point. 'Towards the end of the Second World War there were many in Allied command who believed assassinating Hitler was a priority, and for a while it was. That is, until they realised if you're going to wage all-out war to the bitter end then it's better to do it against the devil you know.'

Everyone was now nodding their approval and Sloan shot Munroe a knowing smile as the deal was cemented by Remus, who sat back in his chair and crossed his arms with satisfaction.

'McCitrick strikes back, huh, Ethan.'

'Damn right,' Munroe replied with a confident stare. 'And we, ladies and gentlemen, have a date with North Korea... Let's get to work.'

Chapter 17

'I told you, no playing,' Hans Bauer yelled into the receiver of his phone, pushing back in his thick leather business chair with such force it almost tipped over. 'Once is a travesty, twice is total incompetence. My patience is wearing thin and my faith in you is waning. What the hell are you playing at? You of all people realise the seriousness of finding this vault, but you appear to be deliberately pissing into the wind and laughing at me while you do it.'

There was silence and then Davit Gasparyan came back on the line, his tone sincere but lacking none of its usual smugness. 'I'm not laughing at anyone; I've lost some good people and I don't have to remind you that it was you who let them run for us to chase in the first place. You knew how good they were, so you know what I'm up against. I'd appreciate some patience, my führer.'

There were many things Bauer would like to have said to the man he once called friend, but that would come in time and for now he wanted to act as he normally would and not give the psychopathic killer any cause for concern. Besides, Bauer needed the hunt to stay relevant in the eyes of the British prime minister and his Allied counterparts, but these failures were now making him look bad. The escape of Marcel Lavigne had been a painful one to explain, and fortunately the French security detachment on guard that day had taken most of the blame, but if he and Blackstar could not show progress soon then he had no doubt he would be dropped like a bad habit. And that could not be allowed to happen.

'My führer?'

'Yes, I can hear you, Davit. But I don't like what I'm hearing. Ethan Munroe won't be a problem, you said. DSV have run out of road, you said, but so far all you've done is lay down extra fucking tarmac for them. I won't accept any more of your screw-ups. In days, the chancellor's inauguration will cement our ties with the coming new world. I need all your attention on finding Phoenix. That is your priority, understand? DSV have made you look like an idiot and your mission may be intertwined with theirs, but they are a secondary concern. Let me say it one last time because you appear to be suffering from selective hearing of late: Phoenix is our priority; DSV are a means to that end, so leave any personal vendettas out of it.'

'Believe me, I understand the importance and the time frame, and once I reach the vault first DSV will have no skin in the game. Literally. I promise you; I will skin them alive myself.'

'Promises, promises!' Bauer shouted back, and for the first time he felt a sliver of nervousness flicker down his spine. 'You have one more chance, Davit, and then it is I who will be skinning you. I will not accept any more failures, understand? There's too much at stake to be fucked up by one man's incompetence.'

There was no reply and Bauer let his words hang in the air for a few seconds. 'At least we have Gruber. That treacherous little bastard may be useful yet, and I'm hoping he can provide us with Miss Freda Wilter.'

Before Gasparyan could answer, a heavy knocking came from Bauer's main office door and he placed the receiver to his chest.

'Fuck off, please.'

The insult was followed by a heavier set of knocks and Bauer now gripped the telephone handle tightly as if to strangle it, but his composure quickly returned to him.

'Come in.'

A young man in his twenties, wearing a blue-checked suit and tie, poked his head from behind the door and in a hushed voice said, 'Mr Bauer, your jet is waiting on the runway. If we don't leave now you will be late for your appointment with Prime Minister Previn.'

Bauer had been allocated a weekly meeting with the British prime minister since taking on the role of tracking down DSV, or as he always referred to it 'the Disavowed', probably because the term sounded more disturbing. Until now he had enjoyed the meetings, running no longer than twenty minutes at a time, allowing him to keep tabs on what information Previn had come into. That was until last week when he had to admit that the only captured member of the terrorist group DSV had escaped from right under his nose. At that meeting he had promised the prime minister that he would speed up the apprehension of these freedom-hating psychopaths. Now here he was, and with not only nothing to report but, thanks to Gasparyan, nothing to look forward to.

'Give me one minute, Toby, I'll be right with you.'

The young man raised his finger in the air in acknowledgment before disappearing through the door, pulling it closed with a thud. Toby was a good lad, young and straight out of school. Of course, he had no idea of the real identity of Hans Bauer, few did. To them he as a brilliant businessman, an entrepreneur at the head of one of the largest private military and weapons companies on earth. Yes, Toby was a good boy and intelligent too although he had become a little too organised of late and had come across some Daedalus files that were not for him to see. Nothing serious, but Bauer couldn't be too careful. He chuckled to himself. It was a shame he would have to be killed.

All is fair in love and war.

'Hello...? Hello!'

Bauer pulled the receiver from his chest and placed it back to his ear.

'So, did you hear me, Davit? Let's put Karl Gruber to work and track down Freda Wilter. Is he with you?'

'Yes, he's with me now. Safe and sound, but he doesn't know anything – although I've only just got to working on him,' Gasparyan lied, but so what? So long as he reached the vault first, Bauer wouldn't care.

'Get to work on it right away. And, Davit, I know I'm repeating myself but if you screw up I'll have you slowly strangled with a piano wire and then hung from a meat hook in the woods so that the scavengers can pick at your carcass. I've had enough of your bullshit and frankly I'm wondering what worth you bring to Daedalus these days.'

The threat was said with such lethargy that anyone listening could have mistaken it for some idle insult, just someone being an obnoxious prick but anyone who knew the man would also know that he would go through with it – and enjoy the process.

'I'm sorry I do not hold your confidence, but I assure you I won't let you down.'

'Better not, Davit. I'll be watching and waiting.'

Bauer dropped the receiver into the charging station and got to his feet. He tucked in his white shirt, straightened his tie, made for the door and almost bumped into a concerned-looking Toby on the other side.

'We'll just make it, sir.'

'Of course we will; do you have the relevant files?' Bauer said as in front of him two large, suit-wearing security guards peeled off from either side of the main reception and marched a few metres ahead of him as the procession made its way down the short flight of stairs to the black limousine waiting for them, parked up by the curb. The security guard opened the nearest back passenger door and as Bauer came to a halt, along with Toby, he sucked in a deep breath and looked onto the Rhine River, which snaked along the western edge of the city.

'Ahh, Dusseldorf. I do love this city!' Bauer exclaimed, stealing a moment to just take it all in. 'I spent part of my childhood growing up here, you know, Toby. Clean air, fashion capital of the world and the origins of pounding Techno. I guess one can't have it all.'

Before Toby could even reply, Bauer had slipped into the back seat and he was hastily followed by his assistant who once seated closed the door behind them as both security guards entered the front seats and started up the engine.

The cool interior of the limo was just as Bauer liked it, with every electronic toy available installed. Specially made Bose speakers allowed perfect surround-sound of the thirty-inch 4K flatscreen television that popped up from its storage position on one side whilst a telephone and computer screen were positioned on the other. The seats were fashioned from tanned crocodile hide and the stocked drinks cabinet was highlighted with a white neon light, which wrapped around the glass casing holding crystal tumblers with a funnel-shaped bottle of Beluga Epicure vodka at the centre of the display.

'Let's go.' Bauer spoke the order into the small wall phone connected to the security guards in the front seat, out of sight and hidden behind an electronically activated velvet divider. If one wanted to truly go to hell, then there was no need for a lifetime of sin but just a single step into the back of Hans Bauer's limousine for crimes against fashion.

'Sir, I just wanted to say how sorry I am for my indiscretion,' Toby announced as the car took off at great speed on its way to the private airstrip less than ten minutes' drive away, located on the outskirts of Dusseldorf. 'I hope you know it was only my wish to make sure you had everything you need at your disposal.'

Bauer grasped the walnut-wood wrapped TV remote and clicked the on button, setting off the sound of air hydraulics as the thirty-inch flatscreen rose up and in to place.

'Not a problem, Tony.'

'It's Toby, sir.'

'Ahh, yes, Toby. It's not a problem, Toby. I know you've only my best interests at heart and on the wage I pay, you ought to.' Bauer opened the drinks cabinet and then sat back in his seat before staring at Toby who immediately got to work fixing his boss a drink. 'Not too much Red Bull, it gives me gas.'

Toby nodded and continued with the drink as the flatscreen lit up, displaying a live feed of the New York stock market.

'Thank you, sir. I appreciate that.'

Toby finished mixing the drink and after passing it over he sat back, looking conflicted, and it was only after a few minutes that Bauer noticed the odd look on his assistant's face.

'What is it, boy, you look like a bulldog chewing on a wasp?'

Toby continued to stay silent, until after a few moments Bauer sighed heavily and with dull eyes turned off the flatscreen, dropped the remote into his lap and placed his drink in the cup holder.

'Well?' Bauer asked, now folding his arms. 'Woman trouble?'

Toby said nothing, and Bauer simply continued with his line of questioning. 'It's a woman, isn't it? Look, how many times do I have to tell you... You are an ugly man, almost rat-faced really. The only women you're likely to get are those in dire straits and in need of financial help. So, don't worry, do your job right and the money you earn will get you any woman you want. You see, there's an equilibrium to the universe, Toby, and one of its laws is that ugly men become more attractive the more money they have. It's an evolutionary thing, it's in the DNA. Anyway, don't worry, you're not that ugly.' Bauer expelled a loud laugh and he took a slow sip of his drink, enjoying the burning sensation trickling down his throat before placing it in its holder and then reaching over and slapping Toby's arm. 'No, I can't lie. You are one ugly bastard.'

If Toby found all this amusing it didn't show, in fact he didn't appear to even care, and once Bauer's laughing had subsided he looked over with an apologetic gaze.

'It's just I feel bad, sir. I should never had looked in those files and I only wanted to say that I would never mention it to anyone.'

The atmosphere in the limousine went suddenly cold and Bauer stared over at the young man with an irritated look in his eyes. 'And what did you see... Toby?'

'The Daedalus accounts, sir. I know they're off the books, but I wanted you to know I would never mention it to anyone and if I can ever be of help in that area of your business, I would be more than happy to be of service.' Toby looked at him with wide eyes. 'I mean, it's a lot of money, sir.'

In Bauer's mind the young man was either trying to get involved with his personal dealings and cement his position with his boss, or he was having a stab at blackmail. Either way, it was a foolish thing to do, and Bauer took another sip of his drink and mulled over his response whilst studying his assistant's expression.

'Are you...' Bauer said, as his chin dipped towards his neck and he looked from left to right in shocked surprise. 'Are you trying to blackmail me, Toby?'

The mention of the word had the young man reeling backwards in his seat. 'No, sir. I would never... that's not what I meant... Never. I just thought I might be of help.'

Bauer eyed him some more and then deciding that young Toby was merely attempting to cement the relationship with his boss said, 'I didn't think so because there's nothing there to blackmail me with. I do though appreciate the offer and perhaps, Toby, in the future I may take you up on it... but not today.'

His reply drew a relieved and happy smile from the young man and Bauer smiled back. 'Did you know that this vodka costs around eight and a half thousand pounds a bottle, which, if you drink it the way I do, means it weighs in at about eight hundred and fifty pounds a round.' Bauer raised his glass high and grinned. 'I toast this drink to you, my young assistant, all eight hundred and fifty pounds' worth.'

Bauer brought the glass to his lips as his side window darkened, followed a split second later by solid impact as a large van crashed into his side of the limousine with such force that the entire vehicle was flipped onto its roof sending both men tumbling to the ceiling. The limousine was still moving, screeching against the tarmac below and filling the entire vehicle with a deafening sound of metallic destruction.

With a thud the limousine hit something, rolled up on one side slightly and then lurched back onto its roof, slamming against the road in a final movement that hurled Toby directly on top of Bauer. They lay there, dazed and bruised, and it was then that the sound of automatic gunfire filled the air. It was loud and it was close and as the thud of bullets hitting the side of the vehicle made their way up towards Bauer's passenger window he pushed the unconscious Toby off of to one side and then thrust himself upwards to the security box on the seat arm and pressed the small circular metal button located on its surface.

A lid fell open and a black Glock handgun tumbled downwards onto the ceiling beside him. He scooped it up in shaking hands as bullets slammed into the back passenger window, cracking it into multiple spiderweb patterns with every round that struck the thick bulletproof glass.

Bauer, still dazed from the impact and bleeding from his forehead, cocked the already loaded gun and held it against his chest defensively. The gunfire stopped as quickly as it had begun and through the shattered glass he watched as multiple shadows approached. The knock to his head had undoubtedly caused a concussion and with his head still spinning he watched as a closed fist slowly reached down the outside of the window and then knocked two times.

'We know you're in there, Hans. Davit Gasparyan sends his condolences.' The words were spoken in thick German and followed by a grunting laugh as the hand now rotated to reveal a grenade being held in it.

Bauer's vision was blurred but he pointed the gun at the window and began unloading his magazine clip into the shattered bulletproof glass. One bullet broke a hole in the glass, sending the shadow outside reeling backwards with a yelp, but the rest did more harm than good. Spent bullets ricocheted around the interior of the vehicle as Bauer screamed in a rage until all he heard over the ringing in his ears was the muffled clicking of the Glock's firing pin as it was released into the now empty firing chamber.

In the distance Bauer could hear police sirens approaching along with the sound of a van's engine revving up and taking off at high speed, its tyres screeching in plumes of burnt rubber that blew past the hole that had been made in the window.

A wave of relief washed over him, and he fell back against the ceiling of the limousine and stared upwards at the tanned crocodile seats hanging above him. He began to feel the numbness of a blackout approaching.

'Thank God, I'm alive,' he muttered to himself and turning to his left to see the dead expressionless eyes of Toby staring back at him: a ricocheted bullet had blown the side of his head away and left bits of crimson brain matter on his shoulder. 'And thank God you're not,' Bauer whispered, and as his mind was enticed into the black void of unconsciousness his last thought took shape: an image of Gasparyan, taunting him with a smug smile across his lips.

But not for long.

Chapter 18

The large cylindrical cabin was smothered in darkness with only two red lights above discharging their crimson glow below and lighting up the shifting silhouettes sat upon a single row of canvas-covered seats bolted to the floor. The rumbling sound of passing air outside resonated throughout the cabin as heavy winds buffeted the aircraft, sending a constant ripple of vibrations throughout the interior.

'Coffee?' Munroe asked, holding an aluminium can towards Sloan whose hands were pressed against either side of her head and the large pair of black cushioned headphones she was wearing. She squinted at the can being hung in front of her and slipped the 'phones down around her neck, all the while looking puzzled.

'You mean fizzy drink.'

Munroe shook his head and tipped the drink on its side to reveal a red button on the underneath of the can.

'You don't remember these?' he said and with his finger tapped the button lightly. 'Self-heating can of coffee; they were all the rage fifteen years ago.'

Sloan picked the can from his hand and pressed the activator button as Munroe did likewise and took a seat next to her, the cans placed between them discharging a fizzing sound as they began to warm up.

'I didn't think they made these anymore.'

'Neither did I, but you'd be amazed what you can get in Dubai.'

Sloan looked unimpressed. 'Or on the internet. Save you a flight.'

Neither of them smiled but just acknowledged that each was making the effort to lighten what had been a tough few days. The schedule to arrange the operation on North Korean soil had been as tight as it was taxing. So little time to organise and with so much to do, no one had touched the events surrounding McCitrick's death, and in a way the work had been a godsend. Still, there was a heavy yet invisible cloud of grief that had hung above the team, even if no one mentioned it.

'I got a text from Remus,' Sloan mentioned causally with a smile. 'Gruber won't be a problem for us. Not for a while anyway.'

The news was welcomed by Munroe who chuckled.

'Good to hear. It's always the loose ends that can get you into trouble.'

Usually a man like Karl Gruber would have ended up in the prison facility of Cape Wrath at the northern tip of Scotland – that was before it was blown up. With nowhere to put the man it was Remus who had come up with the perfect solution. A few bribes and some false identification and Karl Gruber was now a patient at the Al Amal psychiatric hospital. He wouldn't be there for ever, but his evaluation would take some weeks and his doctored personal history would ensure he remained out of sight and mind for a few months more and that was enough to finish this whole thing either way.

'You know, the last time I was on a C-130 with you it got shot down over New Orleans,' Sloan said, looking around the empty cabin, and she took her open palm and crash dove it onto the seat next to her. 'You're not a lucky rabbit's foot when it comes to aircraft.'

Munroe blew off the playful insinuation by exhaling from the side of his mouth comically.

'I got us down in one piece, if I remember rightly.'

His response had Sloan nodding in agreement. 'But only to almost get arrested by the NOPD.'

'The word you need to focus on would be "almost".'

Sloan finally cracked a smile and she let out a laugh that was due.

'True, true. You have a habit of finding a way out of even the direst circumstances.'

'And when I don't, you're always there to pull me out,' Munroe replied, and they now stared at each other with a shared respect until sadness fell across her face.

'When I first met you, Ethan. I have to admit... I wasn't impressed.'

'Cheers, Jax. You should know the feeling was mutual,' Munroe replied with a smile and then he fell silent and allowed his team mate to continue to wherever she was going with this, which she did.

'But John McCitrick had so much faith in you it became infectious and I saw what you could do and now I wouldn't want anyone else at my back. And I now realise it was exactly that same faith that John had in me.'

Munroe let the short pause that followed play out before saying anything. 'He had a way of seeing things in people that no one else saw. Underneath the surface.'

'Exactly right,' Sloan agreed, still nodding away. 'When he first brought me into DSV, initially, many of the heads weren't convinced. Thought he'd made a mistake... but not him. He was tough, but fair and able to alleviate any doubt in my mind that this was where I belonged. What I was born to do, and he was right, even when I was unsure.' Sloan wrapped her hand around the nearest coffee can, and on sensing that it was still heating up she pulled back and now stared into Munroe's eyes, unblinking, as she spoke. 'And now that's all gone... I'm going to miss that old, beautiful bastard. God, he could be a pain in the arse, but you have to hand it to him, he was always right.'

Munroe smiled at the mention. McCitrick could be a ball-breaker but he was usually right on the money and he now realised what Sloan was really coming to terms with, apart from the obvious of losing a close colleague. 'We're making the right decision, you know.'

Sloan gazed up at him, the look of concern carved into her face.

'Are we? Breaking into the most closed-off country in the world and stealing one of their scientists? A country with nuclear weapons and the idiocy to use them. Christ, Ethan. If we get caught this could spark off an international incident that could potentially lead to World War Three. That we're not even an arm of the government apparatus means nothing to Pyongyang. They will see this as a direct incursion, an attack, by the very powers who fought them in the Korean War. Things could go south very quickly. It's how all wars start, with a minor incident that snowballs out of control.'

Munroe eyed her with confidence and then he leant towards her. 'Then we'd better make sure nothing does go wrong.' He picked up one of the cans and gave it a shake, feeling the temperature rise sharply and then passing it over to her. 'And if it does, I'll know you'll have my back and pull me out of there. What you said goes twice for me. There's no one I'd rather have watching my back.'

Munroe picked up the spare and opened it and Sloan did the same allowing the heat vapours to flow from the top of the can.

'So let's get this done and we can take down Daedalus and be back in London for a great British fry-up of your choice.'

Sloan's resolve had now returned, and she tapped his can with hers.

'Captain Munroe.'

'Captain Sloan.'

They took a swig of coffee as Lavigne's voice erupted over the aircraft's internal speakers.

'We're approaching North Korean airspace, get suited up.'

–

Munroe shifted his face mask to a more comfortable position, then checked the straps holding it in place whilst sucking in another measured lungful of oxygen which was being delivered to his respirator via a small aluminium gas tank concealed within his jumping harness. The black boiler suit he wore underneath had a long plastic zip running from his groin up to his neck, allowing for quick removal, and his multiple pockets contained everything he would need on – what had been planned as – a short mission.

Get in, meet Wilter, extract the information and get out.

With well over one million soldiers in the DPRK army – not including the numerous security agencies that roamed the provinces – the control of the population was unlike anywhere on earth, ensuring every aspect of North Korean life was watched and controlled. The hermit kingdom and dictator's paradise was like nowhere else, and the limited number of people who had managed the near impossible and defected to the south had risked everything to make it to the other side, including their own kin. Stories of entire generations of families being thrown into the numerous concentration camps throughout the country as punishment was well known. Mothers, sons, brothers and even friends were required to bear the brunt of a defector's treachery and were forced to live out their lives in camps that would have made the Nazis proud. Entire bloodlines sentenced to live out their lives foraging for every morsel of food – worms, rats, insects – before being tortured and raped by guards who, so far as the intel showed, were handpicked for their vicious nature and absolute devotion to the communist regime. Just one misstep and Munroe knew he'd end up joining those poor souls, never to be seen again.

'Four minutes until the drop,' Sloan advised through the transmitter in her own facemask, checking Munroe's harness buckles one last time. 'It's a two-minute descent and you'll have thirty minutes on the ground before pick-up. If the time frame needs to be changed for any reason, then radio it in but make it count because the radio chatter is likely to be picked up immediately and if we have to circle back we'll have MiG-29s up here as quick as they can get into the air.'

Munroe replied with a nod, but Sloan slapped down on his shoulder and looked into his mask.

'Did you hear me!' she growled, staring at him with all the grace of a drill instructor.

She's more worried than I am.

'I heard you, Jax. Don't worry, I'll be in and out. Simple as.'

Sloan gazed at him for a moment longer and then placed her hands on his mask firmly.

'What's your name?'

'Ethan Munroe.'

'What's three hundred and forty-two plus four hundred and sixty-one?'

The demand had Munroe smiling.

'Maths isn't my strong point, Jax, and my oxygen is pumping just fine.'

The French-produced Transall C-160 military transport aircraft they were in had been provided by Colonel Remus and was the perfect aircraft for the mission. How the Frenchman had acquired it wasn't known, but true to his word he'd managed to get all the gear they had asked for. Flying at over forty-thousand feet provided the best defence against the surface-to-air missiles, or SAMs, the North Koreans employed within their arsenal. It also meant they depended on supplied oxygen in the depressurised cabin and any lack of it caused hypoxia, which could, if unchecked cause blackout and death.

The high altitude wasn't a foolproof tactic, the SAMs could go higher, but the transponder they had attached to the aircraft signalled them as a commercial 737 Chinese liner, adding another layer of protection as they sailed high in the dark skies over Hamhung. The North Koreans would be less likely to take a potshot at a Chinese aircraft that appeared to have flown off course, but if their radar showed it circling over the nuclear research facility below then they would be quick to react.

'What's the answer, Ethan?' Sloan repeated her question, still keeping his mask firmly in her grasp.

'Eight hundred and three. Now relax, you're making the women nervous.'

His answer pried a smile from her and she went back to checking his equipment and once assured everything was where it should be, she grasped one of the handrails protruding from the side of the cabin and waited.

'Three minutes to drop.'

Munroe raised his wrist and tapped at the circular altitude gauge attached to his wrist like a watch. He would release his canopy a few thousand feet from the ground and glide into the meeting place that Karl Gruber had organised for them. It turned out Freda Wilter was working at the research facility just outside Hamhung which, given its proximity to the coast, was strategically a stroke of luck. Furthermore, given her high status, she was allowed a decent measure of freedom to move around, although with a security contingent at all times. The meeting place had been set at a communist-hero cemetery just on the coast, although it was Karl Gruber she believed she was meeting – a man with a wish to defect and escape the clutches of Daedalus as she had done. Gruber's access to spy networks and understanding of the West's military strategies in Asia had been the ticket to convincing her he could provide benefit to the DPRK.

There was a problem though. Gruber, so far as she knew, was being smuggled in by boat, paid and operated by an Asian drug cartel. This in itself wasn't the issue, but if she had told the Korean authorities of his impending arrival then Munroe would soon find himself greeted upon landing by a security of AK-47-wielding soldiers and the game would be up before it had even started. Under strict instructions from Remus, Gruber had insisted that he just turn up and throw his expertise at the mercy of the authorities rather than risk any Western agencies potentially being alerted to his defection by their own sources within the North Korean leadership. It was the only part of the legend that DSV had created that was… somewhat flimsy. But with so little time to lay the groundwork for another story, it was the best they could come up with.

Has she held her tongue and agreed to Gruber's wishes? Munroe was about to find out.

'One minute,' Sloan called out over the transmitter, so Munroe got to his feet and rolled his shoulders, ensuring the harness was comfortable before taking a few steps towards the fuselage. He waited as the ramp began to descend, allowing the high winds to enter.

The noise was something Munroe had grown used to, the thrashing sound of wind tearing around the inside of the cabin like an induced mini-hurricane. For him it was a moment to savour, the calm before the storm, his veins picking up speed with controlled bursts of adrenalin, supplying his muscles with a tightness that felt not only pleasant, but calming to his mind.

I fucking love it. The real key is controlling it and not loving it too much. That's when problems occur.

'Twenty seconds,' Sloan yelled out over the transmitter, pulling her finger off the red release button as the ramp thudded into place, the back end of the fuselage fully open. 'Get the job done, soldier, and we'll be in Tokyo for breakfast.'

Munroe flicked his finger in a salute and took a few steps closer to the edge of the ramp when Zeke Dalton's voice sounded over his earpiece.

'We'll be waiting for your call. Enjoy the ride.'

'Cheers, see you soon,' Munroe replied, and as Sloan counted down into single digits he readied himself for the jump. Dalton had been a navy pilot and even flew for the CIA's private air force. He had then moved on to special operations, after which he was invited to join DSV. If anyone could get him back in one piece it was Dalton.

'Three, two, one. Go.'

Munroe raced down the ramp and launched himself into the air, his hands spread outwards as the feeling of weightlessness turned into the sensation of falling and the sound of the C-160 engines faded behind him. He soared downwards towards the overcast and cloudy skies over Hamhung.

The air was cold, even with his protective jumpsuit, and as the tops of the black clouds below got closer he glanced at his wrist and noted the altitude. A drop like this would level out at a falling speed of around one hundred and twenty-seven miles an hour, and he felt a sense of equilibrium return as he reached terminal velocity. He held his head forwards, plummeting into the layer of thick cloud.

For the next few seconds he was in a disorientating misty haze where above and below had no meaning before he crashed thorough the layer into the clear night's sky, giving Munroe his first look at the North Korean coast.

It wasn't the glow of lights one would expect from a Western country with a naval base on the coast further along lit up brightly, which then bled into darkness the further into the residential areas one looked. The national power shortages in DPRK were a daily part of citizen life, all available power supplying the military bases and cities where high-level leaders resided, mainly Pyongyang. This was a good thing for Munroe, and as he plunged towards the long beach running all the way up to the naval inlet, surrounded by old tech naval ships, he prepared to pull his 'chute.

A few miles inland Munroe could just make out the generously lit communist-hero cemetery standing out like a beacon, as it was supposed to in the otherwise dark landscape. He focused his attention on his wrist altimeter and as it approached the red line marking two thousand feet, he pulled his rip cord.

The parachute's black canopy burst outwards above him, slowing Munroe from one hundred and twenty-seven miles an hour to just fifteen in the space of a few seconds, the specially fabricated material creaking as it took the full load. The night air was calm as Munroe grasped the two toggles hanging from either side and positioned himself in line with the illuminated cemetery, which from this distance appeared more like a football stadium.

Through stroke of luck and not timing it was a new moon and the sky was darker than another time of the month. Munroe glided over the rocky countryside and began to mentally run through his checklist for landing.

In the distance the headlights of a truck lit up the mud road it was driving along, on a direct course with Munroe, but it quickly came to a stop and turned away, following another road down a rocky incline until it was out of sight, the spluttering engine fading into the background.

With less than half a mile to go, the cemetery became visibly detailed and Munroe began to pull back gently on his toggles, his mind still focused on his checklist. The landing was nothing more than a peripheral action for him and once he caught sight of a darkened area just beyond the cemetery walls he aligned himself and readied himself for landing instinctively. There were a couple of cars in the large car park on the far side and with no people in sight he heaved on the toggles forcefully, pulling them towards his waist and touched down.

The landing was as gentle as one could have hoped for, but the wet mud on the ground caused him to slide for a few metres until the soles of his shoes hit rock, bringing him to quick stop. The parachute floated over him. He swiftly pulled it down to the ground and rotated his arms in a rolling motion to reel the canopy into a bundle and then, down on one knee, he began removing his harness and the large utility bag strapped to his leg.

Munroe took the roll of fabric and pushed it into a row of bushes lining the base of the cemetery wall before unzipping his jumpsuit and turning it inside out, revealing the true purpose of the garment. The outside resembled a set of weathered farmer's work clothes, complete with rips, mud staining with ragged bindings wrapped around Munroe's actual boots underneath. The material looked exactly like Vinylon, a cheap clothing material made by the DKPR for the poor masses, surprisingly made out of limestone and coal, which was then spun into the uncomfortable fabric.

Remus has outdone himself.

Munroe now stepped over to the bush and retrieved a parcel from one of the pockets on his harness. He opened the plastic bag, pulled out a tan item and began to carefully unfold it. Sloan had put together this piece of kit and it had taken two hours of patient modelling by Munroe. He'd never used one before and as such was wary of the idea at first, but after learning that the CIA had developed such items for just this type of operation he had agreed. Not only had they been successful, but no agent had ever been caught using one and to top it off the piece was extremely durable.

Munroe laid the item out on his knee and looked down at the old, wrinkled Korean gentlemen staring back at him. The mask was impressive, the skin perfect down to the individual pores, with a smear of dried mud along the left cheek. The hair was synthetic, but impossible to distinguish from the real thing. A withered-looking neck had also been included, ending in long flaps that could be hidden underneath his collar, adding to the illusion of continuity. It was all one piece, and Munroe now slipped of his skydiving face mask to reveal the additional make-up around the top and bottom of his eyes, ensuring any gaps around the eye holes in the mask would not be seen. On the inside was an exact mould of Munroe's own face, hence the patient modelling as Sloan had cast it in silicon rubber, allowing the mask to move with his own muscles, giving realistic movement when making almost any type of expression.

Munroe brushed his hair back and then slid on the facial veneer, tucking the neck flaps underneath the collar of his peasant's clothing and pulled out a small metal mirror from his back pocket so he could examine his handiwork. A wriggle there, a straightening, pressing the adhesive edges of the eye openings to his skin, and then he pulled the mirror back and took a good look.

As in the practice run back in Dubai a few days earlier, it looked bloody good. Even under medium scrutiny and lighting you couldn't tell. Anything more though and the minute imperfections could be made out, but on a dark night, even with the lights of the cemetery, he could pass for what he looked like. An old peasant farmer coming home after a long back-shattering day's work in the fields.

Munroe pulled the last piece of equipment from another harness pocket, a micro 9mm handgun, and placed it into the designed pocket underneath his clothing. The firearm was small and round-limited but it packed a punch and was more than enough to take down six people with a good aim. And Munroe didn't miss.

Lastly Munroe picked up the utility bag he'd strapped to his leg and gently unfolded it before attaching it to his parachute harness and connecting a small silver tube to the bag. Finally, he laid his creation out on the floor, ready for when he needed it.

There were no roads he could see running past this area of the exterior wall and DSV's intel had shown that unlike most sites in the DKPR, the cemetery commemorating past communist heroes was open to anyone who wished to see their masters of old. Perfect for a poor old man wishing to pay his respects.

Munroe pulled back his rags and checked his watch before jogging alongside the wall until he reached the corner, allowing him to steal a look. He could see the two cars, one of with a small red party DPRK flag hanging from a small piece of vertical metal attached to the bonnet.

Looks like she has already arrived.

The entrance was flanked by two soldiers wearing olive-green uniforms with a leather strap running across their chest from right to left. Each man wore a flat olive ceremonial hat and AK-47 rifles at their sides, the butt on the floor and the barrel held in their palms.

Munroe donned his practised old-man's posture and then, with a clearing of his throat, he turned the corner and began hobbling slowly towards the main entrance.

The uplighters at the entrance were dimmer than inside the open-air cemetery and he stopped at the stone opening to note the smiling and welcoming image of Kim Jong-un at the top. The two soldiers looked over at him, their eyes examining the old man before them. Munroe offered a gentle bow to them and then to the sacred image above before entering, the underneath of his fabric shoes making a scuffling sound against the stone floor paving.

So far so good.

The cemetery was impressive, with monuments celebrating figures Munroe neither knew of nor cared about. As he ventured into the main area, he came across a long rectangle and well-watered strip of grass with flowers lining its side and running up its centre towards an oversized statue of Kim Il Sung, the founding father of the communist regime, with his head held high and one arm pointing upwards towards the skyline.

The place looked empty, but as Munroe continued slowly up towards the end statue he saw a woman standing in the corner gazing up at a statue of some magnanimous-looking fellow. From the back it was impossible to tell who she was, but the blonde hair and independent swagger suggested someone not native to the shores of the DKPR. He continued to shuffle closer until he was within metres, at which point she turned around on her heel and stared at him.

Freda Wilter looked exactly as she did in the photo that Karl Gruber had provided him with back in Dubai – in her early forties with high cheekbones and a strong jaw. This woman had been Bormann's closest confident, but the distasteful way she was staring at Munroe showed she obviously didn't think much of him.

Munroe offered her a smile and proceeded to shuffle towards her, stopping at the statue, which he looked up at, nodding.

'It is a beautiful statue? Almost as beautiful as you, my lady,' Munroe said in fluent German with a Berlin twinge, his eyes never leaving the stone effigy. 'But then we can't all have such perfect bloodlines, can we?'

The comment had Wilter taking a step back from the old man before her and then her eyes squinted and she craned her head closer and stared at him in disbelief. 'Gruber!'

Munroe turned to face her and as she scrutinised his wrinkled face he could see the glimmer of realisation as she worked out that he was wearing a mask.

'No, Miss Wilter, I'm not Karl Gruber, but a friend he asked to take his place.' He glanced back cautiously to see one of the entrance guards appearing in the far corner of the cemetery and looking in their direction. 'Don't look, but there are eyes on us so I need you to appear relaxed and walk over to the next statue. I'll join you shortly and explain what is going on.'

To her credit she did exactly as she was told and slowly and calmly walked over to the next statue and began feigning interest in the communist icon. Munroe stayed where he was, waiting as he searched his peripheral vision for the blurry figure of the guard and after a few seconds the blur disappeared, instigating Munroe's move to the next statue.

'Where is Karl?' Wilter asked, pretending to pay interest to the inscription at the base of the sculpture.

'He was captured by your old bosses,' Munroe replied, wanting to build up some urgency as well as trust with the woman. 'But my friends and I were able to get him back, unharmed, although like with you they appear relentless in their efforts to retrieve him. It seems that the reason you ran from them is the same reason Daedalus now want him.'

The very mention of Daedalus had her gulping, and Munroe sought to ratchet up her anxiety. 'Hans Bauer. The man who killed your Reichsführer Bormann, wants to cement his position, and to do that he needs something. Something he believes Karl Gruber has, when it is actually information that *you* possess. And he will stop at nothing to get it.'

Wilter gulped for a second time and then she lifted up her chin and attempted to regain her composure.

'Who the hell are you, old man? That mask is convincing but underneath I suspect something far more loathsome than a filthy peasant. What are you, CIA, MI6?'

Finally, the woman was showing her true colours and the revolting nature that lay just beneath her skin.

'Neither, Freda. I'm just someone who can ensure that you never again have to look over your shoulder for the Daedalus assassin ready to cut your throat from ear to ear. And before you speak again, let me explain exactly what's going on and your place in it. Your old organisation will stop at nothing to reach you. I told you that we rescued Karl Gruber from a grisly fate and that is true, but not before he gave up your location, here in this lovely paradise.'

'Bullshit! Karl would never give me up.'

'Oh yes? Then how do you think I found you?'

Wilter breathed in deeply and then she paused halfway through exhaling. 'They may hold a grudge, but there's nothing I can give them… except trouble.'

'Maybe not, but…' Munroe began, now moving to the next statue, followed soon after by Wilter who continued to maintain her distance while just close enough to hear Munroe speaking, '…to keep one's hold over the cesspit that is Daedalus, one needs insurance and Hans Bauer has realised this rather late in the day. Call it a mistake on his part, but for a man so calculating he appears to have forgotten one of the most important lessons when keeping psychopathic, power-hungry Nazis in line.'

'And that is?' Wilter replied defiantly, not prepared to have her background and beliefs belittled by this unknown old man before her.

Munroe glanced back to make sure they were still alone before leaning closer towards her. 'That blackmail is the only way to keep the masses in line.'

Wilter's eyes opened wide and, sensing that she now knew what he was talking about, Munroe resumed his position, although still maintaining his old man's slightly hunched demeanour.

'The Iron Phoenix, and the way Karl Gruber tells it you're the only one who knows where it is.'

Wilter now turned her head and looked directly into Munroe's eyes with a piercing anger that caused her jaw muscles to tense and her lips curling in revulsion as she finally connected the dots. 'DSV, the Disavowed.'

Munroe simply nodded slowly as Wilter's anger slipped into smugness and she let out an ominous chuckle.

'And there I was thinking I was in trouble. With such a good grasp of German inflections you have to be Ethan Munroe? Good God, you and your people are in more trouble than I could ever attract. Terrorists taking us into the age of nuclear terrorism. Thousands of deaths on your hands. Compared to you, I'm a fucking saint.'

Munroe said nothing, wanting her to get it all off her chest before playing his trump card.

'Oh, yes. I know all about you, Mr Munroe. It would be accurate to say that if you had never caused the trouble you did then Reichsführer Bormann would still be alive and I would not be tucked away in this shithole of a country, keeping out of sight. Still, I do take some comfort in knowing it was only a person of our creation who was able to cause so much trouble.'

Wilter gazed upon him with a confidence that had been missing until this moment. 'You do know that you exist only because we decided to create you in a lab?'

Munroe made a clicking sound with his tongue and then he smiled. 'Oh, I've known about that for some time. It's true what they say... you can't choose your parents. But you can choose to feed them to the dogs.'

Wilter was still smiling, arrogance flowing from every pore in her body as Munroe now laid down the reality of her situation.

'Thing is, Freda, we're your only salvation. Bauer is going to come after you for the information you possess and nothing's going to stop him. He has too much to lose. Either way, you're toast. You think you're safe in North Korea? Bauer has a dozen people with more nuclear knowledge than you, and if you don't think that the Kim regime would be willing to trade you in an instant then frankly, my dear, you're as crazy as the nut-job he's sending after you! And when he has his greasy little paws on you it's just a matter of time before you crack. A person can only stand so much torture; everyone breaks eventually, and with a man like Gasparyan wielding the knife...' Munroe shook his head. 'Well, you know what horrors that man is capable of.'

Munroe waited a moment for the blunt and unsettling reality to sink in before walking to the other side of her and leaning in, close to her ear. 'Or you can tell me, right now, and I save your life. DSV gets to the vault first, exposes Bauer and his little firm of fascists to the world, of course leaving you and Gruber out of the picture. Any details of your involvement could be wiped away with ease and then, when the dust has settled, well, who knows, you could go wherever you want and I'm sure a few million from the four and a half trillion Daedalus slush fund wouldn't be missed.'

Freda Wilter eyed Munroe with hope. Expunging one's past for some is a terrible thing, an option to be accepted as a last resort… but Freda Wilter was no average person and neither was her future bright.

Munroe let the offer hang in the air, but by the look on Wilter's face he already knew the answer. As in many negotiations, the offer made has already been refused or accepted in the mind of the buyer long before they say yes, and the middle-aged Nazi, with few options to live the life she wanted, was no different. She looked up at the statue of Kim Il Sung with a daydream stare, most likely imagining what the rest of her life would be like as a servant of her communist masters. Her head then dipped down and with a deep breath she nodded.

'I don't have the location,' she said, turning to face the wrinkled old face of Munroe, 'but I know how to get it.'

It wasn't quite the answer Munroe was hoping for, but it would do. 'Good choice, Freda. We don't have to be friends, but you keep your half of the bargain and I promise you we will as well… Now, follow me.'

Chapter 19

'Don't you have a security detachment?' Munroe asked as the they headed past the long central lawn towards the main entrance.

'Yes, but they don't know I've gone. I rarely leave my house once I've gone in for the night. My regular routine means the two agents assigned have become fairly relaxed and most nights take an hour off for dinner. Not always, but they did tonight.'

Wilter tugged at Munroe's shoulder and brought him to a halt. 'I'm less concerned about my bodyguards and more about how you intend to get us both out.'

Munroe made a subtle calming gesture with his open palm and raised his finger up to his lips. 'You'll see, but from here on in there must be no talking between us. When we get to the front entrance you get in your car and I'll meet you on the south side exterior of the cemetery.'

The unsure expression and frown had him repeating his instructions in more detail. 'Behind the statue of Kim Il Sung, on the other side of the wall. It's all grassland and somewhat muddy, so take it easy.'

This time Wilter gave a convincingly confident nod as Munroe took the lead and staying three metres ahead of her as he approached the front entrance, the two guards still standing stiffly on duty. Munroe passed through first, with barely a glance from either of the soldiers, and turned left, heading back towards where he'd touched down. The beach was less than two miles away and with the use of Wilter's car they could be there within minutes.

Behind him, Wilter now exited the cemetery and although her departure drew more attention than Munroe's did they said nothing and merely watched as she headed towards her green Pronto GS. She didn't look hurried as she went, staying calm as he had expected, but as Munroe reached the corner he glanced back to see a silver four-door Huanghai Landscape F1 pull into the car park. Access to cars and car dealerships were all owned by the state and to have a car you either had to be in the leadership, or on security detail.

Munroe slid around the corner and then turned back to watch the F1 come to a dramatic stop. Both front passenger doors flew open and two black-suited men jumped out and approached Wilter. The taller of the two now engaged her in conversation whilst the smaller stood back and began speaking into a phone he was holding.

Shit.

Munroe watched as the conversation began to get heated, although it was Wilter who appeared the most upset with her hands flapping up and down as she voiced her annoyance at their arrival. In fact, she raised such a commotion that the two cemetery guards began walking over to the small group and brandishing their AK-47s.

Munroe was already pulling his micro-Glock from the hidden pocket within his peasant disguise and preparing to head towards the group when Wilter glanced back at the approaching guards and immediately started to bring down the temperature. By the time they reached her she seemed to have mollified her two chaperones and with a polite smile to the guards she headed over to her green Pronto.

The suited chaperones did likewise and got back into their own vehicle and with the doors slammed shut they waited as Wilter retrieved her keys and entered her own car.

It looked like the assigned agents were to escort her back to her residence and as the guards started their return to the cemetery entrance Munroe made a split-second decision on what he guessed she would do next. He immediately ran back along the wall to the far end, his small firearm holding just six shots gripped firmly in his hand and waited.

'C'mon,' he whispered to himself, willing Wilter to do what he expected, and about fifteen seconds later with the sound of an engine being revved in high gear, his guess was rewarded.

Freda Wilter's green Pronto screamed around the far corner towards him, sliding in the mud as it went and sending a dark spray of dirty water back towards the corner she had just come round. Munroe was already waiting as the car slid to a messy stop and he pulled open the door, pushed her over the gearstick to the passenger side and got in just as the silver F1 appeared from around the wall.

With the automatic gear slammed into drive and his ragged shoe pushing the Pronto's accelerator to the floor, Munroe sped off, churning up a fresh clump of mud over the windscreen of the F1, which had closed the gap.

'That went well,' Munroe yelled as he manoeuvred the Pronto down the steep and muddy stretch of grassland in the direction of the beach, swinging back and forth as he countered the sliding of its wheels as they struggled to grip the earth beneath them.

'Where are we going?' Wilter shouted as they flew over a dip and slammed down hard on the other side before crashing through a wooden fence, bringing them onto a tarmac road. The tyres smoked rubber as Munroe pulled a sharp ninety degree turn and then accelerated.

'The naval base is only a few miles away; they'll have dozens of units on our location in no time.'

Munroe ignored her, focusing on the empty stretch of road he was speeding down; he knew the response time would be swift and giving his passenger a detailed brief of the escape plan wasn't going to help one damn bit.

Behind them the silver F1 was catching up with flashing red lights in the corners of its windscreen, honking its horn as Munroe pulled hard on the handbrake and skidded off to the left when he reached a set of crossroads. He then hit the brakes and continued to skid closer to the left side of the road, causing the following F1 to turn wide to avoid crashing into them, bringing the two cars level with each other as Munroe slammed down the accelerator again.

Both cars were evenly matched and Munroe glanced over at the other car to see the suit in the passenger side staring in confused surprise at the wrinkled old peasant giving them a run for their money. Munroe offered the man a smile as the sides of the cars slammed together briefly, but in return he got to stare down the barrel of a gun as the suited passenger raised the weapon and aimed it directly at Munroe's head.

Munroe spun the steering wheel to the right, sending the green Pronto slamming into the side of their pursuer's vehicle and sending it off the road and up onto the mud embankment, which not only slowed the vehicle but knocked the gun from the passenger's hand.

'They won't shoot. I'm a high-value asset,' Wilter shouted as Munroe attempted to put some distance between the two cars. 'They'd be shot themselves.'

Munroe managed a nod as his wing mirror exploded into shards and another bullet struck the back window, causing it to internally shatter as yet another bullet ripped into the opposite wing mirror, making him blind to any rear view.

'They may not know that,' Munroe yelled back as the F1 bore down on them and attempted to clip the back of the vehicle and push them into a spin. 'Either that or you're not as important as you thought.'

Again the F1 slammed into their back-right tyre, attempting a pit manoeuvre which would send them careering off the road, but Munroe held the green Pronto straight and it was then that he saw multiple sets of flashing red lights approaching them from further down the road.

'Jesus, that's a quick response time,' he yelled, his focus on what must have been military units maybe two miles away and closing. 'Hold on.'

Munroe tapped the brakes just hard enough to send the F1 flying past them, their reactions slow, and then he wrenched the wheel hard to the right and slammed his foot down on the accelerator. The move resulted in doing to the F1 what they had been trying to do to the Pronto and they watched its passenger side window literally slide around the edge of the Pronto's bonnet, over onto the other side, so the car was facing the opposite direction and hurtling backwards at high speed. Munroe caught a glimpse of the panicked-looking F1 driver before the car flew off the side of the road and flipped over as the wheels hit a rocky outcrop.

Munroe couldn't tell how bad it was because all his mirrors had been shot out, but it was enough damage to put them out of the chase for good and he skidded off the road, smashing through another wooden dividing fence and heading back in the rough direction of where they had come from, no closer to the beach.

With the flashing red lights of military vehicles getting nearer to their position but still a good distance away, Munroe passed over to Wilter the micro-Glock he'd wedged on the seat between his groin and thighs.

'Hold on to this, will you?' he asked and slid his hand into his disguise's last untouched pocket and pulled out a small rectangle receiver transmitter. The two-way radio was only to be used once because it was unlikely to be picked up by the naval base and bring the military down on him, but seeing as they already were, Sloan's issued protocol was now redundant.

'Ground Rat to Phoenix, Ground Rat to Phoenix. I have the package and also its owner. I'm coming in hot.'

As Munroe waited for a response he made a mental promise to himself that from now on he, or anyone but Dalton, would organise any call signs in the future.

'Ground Rat, understood. Time frame?' Dalton replied in a monotone voice.

'Three minutes maximum.'

'Three minutes acknowledged.'

Munroe dropped the transmitter back into his pocket and accelerated up the grassy hill, the Pronto's tyres thudding against small areas of rock protruding from the earth. 'We'll only get one shot at this,' Munroe stated coldly, glancing over an extremely nervous-looking Wilter.

'One shot at what?' she yelled, her voice straining and her nerves getting the better of her. 'Do you even have a plan?'

Munroe broke through another fence as they approached the south side of the cemetery from where the short chase had begun. 'You're going to have to trust me, Freda,' was all he said as he brought the green Pronto to a sliding stop just metres from where he had initially landed by parachute. 'Out of the car,' he growled, then reached over, pushed open the passenger door and roughly shoved Wilter out onto the wet mud. 'Go by the wall,' he ordered, pointing to the bush where his harness was still laid out on the floor before exiting the vehicle himself.

There was no complaint from Wilter and she hurried over to the spot as Munroe reached to the nearest bush, plucked off a branch and stripped it of its leaves in one thrust through his palm. He then pressed down the Pronto's accelerator, jammed the thickest part of the branch into the opening the pedals retracted into, jamming it in place, and dropped the gearstick into drive.

The green Pronto wheel spun in the direction of the car park as Munroe ripped off his wrinkly mask and winked at Wilter before picking up the waiting harness and securing the straps around his body. 'Nice to meet you face to face,' he said, now spinning the small release valve on the silver tube that he had connected to his leg pack earlier.

Freda Wilter watched in stunned silence as a silver fabric balloon swelled from the helium being pumped in to it and began rising steadily into the air, attached to a cord linked to Munroe's harness.

'You have got to be fucking joking,' Wilter gasped, glaring at him as if he were insane. 'A skyhook!'

Munroe unfolded the connecting harness attached to his chest straps and waved her towards him. 'You want out and a new life? Or do you want to stay here?'

The sound of AK gunfire erupted on the other side of the cemetery and just as Munroe had hoped they had taken the bait of the speeding green Pronto driving out of control, slamming through anything in its way. The last thing he wanted was for the balloon to be noticed and the guards taking potshots at it.

'Time's up,' Munroe said with a smile as overhead he could hear the C-130 aircraft's engines approaching at low level and to his right the sirens and red lights of the military unit headed up the grass embankment, just two hundred metres from their position and closing fast.

'Shit,' Wilter yelled, and she leapt into his chest and slid on the attaching harness as Munroe pulled the straps tight and ensured the buckles were fastened.

High above them the silver balloon reached its required altitude and emitted a yellow, LED flashing guidance light as the C-160 aircraft lined up and streaked towards it, the V-shaped catching devices attached to its nose ready and waiting to snag the cord holding the balloon connected to Munroe's harness.

'These things are death traps,' Wilter yelled as the military van's lights cast red shadows across their bodies and at the far edge of the cemetery the two guards appeared, having apparently given up on the green Pronto and instead attempting to converge with the military unit.

'Piece of cake. I've done it a bunch of times and I'm still here,' Munroe reassured her as the C-160 approached them, now taking sporadic blind fire from the guards.

'How many times?' Wilter yelled over the sound of the aircraft, which flew over them, catching the balloon cord as it passed.

'Actually,' Munroe yelled back as camouflaged soldiers began pouring out of the nearest military van. 'It's my first.'

Both of them were catapulted backwards with such force that Wilter's head looked as if it were about to snap off due to the immense force of the pick-up, and they were dragged high up into the air as the C-160 turned sharply and headed out to sea. The guards turned into small dots within seconds and the red flashing lights and the cemetery faded into the night. There was no way for Munroe to tell how quickly they were being reeled in, or if they were even being reeled in, as they were both flung from side to side, the cold night air buffeting their bodies around like a piece of ribbon in a wind tunnel. The pressure on his shoulders was near bone-snapping as he took not only his own weight but Wilter's too. They continued to be tossed about in the thrashing air that slammed against his back.

Through streaming eyes, Munroe looked back at the darkened outline of the North Korean coastline when a bright, hazy light exploded from near the beach and began to rise into the air. He squinted his eyes tightly, giving himself a just a semblance of clarity, and realised what it was.

The SAM released its fiery trail as it streaked towards them, its white cone tip becoming larger with every passing second. Munroe felt them being pulled higher towards the clouds as Dalton prepared to evade the incoming missile. Munroe attempted to turn his head to see behind him, managing to steal a momentary glance of the tip of the C-160's left wing. Good news was that it looked close, meaning they were being reeled in quickly. The bad news was aircrafts and surface-to-air missiles didn't mix well, and with only one reliable deterrent, he knew what was coming next.

Munroe watched the missile streak towards them, passing air vapour fluttering across its nose cone, which was just visible as from behind all around them the sky was lit up in dozens of bright balls of light, which then flew past them in the direction of the SAM. The first round of pyrophoric decoy flares was ignored by the missile and it maintained its collision course as a second then third were deployed. Soon dozens upon dozens crackled in the air around them in a burst of blinding light.

Munroe watched through half-closed eyes as the missile exploded into a flaming fireball less than a few hundred metres behind them with such fury that he felt the heat searing on his cheeks and he watched as shards of debris fell to the ocean below until they were out of sight.

Suddenly something slammed against his back and he managed to turn his neck to see the edge of the C-160's rear ramp as he made contact with it again, only this time he stuck to it, the cord still reeling them both inside until it came to a juddering stop and the ramp began to close.

A voice called out to him and he felt a hand grasp his shoulder, but it was not until the whine of the hydraulics had stopped and the ramp closed fully with a heavy metallic thud that Munroe could make out the words.

'Ethan. You all right?'

Munroe craned his head to see Sloan looking down at him and smiling, and he smiled back and then groaned.

'Get her off me, will you?'

Freda Wilter lay passed out on top of him, her blonde hair spiking out in every direction like one of those old movies where someone has a barrel of gunpowder blown up in their face. Sloan unclipped the harness and rolled her off him and onto the floor of the aircraft. She then gripped his hand and helped him to his feet.

'Are we in the business of collecting Nazis these days?' she said, giving Wilter a nudge with her boot tip.

'Had to,' Munroe replied. He took a moment to compose himself, his short flight backwards had pulled many of the muscles around his neck and shoulders and the initial whiplash he'd received during take-off had thrown his balance. 'She doesn't have the intel but she can get it, so I offered her a way out. She's alive, isn't she?'

Sloan glanced down at their unconscious passenger and nodded.

'She's breathing.'

'Good,' Munroe said, then he sat down on one of the seats bolted to the floor of the aircraft as Sloan moved beside him and grabbed one of the overhead bars for balance against the turbulence that was now causing the C-160 to shake unpredictably. 'Christ, that was close.'

'I know, I was watching from the cockpit's surveillance cameras. Hell of a job, Ethan. That one will go down in history. Hall of fame stuff, and not bad for a wrinkly old farming peasant.'

Munroe rubbed his neck and then stretched it to one side. 'Your mask performed perfectly. No one even suspected.'

'Told you.'

'Yeah, you did,' Munroe replied, leaning back against the metal cabin wall. 'Any news from Talon and the others?'

The sly smile on Sloan's face confirmed his hopes and he nodded, glad at the news.

'Our mysterious contact Saviour provided all the information we needed as promised. Hans Bauer now believes that Gasparyan, his faithful henchman, attempted to assassinate him. Barbeau said the operation went off without a hitch, although Lavigne took a flesh wound to his hand. Apparently, Bauer emptied a full magazine into the bulletproof glass from inside the limousine. He not only killed his associates with a rebound but a fragment of the bullet made it through and clipped Lavigne as well. Not exactly how we wanted it to go down but it appears to have worked.'

'Understood,' he replied, his dizziness subsiding and never enjoying the unexpected collateral of a mission. 'And so the internal war of Daedalus begins and that—'

'Presents opportunities,' Sloan finished the sentence for him and they both chuckled. It was good to feel like they were back in the driving seat. Munroe sucked in and expelled a deep breath before looking over at the motionless body of Freda Wilter, still rolled on one side and sleeping like a baby.

'If she delivers then we can take down this whole rotten house of cards.'

'And if she doesn't?'

Munroe thought about it for a second. 'If she doesn't, then I'll cut her loose and deliver her to the wolves myself.'

Chapter 20

'The prime minister will see you now, Mr Bauer.'

Hans Bauer forced a smile, the stitched-up cut on his lower lip only allowing for a pained grimace.

'Thank you,' he replied, and stiffly made his way towards the door being opened for him. He leaned heavily on the ebony derby cane, with a silver wolf head handle that he squeezed tightly in his grasp.

'We do have a selection of wheelchairs, if that would help get you back to the car park.'

The insinuation of weakness tempered the sanguine demeanour Bauer was attempting to project and although he manged not to grit his teeth in annoyance, his voice did sound raspy and frustrated.

'Thank you, but no. It looks a lot worse than it is.'

The secretary offered an understanding nod before raising her hand to the top of the door and allowing Bauer to pass beneath her as he shuffled inside the UK leader's private office at 10 Downing Street. Inside, Prime Minister Andrew Previn was finishing up the phone call he was on and he glanced over, raised his finger into the air and offered a smile before looking concerned at his guest's troubling appearance.

The surprise attack on Bauer's limousine the day before had left the Daedalus führer with a ruptured hamstring, a serious concussion, temporary deafness in his left ear and multiple cuts upon his face. He had, of course, needed to cancel his appointment with the prime minister but after hearing of the 'car crash' that had occurred, the PM been gracious enough to fit in this meeting a day later. And so here he was although not in the way he would have liked or indeed expected. First, he'd been asked to enter by the back entrance, most likely so as to avoid even the possibility of any journalists taking an interest in him – later that day the prime minister of Norway would be visiting and the photographers had been camped out since sunrise. Second, Number 10 had initially attempted to push his meeting back by a month, which did not bode well in Bauer's eyes. For the PM to casually tell the man he had tasked with finding the DSV terrorists 'don't worry we'll talk in a month' had been a serious cause for concern. Since Marcel Lavigne's escape for military justice, Bauer had the sense that he was on the precipice of being pushed out of the inner circle he had worked so hard to cultivate. And that was not acceptable. All his effort over the past year in cementing his place at the table of the powerful and now this 'car crash' and lack of progress in locating the Iron Phoenix. All in all it had Bauer feeling the very real chill of angst. Adding further to his worries was Davit Gasparyan who was perhaps causing him the heaviest feeling of dread in the pit of his stomach. If there was one person who knew where all the bodies were buried, it was Gasparyan, and to have him turn his considerable fangs on his führer was, if one put aside the betrayal, unnerving to say the least. At any other time Bauer would have met such treachery with a reprisal of unreserved violence – he had never been a supporter of 'keeping one's enemies closer' and preferred to send a top-down message with swift punishment and dismemberment – but this wasn't the time to do it. On this occasion, something more was needed. At least neither man could allow Daedalus to be exposed at any cost. It was for this reason that Bauer had not made any accusations during the phone call to the assassin shortly after the attempt on his life. He had accepted Gasparyan's well-wishing and his solemn oath to track down and kill those involved. The betrayal was, of course, to be acted upon, after the vault and all its information had been secured, because that was Bauer's absolute top priority.

He could not enlist the help of anyone else – if others within Daedalus discovered that blackmail was *not* at his fingertips then it would be a blood drenched free-for-all and that could not be allowed to happen. Not now. Better instead to play ignorant and until the vault was within his grasp, then he would exact the bloody revenge.

His phone call to Dupont guaranteed it. His protégé was still shadowing Gasparyan and when the moment was right and the vault in his possession it would be he who carried out the death sentence.

Bauer watched as Prime Minister Previn said his good-byes and then place the phone back in its cradle before making his way over to where Bauer was standing and gently grasping hold of his arm, concern written all over his face.

'My God, Hans. You look terrible. How do you feel?'

'I'm fine. As I told your secretary, it looks worse than it is.'

Previn pulled back and nodded. 'Well that's good to hear. You're a tough one, Mr Bauer. There's no denying that. If I can get straight to the point, I wanted to see you face to face rather than giving you a call. Please take a seat.'

Bauer smiled pleasantly but inside he could already feel anger beginning to rise within him. He had the sense this was not going to go well and he made his way over to one of the chairs and carefully sat down on it and placed the cane across his lap as Previn strode around to the business side of his desk and sat down.

'I firstly want to say that you have been of great help at a time when it felt like the whole world was going to hell. The monstrous business in New York will take years, decades to come back from and even now we see what a hit America has taken. The economy, GDP, the stock market near crippled. That single terrorist attack has, I fear, set us down a slippery slope to the depletion of American power around the world. It should have galvanised the American spirit, but in the past twelve months all it has done is push the markets in the direction of the emerging countries. This attack has caused most Western nations to focus their efforts on the protection of their own borders, and although NATO has never been stronger, there is real fear out there that in the near future America will no longer be able to offer the financial backing, the glue, that has held the West and the world together for decades.'

Previn sat back and made a cradle with his fingers. 'In short, the landscape of power is shifting in people's minds as it did at the end of the Second World War, and that has caused many – the EU, India, Russia, China – to be bolder in the assertion of their own power. It won't happen overnight, but I think we are witnessing the beginning of a total reordering of world power. The pecking order is in flux and if anyone found out the truth about DSV and what they've been up to for all these years, culminating in such a devastating tragedy, I do believe it would cause a complete collapse of confidence in our national institutions that have kept the world in relative peace for so long. There's a change happening, Hans, a skewed perception out there, and it's for that reason I am asking you to step down in your role to bring the real terrorists of New York to justice. It's just too sensitive and after... who was it?' Previn pulled open his desk drawer and pulled out a red binder labelled 'TOP SECRET' across its front and opened it up. 'After this Marcel Lavigne's escape, it's not worth it. If the papers found out that a secret military court had been operating for the past seventy years to execute individuals deemed dangerous to what were the Allied powers... well, it could bring down governments, especially the Americans, and destroy our credibility as fighters of democracy at a time when trust and faith is at an all-time low.'

Previn placed his elbows on the table and leant towards Bauer. 'Don't worry, we'll get those bastards, sooner or later, but right now we need to lower the temperature and focus on keeping all this out of the public eye.'

Bauer loosened the grip around his cane and the whiteness in his knuckles began to fade as Previn stared at him confidently, gently nodding his head. The UK's leader might have sounded like all this was a positive, but when it came down to brass tacks this was what one called the rub-down or being given the cold shoulder, and Bauer knew it.

'I understand, Prime Minister,' Bauer replied, using the title as his acknowledgment this was now an affair of State and not, as it had been, a private understanding between the two, 'but there is something you need to be aware of. Information that I only received this morning from my people at Blackstar.'

Previn continued to stare with his eyebrows raised questioningly. 'And what would that be?'

'We've tracked them down and they will be taken into custody during a meeting they'll be attending within the next forty-eight hours. From what we've learnt this gathering represents the beginnings of a new organised terrorist attack.'

The mere mention of the word 'attack' had Previn sitting back in his chair.

'Where, when?'

His tone had Bauer feeling resurrected from the pits of despair. It was all bullshit but he was now playing for time. Time to reach the Iron Phoenix, and with the protection of the various judicial organisations his initial agreement had allowed for.

'We won't know that until we bring them in, but Blackstar has the ability, right now, to scoop up this venomous group of traitors and deliver them to justice... and it's all off the books. You'll be able to deal with them in whatever way you deem necessary to ensure national security for not only the UK, but the US and France.'

Prime Minister Previn placed his fingers together and considered the offer. Bauer knew the man's greatest concern wasn't for the country, or anyone else's. He was worried about his own involvement and direct connection to an operation that could reveal many political problems, and that he had hired a private company to do the dirty work made it all the juicier. Oh yes, Andrew Previn was concerned all right, but concerned for his own arse.

The silence confirmed the prime minister was having second thoughts and he immediately seized upon the man's indecision to push for what he wanted.

'Sir, I told you I would bring these… people to justice and it is now within my grasp. Please, I beg you, allow me forty-eight hours to fulfil the promise I made to you.' Bauer looked like he was on the verge of tears and he gently tapped upon the cane lying across his lap in desperation. 'To be frank, Prime Minister, I don't think I could ever forgive myself for failing you on such an important promise.'

Previn continued to stare, his expression deeply troubled, and after almost ten seconds of silence he breathed in deeply and nodded. 'You have your forty-eight hours and your clearance stands until then.'

What a moron, Bauer thought. He followed Previn in shakily rising to his feet, his cane back at his side, and grasped the hand being offered.

'But this is the last chance. In forty-eight hours' time I will be taking a new direction, as we discussed.'

'I understand completely, sir, and thank you. I will deliver these sickening harbingers of death to the military courts by the time we see each other again. They will know justice, a justice I hold so dear to my heart.'

Take it easy, Hans, don't overdo it.

'Good,' Previn replied, releasing his handshake before heading towards the door. 'This journey of ours has not been an easy one, but you have shown yourself to be everything those you chase are not.'

'Thank you, sir.'

'You're a good man, Hans,' Previn added, pulling open his office door. 'You're an honourable man.'

And you're a fucking moron.

'Thank you, sir. I feel the same way.'

'Melissa, have someone escort Mr Bauer to his car, please,' Previn said to his receptionist, but Bauer waved away the offer with a gentle flick of his hand.

'I'll be fine, but thank you,' Bauer said, and he begin making his way towards the back entrance of Number 10, offering a gracious nod to the receptionist as he passed.

I'm going to be fine, and when Phoenix is within my grasp and Gasparyan has been skinned and boiled alive, I'm going to be even better.

Chapter 21

'Good morning, how may I help you?'

Freda Wilter peered over the top of her tinted Gucci sunglasses at the man's gold name tag and smiled before popping her Louis Vuitton handbag on the counter, slipping off her white gloves and resting them on the top of it.

'Good morning... David. We'd like to see the manager, please.'

The jacketless bank teller instinctively stroked his red tie and glanced over at the man accompanying her before returning to her gaze.

'Do you have an appointment?'

'Yes, nine thirty,' she replied, motioning to the oversized gold-rimmed Mondaine wall clock on the wall behind him. 'And we're right on the dot.'

The young man nodded courteously before picking up the phone and pressing one of the green buttons.

'Mr Emerson, your nine-thirty appointment has arrived... May I have your names, please?' he said, glancing over at them both.

'Mr and Mrs Loathlife.'

There was a momentary pause as the bank teller processed the odd name and then he repeated it down the line.

'Mr and Mrs Loathlife... Of course, sir. Right away.' He quickly replaced the phone in its cradle and pointed to the cosy, walnut-panelled waiting area to the right and directed them to the green sofa nearby. 'If you would like to wait over there, Mr Emerson will be with you shortly.'

Wilter smiled and they made their way over to the sofa and sat down, the man picking up a copy of the *New Yorker* and flicking through its pages.

'My neck is still aching. I'm surprised it's not showing bruises,' Wilter complained, massaging the back of her neck.

Munroe looked up from the pages of his magazine and raised his eyebrows.

'Well it was either that or foraging for cockroaches in a North Korean concentration camp. All in all, I think you've come out of it pretty well.'

She lowered her glasses and shot him an unamused glare before sliding them back up the bridge of her nose and putting her bag to one side.

'You just keep your word and we'll be fine.'

Freda Wilter had not woken up until they'd landed at the small airstrip in Japan, outside Okayama under the pretence of using the airport as a stepping stone for delivery to a private aircraft collector in mainland Russia. Remus had organised two sets of false passports for the team and an additional set for the unexpected Freda had been put together, care of Sloan who had brought the necessary forging tools with her on the C-160. Upon arrival they had made it through passport control and then caught a taxi for the eighty mile trip to Hiroshima International Airport. From there, using their new identities, they caught a flight to Washington DC. A waiting rental van drove them to the Wells Fargo Bank just off Pennsylvania Avenue, less than a mile from the White House.

Wilter, so far, had kept her word and her disclosure that the bank's security box at Wells Fargo held directions to the Iron Phoenix vault had been impossible to confirm. But just to make sure she kept up her end of the bargain, Munroe volunteered to go into the bank with her in case she tried to hustle a new deal for the information.

According to Wilter, only she and the late Reichsführer Bormann had access to the security box in case of unforeseen circumstances, which Munroe took to mean if someone like Bauer attempted to force the information from Bormann. If so, Wilter could have closed the Wells Fargo account and hidden the information elsewhere and in so doing, maintain the method for blackmailing all Daedalus personnel.

Jesus, Munroe had thought, *no wonder the bunch of neo-Nazis were so paranoid. With that many snakes in your house someone was always going to get bitten.*

'Mr and Mrs Loathlife. It's a pleasure to meet you. I'm John Emerson, the manager of this branch.'

Munroe looked up to see an older man, late fifties, wearing a blue Armani suit and jacket. With polished leather brogues and a white shirt and navy tie, he looked exactly as one would imagine an upmarket banker should look. He was immaculate and his teeth appeared to glint as if covered in Vaseline, his smile unyielding. Oddly, the effort made paled into significance by the uneven rug that sat on top of his head. The dark black toupee refused to sit still on his dome, shifting slightly and unnaturally with any movement he made, and it exuded an almost hypnotic power, urging Munroe to stare at it. The hairy accessory had also drawn Wilter's attention and she stood up and shook his hand, trying not to fall under its spell.

'Nice toup— to meet you,' she said, correcting herself instantly as Munroe also got to his feet and shook the banker's hand. 'And it's Doctor, and that's my husband, Frank.'

'My apologies, Dr Loathlife,' he rectified, offering a welcoming nod to Munroe. 'Frank. Let's go to my office.'

With smiles all round, they followed Emerson back down the corridor and through a security door before entering his office, where he politely invited them in and offered the two seats at his desk. Apart from a desktop computer and a set of shiny mahogany filing cabinets it was clear this man was a person whose office space was for just that. Office space. A single oil painting offering a skyline view of Capitol Hill hung on the wall behind his brown leather chair and a set of double windows offered a view down onto Pennsylvania Ave, leading all the way to the White House, which was out of sight. On his desk sat a brass double picture frame showing, presumably, his wife on one side and a young boy on the other and they were positioned so anyone entering was able to get a good look.

Anything to make a banker look more human.

Wilter and Munroe took their seats as Emerson made his way past them and fell down into his leather chair energetically, the rug doing a little boogie from side to side as he did so.

'Well, Doctor,' he said, now only using Wilter's fake title as he guessed she wanted it, 'how may I help you?'

Wilter took off her sunglasses and slipped them into her handbag before dropping it to the floor and placing her hands in her lap.

'My brother and I have a shared security lock box and I would like to gain access to it today.'

'Of course, not a problem, but you could have asked one of the tellers. They would have been happy to help.'

'Yes, I would have, but we had a particular arrangement with the last manager, Mr Kleopold, who kept our key until it was needed.'

Emerson looked doubtful. 'That's not a service we carry out at this branch, for security's sake. The client keeps all keys.'

'Not this one, and if you could check your records, I think you'll see I'm correct.'

The doubt remained on Emerson's face but after a few seconds he reached over to his keyboard and began tapping away until he paused, sat upright in his chair and stared over at his client.

'That's very unorthodox and against policy, but you're right. Mr Kleopold has written a note on your file and...' He turned back to his screen and his eyes widened as whatever he saw caught him off guard. 'It says you pay three hundred thousand pounds a year to have Mr Kleopold take charge of your deposit box key!'

'That's correct; as I said, we had an arrangement, but I heard Mr Kleopold died a few months ago, heart attack, I believe?'

'Two, to be precise; that's when I took over the position.' Emerson still stared at the screen curiously. 'These fees you pay, they don't appear on the bank's central books.'

Wilter crossed her legs and leant back in her chair.

'As I said, we had an arrangement. The payment goes, or went, to Mr Kleopold directly.'

Her reply now had Emerson turning away from his computer and back to Wilter, his face full of concern.

'I'm sorry, Dr Loathlife, but are you aware that's outside of our company policy and, if I may be blunt, bordering on illegality?'

Wilter looked unmoved and Munroe watched as a devilish smile crossed her glossy red lips.

'Bordering is the only important part of what you just said, Mr Emerson. My brother and I pay for peace of mind and I now ask you honour that agreement, except we will be happy to pay you half a million dollars, each and every year, for the same service.'

The calm that descended upon the room was, for Munroe, difficult to read. On the one hand the bank manager was not showing any signs of outrage at the idea, but neither did he look on board. For Wilter's part the old Nazi held his gaze and waited patiently, her silence demanding he answer, and Emerson now began tapping his finger lightly upon his desk before leaning in closer towards his two guests.

'If I were even to consider your proposal I need to know why it is worth paying me so much money – are any laws involved?'

Just the question alone convinced Munroe he had taken the bait and Wilter smiled at him.

'I can assure you it's nothing that you're thinking of. Consider it a peace pact between brother and sister, a show of trust for a turbulent relationship and the extremely vast inheritance that was left to us both.'

It was clear Emerson wasn't exactly sure what she as talking about, and neither was Munroe, but it seemed enough for the bank manager to warm to the idea and he glanced over at Munroe and then back towards Wilter.

'OK, I think I get the gist. I believe I can accommodate your request.'

'Good,' Wilter said, offering her hand, which was gently shaken. 'The box number is seventy-seven and I believe you will find the key to it in the wall safe you have behind your desk, where Mr Kleopold kept it... I hope you have access?'

Emerson looked down to one side and to the small wall safe popping out just above the skirting board.

'Yes, I do, although I've not had the chance to rummage through it fully.'

'Well now's your chance, Mr Emerson.'

'Call me John.'

Emerson now looked more than happy at the arrangement and he pulled open his top desk drawer and slid his fingertips to the back of it. He then groped around for a few moments before producing a silver key, which he held up like a prize.

'Let me take a look for you.'

As he got down on one knee and began opening and then searching the safe's contents Munroe looked over at Wilter, his eyebrow raised. Even though this was exactly how he had hoped things would transpire, he couldn't help but feel it was far too easy, and he shifted in his seat and looked up to the ceiling for any telltale signs of a hidden camera. Satisfied there wasn't one, he turned his attention back to Emerson who closed the wall safe with a click and stood back up, a single white envelope in his hand with the number '77' written on it in red ink.

'This, I believe, is yours.'

Both Wilter and Munroe got to their feet and it was she who plucked the envelope from his hand, ripping open the envelope, allowing the brass lock box key to slide into her palm. She then pulled out a silver-topped biro from her handbag and began writing a number down on the torn envelope which she then passed back to him.

'If you can text me your bank details I will have the fee passed over to you by the end of the day.'

'Pleasure doing business with you, Dr Loathlife,' Emerson said, before picking up the phone and pressing one of the internal numbers. 'David, would you come to my office and take Dr Loathlife and her husband down to the vault, please? They will be making a withdrawal.'

'You're not coming?' Munroe asked as Emerson replaced the phone down on its cradle. He shook his head.

'No, Mr Loathlife, I'm happy with your explanation of the situation and more than satisfied with our arrangement. But when you're finished, please return it to David at the desk. I will keep it safe until you require it next.'

'You're not curious?' Munroe asked, genuinely surprised at the man's restraint. Emerson expelled a nasal chuckle.

'I'm very curious, Mr Loathlife, but in my trade, I've found that the saying "curiosity killed the cat" to be a rule rather than a guideline.'

The reply seemed appropriate and besides, Munroe had never known a banker refuse a large sum of money. He shook Emerson's hand and, along with Wilter, headed outside the office to be find the David already waiting for them.

Half a million dollars a year buys a lot of discretion. Shame the man won't see any of it.

'If you'd like to follow me, please,' David said courteously and as the office door closed behind them the trio made their way down to the lower floor by a key-activated elevator that opened into a large concrete room.

The room's lilac-coloured walls were empty and there were three surveillance cameras set into the ceiling within protective white casings. In the middle of the room was a set of steel bars, which separated the void into two areas: on one side the elevator they had arrived in, and on the other a large cylindrical metal door allowing access to the vault beyond.

'Just through here,' David announced, opening the barred divider before leading them over to the vault entrance. Munroe and Wilter waited patiently off to one side as he placed his palm on the transparent plastic surface of a fingerprint scanner protruding out of the wall and waited as a beam of green light passed once and back again.

'We have one of the most secure vaults in DC,' David said proudly, now tapping a code into a keypad with a shield covering and protecting it from any prying eyes. 'Rest assured your valuables are safer here than in Fort Knox... Not that I'm biased, of course.'

Munroe acknowledged him with a grunt as the sound of oiled hinges beginning to swivel filled the air, followed by a series of hefty metallic creaks as the bars of the locking mechanism released. Then there came a heavy clanking sound causing the large circular metal door to swing open automatically, revealing its interior.

'Please,' David said, ushering them in with his palm open. 'I will wait for you here.'

Munroe followed as Wilter made her way inside and began noting the hundreds of numbered safe boxes covering every inch of the four walls. A shiny metal table, bolted to the floor, sat at the middle of the vault. They both began looking for the corresponding number, which they found within seconds.

'Seventy-seven, there we are,' Munroe said, and as Wilter stepped over towards it he snatched the key from her fingers. 'I think I'll do the opening, Freda, if it OK with you.'

Wilter's lips tightened and she looked offended as Munroe now slid the key into the lock and turned it clockwise until there was a click. The small metal door popped open and swung back slowly on a pair of springs. He then gripped the brass handle welded onto the front of the box and pulled it out towards him, the fit in the wall so perfect that they heard a pressurised squeak being emitted as it was extracted fully.

Munroe laid the box on the table and with one of his hands on either side of the lid he glanced over at Wilter and opened it.

'Hello, what have we got here?'

A bundle of thousand-dollar bills tied together with a brown elastic band hugged the side of the box along with three passports, which Munroe flicked through, seeing the now deceased Reichsführer Bormann's face. The British, American and French EU IDs all had aliases and he passed them over to Wilter. 'A memento?'

'No thanks,' she replied coldly, and dropped the passports back in the box, then picked up the bundle of cash, which she slipped into her handbag. 'This will do me fine though.'

Munroe let her take it before delving back into the box and pulling out the only other item in there, a brown envelope with the words 'Dr Loathlife' printed on the front and a red wax 'SS' seal securing the back flap.

'That's it,' Wilter acknowledged, zipping her handbag up.

'Your old friend really had a flair for the dramatic, didn't he?' Munroe noted as he placed his thumb and forefinger on the wax seal and cracked it in half, but before he could take out the piece of paper inside Wilter grabbed it from him and took the first glance for herself.

'Oh come on,' was all she said as Munroe snatched it back just as a voice crackled in his ear.

'Ethan, can you hear me?'

'Sloan,' Munroe whispered, glancing back to check David was still minding his own business with his back to them, which he was. He pressed his finger to his ear and the small micro earpiece hidden deep inside.

'Code black. You've got maybe a minute and a half.'

Munroe had already closed the safe box and was slipping it back into its rectangular hole in the wall before she had even finished her sentence.

'We've got to go, *now*,' he hissed.

Wilter's eyes widened and they both rushed back to David who looked surprised at the pace with which they were heading back towards the barred divider.

'Everything all right?'

'No, it's not,' Munroe groaned, clutching his stomach. 'I need to use the restroom, immediately.'

The young bank teller chased behind them as his two clients quickstepped it over to the elevator.

'Damn it, Frank. I told you not to eat those tacos. How many times do I have to say, you're more likely to get herpes from a mobile kitchen than a full stomach,' Wilter scolded, adding to Munroe's little act.

'I need to close the vault before we go back up,' David declared, looking worried by the urgency with which Munroe appeared to be moving as he slammed his fist against the elevator door.

'Listen, my friend,' Munroe said, doubling over in pain, 'you either meet us back up there or spend the next half an hour cleaning up the sloppy shit that's about to hit your nice clean floor.'

'Pure class, Frank,' Wilter added, shaking her head. 'Don't worry, I've got some Imodium in the car.'

'I'm not going to make it to the car.'

This final comment had David making the split decision for them, his nose wrinkling at even the idea of such a foul job.

'No problem,' he said, unlocking the elevator door. Munroe and Wilter piled inside and began jabbing at the reception button as Wilter offered a wave.

'I apologise for this, David. We'll see you back in Mr Emerson's office.'

The doors closed shut as the bank teller let out a sigh of relief and, as the elevator began to rise, Munroe straightened back up and tucked in the front of his shirt he had pulled out during his scene.

'What the hell's going on?' Wilter asked as Munroe pushed against the micro earpiece in his left ear.

'Be with you in thirty seconds, have the van running,' he said, then he glanced over at Wilter who was still waiting for an answer. 'Code black. It means they've picked up a police call coming to the bank.'

'For us? How?'

'I don't know,' Munroe replied, referring to both her questions, 'but we're not hanging around to find out.'

The elevator doors opened and Munroe exited first, followed by Wilter, as he made a direct line past the teller windows towards the glass entrance doors and the beige Rumpo transit van parked up against the curb outside.

'Doctor Loathlife, I need to speak with you.'

Munroe looked back to see Mr Emerson staring at them both, jabbing his finger furiously. He ignored the man and kept going for the door, seeing the passenger door of the Rumpo being flung open and Sloan waving him in.

The glass doors slid open and Munroe strode out onto the concrete pavement, the damp, humid air hitting his body like a spray of water. He turned back just in time to see the entrance doors slamming shut behind him and Freda Wilter's palms pressed up against them.

'Shit,' Munroe muttered, and he leapt back to the doors and attempted to pry them open as from a few blocks down Pennsylvania Avenue two police cars appeared, their red and blue lights announcing their approach.

'Emergency doors, locked tight,' he growled, still trying to pull them open as Emerson glared at him from behind the teller window, obviously having activated the system himself.

As for Wilter, there was no fear in her expression but only sheer fury as she yelled back something in Emerson's direction before slapping both fists against the security doors, the sound of it barely audible to Munroe on the outside.

'We'll find where you're going and get you out,' he mouthed silently, not just because he knew she couldn't hear a thing but also not wanting to announce his intentions to the passers-by who were already gathering at a distance, curious to see what was happening, their phones being pulled from their pockets.

There was nothing else he could do, and Munroe leapt into the back seat of the Rumpo and slammed the door shut as Dalton sped away in the opposite direction to wailing police cars, leaving Wilter pressed against the bank's security doors, still banging her fists against them.

'Fuck!' Munroe yelled, punching the ceiling of the van as in the rear-view mirror the police cars pulled up outside the Wells Fargo Bank, unaware of the Rumpo van taking its immediate first left and disappearing out of sight.

'Did you get it?' Sloan asked, getting straight to the point as Dalton repositioned the Rumpo's rear-view mirror and glanced back at him in anticipation.

Munroe held up the piece of paper he'd taken from the brown envelope with the red wax seal back at the bank and shook it.

'Yeah, we got it.'

'Thank God for that,' Sloan replied, now turning her attention to the one they left behind. 'Wilter's cover is blown. There's nothing we can do.'

Munroe looked out of the Rumpo's window and watched the cars pass by, considering what to do next. His silence drew a complaining look from Sloan that he saw in the window's reflection.

'You're not thinking of breaking her out?'

Munroe didn't reply, and it was now Dalton who chimed in.

'Saving Nazis is kinda becoming a thing for us, huh, Ethan?'

Munroe turned away from the window to face his two colleagues and the unenthusiastic looks they were giving him.

'She knows where the Iron Phoenix vault is. If she talks, it could cause us problems.'

'Not as many problems as trying to break her out from a DC police station,' Dalton remarked, before turning his attention back to the road as Sloan continued to glare at him.

Breaking into a police station, especially in DC was suicidal. They were low on gear and Remus and the rest of the team wouldn't be with them until the next day.

'We get her back first. If Daedalus reaches her then our whole plan goes to shit.'

There was little response from his team, but a silent acceptance of what had to be done.

'So where is this bloody Nazi vault?' Sloan asked, keen to keep the conversation moving.

Munroe unfolded the sheet and once he'd read it and only then did he realise why Wilter had sounded so pissed off when she saw the destination for herself.

'Well?' Sloan demanded.

'New York City,' Munroe replied, with a deep sense of foreboding. 'Ground Zero, where the nuclear bomb went off.'

Chapter 22

'All she'll give is her name. Freda Wilter. No ID. No fingerprints on file. Like I said, she's a ghost.'

Sergeant Ricardo Tuttle looked up from his paper-covered desk.

'She say anything else?'

'No, sir. Tight-lipped and demanding a lawyer.'

Tuttle thought about it for a moment.

'Give her a phone call then. Besides, there's only so long we can hold her. Apart from what that bank manager told us about the attempted bribery, she's clean. What was his name?'

'Err,' the officer flicked though his notes, 'Emerson, John Emerson.'

'Well, get his statement along with the bundle of cash she had on her and we'll pass her off to justice. They can deal with it.'

Tuttle watched as the officer disappeared in the direction of the cells and rubbed his forehead. A banker not accepting a half a million-dollar bribe! What was the world coming to? The call from Wells Fargo Bank had the nearest patrol units attend immediately. Not because it was a suspected bank robbery, although the way Emerson had spun it you'd think there had been a full assault in progress, but the bank was used by the elites up on Capitol Hill. Senators and governors alike used the place and the last thing anyone needed was one of those assholes causing the department trouble.

Tuttle shook his head and rolled his eyes. What the hell was going on with those clowns? If they weren't trying to disband the police, then they were accusing them of everything under the sun. Difficult times, and even though the unknown woman being held in the cell block was the least of his problems, there was something about her that had the hairs on the back of his neck rigid.

'Sarge, there's someone who wants a word,' the officer said to him, seeming to appear out of thin air.

'Who is it?'

'Says he's a fed and he's here about the woman with no identity on her.'

Tuttle looked up at him in pleasant surprise. 'Great, they can take her off our hands. Where is he?'

'Out front,' the officer directed, and then disappeared back into the crowd as quickly as he'd arrived.

The police sergeant jumped to his feet enthusiastically and strode towards the front entrance, stopping to acknowledge the mop-haired man in shorts, torn red T-shirt and flip-flops.

'Hello, Jackie, what did you do this time?'

'Nothing,' the giant mat of hair replied, shaking his head like an unhappy Afghan hound with a wet coat. 'There always picking on me for no reason. I feel it's unfair.'

Tuttle paused and stared down at the unshaven Jackie.

'Well that's how most of the women feel when you peep through their windows whilst playing with yourself.'

Jackie slung his hair back and offered no reply as Tuttle shook his head in annoyance before resuming his short walk to the station's front entrance, where he found a well-dressed man in black suit and tie – which for a fed was a bit on the nose – who noticed his badge and quickly moved to greet him.

'Sergeant Tuttle? I'm Special Agent Ramone, DC office. I believe you have one of my people in custody.'

Ramone flipped open his identification and after a brief glance from Tuttle he slipped it back into his inner jacket pocket and smiled.

Tuttle looked surprised and he scratched his cheek and rubbed his nose with his thumb and forefinger. 'She's FBI?'

Ramone raised his eyebrow to indicate that he wasn't going to say too much but as the sergeant continued to stare, he shrugged.

'We've been stinging bankers we believe may or may not have been taking bribes and with respect we were unsure whether any judicial agencies might be involved as well which is why she didn't give up her real identity to you. Cartel money is the centre of the investigation and there is a lot of it. Mr Emerson has been in our sights for a while, but nothing conclusive. We'd hoped this could be the day he gave us something… Apparently not.'

Tuttle attempted to hold in the laugh that was desperate to come out, but he failed miserably and let out a holler.

'That guy either knew you were coming or he's a damn unicorn in a profession of sharks. He was crying attempted bribery from the moment we arrived and I'm glad you realise our department is clean as well, Special Agent.'

Ramone looked sheepish and the corner of his mouth curled up as he sighed.

'Maybe so, but if you don't put out the bait you never catch the fish.'

'True.' Tuttle nodded in agreement, taking a measure of the man. Most of the feds he came across acted like they had a nose up their ass, smelling the sweet scent of flowery perfection, but then you came across one who was down to earth and Ramone seemed to be from that stock. 'She's not been charged with anything, but the stack of cash on her was a concern.'

Ramone shot him a look of understanding and he patted his outside jacket pocket.

'That's government money, used in the sting. I'll be needing it back.'

'Sure thing, I'll get the paperwork and you can take her too. My cells are busy today.'

Tuttle called out to a passing officer. 'Mike, can you bring out the German mystery for me?'

The officer gave a wave and disappeared through a door labelled 'Holding Cells 1-12' as Tuttle continued with his conversation.

'With no ID we've been calling her that since she came in. Haven't heard an accent that thick for a long time.'

Ramone gave a reassuring nod and tapped the sergeant on the arm. 'She's with the German Federal Intelligence Service. She's on loan to us. Cracked some pretty big undercover banking stings back in Europe.'

Tuttle looked impressed and he now pointed back to the main office. 'Let me get the paperwork and you can be out of here in no time.'

'Thank you, Sergeant, I appreciate your help. It's good end to an otherwise unproductive day.'

'We do what we can,' Tuttle replied and ambled back to the office, leaving Special Agent Ramone standing alone in front of the reception desk. He placed his finger to his ear and after glancing around to make sure he was alone, muttered something before the holding cell door swung open and out came the same officer with Freda Wilter by his side.

'Thank you, Mike,' Ramone said, once again showing his ID. 'She's coming with me; Sergeant Tuttle is getting the paperwork,' he said, now turning his attention to Wilter. 'Sorry about that, Freda. Looks like I owe you that drink.'

Wilter stared at the man with hesitance at first and then she smiled.

'You owe me more than one.'

'You've got a deal; let's get you back to the office for the debrief. I'll fill out the paperwork and we're golden. Mike, would you mind reminding the sergeant I'll need the money as well?'

The officer barely gave it a second thought. 'Sure, I'll tell him.'

With that the officer sloped off into the back room as Ramone gently grasped Wilter by the arm and led her towards the entrance.

'Munroe's waiting outside. You're lucky we didn't leave you here to rot.'

Wilter needed no further encouragement and she followed Special Agent Ramone through the double doors and across the plaza outside to a waiting dark blue Cadillac. Once they were in the back the vehicle drove away at a leisurely speed as back in the police station Sergeant Tuttle returned to the reception desk. He looked around, and from behind him the reception officer called over to him.

'The agent wants to sign for the money as well.'

Tuttle looked back, glared at the returning officer, his nostrils beginning to flare. 'What agent?' he demanded, waving his hand across the empty room.

The reception officer looked clueless. 'He was right here.'

As the two officers began to argue, a blonde woman, wearing a tan-brown suit, entered through the front doors and sauntered over to the main desk where she rested her elbow on the counter. She waited as the officers argued for a few more moments and then watched as the policeman ordered his subordinate to make a call. She raised her hand to get his attention, but immediately dropped it to her side as the sergeant continued to lambaste his colleague.

'You better find her, Mike, or I'll have the name Freda tattooed across your goddamn forehead.'

The woman slowly pulled back from the counter and began to head for the main entrance doors when Sergeant Tuttle noticed and called out to her.

'Can I help you?'

'I'll come back later. There's no rush, and besides, you guys look like you've got enough on your hands at the moment. No problem, really.'

Tuttle accepted the reply and watched the woman exit the building before returning his attention to the increasingly worried-looking reception officer who was already in mid-conversation with the local FBI office.

Outside, the woman made her way a short distance before pressing her finger to her ear.

'Ethan, they've already got her. We just missed her.'

There was a short silence and then Munroe's voice came though the earpiece.

'Damn. OK, head back to us. We've got a plane to catch.'

Sloan said nothing and began walking towards the side alley where their van was parked up, cursing under her breath. She must have missed them by a few minutes and it riled her. There was nothing she could do but head back to where this whole nightmare had begun, and she muttered to herself as she walked.

'Big Apple, here we come.'

Chapter 23

The skyline of Manhattan looked uninviting as dusk settled over the fated city, and as near darkness reigned from the southern tip of the financial district up to the north end of Harlem, where the twinkling lights of construction crews peppered the night air. The one-kiloton nuclear bomb that had detonated inside the United Nations building almost a year earlier had left nothing but a three-hundred-foot crater and had levelled everything within a third of a mile. For a further half a mile most of the buildings had such catastrophic damage that many had needed to be pulled down, including the iconic Chrysler Building. From the southern corner of Central Park to the northern tip of Korean Town, the damage had been extensive, and the quarter of a million people killed instantly were only the beginning of what was to come for the resilient citizens of New York. They had seen the total annihilation of the city's barriers dividing the East River, causing millions of gallons of water to seep inwards as far as the Theatre District. The severe flooding had drowned many of the people who managed to survive the nuclear fireball, and it ruined buildings that had not collapsed in the initial blast.

The Queens-Midtown tunnel was gone, evaporated along with the millions of gallons of water in the first moment of the detonation, and on the other side of the

East River, from Astoria Park though Long Island City to the Williamsburg Bridge, homes and businesses had been abandoned. There had been serious damage to these areas, but they now remained empty and cordoned off for the same reason that most of Manhattan lay desolate.

Fallout.

Whatever additions Daedalus had made to the Russian suitcase bomb used in the terrorist attack, it had thankfully produced less radiation than would have been expected from such a low-yield nuke. The levels had decreased over the past ten months and along with measures such as the gigantic concrete dome which had been constructed over the crater, construction workers in hazmat suits had been able to enter the devastated city and begin the clean-up. Despite thousands of men and women entering in shifts around the clock to minimise exposure, the progress had been slow and only a few of the north-western areas of Manhattan could be repopulated within six months of the attack. But the fear of radiation causing cancer and with millions of people up and down the East Coast thought to have been affected by its wind trail, it was hardly surprising that New York was still a ghost city. The prevailing storms after the attack had blown the fallout as far north as Stamford a few hundred miles away and who knew what the totality of the devastation would be.

Wall Street and a new financial sector had been relocated to Washington DC, causing huge political debate, and the millions of displaced residents had been pushed further towards the border limits of the state, putting unyielding pressure on all services. Others had left entirely to begin a new life in other parts of the country, causing the term 'NY Orphans' to enter the common vernacular when referring to the many dispossessed.

The only positive thing to come out of the attack, if one could call it that, was the realisation of what a nuclear war would look like in the modern age. The Daedalus bomb used had been only one kiloton and by the measure of the twenty megatons in each tactical warhead it had given many around the world a sobering wake-up call to what a nuclear exchange would bring. The damage caused to Nagasaki and Hiroshima was, for many, difficult to fully comprehend, even via textbooks, but seeing it in the flesh was different: an effect that was now playing out on the political world stage. Calls for a more united globe had seen support grow immensely in recent months. The goodwill of nations had become amplified since the attack and cooperation was at an all-time high, and this time those olive branches were not hollow. There was real change in the air throughout Western countries and even China, Russia and Iran now sought closer political ties amongst their own nations, offering the possibility of smaller clumps of nation states around the planet. Would it last? Probably not, but as Munroe sat in the driving seat of the red Ford Bronco he tuned in to the radio reports of the world leader summit happening that night just three miles away on Liberty Island.

'Turn it off,' Sloan demanded from the front passenger seat as in the back Colonel Remus and Jean Barbeau adjusted their own green hazmat suits, staring ahead at the military blockade that had been set up across the road from Holland Tunnel and allowing access to the south-east portion of Manhattan. With security IDs attached to their chests, they looked indistinguishable from the dozens of other workers heading for their shift of clean up on the near deserted island.

'Relax, Jax,' Munroe said, but he swivelled the volume knob. 'Most of these guys will be listening to the reports. It would be odd if we weren't.'

Sloan had been unusually on edge since they had slipped away from Wells Fargo Bank in Washington. She was a woman who was usually so in control of herself, so even the smallest change in demeanour was quickly noted, and although Munroe had not been the only one to see it he had decided to not bring it up with her. Maybe the death of McCitrick was still causing the distraction. Or possibly it was because they missed Freda Wilter, allowing her delivery to Daedalus operatives and most likely a gruesome end. The woman may have been a Nazi but leaving assets behind during an operation was not their style. Or maybe the past ten months of being on the run with their own people hunting them down had begun to take its toll. If any soldier was trapped behind enemy lines, they needed the idea of home to keep them going, but having nowhere to call home and always being one moment away from capture or death had a way of making a deep psychological impression. Especially after such a long time in the field.

Munroe wasn't sure, but if tonight yielded the results they needed to resurrect DSV and everything went to plan, they could begin to put the whole shit show in the rear-view mirror. And if it didn't, then that was that: their last hand was played. Either way, it ended tonight, and as Munroe pulled up to the military roadblock and rolled down his window, the sense of finality gave him strength.

'Identification, please.'

Munroe handed over the four laminated ID cards to the waiting US soldier with an M4 automatic rifle slung over his shoulder. He glanced over each one and peered into the car, identifying the four passengers.

'Where's you work detail tonight?'

'Lower East Side,' Munroe replied, taking back the ID cards. 'We're on a four-hour shift.'

The soldier nodded and then pointed to his hazmat suit. 'You got your rad detectors?'

Munroe reached into his waist pocket and half pulled out the small red digital reader before dropping it back inside and patting it with his hand.

'Never leave home without it.'

The soldier looked happy with everything and he stood back and waved them through.

'Have a good one.'

'We will,' Munroe replied as he took off slowly down the tunnel, winding the window back up. The ID cards had been sourced and copied by Remus with ease and they had all taken the potassium iodine anti-radiation tablets, which would cover them during their time on the island. When Munroe had said a four-hour shift he had meant it. Any longer and possible exposure to the contaminated area could cause serious long-term issues and he hadn't come all this way and gone through so much to end up in the cancer ward later down the line.

The red Bronco exited the tunnel under the bright glare of construction lights overhead and headed slowly towards Soho, leaving the Hudson River behind them, along with the dozens of boats and support barges occupying it.

The sight was ominous and something right out of one's nightmares, or any high-budget disaster movie.

'I've been in some strange places but damn,' Barbeau said as they made their way up the dark, foreboding shell of what was once one of the greatest cities on earth. The central power grid now only served parts of the city, and only the streetlights were operational. The stores and shops lay in darkness, like something from an apocalyptic wasteland – windows had been blown out and there were thick cracks in parts of the tarmac, splintering across pavements. Green moss had taken to filling the fractures in the road and after ten months of growth it gave the term 'urban jungle' real, tangible meaning. The faint glow from lights beyond their sight gloomily lit up the tattered skyline, revealing the enormous damage done to so many building tops, many whose tiles and outer edges been stripped away, leaving the blackened husks of people's bedrooms and personal spaces.

The further into the city they got, the worse the damage became and Munroe found himself drawn to the flashing neon green sign reading 'open' which flickered intermittently, revealing the caved-in front of an Irish bar. Amongst the rubble sat a cat licking its paws and it paused and looked over at him before quickly scurrying away into the decaying mess of twisted metal and brick.

'At least something survived,' Barbeau said with a heavy breath, having noted the feline himself.

'Take Sixth Avenue,' Remus directed, and Munroe obliged and swung left, past a set of traffic lights that were bent in half and stuck on red, spreading an eerie red haze across the pavement. He navigated the dozens of cars and vans that had been bulldozed to the road's edges to allow the construction workers access around the site, and then onwards, deeper into the shadowy abyss and what had once been the great city of New York.

'I did some intelligence work back in China during the noughties,' Munroe said as the others took in the sheer empty desolation outside. 'Me and a colleague ended up meeting an asset in the one of the dozens of new cities the Chinese built during their expansionist period. A whole city, shops, residential areas, high-rises, parks, all completely empty. Void of anyone except the animals who'd taken back their territory. The place was creepy, like something out of an episode of *The Outer Limits* but,' Munroe explained as he slowed to take a right on to West 4th Street, 'this is so much worse.'

It was hard to believe that only ten months ago they had been here as the nuclear bomb went off. New York City, bustling with millions of souls, from shop owners to teachers, to hustlers to cops, and now the entire place was one gigantic ghost town.

'Ever seen *Escape from New York*?' Lavigne said. Apart for the low hum of the Bronco's engine, there was unnatural silence all around them.

'Yep,' Remus said with a grunt and he tapped his forefinger against his window, 'but that place looked more hospitable than this.'

Munroe brought the Bronco to a stop and leaned closer to the windscreen, then he pointed to the stone platform area on his left, lined with leafless, blackened trees, their branches wilted long ago.

'That's Washington Square Park… least it used to be, which means,' he said, turning and pointed over to the other side of the street, 'that's our place.' The single doorway in between two large buildings now became everyone's focus.

Munroe exited the car and waited by the bonnet as Barbeau and Remus went to the boot and came back moments later with two powerful torches and four Smith and Wesson automatic rifles, which were passed around.

'So this was the address you got from Wells Fargo Bank?' Barbeau said, sounding sceptical. 'Doesn't look like the place for a secret vault. There's a jazz club around the corner from here, least there used to be. I went to a couple of times.'

'Sounds the perfect place for a secret vault. Hidden in plain sight,' Munroe said, he nodded to Remus. 'Let's go. I'll take point.'

With the others close behind him, Munroe made his way over to the single door and the heavy-duty number lock securing it. He reached into his pocket and pulled out the piece of paper he'd acquired back in Washington and noted the number below the New York address. He forcefully tapped the code in and then stood back cautiously as the door slowly swung open on its oiled hinges.

Munroe held up one of the flashlights and slipped the written note into his pocket once more before holding up the muzzle of his gun and entering the narrow passageway, followed by the others.

The hallway corridor had three doors leading off it and Munroe flicked his finger the right side before venturing further towards the other two. Sloan broke off to check the first room and Barbeau was instructed towards the other, and after closing the entrance door Remus caught up to Munroe, who was already passing over the threshold and into the last room at the far end.

'Clear,' Barbeau called out from behind them as Sloan confirmed her own clearance and they came through to join Munroe and Remus who were checking out what had turned out to be a large kitchen.

'There's no upstairs so far as I can tell,' Sloan told them, and she received a confirming nod from Barbeau. 'Just a living room.'

'And a bedroom.'

'And this kitchen,' Munroe said, once more surveying the white-tiled room with his torch.

'Hold up,' Remus ordered, and they all turned to see him pull the rad detector from his pocket and note the read out. He then slipped it back in his pocket, unzipped his hazmat suit and completely stepped out of it. 'Radiation's nominal in here and I am not wearing that fucking suit any longer.' He looked over to Barbeau and motioned back to the main door. 'Get the slimlines from the Bronco, will you?'

The slimlines were new tech, military-grade hazmat suits that Remus had acquired whilst organising their North Korean gear back in Dubai. The specially developed tight-fitting fabric was far less cumbersome than traditional hazmat suits, which the team had employed merely to fit in with all the other workers entering Manhattan that evening. The slimlines were also extremely expensive, which meant they weren't for commercial use and the clean-up taking place around the city.

'I feel like I'm wearing a plastic bag,' he added as Barbeau arrived back with the requested gear and passed them out. Once on they looked far more like a one-piece of cargo trousers and tactical vest, and the full-face mask allowed the entire visual of one's face with the rebreathers wrapped around the collar.

With each leaving their face mask off and hanging down their back, Munroe shot Remus a questioning look.

'Happy?' he quipped, even though he had been finding the plastic bags uncomfortable to navigate in.

Remus ignored the jab and with their Smith and Wesson semi-automatics back in their grip, they headed into the kitchen, the last unchecked room in the house.

Nothing stood out: a fridge freezer, electric hob, stainless steel sink. With no windows it had not been spoiled by months of weather seeping in. It was just a kitchen, but as Munroe moved closer to the table, he felt the linoleum flooring change in thickness from solid to soft and it creaked underneath his boot.

Remus was already sliding the table over to one side as Munroe slung his rifle around his shoulder and slid his fingers along the floor until he felt a break in the linoleum flooring.

'Here we go,' he said and pulled back the section of plastic covering to reveal a wooden hatchway set into the concrete floor.

'That's more like it,' Sloan said as Munroe grasped the aluminium ring handle and with a pull heaved open the entrance panel to reveal a metal staircase leading down into the base of the house.

Munroe made his way down the stairs and into a bare concrete room with a large grey door containing a keypad, which he was already examining as the others joined him.

'Now that looks like a vault,' Sloan voiced as Remus joined Munroe and eyed the small black keyboard sticking out of the wall, waiting to be tapped upon.

'OK,' the Frenchman said a husky voice, 'so how do we get it open?'

Sloan pulled out the sheet of paper Munroe had given to her and passed it over to him.

'There's nothing else on there, unless it's the same number as the front door.'

It seemed unlikely, but Munroe gave it a try only to receive a monotonous beeping as the code was rejected.

'We've got some C4 in the Bronco. We could blow it,' Barbeau suggested, ready to go back up to collect it himself.

The idea fell flat, and everyone went quiet as they focused on Munroe who was still hovering over the keyboard, his eyes distant and in deep thought. He stayed that way for a while and then he stood back up and shook his head.

'Could it be that simple?'

Munroe carefully typed in the only other code he had, spelling out the letters as he went and then hovered his finger over the 'enter' button. 'Dr Loathlife.'

A display flashed green in recognition of the correct code and they all watched as the sound of releasing pressure hissed from around the edges of the grey door as it swung backwards to reveal only pitch darkness. Moments later, lights began to flicker overhead and one by one rows of boxes materialised from the darkness, revealing the large space beyond the vault door.

It wasn't warehouse size but the number of storage boxes, both wooden and plastic, took up much of the space and on all sides ran air filters and heaters used to maintain a steady temperature for the precious Daedalus items that had been stored diligently within.

'So this is the where all of Daedalus's secrets are kept,' Barbeau said, taking a step inside behind Munroe.

'Their very own blackmailer's cache,' Sloan added, and Remus threw her a look of genuine excitement. There must have been hundreds of boxes, but they were all organised alphabetically into sections and as the others began to venture deeper inside, one of the categories caught Munroe's attention.

Surveillance.

Munroe strode over to the sign and looked down at the shiny aluminium transport box beneath it and he bent down on one knee, released the two clips, and looked inside.

Foam layers sat one upon the other, the top having multiple slits and holding identical metal memory sticks, individually labelled.

Munroe thumbed through them and coming to a stop on one marked, 'Bauer', and he pulled it out and held it up before him.

'Jax, you may want to look at this.'

Sloan headed back to him as the others continued their inspection and knelt down beside him, taking the memory stick from his fingers.

'Bauer,' she murmured curiously before turning her attention to the other rows of digital storage devices. 'And what's this? Ursula Schneider. The German chancellor!'

Her excitement was infectious, and Munroe couldn't help but be caught up in her enthusiasm.

'Why don't you get the laptop? There's a lot to go through, and we have less than a few hours to sift through this stuff.'

While Sloan headed back to the Bronco, Munroe began checking out the other boxes. No wonder Reichsführer Bormann had managed to maintain such a strong hold over power-hungry psychopaths like Bauer and the rest. With the likely information contained here, it was mutually assured destruction. Anyone tried to take him down and he took everyone with him. Course, it hadn't worked in the end, but you had to give the old Nazi credit – he'd never trusted Bauer with its location. And why would he? Daedalus was a ship of scurrying rats, each one ready to slit another's throat in order to gain the reins of power. In truth, Munroe found it incredible that the organisation hadn't eaten itself long ago, but like with organised crime, fear, violence and money kept them in line. That was unless tonight they took down the whole rats' nest at once.

'Ethan.'

Munroe looked up to see Remus beckoning him over and he moved over to the central row to find Barbeau already examining boxes underneath a sign labelled '*Projects*'. Remus said nothing and gave Munroe a gentle and reassuring slap on his back as he knelt down to see the printed label on top of a metal box reading '*Project Icarus*'.

Munroe reached towards the box and hesitated momentarily before shrugging off his apprehension and pulling open the lid. Multiple files, neatly packed, greeted him as he gently began searching through them. Project Icarus had been what had started him on this whole journey, the genetic-engineering programme that had not only created the perfect politicians and assassins, but the serial killer known as Icarus. He had discovered that he, Ethan Munroe, had been a result of the wretched lab experiment as well. Since finding out that truth deep within the bowels of Blackstar's research and development department, he had not thought about it as much as one might think. That he was bred from the best Aryan stock the Fourth Reich had to offer should have left him with a bad taste in his mouth, a feeling of shame and revulsion at the very body he inhabited. Instead, he had found strength in it, and having the chance to be a part of DSV and take apart those that had sought to corrupt him, even on the genetic level, was the most gratifying thing of all. What was that Shakespeare quote, 'the sins of the father shall be laid upon the children'. Great line, but for him personally it had no meaning. Growing up as an orphan had meant his bloodline began with him and him only. Unlike many, he had managed to find independence in it even if it had taken many years to surface.

Sloan appeared at the vault door and she pulled down the nearest box and then dragged it next to another before sitting on one and placing the laptop on the other.

'I'll need some time,' she said, inserting one of the metal memory sticks in the laptop's port.

'You've got five minutes, Captain. Do your thing,' Remus directed, standing up to begin taking a look at the other sections. But Munroe stayed where he was. Not because the Icarus files held any more interest for him, but instead because of the box just behind it, which had caught his attention. He grabbed hold of it and slid it towards him.

Dr Loathlife

'We keep coming across this name, over and over again. What the hell is Dr Loathlife?' he said out loud, and Remus, who was still standing next to him, shook his head.

'Open it up and take a look,' he said, before wandering off into the vault to see what other gems the place held that could be used in burying Daedalus once and for all.

Munroe unlocked the case, which released a gust of air with an ear-popping squeak, causing him to shift back on his haunches. He carefully pushed open the lid with one hand and looked inside.

Contained within was a box within a box, the lid comprising an oval viewing window made of glass, the edges of which were frosted, and as Munroe touched it a light flickered inside, revealing a single vial of red blood, hermetically sealed and held in place by two metal rings that attached directly to the bottom of the case.

'Looks like blood,' Barbeau noted, appearing over Munroe's shoulder. 'But whose?'

Munroe turned his interest to the side of the case and the tan folder that was in a break in the foam packing. He pulled it out, flipped it open and began to skim through the first page with his finger before coming to a sudden stop at a familiar name.

Barbeau saw it too and he craned his neck closer.

'Why is your name in there, Ethan?'

Munroe appeared somewhat taken aback. He said nothing, and as he flipped the page to the corresponding number, Remus made his way over to them both, having been listening from a distance.

'It's probably Project Icarus,' he said as Munroe flipped to a page filled with a red swastika and a banner title, which he muttered to himself quietly. 'Operation Wolf Fang, codename Dr Loathlife... resuscitation... genome reintegration... subject... Jesus Christ,' he said loudly, looking over at the vial of blood stored safely in the mini freezer. 'It's Hitler's blood!'

'What?' Remus said, looking at the innocuous little red vial.

'The letter we found at the Odessa base. The one addressed to Hans Baur, Hitler's pilot. This is what he wanted smuggled out, to be placed in his vault of treasures wherever it was originally. This is what he saw as the saviour of the German Reich. His own bloodline. This is the Iron Phoenix!'

Such a twisted notion, like everything with hindsight, became abundantly obvious the moment Munroe said it.

'Doesn't it make sense that a man like Hitler, obsessed with the belief that true greatness could be measured by genetics alone, would judge it was his own blood alone that could guide them to victory? Through the belief that he was the pinnacle of significance, almost supernatural in being, having saturated himself in his own wretched narcissism.'

Barbeau glanced down at him with a frown. 'Fancy talk aside, you mean like a clone?'

As usual, the Frenchmen stripped away the veil of drama and got down to the bare bones. It was a trait Munroe liked and he nodded agreeably.

'Yes, Iron Phoenix was a project to resurrect a clone of Hitler to lead the Fourth Reich.'

Barbeau asked and looking puzzled.

'But they didn't have the technology back then, what, eighty years ago?'

'Not then... now,' Munroe stated, morbidly fascinated by the idea, the foresight, the arrogance that must have prevailed until cloning became a feasible notion. 'And operation Wolf Fang was the project.'

Munroe flipped to the next page and his eyes widened as did the other's when they saw the picture taking up half the page. 'That's impossible, that... that can't be.'

Both Remus and Barbeau remained silent as they read the information below and, in the silence, it was Sloan who looked up from her computer and stared over at them.

'Well, is it Bauer?'

Munroe slowly looked over at her, his eyes slightly glazed. 'No. It's not Bauer... It's me.'

Sloan's mouth dropped open, and then she was her shaking her head.

'That's impossible, you don't even look like him!'

Before Munroe could answer he now noticed the gun barrels poking from either side of the vaults doorway and a familiar voice delivered an order.

'Anyone moves and they're dead. Drop the guns, slowly, or Captain Sloan is first to get one in the head.'

From the darkened entrance the face of Davit Gasparyan appeared as on the other side an unknown face joined him.

Sloan was already shaking her head, but Munroe knew most of them would be dead immediately because from where the guns were positioned, it would be like shooting fish in a barrel.

'Well, Ethan, that's one hell of an omission. Frankly, I'm stunned. I don't know whether to hug you or kill you.'

Gasparyan looked absolutely shocked by what he had just heard, and he breathed out a sharp, stunned chuckle. 'Ethan Munroe, the truth behind the legend of the Iron Phoenix.'

Chapter 24

'Now drop your guns, gentlemen, or none of you will even make it past the pleasantries.'

Barbeau had his rifle still slung around his back and by the look of him he had no intention of dropping it, and neither did Munroe, whose rifle was also slung around his back.

'Colonel, be a good boy and tell your men to do as I say.'

Remus stared over at the Daedalus killer with contempt before slowly placing his rifle on the floor.

'Do as he says.'

There was still a moment of hesitance, but despite Sloan's glare that was urging them to start shooting, both men eventually nodded and did as they were told, laying their rifles on the floor and sliding them over.

'Good,' Gasparyan said with a hint of glee and he now fully entered the vault, calling back to the other gunman. 'Mr Dupont, would you do the honours, please?'

Ernst Dupont appeared at from behind the vault wall and quickly stepped over to the rifle, which he collected swiftly before joining Gasparyan.

'Easy, Captain Sloan,' Gasparyan growled, holding the barrel of his Glock to the back of her head and foiling any attempt she might have made to grab the rifle next to her. 'Colonel Remus, Captain Barbeau, I would ask you to stay where you are, we don't want anyone to lose their heads, do we… starting with this young lady.'

There was only one way the killer could have found them, and it was the same loose end Munroe wished they had managed to wrap up back in Washington.

'You picked up Freda Wilter then.'

Gasparyan didn't reply at first, his focus on Munroe as Dupont covered Remus and Barbeau. He now pushed Sloan towards the other three and pointed his Glock at Munroe's chest.

'Freda was extremely helpful. She gave you all up with very little pressure, but I wanted to play with her a bit so, I'm afraid, we got here later than we wanted, but rest assured, the old cow got what was coming to her. Impressive extraction from North Korea, by the way.' Gasparyan shook his head, now looking disappointed. 'Oh, Ethan Munroe, what a benefit you could have been to us… and what a pain in the ass you've been to me personally. Never in my wildest dreams did I consider that you could be the one we talk about during the long nights. The tale of Reichsführer Bormann and his genetic side project and the information he had stored in his precious vault, his Iron Phoenix.'

Gasparyan looked completely astounded at the notion and he began to examine Munroe's face but from a safe distance, then he glanced over at Dupont.

'What do you think, Ernst? You've heard the stories.'

Dupont did look somewhat shocked at first but it quickly turned to disbelief.

'He doesn't look anything like Hitler.'

'He's not a complete clone, but as the story goes it was Hitler's wish to be reborn at a time when medical science could perform such miracles. To retake his place at the head of the Fourth Reich and ensure world power was returned to us. They may have tinkered with his DNA profile to amplify some of the physical aspects, but they tinkered with his genome from the best stock we have to offer. I assure you the blood running through his veins is the führer's and it's as pure as the driven snow.' Gasparyan shook his head in wonder, his eyes wide. 'They say that Bormann regretted the procedure soon after, having second thoughts that the child might usurp his own position when he came of age, so the child was murdered, the project disbanded, but what a twist of fate that here you are, now, before me. I never believed it was possible, just a tale one told to their children, the messianic power of the man that began it all, but here you are. Truly astounding. Oh dear, Ethan, what a predicament you are in. To think that DSV was brought into existence to destroy the very thing that now stands before them.'

Munroe continued to remain silent, expressionless, and his breathing became heavy, but measured, as he considered the harsh reality being laid out before him.

'Feeling a bit of a sting, I'll bet,' Gasparyan mocked, licking his lips like a man preparing to gorge on his favourite dish. 'Oh, the questions that must be running through your mind. Quite the mindfuck I'd wager, but if it makes you feel any better I feel the same way. One hell of a mic drop.'

Munroe glanced over at his three colleagues, their eyes holding no malice but each visibly shocked at the disclosure, and then he turned back to face the psychopath who now raised his right hand and pointed it towards the ceiling.

'Heil Hitler!'

The very act of such a devilish salute brought pride to his face, but what had no doubt been a condescending display had the opposite effect upon Munroe, who stood proudly and eyed them both. He still wasn't ready to accept what was in effect being dropped on him with all the weight of a steel anvil and he said nothing as Gasparyan appeared to lose interest in a legendary story told within the ranks of Daedalus.

'So, enough of that, let's deal with the issue at hand,' he cried out, and allowing his weapon to drop to his side as Dupont kept them covered. 'Here we all are, together again. An audience with the terrorists DSV... and their world-famous Nazi leader thought dead for the past eighty years. How often do you get to say something like that?' Gasparyan joked to Dupont who looked wholly unamused. 'The Disavowed, although you seem to have shrunk in number. No matter, I'm sure they're nearby. We'll mop them up as we go. I keep expecting McCitrick to appear like the mole he is, but I guess this little venture of yours to find this holiest of holies is a bit too dangerous for a man who hides behind his desk.'

It was obvious Gasparyan had no idea McCitrick was dead and Munroe was not about to inflate his ego further than it already was.

'What! No patronising or plucky remark, Ethan? You're becoming far too serious these days and, I'm afraid I don't have anything but bad news, so let me tell you what is going to happen. I'm going to shoot your two friends dead and then, after I've tied you up, I'm going to do some terrible... terrible things to Captain Sloan over there. And after you've watched me degrade and humiliate her for my own amusement, then, and only then, will I slowly peel your skin off and watch you bleed out. A fitting end to a son of a bitch such as you.'

'No, Davit. We wait until führer Bauer arrives,' Dupont said with such a finite tone that Gasparyan was caught off guard.

'Hans is coming here, to the middle of this radioactive dustbowl?'

Dupont offered a slow nod of his head.

'He wanted to see the vault first-hand and of course take charge of its secrets personally.'

Gasparyan thought about it for a second and then he appeared sanguine at the idea.

'Our new führer is braver than I thought. Good, I can wait, but first I think I'll indulge in a bit of playtime before he gets here.' The smug fun-loving demeanour vanished near instantly as if a veil had been pulled down over his face and it was replaced by the caricature of a wide-eyed maniac. The man's pupils dilatated so his eyes now appeared black and he retrieved a leather-covered switchblade from his pocket and flicked it open then placed it next to Sloan's laptop on the box. What followed was a transformation of truly hideous effect as his lips curled upwards revealing his white teeth, and as he licked his lips saliva began to drip down his chin.

It was chilling to see the face that so many of Gasparyan's victims had witnessed personally and Munroe was already tensing at the sight. If this was it then they were going out fighting and as from his peripheral vision he noticed his other three teammates stiffen in preparation for the same thing he was planning, it was Dupont who cut through the ever-chilling atmosphere.

'Think we've had enough of you,' he said, and swiv-elled his gun towards his colleague and blew the man's brains out, sending blood and brain matter onto the wall opposite.

Davit Gasparyan wobbled at the force of the shot, but he remained standing for a few moments until his eyelids drooped and then he fell to the floor in a heap, the maniacal grin still hanging from his lips.

'Captain Munroe, it's a pleasure.'

For Munroe everything fell into place, and the timing could not have been better. 'You're McCitrick's contact... Saviour.'

Ernst Dupont nodded and put his gun back in its holster as Remus and the others immediately retrieved their rifles, and Sloan barely acknowledged the man who had just saved them and shot back onto her laptop.

'Yes. And I have no idea if this whole Hitler thing bears any weight, but it means nothing to me, I can assure you. We have bigger concerns facing us all. Firstly, you have my condolences for John. He was a good man. I had hoped to meet him again... real shame. Now, we have to go; what I said about Bauer is true. He's on his way right now. He wants this place for himself.'

There was real urgency in his voice, but Munroe needed to know who the hell this guy was and more importantly *what* he was.

'Start loading as much as you can into the Bronco. Focus on the surveillance intel and place a few charges, enough to set this place alight,' Munroe ordered Barbeau, who took off immediately as Remus moved to Munroe's side and shook Dupont's hand.

'Nice to meet you finally, Mr Dupont. Or should I call you "Saviour"? So how about you answer what both Ethan and I are thinking. Why the change of heart? You were born into Daedalus, weren't you?'

Dupont still looked anxious to leave and Munroe noticed it right away.

'We can't leave until we have this intel packed up, much as we can, so we've got a few minutes. We just need to know why you're doing this.'

The effort to mellow the man worked and Ernst Dupont stepped back and sucked in a deep breath.

'OK, and call me Ernst but, the short version, because he'll be arriving in about twenty minutes. You're right, I was born into Daedalus and ended under the tutelage of Hans Bauer. I don't mind telling you I was a nasty bastard in my youth. Just as I had been taught to be, and I'll be happy to give you all the details later. All you need to know is that something happened and it changed my whole ethos. About a year ago I ran into McCitrick, or he ran into me more like it. Soon after you lot got thrown to the wolves by your own governments. My way out was unachievable until I heard from him again, and by then I was already planning to take out Bauer myself.'

The man wasn't kidding about keeping it vague and Munroe now pushed for more as Barbeau arrived back for another box.

'What exactly did Bauer do? Must have been a hell of thing to turn you against all you've known.'

Dupont suddenly seemed uncomfortable and he looked away from their gaze momentarily.

'I was groomed for governmental infiltration, which is exactly what I achieved within the corridors of French political power. All behind the scenes, but it's not unlike the mandarins of the civil service in the UK. Leaders and their political parties come and go with passing elections. The style and substance of leadership changes like the wind, but the mandarins are constant, they rarely change, and with that comes a high degree of power and persuasion to whomever yields it. 'Course it's not absolute, nothing ever is, but you would be surprised how much can be accomplished with the right people in the right unelected positions. My dealings with Daedalus became less and less, a phone call here, a meeting there, but I was always ready if called.'

Dupont's demeanour now became more morose, and Munroe could see he was approaching the real reason for his betrayal.

'That is until I met someone. Someone I fell deeply in love with, and she was a person Bauer took a personal exception to.'

Munroe had an idea of what was coming, and he suddenly found it cut very close to the bone for him. Too close, perhaps, and Dupont saw it in him.

'Yes, Ethan. It is a pain that you will understand more than anyone else. I fell in love with a Jewish girl and Bauer murdered her simply for loving me just as he did your wife and child.'

Munroe felt a rage filling his chest he had not felt in a while, but he contained it and allowed his new colleague to continue.

'But whereas yours he killed in a car bomb, he had mine strangled right in front of me as others held me down until the light had been extinguished from her eyes and right there and then I resolved to take down that wretched organisation that had consumed my life since my earliest memories. Of course, he had others do it and swore he was not involved, but I knew the truth. I saw it in his eyes. The gloating, underneath the surface.'

There was silence at first and then Remus touched Dupont in the shoulder.

'I'm sorry, Ernst, but I am glad to have you with us. I'll get things wrapped up here and we'll get going.'

The colonel left the two men alone, staring at each other, and understanding the other's pain.

'I'm sorry.'

'As am I for you, Ethan. Hans Bauer is a man the world could do without, and that goes the same for Daedalus. I could have killed him many times but another like him would have taken his place, and I won't let that happen. They say you cut off the head and the body withers, but for Daedalus, like a lizard replacing a severed limb, heads spring eternal.'

'OK, let's go,' Remus called out to them as Slone slapped her laptop shut and pulled on her mask.

There was only one thing Munroe could say.

'Let's finish this.'

Within moments they were all in the kitchen and Dupont quickly slipped on one of the yellow hazmat suits both he and Gasparyan had worn.

'Are the charges set?' Munroe asked, and Barbeau gave a firm nod and flung the backpack containing the last of their ordnance down the stair well before showing the small handheld detonator in his hand.

'You finished, Jax?'

Sloan shook her head.

'I need a few more minutes, but I can finish it the car before we go live.'

The others were already out the door and heading for the red Bronco but Barbeau walked straight past it and over to the black Range Rover parked next to it.

'It was open, so why not. You got the keys?'

Dupont rummaged in his waist pocket, the hazmat suit rustling as he did so, and threw a set of keys towards Barbeau, but they were intercepted by Munroe's outstretched palm.

'I'll drive. Everyone in. Jax, you're in the front with me.'

With three in the back it was a tight squeeze and Munroe was thankful they had the slimline rad suits on. As he reached the driver's side he noticed a small red dot racing along the ground towards him. It was then that instinct took over and he flung open the door as the dull sound of bullets thudded against the other side of the door and he jumped into the seat and turned on the ignition.

'Contact!' he yelled, as the from behind them gunfire hit the back corner of the vehicle, shredding the body-work but missing the tyres as Munroe slammed down hard on the accelerator. The bright lights from two SUVs flashed into life and took chase. 'Blow the vault.'

The building behind them exploded into a fireball, sending fiery debris into the road, and the key-pad protected security door they had entered by buckled it hinges and was blown violently into the road and with such force it clipped the nearest SUV which spun thirty degrees on its axis. The damaged vehicle was back in the chase within a few moments as Munroe sped away, his engine revving loudly, into the depths of the rubble-filled wasteland that was once Manhattan.

'How long do you need?' Remus shouted from the back seat as he and Barbeau wound down their windows and began returning fire.

'Give me ten minutes,' Sloan shouted back over the deafening noise being amplified in the vehicle's interior, and as the screen of her laptop lit up, she began to tap away at the keyboard furiously. 'I need to string this all together and then we can go live.'

Behind them sporadic flashes of light lit up from the sides of the pursuing SUV as M4 rifles were stuck out of its side windows and unloaded into the back of the Range Rover as Munroe fought to keep the distance between them.

'You said five and that was twenty minutes ago,' Munroe yelled as he skidded around the corner and headed north up 3rd Avenue, passing rows of cars that had been bulldozed back onto the pavements.

'Well I need another ten.'

'You've got five and make it count.'

'Shit,' Sloan yelled, pulling back off the keypad and clenching her fist tightly in frustration. 'The satellite signal is too weak; we'll never get it out.'

'Why not, what's the problem?' Munroe shouted back as another spray of bullets hit the rear bumper, this time shattering the back window and flooding the whole car with the cold night air.

'Could be the radiation, could be the satellite. We need to get some height.'

'Heading back to the security exit would be undesirable, not with the number of soldiers guarding it,' Dupont yelled, fogging up his visor. 'We wouldn't get through the roadblocks without turning this car into Swiss cheese and us along with it.'

'He's right,' Remus shouted above the noise of his semi-automatic rifle that he was now firing in short bursts at the SUV, which was beginning to close the gap. 'We need a new plan.'

Barbeau joined in, taking aim at the nearest SUV as Munroe searched for a solution. They hadn't come this far just to get screwed by shitty WiFi.

'We got another problem. Looks like Bauer's called in the troops. I've got multiple calls for back-up to our location,' Sloan added, ramping up the challenge they now faced as she tapped at the small window on her screen that was tracking military noise chatter. 'They'll be on us in minutes.'

As the other two let off more rounds from the back seat, Sloan stared over at Munroe and an idea flickered into his mind.

'Is the main electrical grid still operational throughout Manhattan?'

Sloan looked unsure, but she nodded.

'Yes. But most of the buildings have been disconnected.'

Before Munroe could say anything a series of high-pitched beeps filled the car and Sloan immediately squeezed her fingers deep into her front trouser pocket and pulled out the black compact radiation sensor. 'Radiation levels going up; we're getting too close to Ground Zero.'

In the distance, through the levelled destruction of concrete and brick rubble that had once made up the fancy New York residences, they could just make out the huge protruding dome covering what had been the United Nations building looking like a gigantic, shelled monster lying in slumber. The top of it just cut above the skyline, offering a remembrance, a mausoleum, to the thousands of souls lost within the blink of an eye.

'We can't get any closer,' Sloan said, her stare fixed upon the cupped monolith. 'If we do the radiation we'll soak up will be irreversible.'

Decisions, decisions, decisions.

'Hold on,' Munroe yelled, and he tapped the brake and skidded around the approaching junction on to East 23rd Street as Remus and Barbeau returned fire, causing one SUV to oversteer and come to a screeching halt. Having sailed past the junction, the other narrowly missed and went slamming up onto the pavement, crashing to an abrupt halt as it collided with a lamppost.

'Where are we going?' Sloan yelled above the sound of gunfire as both SUVs reversed and skidded ninety degrees before tearing off after them again with M4s blazing.

'Just get it finished, Jax,' Munroe yelled as he drove over a wooden ramp that had been placed across a deep four-foot rip in the road and slammed on the brakes. 'Cover me,' he shouted, already out of the driver's side door as the SUVs continued their approach, with Remus and Barbeau's shots ricocheting off their bulletproof windows and front grille in a multitude of sparks.

Munroe reached down and heaved up the wooden ramp, grunting at its weight, before dropping it into the deep crack. He then raced back and leapt in the driver's side, slamming his foot down hard on the accelerator before he was even fully in the driving seat.

As they sped away, both SUVs came to a shuddering halt just feet away from the tear in the road and then screeched back in reverse, the M4s now silent, and for second Munroe caught sight of the screaming face of Hans Bauer as he barked orders.

'Well, that's definitely Bauer in there,' Munroe yelled as Dupont, who was squeezed in the middle of the back seat, attempted to take a look for himself, but was hampered by the bulky helmet of the hazmat suit.

'Should buy us a bit more time,' Munroe said as Remus and Barbeau sat back in their seats and without a word began reloading their rifles as Sloan busily tapped away, her eyes glued to the laptop screen.

Dupont also began checking his clip and Remus leant towards him and shook his finger.

'Please don't use that until we get out of this car,' he said, referring to the burdensome hazmat suit. 'You're more likely to shoot one of us by mistake.'

They took a left onto 5th Avenue and sped down it, only slowing slightly to manoeuvre past a stack of rusting cars nearly blocking the junction a few hundred metres along, and then onwards before Remus's own patience wore thin.

'Where the hell are we going, Ethan?'

Munroe pointed through the windscreen to one of the only buildings left untouched by the blast and the water damage from the East River that had followed it.

'Right there. High enough, Sloan?'

They all craned their heads upwards and stared towards the towering building they were closing in on, its shadow casting a long silhouette across the tangled ruins of misshapen debris of the city below.

'The Empire State Building! Do you know how long it will take to walk up to the top?'

'We shouldn't have to,' Munroe said, now guiding their attention to the row of lights near the top of the structure with his finger. 'If the power's still on then the elevators should be as well.'

'Good a plan as any,' Remus said with a grunt, and Sloan buried herself back in the laptop balanced on her knees as Munroe pulled around the corner and headed at high speed to the main entrance before bringing their vehicle to a tyre-burning stop right outside the double doors.

'Everyone out,' Remus ordered, exiting the vehicle and running towards the double doors along with the others, whilst Sloan slapped her laptop shut and followed.

'Are you done?' Munroe asked as Remus and Barbeau pushed against the doors and, on finding them locked, pulled out their Glocks and took aim.

'Almost,' Sloan shouted over the gunfire as a single glass panel of the door shattered and was then kicked in, creating an entry point. 'I'll finish the rest on the elevator trip.'

Her reply sounded condescending and Munroe managed a smile as Remus and Barbeau made their way inside the darkened building.

'Have I ever let you down before?' she asked resolutely, shooting him a cheeky smile and ducking down then making her way through the gap. 'Always a first time, though!'

Chapter 25

'I would like to thank everyone who travelled from around the world to join us here tonight. Such a show of world unity to honour the terrible attack that took place here less than a year ago. We are at the dawn of a new era, one of cooperation and of putting behind us the problems of the past and seizing the opportunities of the future for all countries of the world. As you will have heard, the breakthrough in nuclear fusion, although in its infancy, gives us an opportunity to provide the world with cheap, unlimited energy. Once confirmed as President of the UE, I intend for this to be my first order of business and with the concerted effort of all countries we will rid ourselves of the shackles of the petrol-dollar that has allowed us such tremendous strides in civilisation whilst at the same time divided the globe into the haves and have-nots.'

Ursula Schneider smiled and looked down at the crowd of world leaders who were attending the rebranding of the United Nations into the new organisation of 'The United Earth'. The event would also mark her ascension as the first president of the 'UE' lasting four years, whereupon a new candidate would be put up for election. The new rules stated that no sitting president may serve longer than three terms and for her, just one would be all she and Daedalus needed in order to cement the legal foundations that would facilitate a Fourth Reich in the decades to come.

Behind her, the Statue of Liberty soared high into the sky, lit up by spotlights as beyond Liberty Island, across the Hudson Bay, the City of New York was illuminated by a sprinkling of lights as construction continued through the night.

Schneider took a moment to enjoy the applause, expressing gratitude for not only her own role in such a monumental shift in world politics, but for all the leaders of countries who had signed up to such a politically radical venture. It would be a few years before the UE had any real political and military teeth, but the ball was rolling exactly as Hans Bauer had said it would.

It was strange that her führer had not managed to make it that night, prior engagements calling him away. They must have been incredibly important for him to miss an event Daedalus had worked towards for so long. Still, she thought, not having forgiven him for the disgusting things he had asked of her back in her office just a few days earlier, once she had settled into the role she would make it her top priority to dispense with Bauer in the most painful way imaginable.

It is time the Reich has a female in power. Totalitarian rule isn't exclusively for men.

'Presidents and prime ministers, ladies and gentlemen, let tonight shine as the first example for many to come, of an idea that for millennia has been pursued with the gears of war, only now to be fully realised by the extended hands of peace. On this night I formally accept the presidency of the United Earth and offer my service to the nations of the world. I will not fail you.'

Schneider stood back from the podium and raised her hand, pointing to a spotlight which lit up the sky with the new logo of the UE as fireworks began exploding around it and cheers and applause filled the air. Everyone looked to the heavens in excitement... except for a single man, who had his finger pressed to his ear and an eye on the hundreds of multinational security agents on watch.

'How's it going, Zeke?' Marcel Lavigne whispered, barely moving his lips. 'Fifteen minutes until the big game.'

Over by the huge almost one-hundred-metre-tall LED screen projecting the evening's events and speakers, DSV members Zeke Talon and Jack Dalton were serving punch to the guests, each wearing a white tuxedo and black tie. Talon finished with his customer and dropped his chin slightly to speak into his hidden lapel microphone.

'Understood.'

Talon offered a smile to the old lady drenched in diamonds and getting a crystal cup full of alcoholic punch from Lavigne, who also sported the same cheesy smile.

'I'll do my Champagne rounds,' he said, and with a nod from Dalton he picked up the silver serving tray filled with filled Champagne glasses and began to make his way into the crowd of guests. By the time he reached the far side, his tray was almost empty, having left many happy drinkers in his path. At $18,000 a bottle, the Cristal Brut was not something any of the guests were willing to miss out on, and as Talon edged towards his destination the last few glasses were snatched up, leaving him with an empty tray.

Shit, greedy bastards.

He courteously placed the empty tray under his arm and headed for the small black portable ready-room, with no windows. It may have looked empty, but you could be sure that inside sat the heads of the various security services, all of them organising the spread of agents on Liberty Island that night. Sometimes a heavy judicial presence made covert operations easier, blending into the crowd being one of them, but as Talon approached the portable ready-room he felt a firm grasp on his shoulder.

'Can I help you, sir?'

Talon turned around and smiled at the black-suit-wearing security agent who stared at him with dead eyes and a chiselled jawline.

'Champagne duty,' Talon replied, holding the empty tray before him.

'This is a restricted area, sir,' the agent said, looking down at the tray. 'Seems like you need a refill.'

'Oh, yes. The Cristal Brut Champagne is popular.'

His attempt at conversation was met with a stony expression and Talon immediately moved on to his question.

'Agent Dawes asked me to provide some coffee for the ready-room. I was about to get their order.'

The agent didn't reply, but instead raised his hand and spoke into the small black microphone jutting out from beneath his shirt cuffs.

'This is Tango 2. Need confirmation on a drinks request by Agent Dawes.'

Whatever the reply had been into the agent's earpiece it did the job and the man gave Talon a nod.

'Just coffees, black, and bring them back to me. I'll take them in.'

'Of course,' Talon replied, and he made his way back through the crowd to the punch bowl, once more whispering into his hidden mic.

'The bait's been taken. About to deliver.'

Dalton was already waiting for him with a large silver thermos of coffee and a short stack of brown plastic cups, which he passed over, and then he got back to dishing out the punch. Within seconds, Talon had danced his way through the crowd and was at the agent's side, passing the refreshments over.

'If you need milk or sugar, just ask.'

The agent, still refusing to smile, nodded and then waited for Talon to move off again before turning to the ready-room and delivering a couple of solid knocks on the door.

'Here we go,' Dalton said over their internal earphones, watching Talon pass back to the punch bowl as the agent disappeared into the private security room. His hand had healed well from the flesh wound he'd received during their false-flag operation, although he kept his hands crossed to hide the short row of stitches. If it hadn't been healing well then he would have been serving the punch and having to make small talk. Jack Dalton had no qualms about flying a plane into North Korean territory or dodging a surface-to-air missile with two of his passengers hanging from the plane fuselage, but small talk was where he drew the line. He only had so many brain cells to lose.

'We're good.'

Lavigne watched as both Talon and Dalton slowly began to make their way towards the rear end of Liberty Island and the area designated as a service entrance for all the incoming refreshments. It was how they had arrived and how they would be leaving, and having made up only a small part of the service team, they would not be missed for another ten minutes.

The three men came together at the edge of the dock and fell into a line as they strolled down the pier to the dark blue bowrider boat and hopped into it. Within moments they were speeding away, leaving the Statue of Liberty behind them, standing guard above the dark waters of the Hudson River, the glitzy party below shrouded under the cover of the UE emblem being projected high above them. The next ten minutes would signal triumph or defeat. They stared out at the darkened skyline of Manhattan to the blinking light atop the Empire State Building, with no idea what was happening up there at that very moment.

Chapter 26

The musty smell of dust and disuse caused Munroe's nose to wrinkle as he joined the others in the centre of the reception area. He and Barbeau switched on the bright torches they had brought. The brown marbling on the walls and floor looked dull and the small gift shops on either side of them seemed to be fully stocked with mementos and trinkets covered in layers of grey dust, no security shutters pulled down. And who would have bothered, given the terror of an atomic detonation taking place just under a mile away? To Munroe it was remarkable that the skyscraper was in the condition it was, and he shined his torch light on the large mural of the building they were in etched into the far wall.

'They don't make them like they used to,' he said as Barbeau moved ahead to escalators on the right-hand side and waved them over.

'This way,' he said, climbing up them, followed closely by the others. 'I lived in New York for two years back in the noughties, and I only visited once, but I'm sure the elevators are just up here.'

With Barbeau as the tourist guide, they climbed up the static set of escalators to find they led into a large foyer and guest area with small information attractions about the building itself spread around the room. Baby strollers, suitcases and an array of backpacks littered the walkways, another testament to the speed at which the numerous sightseers had dropped everything and run for the exit on that terrible day.

For Munroe, seeing the explosion from the outside had left a wildly vivid impression, one might say a scar of a memory burned into his mind, but only now did he consider what the same detonation must have felt like to those trapped inside these huge buildings. The initial blast wave would have felt like the mother of all earthquakes, but far more focused as the energy of the one-kiloton bomb was unleashed all at once. The instantaneous cracking of the walls, now filled with black dusty residue, snapping overhead and dropping plaster down on the crowds. The blinding light causing complete blindness in a blink of an eye as their retinas were burned away, leaving people disorientated and lost in pitch darkness as the crowds of terrified and screaming tourists all raced for the exit. The idea was terrifying enough for a hardened military man like Munroe, let alone for a mother and baby or some fifteen-year-old kid, playing truant from school and realising there was no one there to protect them.

For anyone watching the TV reports around the world they would know the first job of the clean-up crews had been to recover the bodies, although thousands were never recovered, and it was as Munroe scanned his surroundings that he wondered how many had died on the spot. Some of them, perhaps all of them. This shell of a building was now more of a tomb than the place builders had originally envisaged it to be.

Barbeau led them in a line past the deserted ticket desks, and true to his word, they arrived at a row of elevators, which if the brown-stained sign was correct, headed up to the observation levels on the top floor. With a confident glance at Sloan, Munroe reached over and pushed the blackened button.

Nothing.

Munroe tried again, tapping it in quick succession, but his efforts were met with deafening silence and he turned around to face the other four, of which it was Sloan who looked the least impressed.

'Don't you ever get tired of being wrong,' she quipped, and Munroe managed a smile.

'There should be a fuse box,' Dupont said as they all began to look around for signs of any cabling.

'Everyone spread out and let's make it quick,' Munroe stated, and he took off in the direction of the ticket desks they had passed, as the others fanned out in opposite directions. Upon reaching the counters, he leapfrogged over onto the other side and then headed to the staff offices at the back. They were all empty of the items that had littered the guest area and his nose twitched as he approached office doors with flaking brown varnish. He smelt traces of an odour he'd not come across in a while. Munroe grasped the metal door knob and pushed it open, his torch lighting up the small room and the unpleasant smell becoming so potent now that he pulled up his shirt and pressed it to his nose. Slowly, he moved the torch beam around the room from left to right, bringing it to a complete stop on the decaying body of a man on the chair next to a central desk. Strips of dried skin clung to the skeleton making it look like something you'd find in a storefront for Halloween, and although the hair remained attached to the decayed scalp, the eyes had completely liquified. The person's last meal lay on the table in front of him and had not fared much better, now only a plate with a brown congealed mass upon it.

Though body retrieval had been the first order of business after the attack, not everyone had been accounted for.

He shifted the torch light away from the carcass and moved it along the wall until he found what he was looking for – a large grey painted metal box stretching from near the ground to the roof, secured to the wall, with thick cabling dropping from its underneath.

He now entered the room fully and made his way over to it, offering a respectful nod to the corpse, and released the black plastic catch, allowing the panel door to swing open to reveal rows of circuit breakers.

Munroe ran his forefinger down the labelled switches until he came to the one marked 'Reception Guest Elevators' and, with a heavy push, clicked the fuse switch into place. There was no sound and, not wanting to create a beacon of light for Bauer, he left the others untouched and headed back to the elevators.

He was rewarded with a glint of light emanating through cracks in the blackened plastic buttons and felt a wave of relief.

'I've got it,' Munroe yelled, and the first to appear was Barbeau who moved over to him quickly and did the honour of pressing the button as Munroe flashed his torch beam around the guest area, looking for signs of the others.

The sounds of approaching footsteps in the distance and flashes of light had him joining Barbeau and guarding the elevator, both their rifles raised. Neither man said anything as the footsteps got closer when something caught the Frenchman's attention in the direction of the escalators.

'What the fu—' Barbeau's chest exploded just above his breastplate causing his hands to drop to his sides and shake as a second bullet ripped through his thigh, flipping him backwards to the floor. Munroe spun around whilst dropping to his knee to see someone in black tactical gear deliver another shot that whizzed just inches above his head, whereupon he returned fire, the first burst catching the killer in the chest as the sound of multiple boots echoed from behind him.

'Jean!' Munroe yelled, with his rifle still pointing in the direction of the escalators, he began delivering short bursts of volleys as he dragged his wounded colleague behind a stone flowerbed display for cover.

Behind him, Remus and Sloan appeared, sprinting towards the elevators with their guns drawn, followed closely by Dupont, all laying down suppressing fire in the direction of the escalators, at the shifting shadows around the top step.

'It's got to be Bauer,' he yelled as Remus and Sloan took up defensive positions behind a wooden counter with a viewing monitor. Dupont joined Munroe, allowing him to slap his hand against the elevator call button once again before ripping open Barbeau's shirt to inspect his wounds.

'We've got incoming,' Remus shouted, poking his head up to steal a glance over at the escalator as the haze of bobbing torch lights headed up towards them. 'It's Blackstar security. Shit, it might even be the army.'

As the others began clipping off defensive shots, Munroe pulled out a white surgical rag from his pocket and began to attend to the gaping hole in the left side of Barbeau's chest. The wound was spilling out blood and Barbeau's breathing was short and heavy, but at least his lungs were intact. He was conscious and alert, but in great pain, and he clenched his teeth together and began to shake.

'You're OK,' Munroe reassured him as he pulled another bandage from his pocket and flung the used and bloody rag to the floor. 'Don't you fucking dare pass out on me, Jean.'

The sound of automatic gunfire had Remus and Sloan digging into their positions as Dupont took potshots at the men attempting to breach the top of the elevator, and it was clear by their outfits they weren't military.

'They're Blackstar mercenaries,' Dupont shouted as all four of them now laid down a barrage of bullets, forcing the horde to retreat down the stairs with at least two lying dead on the guest area's entrance floor.

Ding.

The elevator door slid open, shining light onto the thick pool of blood surrounding Barbeau as Munroe grabbed him by his jacket's shoulders and dragged him inside. 'Time to go,' he yelled, and Sloan crawled her way over to him, picking up Barbeau's backpack whilst Remus provided covering fire. The colonel spent a few more rounds before something small was lobbed in their direction, but Remus was out of cover even before it hit the floor. In one swift movement he caught what turned out to be a green pineapple grenade and he threw it back down the escalators before diving towards the elevator where the rest of the team had taken shelter.

The thundering sound of an explosion filled the reception area with a blinding flash just as Remus crossed the threshold of the elevator, the minor shock wave thrusting him forwards as the doors slid shut and the sound of an electric motor jerked into motion.

The fact that Remus had just pulled a near superhuman feat was not even mentioned and he turned his attention to Barbeau immediately.

'How you doing there, Jean?' he asked as Munroe moved aside and allowed Sloan to take over the triage. The wound was a bleeder, but so far as Munroe could tell the bullet hadn't clipped any of his major organs.

'I'm good, sir,' Barbeau replied in nothing more than a pained hiss and Remus ran his hand over the young soldier's head.

'Good, because we need you, understand?'

Barbeau nodded, his head jerking as Sloan attended to the wound with the fresh bandages she had on her.

'I can give you a morphine shot to stem the pain—'

She didn't even finish the sentence before Barbeau shook his head firmly.

'Last thing I need right now is to be woozy, Jax. Patch me up and give me a gun.'

Sloan shot him a smile and gave him a pat on his head as she went back to completing the bandage before turning to the graze on his thigh, which was only skin deep.

'Here you go,' Dupont said, placing his own Glock into Barbeau's waiting hands. 'I'll use the S and W,' he added, picking up Barbeau's rifle and leaning it against the elevator wall. He then unzipped his hazmat suit and pulled it off himself.

'Are you crazy?' Munroe growled, but Dupont looked undeterred.

'If I can take out Bauer and Daedalus tonight, then it's worth the risk.'

'Actually, we're good,' Sloan confirmed, holding her rad detector up in the air. 'The radiation's nominal in here and the higher up we go the better it'll get.'

As Dupont reloaded his weapon, Munroe locked stares with Remus and then together they pulled back their masks and sucked in the musty and dank air of the elevator.

'Shit, it smelt better with the mask on,' Munroe said, and Barbeau began to laugh but caught himself as the pain in his chest intensified.

Sloan then followed their example and removed hers, and with an urging from Barbeau himself Sloan pulled his off, leaving everyone in the elevator maskless.

'I hope that rad detector is working right,' Munroe said questioningly, and then he glanced around the confined space and his teammates stuck within. 'Not sure how many we've got down there, but they'll be coming up to pay us a visit, no doubt.'

'I counted ten of them,' Remus growled heavily, still catching his breath as Munroe reloaded his Glock and cocked it back. 'Automatic rifles and full body armour.'

'Expect nothing less,' Dupont instructed as Munroe turned now to Sloan.

'You need ten minutes to do your thing, right?'

'Not a minute more, sir.'

Munroe looked over at each of them individually and nodded.

'Then we'll get you that ten minutes.'

Chapter 27

The adjacent elevator was already rumbling when Munroe stepped out onto the eighty-sixth floor of the Empire State Building and checked all his blind spots for movement. Once confident they were clear, he quickly motioned for the others to join him. Remus and Dupont made their way past him with Barbeau, his arms draped over their shoulders, as Sloan picked up one of the dusty metal chairs lining the walls and jammed it between the elevator's sliding doors.

Given that their own trip to the top had taken over three minutes, with the elevator straining all the way up, Munroe gave it about two and a half minutes before they had company. Whether Bauer would make the trip up to them in person was debateable, but a shot at taking down the head of Daedalus was a luxury at this point, and he sensed Dupont knew it as well. They had one mission and that was to hold Bauer's henchmen and give Sloan time to enact their plan. There was no room for error and the next ten minutes would either see DSV's return to the fold, and their lives given back to them, or the beginning of Daedalus's grand plan to enslave the world. The stakes were high. As Munroe watched his team carry Barbeau up the short flight of stairs towards the observation area he had more than a few misgivings. It was a common feeling when faced with overwhelming odds, but the team – his team – had come up against it before, though this time it felt decisive.

Munroe locked the thought back in its box, feeling a surge of adrenalin restore his focus, and he followed the others though the double doors and out into the cool night air, his resolve returned to him.

Munroe was already scouting for a tactical position and he pulled off the backpack slung over his shoulder and drew out the two Claymore mines.

'Get that laptop running, Jax, we'll make our stand around the corner. Remus and Dupont at one end, me and you at the other.'

Sloan and Dupont made their way down the wide walkway supporting Barbeau's increasingly limp body, his arms slung over their shoulders. The Frenchman's legs had lost all mobility and his feet dragged against the floor as Sloan glanced back at Munroe with a look of dire concern at the injured man's ever-weakening state.

Munroe said nothing; he sensed what was coming and instead he tossed Remus a Claymore and began placing his own at the edge of the doorway and out of sight for the next person coming that way.

The walkway ran all around the top of the Empire State Building, offering solid strategic positions at its corners and creating a funnelling effect for anyone trying to reach them. Large thick-mesh security fencing was erected to prevent tourists falling, or jumping, over the edge, and with the building exterior wall on the opposite side it created the perfect kill zone. Like shooting fish in a barrel, or fish in an alleyway.

'The only thing that'll screw us is our ammunition,' Remus said, pulling back from the Claymore he had just placed. 'We have about nine minutes, by Jax's count.'

Munroe pulled half a dozen filled magazines and four grenades from his backpack. 'We'll make the time, but after that...'

Remus didn't acknowledge their lack of ammunition but instead took a couple of the magazines and together they began jogging along to the first corner. 'I never thought our designation, the Disavowed, was appropriate,' he said, reloading his Glock as they moved.

Munroe grunted a chuckle. 'Should have been the Expendables... the movie ruined that one for us.'

They turned the corner to find Jax, her back against the wall and already hard at work on the laptop balanced upon her lap whilst Dupont tended to Barbeau as best he could. The Frenchman was white as a sheet and the bandages wrapped around his chest soaked in blood as Munroe now knelt down and helped stop him from slumping forwards, face first, to the walkway floor.

'How you doing there, Jean?' Munroe asked and Barbeau only just managed to raise his head to face him and straining to keep his eyes from rolling back into their sockets.

'I've been better,' Barbeau managed, his breathing becoming more erratic. The change had Sloan drawing her focus away from the laptop and on to him.

'No,' Barbeau hissed, each breath clearly painful for him. 'Get it done.'

Sloan hesitated for a moment but then she leant over and kissed the top of his head before returning to her keyboard and frenziedly tapping away.

They all knew where this was heading and Remus gently placed his hand on Barbeau's shoulders as Munroe gripped his bloodied hand.

'Get the job done.'

'You can count on it, Jean,' Munroe replied as the last vestiges of life drained from the wounded man's body and he now looked up at into the night air and a smile spread across his lips.

'I know I can.'

Barbeau's grip loosened and then slid from Munroe's grasp, dropping to the floor limply as he expelled his final breath and his eyelids drooped as the walkway fell in to silence. Sloan shook her head slightly at the loss and a heavy sigh sounded from Remus as Munroe reached up and gently ran his palm downwards over his teammate's eyes until they were closed. The few moments pause felt like an eternity and then they were all back in the game.

We will grieve later.

'Take these,' Munroe said, placing two magazines down on the floor beside Sloan's already loaded Glock and the he turned to Remus and passed over two of the grenades, which the colonel stuffed into the side trouser pocket of his slimline.

Dupont took the additional magazines he was passed. He said nothing but gave Munroe a confident smile before heading to the far corner and preparing for the onslaught.

'Well, people, this is it,' Remus said, and although Sloan never looked up from the screen she reached over and gave him a pat on his shin.

'It's been a pleasure, sir. If I don't get the chance before, I'll see you in the next life. Maybe I'll be in charge next time around.'

A look of genuine pride spread across Remus's face and he leant over and placed his palm on the top of her head, giving it a gentle squeeze.

'I'd be honoured. But that's bullshit, we're not finished with this one yet. I see you when it's over.'

Remus now looked to Munroe as in the distance they could just make out the beeping sound of an elevator arriving, and he offered his hand and it was taken and squeezed briefly. They said nothing, Remus only giving him a look of satisfaction, and then he simply nodded before heading off down the walkway at a fast pace to take up his position at the far corner, with Dupont behind him ready to take point during magazine changes.

Like during any operation, Munroe never really considered the possibility of dying. Sure, the thought may make an appearance pre-mission before it was quickly locked back up, but once an operation began he never thought about the possibility, like flicking a switch. All focus was on the task at hand, and then maybe on getting back home. As he readied his weapon and took a crouched position by the corner, he did have a flash of the only home he'd ever had, of Strawberry Fields Orphanage, and he drew on the strength it gave him. If this was it then he was going out the way he came into this world. Kicking and screaming.

'Bet you'd never thought you'd have Hitler's clone protecting you,' he whispered, and Sloan now glanced over at him and punched him hard in the thigh.

'Fuck off, Captain Munroe,' she growled, and then returned to her laptop. 'One of my best friends once gave me some of the best advice I ever heard, and I never forgot it.'

Then comment had Munroe chuckling and they now spoke in unison.

'I never saw a wild thing look sorry for itself.'

The thunderous sound of the first Claymore being tripped had Munroe checking around the corner to see a balloon of smoke erupting from the observation entrance.

It was quickly followed by the detonation of the second mine, which sent what was left of the double glass doors exploding into the security fence and blowing out a small section of it.

Munroe took aim as the sound of howling could be heard and from the tattered entrance the hazy silhouette of a man stumbled through the dust and stood staring into the night sky. He attempted to raise his left hand, but instead only a bloody stump poked upwards as squirts of blood spat sporadically from the gaping wound before he dropped to his knees and fell face first to the floor.

An unnatural calm descended on the walkway. Munroe fixed his gaze on the fading clouds of smoke while a pool of blood gathered around the corpse of the Blackstar mercenary as the stump of his arm continued to drain. A few moments passed and then a head wearing a balaclava poked into view and Munroe immediately took the shot, dropping the man on top of his fellow dead mercenary.

A familiar hiss now filled Munroe's ears as a grey cylindrical canister was lobbed down towards him and erupted twenty metres from his position, and as soon as the walkway became thick with heavy smoke he heard the scuffling of multiple boots against the stone floor.

Everything then went silent; the concealed mercenaries having taken up their positions before the haze lit up in dulled flashes of light as a wave of blind gunfire was let loose in Munroe's general direction. The bullets mainly hit the walls and security fencing but a couple ricocheted off within inches of his face. Munroe remained still, not yet returning fire.

He could hear the whispers of two voices coming from somewhere in the distance and then silence, the only noise coming from Sloan's laptop as she struck the keyboard with her fingers.

Automatic fire lit up the haze once again as two mercenaries wearing balaclavas and protective armour sprinted through the smoke, swirls of grey mist trailing them as they broke through to the other side, their machine guns firing wildly. The first one took a direct hit to the temple, causing the mercenary behind to trip over the falling body and allowing Munroe to put one in his shoulder and then the top of his scalp. The failed manoeuvre was followed up by two more attackers employing the same tactic, but this time Munroe took out the front runner's kneecap. The shot caused the man to fall forward, exposing the man behind and allowing a further two shots to be delivered to his chest, dropping him to the floor and adding height to what was becoming a human barrier of corpses.

The mercenary who got kneecapped was writhing in pain and unloading his entire magazine, causing Munroe to pull back from the corner's edge temporarily, but once the weapon had emptied he popped back out and landed a kill shot to the side of the masked man's head.

The foggy walkway fell silent once more as Remus began laying down fire from the other end of their position. The wisps of smoke blowing by him suggested the same tactic was being employed, but after unloading a full magazine from his Glock and with the last few shots being taken by Dupont while Remus reloaded, the night air once again fell silent.

Munroe glanced over at Sloan who seemed to sense his stare and without looking up she gave him a thumbs up and then returned to her screen. Munroe wasn't sure if it meant she was close to finishing or it was for a 'good job, keep it up', but he turned back to the walkway to hear the hiss of the smoke grenade fizzle out.

The breeze in the air was surprisingly soft that night and even at this height the smoke hung where it was as it slowly began to fade away. Munroe continued to stare down the walkway when the bulky mass of a silhouette started to take shape. It was distorted at first and then it morphed into the outline of a figure, but shorter and thicker than he would have expected. A sharp spear-like shape protruded from where a head would normally be and as a light gust of wind blew away the last dregs of smoke he got his first clear view.

'*Get down!*' he yelled, leaping back towards Sloan and pushing her to the floor as the kneeling mercenary with an RPG rocket launcher launched a missile in a bright flash of light, propelling it screaming towards them and impacting against the wall opposite.

The explosion sent shockwaves rippling through Munroe's body as he lay huddled on top of Sloan. Masonry burst into fragments sending pieces scattering in all directions, the sharp splinters cutting through anything in their way. The accompanying fireball thankfully exited through the gaping hole in the observation wall, but it left a black and cracked-open drop-off point to a one-thousand-foot plummet to the sidewalk below.

At the other corner, Remus and Dupont were taking it in turns to lay down fire from their position and while Munroe's ears were ringing from the explosion, Sloan pushed him off her to one side and raised her Glock just in time to catch the first mercenary appearing at the corner, putting two in his chest, stopping him dead.

Munroe lunged to his feet, his balance still off, and hugged the wall for stability just in time to grab the rifle off the second man who sent his barrel around the corner. Munroe thrust the gun upwards into the air and then brought his knee up hard into the attacker's groin. Then in one motion he swung him around and allowed the momentum to carry him out through the hole in the wall, the man's screams fading into the night until they abruptly stopped when he reached the sidewalk.

Munroe snatched his gun from the floor and Sloan returned to her laptop as if nothing had happened as Remus pulled the pin from one of his grenades and threw it along his own walkway. Both he and Dupont crouched and waited.

Munroe barely registered the small explosion, his hearing still impaired, and he allowed his magazine clip to be ejected to the floor before slapping in a fresh one and digging in against the wall once more.

At this rate Bauer is going to run out of men before we run out of bullets.

Once again silence descended upon the top floor of the Empire State Building, the darkened flashes of a brewing storm lighting up the clouds, way off in the distance. As Munroe stole a glance around the corner the sight that greeted him had him reaching into his pocket and pulling out a grenade.

Two black ballistic riot shields covered the breadth of the walkway and through the small clear-carbonate viewing windows, Munroe could see four more mercenaries lined up in rows behind each protector. Each shield had a hole from which protruded the barrels of AK-47 rifles, and without pause they began to advance swiftly as rhythmic barrages of shots were fired off, forcing Munroe to duck for cover.

Munroe waited patiently as the sound of heavy movement drew nearer, the shifting of battle armour and scuffling of boots filling his ears until the right moment when he pulled out the pin of his grenade, judged the distance and flung it in an arc around the corner.

The scuffling suddenly stopped, and a powerful explosion erupted. Far off at the other corner, Remus and Dupont took it in turns to open fire as Bauer's men attempted to flank them.

Munroe waited for a few seconds before stealing another peek to find all four men in different states of dismemberment, the ballistic shields nowhere to be seen. His grenade had landed just behind them, allowing for the maximum devastation, and Munroe now finished off the only man still moving with a single bullet to the head, his protective helmet having been blown off by the blast, adding him to the new pile of corpses being created.

Munroe stayed in his position as the seconds past and then a voice he had expected to hear at some point called out to him, sounding remarkably calm considering the damage his men had taken.

'You can't keep this up, Ethan. But I appreciate your guile,' Bauer's said, his voice travelling down the walkway but the man was nowhere in sight. 'I have another contingent of Blackstar on their way over and I can do this all night long. You must be getting low on supplies. You can't last forever.'

Munroe looked over at Sloan who put two fingers in the air, giving him a time frame for her completion, and he moved as close to the corner as he considered wise.

'Don't worry about us, Hans. We're in no rush. Kind of enjoying it actually. Haven't visited the Empire in years and the activities aren't half bad.'

There was a pause before Bauer called out to him again, but this time sounding less cavalier.

'You've lost, Ethan. The vault may have taken a hit but the those boxes you left in the Range Rover are proving very useful. I only gave them a preliminary look, but you are aware that the bank records I need are amongst them, aren't you?'

Munroe looked over at Sloan who was already shaking her head and he did likewise. It was the one thing he had forgotten about.

Shit.

'I'm guessing you've traipsed all the way up here to get a signal for whatever your planning, so, I'll make you a deal. Give me what you have and I will let you walk out of here to chase you down another day. C'mon, we've done this before, you know I'll keep my word... I enjoy the hunt, especially when you're the prey.'

Munroe glanced over towards Remus and Dupont in the distance who could obviously hear because the Frenchman raised his middle finger in Munroe's direction before resuming his covering position.

'No, I don't think so, Hans. Were done running. This ends tonight.'

'That's a shame, Ethan. I have enjoyed our game, but so be it.'

The sound of pressured popping echoed in the distance and a thud from behind had Munroe spinning around to see a small bullet-shaped smoke canister land at his feet, which began to ooze black smoke. He immediately reached down and with his hand flicked it over the side of the safety barrier as more shells rained down around him and flared up into thick puffs of smoke, filling the air with more blinding and nauseating black fog.

In the midst of it all, he could hear other smoke capsules dropping to the floor, coming from a grenade launcher located out of sight, and he caught his last image of Sloan as she pulled her shirt up over her head and continued with her work, disappearing out of sight.

The inky discharge was irritating, not suffocating, but as Munroe held his Glock out before him he couldn't even see his own hand, just a disorientating wisp of black, and he now dropped his head slightly and placed all his focus on his hearing.

There were no footsteps nor the sound of battle armour shifting against their wearers and he now waited, lost in a sea of black, for any sound of movement, his finger lightly pressing on the trigger.

Munroe closed his eyes momentarily and built a mental image of his surroundings, the hole in the wall, his position in relation to Sloan. He remained glued to the spot, not wanting to throw off his imagined location, when off to his left something scuffled and he shifted his barrel towards it and unloaded a single round.

The smoke was so thick that the flash from his Glocks muzzle was barely visible and no sooner had he fired than he felt the blade of a knife slice through his shirt, delivering a deep cut across his waist.

Munroe swivelled and fired twice, listening for a thud to the ground but none came and he remained in that position as the sharp stinging pain of a thrust blade was stabbed into his lower back and he spun around and shot twice.

Again there was no sound suggesting he had hit his mark, and as he reached down and checked his latest wound, his fingers becoming sticky with blood he felt a knife slide up against his neck and he froze.

'Don't move, and drop the gun,' Bauer's voice hissed in his ear as pressure was applied to the blade, and Munroe grudgingly dropped the gun and loosened his shoulders offering no resistance.

The sound of the smoke bombs began to fizzle out, one by one, and as the smoke began to clear he saw what he expected to see, two mercenaries wearing heat-sensing goggles who had taken positions with one pointing his rifle directly at Sloan's head and the other on his haunches and aiming in the rough direction of Remus, who was still beyond the clearing haze.

'Nice and easy, Ethan,' Bauer whispered into his ear, keeping a tight grip on the blade at Munroe's throat while he removed his own thermal goggles and dropped them to the floor.

With a nod from Bauer, the nearest mercenary slid away Sloan's gun, pulled back the shirt covering her head and placed a finger to his lips before taking the laptop from her and examining it, his rifle still aimed in her direction.

Up ahead, the mist cleared in a gust of wind and Munroe caught sight of Remus, still covering his walkway, as a shot rang out, clipping the colonel in the side and spinning him to the ground where he now lay motionless. It was followed by another, which hit Dupont in the chest dropping the man to his knees as he clasped his wound, his face etched in pain before he collapsed to the floor.

Bauer saw his protégé and a deep look of disgust crossed his face.

'Bring that traitor over to me at once.'

The nearest mercenary took off at speed and proceeded to drag Dupont to his feet, the blood spreading across his shirt from his chest wound, and roughly dragged him back down the walkway to where Bauer standing, his grip on the blade at Munroe's neck never loosening.

'You're a sad sight,' Bauer spat, looking wholly disgusted by the man. 'You could have had it all, you idiot, and instead you throw it all away for a Jew.'

Dupont was barely conscious but his eyes flicked as blood dribbled form his mouth and he attempted to raise his arm aggressively, but it fell back down to his side, his energy and life force draining from his body with every passing moment.

'You should have trusted me, but to see you run out of that vault with this band of scum is like a knife through my heart.'

Dupont grunted heavily and he once more strained to raise raised his arm upwards in a grabbing motion but Bauer had already lost interest.

'Please would someone shoot this traitorous piece of shit?'

The mercenary holding him pushed Dupont back to the outer edge of the walkway and without hesitation shot him in the temple, jerking back the man's head as the lower part of his skull exploded into pieces. His body then slumped forwards as his knees buckled and he dropped to the floor as Bauer snorted uncaringly.

'There's nothing worse than a traitor, Ethan. It's what he deserved, and I would consider your loss worthier than his, any day of the week… Now, with that unpleasantness done, let's get back to business. Cover him,' Bauer ordered, and the mercenary got to his feet and aimed the rifle directly at Munroe's head as the other passed over the laptop and then pulled Sloan to her feet.

'Now, what have you been up to, Captain Sloan?' Bauer teased condescendingly, releasing his blade slowly from Munroe's neck before turning his full attention to the screen.

'Just seeing how the chancellor's little shindig is playing out over on Liberty Island,' Sloan said angrily as Bauer swivelled the laptop on his palm so they could all see the real-time view of the inauguration in process. Ursula Schneider was standing on the stage, shaking the American president's hand as an image of the new UE emblem filled the entire outdoor screen behind them. The crowd were already raising their glasses, and Bauer moved his finger to the flashing command window reading 'execute'.

'Well whatever you're doing I'm afraid you won't have the chance to carry it out,' he said, pressing the delete key, which made the command window disappear, leaving just the view of the ongoing event. 'So, what is it that you were so desperate to execute?'

'Just a montage Captain Sloan put together using the surveillance footage and other files from your vault,' Munroe replied, rubbing his neck as his jaw muscles flexed in anger. 'But, well done, Hans, you've saved the day again. If you weren't such a pathetic little shit I would be impressed.'

Bauer let out a smug chuckle then placed the laptop on the edge of the observation wall and flicked his finger over at the bleeding cut on Munroe's waist. 'I would suggest getting some medical attention for your wounds, but there isn't really any point, is there? And don't be too annoyed, Ethan. You were never prepared for the sly recesses of my mind. You just weren't designed that way.'

Bauer now turned his attention to Sloan and he looked her up and down before biting his lip. 'How frustrating it must be to have been on the cusp of exposing Daedalus to the world only to have it all come to nothing. Painful, no?'

Sloan now locked in on his gaze and she shrugged.

'Oh, wouldn't say it's that bad.'

Her answer produced a look of concern from Bauer and he craned his head forwards. 'And why would that be exactly?'

Sloan smiled over at Munroe and then returned to his questioning gaze.

Bauer's demeanour appeared to crumble, his whole body sagging, and his neck snapped around to the laptop screen for what he saw caused his entire body to stagger backwards in disbelief. On the giant screen behind Chancellor Schneider and the American president flashed images of her offering the Nazi salute proudly, with Bauer looking on as the late Reichsführer Bormann returned the salute. The screen now flickered to a video clip of Bauer and the chancellor mid-conversation and although the volume on the laptop was muted it was clear by the shocked look on the American president's face that whatever was being said was damning. Then followed photos of Bauer, Schneider and Gasparyan amongst others, all under the banner headline 'wanted for treason' with swastika emblems stamped across their faces as the showreel continued.

'Sorry to break it to you, Hans, but the Daedalus files in your vault have also gone out to every major media outlet in the world. There's as more documentation than anyone would need to crucify your fucking arse, and all your Nazis buddies as well.'

Bauer stood there, his jaw now dropping open as he watched the German chancellor rapidly make her way off the stage amid a now raucous crowd that had moments earlier appeared excited and supportive.

'What have you done?' he muttered, lost in shock as the blood drained from his face, his cheeks becoming sallow.

'Just what we had to do, Hans,' Munroe said, motioning to the two mercenaries whose eyes were also transfixed on the screen. 'This game of tag has turned, lads. Seems we'll be hunting you down from now on.'

Sloan moved with unbelievable speed and grabbing the nearest mercenary's gun barrel, pushing it into the air as she brought her boot hard into his groin. In the same instant Munroe rushed the other one, the mercenary getting a single bullet off which just missed Munroe's arm as the two men wrestled for the rifle. A hard punch to the killer's side, just between the chest armour he was wearing, made him jerk forwards before Munroe delivered a headbutt and drove his boot into the crux at the back of his leg, dropping him down onto one knee. This was followed by a swift smack to the side of his neck with the butt of his gun, sending him unconscious to the floor as Munroe now turned his attention to Sloan who was still struggling for control of the rifle. A single shot to the mercenary's chest sent him tumbling backwards, dead before he even hit the concrete, and they as they both turned their weapons on Bauer, who surprisingly hadn't moved an inch, his eyes still locked on the screen.

The other team, comprising Talon, Dalton and Lavigne, had done its job well by getting a receiver and blocking device into the main control room in the bottom of a coffee dispenser. The installed tech meant that not only was it hijacking the screen, but also stopping anyone from shutting off the live feed, which the event's security services would have tried to do the moment the footage began to roll. No one was stopping the signal, meaning the tens of millions of viewers around the world would see the whole damning presentation uninterrupted.

'I've got him, Jax,' Munroe said, motioning towards the still body of Remus at the far end of the walkway. 'Check on Remus.'

Sloan shot Bauer a look of revulsion and then took off in a sprint towards their fallen colleague as Munroe moved around Bauer until he was directly in front of him.

'It's over, Hans. Your world's gone to shit, I'm afraid. To think of all the plans, the murders, the subterfuge and God knows how much money spent and here we are bringing to a close the end of a nearly eighty-year shit stain in history.'

Munroe leant forwards as Bauer finally managed to pull himself away from the screen and glared over at him venomously, his right eye twitching erratically.

'Your Fourth Reich is all gone. Destroyed by the very vault created to protect it.'

Bauer's nostrils began to flare in anger and then suddenly his composure returned to him and was replaced with the same smug veneer that Munroe had come to expect.

'It's not the end, Ethan. Just the messy end of a new beginning. With the money and connections we have, we will just have to rebuild. All you've done here tonight is stall the inevitable. You've achieved nothing. I'll never end up in a prison cell. People with this much money never do. I'll beat it somehow and when I return, I will pick off you and your DSV idiots one at a time. You can't win, Ethan. You never could. This game you've chosen to fight was rigged from the beginning.'

Munroe considered the threatening reply for a moment and then he glanced up the walkway to see Sloan placing her head under Remus's shoulder and dragging him to his feet as he managed a weak, but solid, thumbs up.

The old man was as tough as they got.

'I was worried you were going to say that,' Munroe replied, turning back to face his nemesis before he jabbed the side of his gun into Bauer's face, sending him crashing into the wall behind him. He then dropped his weapon and delivered a hard punch to the Bauer's gut. 'That's for me,' he growled, and then slamming his elbow across Bauer's nose, cracking it at the base and bending it off to one side, the Nazi letting out a pained yelp. 'That's for Barbeau.'

Munroe now grabbed him by the scruff of his neck and dragged him along the walkway as Bauer pulled a blade from his pocket and attempted to drive it upwards towards Munroe's chest, but it was ripped from his grasp. 'This is for John McCitrick.' Munroe snapped Bauer's forefinger ninety degrees to one side and as Bauer screamed in agony, Munroe slammed the sole of his boot into the side of his knee, feeling the joint give way and dislocating it at a ninety-degree angle.

Bauer's screams now became high-pitched and his body shook as he started to go into shock, but Munroe slapped him across his face, keeping him from passing out, and continued dragging him along the walkway until he reached the hole in the observation wall.

'I wanted you to know one more thing, Hans,' Munroe growled, leaning in to within inches of the Nazi's face until they were almost nose to nose. 'Iron Phoenix, the legendary tales your brethren tell their children late at night? Dupont told me all about them. Well I just wanted you to know… It turns out that I wasn't just a product of Project Icarus… I *am* the Iron Phoenix.'

The admission had Bauer looking startled and he began to shake his head, his whole body twitching as he fought the pain in his fingers along with his dislocated knee.

'That's impossible,' he managed to say in nothing more than a hiss as spittle ran down his chin. 'That can't be.'

'Oh, but it can… and it is, you pathetic ponce. It was all in the vault.'

It was difficult to tell what hurt more, his broken bones or what he was being told, and Bauer's eyes flickered from side to side as he considered the possibility as Munroe now dug in the proverbial knife and twisted it with relish.

'No wonder I got the best of you, because my blood was always purer than yours, you disgusting half-blood.'

Munroe didn't believe a word of it, but that didn't matter because he knew Bauer did and he knew it would hurt more than anything else in the world. It was all the man truly cared for and he now smiled menacingly. 'You're not even pure enough to lick the shit off my shoes.'

Bauer's expression crumbled and for a moment he looked broken, and it was a beautiful sight as Munroe pulled out his last grenade and jammed it into Bauer's jacket pocket before flicking the pin out and letting it drop to the floor below.

'And this is for my wife and child, you fucking piece of shit.'

Munroe raised his boot and slammed it hard into Bauer's chest, sending him airborne through the hole in the walkway and watching the man, who caused so much misery for so many, disappear into the darkness, screaming as he went. The screaming continued until it was barely audible as the ex-Daedalus leader tumbled down the thousand feet to his death, and Munroe didn't move an inch until the sound of a grenade exploding echoed across the broken skyline of the wasteland that had once been Manhattan.

Chapter 28

The sun was still rising over the shimmering waters of Loch Goil as the small group of mourners stood around the grave, each taking their turn to gently drop a shovel of soil down upon the glossy wooden casket within in it. No one spoke as each paid their last respects in this traditional symbolic gesture to their friend and mentor, and after the last attendee had finished they slowly retreated sombrely to the edge of loch and looked out at the Scottish mountain landscape before them.

They remained silent and all took in the moment as Munroe put his arm around Sloan and she reciprocated by slipping her arm around his waist, both of them sharing in the grief that they had for their friend John McCitrick.

Almost two weeks had passed since New York and in that time the story of Daedalus and their eighty-year-long murderous endeavour to establish a Fourth Reich had circled the globe, and the story had lost none of its momentum. In fact, it continued to gain speed, and the knock-on effect and consequences of such a truth had only just begun. The press packet that Sloan had sent out back in New York had not only included Daedalus members but their entire history, with photographs and video leading in calls to rewrite the history books and acknowledging the gigantic con that Hitler and the Nazi elite had been able to pull off at the end of the Second World War. Investigative journalists from every country were now scouring the globe in a bid to unearth any and all information of this lost saga, and governmental commissions had been set up to explore the secret pact that Churchill, Roosevelt and de Gaulle had signed tasking DSV in bringing them to justice.

There were also many political careers ruined, including that of the British prime minister, Andrew Previn, who had been forced to resign under the outcry of his dealings with the modern-day führer, Hans Bauer, after his personal friendship with the man had been exposed.

Further afield, most governments still clung to the idea of the nuclear terrorist attack in New York being carried out by Iranian terrorists but this too had begun to fall apart as more information was brought to light about those actually responsible and Daedalus were now in the firing line for the atrocity. The news had led to the arrest of hundreds of the organisation's agents and associates and those not scooped up initially were now on the run, being hunted down; it was only a matter of time before their moment of judgement arrived. As such, the preparation for the invasion of Iran had been placed on hold and diplomatic channels opened, although only time would tell what the final outcome would be.

Chancellor Schneider had also been relieved of her post and taken into custody by the German authorities and though the long process of her trial was still in its infancy, Munroe was confident that over the coming months and years the prosecution of this long, twisted chapter for all involved would see fruition.

One positive thing to come from the whole mess was the ploughing ahead of the newly formed United Earth, but instead of the erstwhile chancellor, the American president had been nominated to lead it, though on a rocky foundation. A change in laws allowing sitting leaders to assume the post was something that might just survive. Many were still wary of the idea that each new UE president would only do what was right for their own country, but no doubt, over time, it might morph into something that most nations could get on board with. The idea of all countries working together for the benefit of the globe was too alluring to pass up, and who knew, perhaps it was the first step, the first foundation stone, towards a new kind of global politics for the twenty-first century. Munroe had his doubts, but frankly anything was better than having Daedalus pulling the strings.

And after all was said and done, and with the dust not even beginning to settle, there was DSV, the Disavowed, or what was left of it. The whole team were initially arrested coming out of Manhattan and had spent the first four days being interrogated by every agency known, and some not so known, but once more information came out via the media the three allied governments of the UK, US and France had granted them clemency and preferred that they all disappear away from the public eye. So far not one of them had been brought up in the news, not even a single column inch, and that was fine by all of them. The one thing that governments detested more than anything else was being forced to admit they were wrong and given that DSV members' names and identities had only been known within the intelligence community, allowing them to just melt away into the background noise had been the preferred choice. The public would ever know the true extent of their involvement and although the tale of Daedalus was on the lips, pen and keyboard of every journalist out there, the secretive organisation set up to take them down remained unknown.

It was probably for the best, but where all of them went from here was still a question to be answered. They had all attended Barbeau's funeral just days earlier in a private ceremony, with full military honours. He, like the rest of DSV, had no real family to attend, but his brothers and sister of the Disavowed had given him a respectful send-off, as they were doing today for McCitrick, whose last will and testament asked for him to be buried where they stood, in the highlands of Scotland. No one had even known he was born and raised here and with no shred of an accent it was a surprise to all but, with a view over the dark blue waters of Loch Goil and the stunning peacefulness of the Highlands, it seemed a fitting final resting place for a man who had barely rested once in his long fifty-year career.

Munroe looked down the line at Remus, who was recovering nicely. The shot he had received miraculously missed all his organs, with the bullet entering his shoulder and ending up lodged just below his collarbone. As it turned out, the impact of the bullet had slammed him back against the wall, knocking him out, and apart from a concussion and a nasty flesh wound, the colonel was in good shape.

Next to Remus, Talon, Lavigne, Dalton stood sombrely because of the funeral, but they were all doing OK. Once things had settled down maybe they would pick up where their own military careers had left off before they join DSV. Talon and Dalton had mentioned going into the private sector. There was always a good pay cheque waiting for people with experience like theirs.

As for Sloan, the whole experience had left a bitter taste in her mouth and given that her own people had turned on them, who could blame her? There was mention of retiring early with a full pension, which was thankfully still on the table, but the idea of someone like Sloan settling into a quiet life as a lady of leisure was something Munroe couldn't imagine. She'd be bored out of her mind within a few months. But she had options if she wanted them.

For Munroe, the future was a blank slate. Much to his everlasting gratitude, the team had decided to keep knowledge of his family tree just between themselves, his actual family, and honestly, he hadn't thought about it that much. There had been too much going on. He was sure he would have to face it at some point, but now was not that time. Munroe had considered getting back into hostage negotiation, but after the whirlwind events of the past year he didn't know if he could face it. Compared to tracking down secretive organisations across the world and the adrenalin spikes of the adventures he'd had, it all seemed a bit mundane, and boredom was something that scared him more than facing down the barrel of a gun. No, his future was yet to be decided, and he figured for the time being he would see where the wind took him. Besides, one never knew what was around the next corner, and for now that was in itself an exciting prospect.

'Captain Munroe.'

All six of them turned around to see two men in black suits making their way over. Sloan pulled away from Munroe and he raised his chin.

'Who wants to know?'

One of the men held back a few metres as the other pulled out an ID card and flipped it open to reveal MI6 credentials before returning it to his pocket and then looking at the other members of DSV who were slowly making their way over, each of them looking suspiciously at the new arrivals.

'My apologies for interrupting. My name is Jack Constantine; I was hoping to speak with you.'

Munroe eyed the man and then he nodded as Sloan and the other members shot him a glance and began to make their way back towards the small wood-shaving covered car park but the agent quickly raised his hand.

'Actually, this concerns all of you,' he said and stopping them in their tracks. 'DSV? Codename Disavowed.'

No one said a thing and they all looked over at Munroe.

'That depends. I've seen the badge, but who's really asking?'

Constantine licked his lips and scanned the face of all six of them before returning to Munroe.

'I'm here on behalf of a joint task force. We're setting up something, something that might be right up your alley.'

Munroe remained silent. Finally after a few seconds Constantine leant in and glanced over at Remus and the others.

'There are many other dangers out there, you know. Perfect for people with your skills. You would, of course, work under a new codename.'

Munroe glanced over at Sloan, then the others, and he watched as each one of them began to smile and then he smiled himself.

'And what exactly would that be?'

Agent Constantine let slip a smile himself and then his expression hardened. 'Codename: *Absolved*.'

Acknowledgements

To Kit Nevile, my editor, whose skill and patience have made writing Munroe so much fun.

To Michael, Iain, Nick and everyone at Canelo.

And, as always, to Alison and Charlotte.